The
HOUR
of the
HAWK

His Dreams
are Becoming
His Reality

The
HOUR
of the
HAWK

JAMES LOGAN

THE HOUR OF THE HAWK
Copyright © 2018 by James Logan

Printed in Canada

ISBN: 978-1-4866-1492-9

Word Alive Press
131 Cordite Road, Winnipeg, MB R3W 1S1
www.wordalivepress.ca

MIX
Paper from
responsible sources
FSC® C016245

Library and Archives Canada Cataloguing in Publication

Logan, James (James Kip), author
        The hour of the hawk / James Logan.

Issued in print and electronic formats.
ISBN 978-1-4866-1492-9 (softcover).--ISBN 978-1-4866-1493-6 (ebook)

        I. Title.

PS8623.O363H68 2017   C813'.6   C2017-903647-5
                                               C2017-903648-3

To my friends of the Duchess Mennonite Church and youth group.
Though the years have scattered us, you all are still in my heart. Jude 24–25

Like a sparrow in its flitting, like a swallow in its flying, so a curse without cause does not alight.

—Proverbs 26:2, NASB

CHAPTER ONE

Grenfel held Morgan's halter and led him down the craggy slopes of the Cabernish Mountains. Darkness was stealing upon both horse and boy now like a thief lurking in the shadows, yet the twelve-year-old hurried his purebred Arabian along, walking with one hand clutched to the halter; the other held the hood of his cloak, which swept around his face to conceal his identity. After all, one was never really alone in Ascar.

As he navigated the rocky slopes like one in a trance, his thoughts turned to Meldrock, whose evil still triggered a fearful response in Grenfel. He shuddered, not so much from the wind but from the icy, spectral finger that seemed to stroke his spine. What could overcome such evil? The problem troubled Grenfel as he led the horse in a tortoise-like fashion down the mountain. His father's priests were no match for such evil; they were like knights riding to battle without weapons.

All is hopeless for Ascar, desolate and lost like I am, he thought. As Grenfel focused on this notion, his thoughts became more real than the rocks under his feet. He stumbled forward, only able at the last second to prevent himself from tumbling downslope by grabbing Morgan's halter with a desperate outstretched hand.

Falling to his knees, Grenfel remembered the dull religious ceremonies he had been forced to kneel through for so many years at his uncle's castle in Heathervane. The cold wind now buffeting his hood seemed no less merciful than his uncle's priests.

The wind picked up Morgan's mane, jolting Grenfel back to reality. It felt like a loving slap across the face from a trusted friend. But that was

not the only reason for coming alert. He heard a voice—bold, powerful, and clear, unlike the others he had heard among the rooms of his father's castle. This was not the voice of merrymakers or knights preparing for battle. This was a voice of authority.

Morgan suddenly locked his front legs and threw his head back, jerking Grenfel to his feet like a ragdoll.

"Easy, boy!" Grenfel shouted as he tried to calm his horse by stroking the great Arabian's neck, holding tightly to the halter with his other hand. Looking into Morgan's eyes and softly whispering his name, Grenfel sought to quiet his horse. As he pleaded with the horse, he felt the fear of them toppling off the cliff and crashing onto the rocks below, where the Bay of Trakai beckoned.

"Sobering thoughts for one so young in years," came that same authoritative voice. The voice reminded him of his father, King Ulrich.

"Where are you?" Grenfel cried, as nervous as a rabbit pursued by a hawk.

"I stand in front of you. Your horse sensed my presence. That's why he threw his head back."

"I can't see anything," spoke a fearful Grenfel, his head moving from side to side as if the movement itself might flush out this stranger.

"Seeing in the spirit is a result of developing intimacy with the Ancient of Days. Getting alone with the Ancient of Days such as in exile is a good way of developing spiritual vision. There are many like me throughout Ascar, with developed spiritual senses, but you would never know it. Not if you rely solely on your natural eyes."

"But I want to see!"

"Yes, I know," replied the voice, "and now it begins with your cry."

Grenfel squinted and soon made out the silhouette of a tall, muscular man.

"Who are you?" Grenfel managed in an unsteady tone. His hand reached for the jewelled knife at his side.

"Relax, boy. I am Estravai, the name I was known by before your father sent me into exile for speaking the truth. Since that day, he has chosen to call me traitor to the crown. I do not doubt that Meldrock's pawns, the corrupt priests of the court, had a say in the matter."

"Are you a sorcerer? Can you turn a staff into a serpent?"

"Such illusions and sleights of hand are common amongst Meldrock's priests," Estravai said. "Through these acts, they obtain court privileges. Are you disappointed, boy? You hoped I could teach you dark secrets to help earn you a name, did you not?"

"Yes," Grenfel admitted. "I hoped if I could cause the sun to go black, or snow to fall on a summer day, Father would allow me to return to Kreniston."

"The Ancient of Days' power far exceeds Meldrock's sorcerers, as you will one day witness. No doubt, boy, no doubt. Trust me on this matter."

"Who are you, then?" asked Grenfel, puzzled, his hand still covering the handle of his dagger.

"I have already spoken my name, but as for my trade, I am not a metal worker, nor a cook, but a humble Revealer of Secrets for the Ancient of Days. That is how I am able to know your thoughts. The Revealer of Secrets discloses knowledge not possible to possess by one's intellect. I work primarily by way of visions and dreams."

"Revealer of Secrets!" Grenfel exclaimed in amazement. "I've never heard my uncle or any at his table in the great hall of Castle Heathervane speak of such a one."

"That does not dismiss the fact that we exist," answered Estravai. "Enough talk, though. A snowstorm is moving in."

"I thought you weren't a sorcerer."

"True, boy. As I have said, I know things as the Ancient of Days reveals them to me. He controls the forces of nature and discloses His secrets as He wills. He told me I would find you here. He gave me a word which will be confirmed with signs in the heavens, a streaking light, and a snowstorm."

Grenfel turned to Morgan, who seemed also to sense something in the air, despite the clear autumn night. Truly Morgan could be trusted, even if Grenfel wasn't yet sure what to make of this stranger.

"Come then, boy, we must move," advised Estravai, sounding a little more anxious. "If you distrust me, I understand. In time, you will grow to love me." He paused to smile. "For now, follow your horse's instinct in this matter, for he was aware of my presence long before you were."

3

The alarm sounded and a groggy Tony Epson looked out from under his covers like a clam in its shell. Trying to focus his eyes on the numbers of the clock, he hoped mental concentration might cause the numbers to turn back one hour—but such would not be the case this morning. As with all mornings, five a.m. was still five a.m.

Tony gave his head a shake, though his mind still resisted his digital clock. His years of fire training had conditioned his body to override his mind and to react, and so Tony stuck out an arm to switch off the alarm, and then swung his feet out of bed, hoping with his movement not to wake his wife Roxanne. No sooner had Tony stood to his feet then Roxanne sprawled across the now vacant place where he had being sleeping and with her face still buried in her pillow half coherently said "You off to work?"

"No, just a strange dream." Tony bent down to kiss his wife's cheek. "I love you," he whispered in her ear.

"I love you" came a faint response from Roxanne before the rhythmic snoring that always reminded him of a whale blowing air.

Guided by the glow of the digital clock sitting on a nightstand next to the bed, Tony walked over to the master bedroom's only closet and opened its double doors just as Roxanne muttered, "Is Jordan up?"

"It's five in the morning," replied Tony as he stood motionless momentarily, listening. Hearing once again Roxanne's rhythmic snoring, he proceeded to yank a patterned housecoat off its hanger.

"I've got to stop eating pizza late at night," muttered Tony. "What a dream."

Stepping through the bedroom doorway, he proceeded left down a hallway to the bathroom with the help of a nightlight, managing to step over one of Jordan's toy trucks parked as if to test those who weren't quite awake yet. Switching on the bathroom light, Tony glanced into the oval mirror hanging above the vanity and noticed the brown stubble of his beard. *Looks like it's time for Roxanne to shave my head again.* He was okay with Roxanne shaving his head, as it was work-related rather than due to a receding hairline brought about by age. Feeling the contour of his chin as he stood before the mirror, Tony remembered the last time Roxanne had shaved his head.

It was a bright sunny afternoon. He was sitting on a wooden stool with a barber's cape on, outside on the front porch. Roxanne had just finished shaving his head and set her razor down on the porch, telling him to wait a moment. Thinking she was just about to undo the barber's cape from behind him, Tony remembered blushing when she cradled the sides of his head in her hands and kissed him on the top of his head. He also remembered looking around nervously as he said, "Roxanne, the neighbors!"

"What of the neighbors?" Roxanne had replied. "Can't a wife kiss her husband's bald head on their front porch these days?"

Smiling at his reflection in the mirror, Tony continued to feel the stubble on his chin as he continued reminiscing. He remembered his moments of nervous fidgeting waiting for Roxanne to unfasten the barber's cape so he could make a hasty retreat into the house. It seemed like an eternity waiting for her to unsnap the cape from behind him and as she did she whispered in his ear. "Maybe when we have our next date night and Jordan's asleep, I'll paint your face blue like William Wallace in Braveheart, put on one of my wool skirts, and a frilly white blouse, with a shawl, and we'll re-enact their wedding scene over a candlelight dinner."

Smiling again at his reflection in the mirror, Tony thought of Roxanne's playful spirit and he remembered that it was the sight of Roxanne that afternoon in the sun with her penetrating green eyes and orange curly hair that had reinforced the idea in his heart of why he didn't mind getting his head shaved, especially when it was Roxanne doing it.

Turning from the oval mirror Tony now stepped into the shower, muttering a prayer that his mind might be washed of the residue of all its unusual dreams.

"Signs in the heavens," Tony mumbled to himself. "Revealers of Secrets…"

After a soothing shower, he made his way back to the bedroom and slipped into his jeans. He then buttoned up an oilskin shirt and warmed his feet with woollen mountain socks—the kind guaranteed for two years; he needed the maximum guarantee, as his toes routinely poked through the worn material.

He took a final glance around the room. Roxanne was still sprawled across the bed snoring, unaware she was being watched. He smiled at her beauty, and thanked God for the truthfulness of His word that he who finds a wife, finds a good thing. Reluctantly, his eyes drifted away from his sleeping wife to the rest of the room. It seemed to be in its usual state of disarray with a few articles of his and his wife's clothing strewn about the carpet. He could live with the state of the room at the moment, though, as the thought of a good cup of coffee was beginning to pull at his neurons.

Having just descended the stairs from his bedroom with a minimum of wall contact, Tony staggered into the kitchen like a rodeo cowboy who had just picked himself up out of the dust after being thrown by a bull. He fought to shake off the last lingering effects of sleep. Comforted by the thought that he didn't have a French Press, Tony pushed the power button of his coffee maker, and then, opening a wooden bread box, proceeded to split a bagel. He then slipped the large knife into its hiding spot behind the kitchen taps, so Jordan wouldn't find it in his daily explorations of the house. He dropped the bagel into the toaster with a click. That, along with the gurgle of the coffeemaker as the last drips of water ran through it, allowed him a moment of normalcy and comfort.

With the preparation of breakfast complete, Tony sauntered across the kitchen with a cup of coffee in one hand and a plate with his bagel on it in the other. Placing his breakfast on the table, he pulled out a chair and sat down to read one of the well-worn Christian magazines stacked in the middle of the table. He thumbed through the glossy pages, not reading anything in particular, with the exception of a few short columns and a full-page ad: nine CDs for ninety-nine cents. He pondered the deal momentarily, considering the advantages of expanding his CD collection, then flipped to the next page.

His eyes landed on another ad:

SCHOOL OF THE APOSTLES CORRESPONDENCE STUDIES
AN END-TIME SCHOOL OF THE SPIRIT
WITH APOSTLE JOHN BRISTANE

Tony and his wife didn't currently attend a church. Rather, they took in the occasion revival meeting put on by travelling ministry groups that passed through Drummingsville.

The most recent being a series of meetings held in the school gym by an Apostle Levi Brandon. Sipping his coffee, Tony recalled his feelings of animosity towards Apostle Brandon before he had even met the man. *Who was this apostle anyway?* Tony remembered thinking, *to deprive him of an intimate date night with his wife on one of his rare days off during the summer fire season.*

Mulling over his thoughts, Tony spread cream cheese on a bagel and proceeded to take a bite. Date night had evolved for Roxanne and himself out of the golden age of their first passionate encounters. Where twenty-dollar lunches had nothing to do with the food but everything to do with the unspoken language of the eyes. Evenings seemed to blend into days, dinners and movie marathons seemed to be all about a huge exercise in sleep deprivation. Those were the days he had thought would go on forever.

Tony shook his head as he wondered how he kept up the pace with work and all. Flipping the page of the Christian magazine in front of him, Tony remembered one specific date with Roxanne at the Backwater Grill where he experienced a moment of Divine enlightenment hearing God specifically say to marry Roxanne because they needed each other. Marriage had come on them quickly, as did the arrival of their son, Jordan—and the concept of date night was born. Mostly date night involved a sitter, but when that wasn't possible Roxanne and he would take turns cooking romantic dinners once Jordan was asleep. Tony smiled before taking a sip of coffee remembering how his personal cooking had grown by leaps and bounds since they had started date night. Yes, it still on his part involved opening a bag, but now it was rustic vegetables and pot roast he was plating for Roxanne, rather than KD and burnt ham.

Tony shrugged as his thoughts of date night once again stirred up his feelings of animosity towards Apostle Brandon. He recalled as he sipped at his coffee how he had voiced his complaint about the apostle and date night to Roxanne on the night of the meetings.

Roxanne had being standing at the kitchen sink doing dishes. She merely took off her yellow latex gloves, placed them on the counter, walked over to him, kissed him on the lips and said, "Get ready, the sitter coming."

Evening did come, as well as the sitter. Roxanne had just given her cell phone number to Beth, the girl they always called on, when Simon and Ruby McKullah pulled up to the front porch in their Suburban with half of their bedroom furniture still tied on top from last winter.

Roxanne said, "We won't be too long. You have my number." Then she exchanged smiles with Beth as the front door closed and they all piled into the McKullahs' Suburban. Roxanne slid into the back beside Ruby, and Tony jumped into the front next to Simon. The next thing they knew, they were heading briskly towards Drummingsville School.

It was as they were driving Tony recalled Simon saying, "Oh, by the way, I hope to catch you during the meeting for a drink." A smile still came to Tony's face as he remembered Simon's bizarre comment. He had not been able to respond, but only to smile back at Simon and think, *really dude, are you for real?* Ruby's random outburst of laughter from the backseat next to Roxanne had only succeeded in making him feel a little more awkward at the time. Then there was her explanation, "You need to remember to tell them, dear, it's about faith and more of the presence of God," followed by another outburst of laughter from her before she had asked him if he thought they were talking about drinking alcohol. Tony remembered his cheeks starting to flush and was grateful when Simon pulled the Suburban up to the front of the school. He also remembered whispering a silent prayer as he got out, thanking God for His timing.

They had all rushed through the front doors of the school like it was a game of British Bulldog. Tony recalled being right on Roxanne's heels as they burst through the gym doors, their hearts pounding to the beat of the music being pumped out through a small PA system connected to a laptop computer sitting on a chair at the front of the gym. Next to the laptop stood a rugged man Tony thought could have passed for an extra in a Jesus film. He had sandy-colored, curly hair with a full beard, and he was dressed in a fishnet sweater with the widest bellbottoms Tony had ever seen. It was the look of wonder in the man's eyes, though, that had stood out in his mind, for it was a look one might have if they had traveled in the spirit with Jesus into space to view the galaxies.

Picking up his bagel again, Tony took another bite and chewed methodically as he continued to work through his feelings towards Apostle Brandon in his thoughts.

Roxanne had grabbed his arm enthusiastically, saying, "Let's go meet the apostle!" Ruby had found a group of ladies that seemed to be as joyous as she had been in the Suburban, and quickly joined them in what appeared to Tony to be backstroking across the gym floor, to songs about being in the River of God. Simon had wandered off towards a group of men that seemed to be miming the art of drinking in another part of the gym. It all seemed a blur, though, from what he could remember—Simon, Ruby, the people backstroking on the floor laughing hysterically, the team member who looked so inebriated he needed to be supported continually—as Roxanne had whisked him towards the front of the gym to where the apostle stood.

The apostle was standing next to the chair with the laptop on it, a guitar hanging loosely from a strap around his neck. He smiled at Roxanne as he unfastened his guitar and placed the instrument back on its stand next to the chair. Roxanne had introduced herself enthusiastically, like one might do when meeting someone in a pub—a little too much, Tony remembered thinking, for his liking.

The apostle had reached out his hand towards him. "Levi Brandon."

Tony remembered not wanting to shake the hand of the individual he held personally responsible for messing up his date night; however, he grasped the apostle's hand and coldly said, "Tony Epson."

It was as the apostle had shook his hand that he had asked Tony a question. He had said, "What is the gold, Tony?"

Tony took a sip of coffee, shaking his head at the memory, and recalled his feelings of embarrassment, the tightness in his stomach the apostle's question had brought on, and his lame attempt to be seen as spiritual with his response,

"Is it the gold fillings people claim to receive at meetings, or the gold dust that falls on certain ones during revival meetings?"

The apostle had just smiled at him as he let go of his hand, then responded. "The gold is the Glory of God, Tony."

Tony recalled as he randomly flipped pages in the magazine how spiritually inferior he felt to Apostle Brandon at that moment. He remembered Simon's hand on his shoulder pulling him away from the apostle, muttering something about Murphy time. He also recalled thinking whilst still glaring at the apostle and being pulled by Simon backwards, *I bet you can't sharpen a Husqvarna chainsaw!* It was the sight of the apostle's hand on Roxanne's shoulder, his seemingly playfulness with her, her bent over at the waist crying, "Yes Lord!" and the apostle's cries of "More, more, more Lord!" mixed with his heavenly language that caused Tony to think of Peter Pan who was attached to his shadow, to the point that when he was separated from it he wanted Wendy to help him attach it again. *Roxanne's my shadow!* he remembered screaming in his thoughts as Simon was insistently pulling him backwards across the gym. *Get your own shadow!* his mind screamed at the apostle before finally turning to give Simon his attention.

I should have been the one experiencing Roxanne's playfulness, Lord, Tony thought as he sipped from his coffee again. He remembered having followed Simon to the middle of the gym to where two individuals were standing, and he recalled it was Simon saying, "Hey dude, meet Karl Weis and James Anderson," that had jolted him out of his dark thoughts towards the apostle.

Karl had reached out a hand to him in between what looked to Tony like a sequence of martial arts moves interspersed with loud expressions of praise to Jesus. James on the other hand had felt the need for personal confession when he grasped Tony's hand, as if he were a priest, saying, "I used to deal drugs out of my hotel room. Now I just do the good stuff: Jesus, faith, and the presence of God." James' introduction ended abruptly as Simon said, "Okay dudes, it's murphy time."

"Yeah!" hooted Karl.

Tony remembered still feeling kind of ornery, and saying, "I don't drink!"

"Why?" Simon had surprisingly asked him.

"It's a rule I have stuck to since high school when I was involved a lot with tabletop roleplaying games. During one game, my party and I faced a giant blocking our path up a mountain. The giant asked, 'Drink or fight?' I chose to drink with the giant, and the result was my whole party's courage stat was lowered for the remainder of the game, and I had to endure their scorn."

"That's harsh!" responded James. "Mellow out, dude, it was just a game."

Really dude, Tony remembered thinking as Simon had explained, "We're really thirsty for more of God's presence. We like to take big drinks by faith from the well of salvation; that's our murphy. Just join in!" Simon encouraged as he, Karl, and James assumed low, sumo-like stances with their arms spread wide as if around large vats of wine. Tony recalled copying their actions with little zeal. There was the repetitive lifting of the mimed drinking vessel to their lips, followed by bending at the waist, and Simon saying, "Again, once more, and again."

A small smile formed on Tony's lips as he recalled James had fallen over backwards sometime between the third and fourth rep, and Karl staggered around praising Jesus boisterously before ending up tangled with Simon. Tony remembered that all he could think at the moment to say was, "Simon, I think you should knock off the murphys; you're driving, remember!"

"Oh yeah!" gasped Simon as he disentangled himself from Karl. "But the presence of God is just so good. Who knows, Tony, God might just translate our whole vehicle right from the school parking lot to your house."

"Wow, cool dude!" Karl had expressed as he punched through what appeared to Tony as a type of karate kata.

"James!" Karl had yelled, "Simon is going time traveling for Jesus!"

Still sprawled on his back on the gym floor between bouts of laughter, James had replied, "Tell Jesus his trips are far cooler than drugs for me."

Tony remembered he had just told Simon to take a moment while he went to collect the girls. He had found them near the gym door looking like they were taking turns trying to practice the Limbo. He had told

Roxanne they needed to let Beth get home and was in the process of gently pulling at her arm when the apostle said over the PA System that the janitors wanted to start cleaning and locking up the school. "Remember, we're holding meetings all week."

"Okay, Tony, I'm coming," Roxanne had said as she pulled her arm away from him.

"There's always tomorrow, girl!" laughed Ruby as she clutched at Roxanne and they made their way out of the gym like two reluctant individuals after last call in a pub.

He remembered standing for a moment facing the gym doors thinking maybe Paul wasn't so far off calling the Galatians foolish, and wondering who had so quickly bewitched them.

"I know," said Simon as he came up behind him, "I like to do that too when there are meetings like these—just stand and linger a little longer in the presence of God before I walk out the doors."

Seeing Karl and James staggering towards them boisterously, Tony had said to Simon, "Come on, we need to get going before another meeting starts." They waved to Karl and James, who were yelling at Simon to do the Philip thing, as they made their way out to the Suburban where the girls were carrying on in the back as if they had never missed them.

Tony recalled the ride home being no more joyous for him than the ride to the meetings. Simon had made a few comments about the goodness of God's presence, and the girls had chattered and laughed in the backseat, and then they were pulling up to their condo and bidding goodnight to the McKullahs.

Roxanne had chatted with Beth for a moment before thanking and paying her for her service. She closed the door behind Beth and then said she was tired and going to get ready for bed.

Tony remembered lying in bed with Roxanne, hoping to spend an intimate moment talking with her before they slept. But before he could voice his desire, Roxanne had reiterated that she was so tired, rolled over, and began her familiar sequence of whale snoring. Normally Tony found the sound of Roxanne's snoring cute, however with the animosity towards the apostle still brewing in his heart, and the replaying of the apostle's interaction with Roxanne in his mind, her snoring brought no sense of the comfort of one's home this time. *Just great,* Tony had thought as he had turned his back to Roxanne and clutched his pillow. *Not only did I miss date night, but now I'm faced with a sleepless night.*

"Murphys!" Tony muttered as he flipped the pages in the magazine back to the ad for the school of the Apostles and refocused his eyes on it. The ad was a full page. In the picture, Apostle John Bristane stood beside the School of the Apostles, surrounded by its well-pruned hedges and fruit trees.

"This could be just the thing Roxanne and I need," Tony whispered to himself as he spread cream cheese over the bagel. "Or at least what I need."

A lot of people had been drifting into town lately claiming to be apostles. Tony had questions about who the apostles were. Unlike his wife, who didn't question the activities of Apostle Brandon meetings, he had questions regarding the manifestations he'd observed at the meeting. What was of God and what was of the devil? He was also tired of suppressing his questions, especially around Simon and Roxanne, for fear of being perceived as one who had just killed a sacred cow.

"Lord, I need help," Tony prayed quietly. He blinked his foggy eyes to prevent tears from welling up. He ripped out the attached application form on the ad, deciding to fill it out.

Dark roast Colombian coffee always makes risk-taking seem more bearable, Tony thought as he took another satisfying sip of his coffee. He sighed as it seemed to carry him to the edge of ecstasy. *Yes!* he thought again, *morning has officially broken.*

Chapter Two

"Watch your step," Estravai said. "You're not walking among the castle gardens anymore."

Grenfel shook his head. "Sorry. I was just thinking about the old stories my mother used to tell when she came to my bedchamber to bid me goodnight."

"Queen Julliet?" Estravai lifted his brow. "It broke her heart to see me exiled."

Without warning, a hawk swooped out of the air, causing Morgan to rear up on his hind legs.

"Steady, steady," Grenfel pleaded with his faithful friend. "It's just you and me."

The hawk's keen eyes had spotted a mouse running between the rocks. She soon flew off with its lifeless body in her talons.

"Like lightning," whispered the Revealer of Secrets as he came to a stop on the mountaintop, marvelling at the majesty of the great bird.

"Estravai!"

At the sound of his name, Estravai broke his gaze.

"Estravai, I can't hold him!"

The panicked cry came from Grenfel, whose lanky arms were being wrenched from their sockets by the boy's horse. Trembling, Grenfel dug his shoes' heels into the slope, but to no avail. He was no match for his horse, who threatened to lift him right off the ground.

Just when it appeared the destiny of both horse and boy was to tumble to their death on the jagged rocks, Estravai's dark and weather-beaten hand grabbed Morgan's halter.

"Be still!" Estravai said in a firm voice.

A moment later, it was as if nothing out of the ordinary had transpired. Morgan stood quietly beside Grenfel, neighing contentedly. He pulled at some tough mountain grass while his young master stood with mouth open, his eyes as round as two river stones.

His voice reminds me of mother's, Grenfel thought.

"As it should," said Estravai, as though he had heard Grenfel's thoughts. The boy felt naked and vulnerable. "The queen has a believing heart, and I'm sure some of her giftings are in you as well, boy. But come, we have tarried long enough. We must finish our descent to the bay and move northward towards the forest of Dresdel, and further yet to the Sienna Desert." Then he looked up to the sky. "It's coming!"

"What's coming?" Grenfel asked, full of curiosity. "Snow?"

"Yes, that." Estravai's voice had a faraway quality. "And also, the hour of the hawk."

⌒

"It's my turn," said the tall, slim man with the salt-and-pepper ponytail protruding out the back of his pilot's cap, as the two friends entered the Backwater Grill.

"Okay, Max," Tony said. "I'll have a cup of the African blend. Is the corner all right?"

"The corner's good," Max responded as he took out his wallet and handed the cashier five dollars and a coffee card to stamp. As Max waited, he slipped his wallet back into his back pocket. Then Max thanked the cashier as she handed over two steaming mugs coffee. Spotting Tony in the corner, Max headed over and sat down. "So, how's life at Forest Tech going?"

"It's okay," Tony said, feeling a little déjà vu. "Dylan made CEO."

"Is that a good thing?" inquired Max.

"It's all right," said Tony nonchalantly. "It just means nothing is predictable anymore. I could be sent out to work at the drop of a hat."

Smiling, Max responded, "Well, isn't that what you smoke-jumpers get paid the big bucks for?"

"Yeah, I guess," muttered Tony, still feeling a little like he was in the Twilight Zone regarding his disturbing dreams.

"Well!" said Max knowingly. "So, what else is new at work besides Dylan's news?"

"Nothing special," explained Tony. "Other than I've being out a couple times behind fire-lines. I had to repel down from the chopper to check out sites to establish a base camp, and to clear out some of the beetle-killed deadfall for the chopper to land, just me and the regular fire team for the most part." Then Tony just stopped talking, for the moment seemingly lost in his thoughts as he gazed at his half-empty coffee cup.

"And?" prodded Max like a housewife desperate for a little more of her husband's time.

"It was very hot," Tony said when he snapped back to reality.

"Well, we can do the java thing another time," offered Max.

"No, no! I'm fine. It's just the meetings and the books I've been reading lately, not to mention the graphic dreams. I think maybe I'll un-hook my satellite TV."

"You're supposed to be putting fires out! Sounds to me like you've got too many fires in your life, and they're all burning at once." Max stuck his chest out like a peacock. "When I'm on the edge, I pack up the wife and head for the mountains. Or maybe we just need to drive out to the mountains and break out the climbing gear in the back of my wagon like we used to on weekends?"

"No, really, I'm not on the edge," Tony answered coldly, trying to believe it himself. Tony shifted his weight like a child waiting for deten-tion to be over before proceeding to vent his thoughts. "Max, you might understand the issues of my heart, since you and Barbara are involved with mission work here in town. I need to ask you something."

Max looked dumbfounded across the table at the guy who had played alongside him for the divisional cup with the Drummingsville

Flames hockey club, not to mention the other countless good times they'd had together.

"Do you have to ask?" Max asked.

"I know we've been through a lot of storms together. It's just that my question is so awkward, I feel like a rookie juggler with it. I just don't know how to begin."

"Try me, Tony. I'm all ears. It can't be as bad as dealing with a ninety-foot wall of fire, can it?"

Tony smiled and nodded. "Here goes, then. What do you think about apostles?"

"You mean the guys who walked with Jesus, sporting long robes and sandals? Those guys?" Max let out a laugh.

Tony paused to fiddle with his spoon; it helped soothe his nerves. "Do you think apostles are around today?"

"Well, I've never seen any shopping at a 7-11, and they're open all hours." Max chuckled at his friend's fantastical inquiry.

"Could they be here, but hidden for a season?" Tony realized he probably sounded relentless, if not a little desperate. "I mean, how would you know, Max? What would they be like?"

Max studied his friend across the table with concern. "Well, Tony, you know what I think? The last time I checked, the letter carrier was still delivering the mail, not Paul the Apostle." Max paused to work on a paper origami swan made from his coffee-stained napkin. "Besides…"

"What?" Tony urged, expecting some further nugget of wisdom, the kind that reveals the mind of God through hours of prayer.

Max held up his paper swan, stalling for time as he gathered his thoughts. "I can make paper planes, too." He paused, putting the swan down. "Apostles, dude? Really?"

"Well, there are people who aren't afraid to call themselves apostles, and you'd be surprised at all the books available on the subject. In fact," Tony went on, sounding now like one of the great defenders of the faith, "did you know the Book of Acts lists at least twelve more people referred to as apostles besides the guys who walked with Jesus?"

"I don't know about that." Max sounded a little tense. "I'd have to see that in Scripture, Tony. Anyway, the early church needed apostles and prophets to set the foundation of faith, but now I'm not sure, Tony. We have the complete word of God, and nothing needs to be added or taken away from it. Furthermore, we're in a different season of God now than the early church. Apostles! Interesting thoughts, Tony, but I'm just not sure."

Noticing the clock on the wall, Tony interrupted his friend's discourse. "I'm not meaning to sound rude, Max, but I've got to get running. Roxanne has to go and get something for Jordan's fifth birthday. Sorry about that. Would you like to do the coffee thing again, say, next Friday?"

"Yeah, I understand," Max said as he stood up. "I have to pick up a roast chicken for supper, anyway. How about we try that new café, John's Java Joint?"

"Sounds interesting. See you then." Tony walked his friend out the door. He turned the opposite direction down the sidewalk, then swung around and called, "Hey Max, I'll leave a message on your machine if I'm called out to work."

Max nodded and waved. "Great! Hope to see you at the Joint."

After his outing with Max, Tony found himself heading home like an A.I. programmed to follow a certain path in a game. *Maybe Max was onto something,* he thought as he unlocked the front door of his condo. Stepping through the front door, Tony yelled enthusiastically, "Roxanne, Jordan, anyone up for camping?" Expecting to be momentarily charged by Jordan in excitement, he smiled in anticipation of his son's greeting. However, his hope of either Jordan's enthusiastic embrace or observing his wife's smiling face seemed to grow less likely with every drip of water from the kitchen tap. He shuddered momentarily as if trying to shake off the disappointment of returning to a silent house, before heading to the kitchen sink to shut the tap off. As Tony passed the refrigerator, he noticed a note from Roxanne pinned to the freezer door, with some of Jordan's bright yellow and blue magnetic letters that had been arranged to spell "I luv U."

Like one pulling a cord on a bus to signal a stop, Tony ceased forward movement. Turning to face the freezer, he frantically pulled the note free, and like a commuter studying a bus schedule to learn how to reach their destination, Tony desperately began to read Roxanne's note for clues to his family's whereabouts.

Apostle Levi came by with his bus. He and his ministry team or having a little get together south of town at the Silver Spur hot springs.

Tony momentarily paused in his reading, thinking it would have been more of a surprise to him if the apostle was not involved with his family's absence from the house. Looking at Roxanne's note again, Tony continued to read.

Apostle Brandon is going to be sharing a little about their signs and wonder meetings in Sarquis, as well as cooking a favorite of his team members, his campfire chili.

Don't worry, I phoned Mrs. Philpots and she has agreed to watch Jordan for the afternoon. I think they're making homemade playdough. Anyways, were dropping Jordan off at her house on our way out of town with the apostle's bus. I know you will find something to eat. Remember there's frozen Pizza Pops in the freezer.

Luv Roxanne

Tony let the note fall from his hands to the floor, shaking his head and thinking, *Roxanne, you're mentioning this apostle a little too much lately for my liking.* Pulling the freezer door open, he grabbed a Pizza Pop, then pushed the freezer door closed, letting gravity seal it. After shredding the wrapper of his Pizza Pop, Tony grabbed a plate for his lunch, popped it into the microwave, pushed the power button on, and stood momentarily watching the plate slowly rotate through the microwave's glass window. He thought as he watched his plate rotate, *Mrs. Philpots, how could you be so available?*

The ding of the microwave set Tony into action like the bell at a horse track starts the race, but as he opened the microwave, retrieved his lunch, and closed its door again, his mind was still absorbed with thoughts of Mrs. Philpots and the apostle. He walked deep in thought to his kitchen table, set the plate on the table, and pulled out a chair to sit down.

Picking up the Pizza Pop from his plate, he fingered it cautiously. Respecting the heat of the pastry, he took a mouse-like bite and set the pastry down on its plate again. Moving the gooey contents around in his mouth to aid in cooling, he realized it wasn't Mrs. Philpots that his feelings of animosity were directed towards, but this so-called apostle holding meetings in their community.

Finally swallowing, Tony continued thinking about Mrs. Philpots. She was a short, dumpy lady with dark wavy hair and Mediterranean features, the owner of a small video rental store with an art studio in the back, next to the town's only general store. *Mrs. Philpots,* Tony thought as he smiled for a moment at the thought of this woman who seemed to always be wrapped in fur no matter the season, "I'm not mad at you," he whispered as he reached for his Pizza Pop again.

However, I can't say the same about this apostle. Tony thought of Samson's statement about the Philistine in Scripture: *you would not have known my secrets if you would not have ploughed with my heifer.*

"Yeah," muttered Tony as he swallowed the frozen, flavorless center of the Pizza Pop, "this apostle better leave my shadow alone."

CHAPTER THREE

A head of the unusual trio of travellers, a white-tailed deer leapt lazily into the underbrush, consisting mostly of willow and fireweed.
The deer's movement seemed to announce the intruders among the forest's tall poplars. At the heart of the forest lay the beautiful, and seemingly bottomless, lakes of the Charvon system, a natural oasis to many of the
local forest residents.

"Come!" Estravai called to Grenfel. "Let Morgan try a mouthful
of this lush forest grass. I'm sure the Ancient of Days has purposed that
we more than admire the vegetation. Sit with me. I'm sure you'll find
nature's blanket more heavenly than any made from goose feathers."

Grenfel lowered his lanky body to the forest floor like a sack of
grain falling off a wagon.

"It's as soft as Mother's embrace," Grenfel whispered, on the verge
of succumbing to sleep. The heat of the sun and the night's journey down
the mountain had worn him out.

Noticing his young companion's state, Estravai reached beneath his
fraying cambric cloak and into a leather satchel hanging from a braided
cord around his neck. Withdrawing his hand, he now clutched a deerskin
package, which he unravelled on the lush forest grass in front of his curious companion.

"There, boy!" smiled Estravai. "A table worthy of a king."

Grenfel raised a mystified eyebrow at the strange fare spread out
before him on the deerskin.

Picking up on his companion's troubled expression, Estravai explained, "It's dry venison, boy, go ahead and try it! It will grant you nourishment and strength."

Grenfel, who lay on his side, reached out a slim arm and caught a piece of meat. He took a bite, nearly ripping a tooth from its root. He touched his cheek in pain. "It's too tough!"

"You have to take it slow, boy." Estravai laughed. "You may judge this food strange, boy, but stranger by far is the way He gives it. Honey from the carcass of a beast, quail off the desert floor, and bread brought daily by the mouths of ravens." He sat up and looked across the grass. "I have hidden a raft amongst some willows at the lake. I have much to say, but not until we get there."

Glancing at Grenfel, Estravai saw the boy had finished eating, so he had them pack up and begin to move deeper into the forest. Soon, they came into view of Lake Charvon, its water bluer than any of the streams Grenfel remembered from his father's castle, and clearer than any of the jewels inlaid in his mother's comb.

Grenfel stroked Morgan's neck as they approached, whispering in his horse's ear, "Wait here, my friend."

But the furthest intention on Morgan's mind was to leave. He didn't wait for an invitation to dine, but set to work immediately, pulling up mouthfuls of the lush forest grass.

Grenfel took off his leather shoes as he watched his beloved horse grazing. He laughed aloud.

"Always thinking of your stomach, my friend, since the day Father gave you to me on my third birthday." Grenfel slipped off his purple gown, revealing a white linen shirt hanging loosely over blood-red woollen tights. He rolled the tights up to his knees and moved into the water.

Estravai was already up to his waist, steadying a raft constructed of poplar wood hewn crudely with a broad ax and lashed together with the guts of a pig. His frayed cloak clung tightly to his muscular frame like an invisible lover.

Grenfel grabbed the side of the raft and pushed his body up onto its small but adequate platform.

"What kept you, boy?" Estravai asked, from where he sat dripping wet upon the hide of a Muskox. Grenfel worked himself further up on the raft and sat upon the Muskox hide next to Estravai. "Do you like it?" inquired Estravai, having noticed Grenfel's amazed look. "It was a gift from another Revealer of Secrets, who took it from the herds found among Ascar's Icefields."

The two new friends sat in silence momentarily as the wind picked up force and began to push their tiny raft out on the lake as if by an invisible hand.

The moments seemed eternal to Grenfel, who sat upon the Muskox hide tightly clutching his knees, and rocking back and forth in an effort to generate some heat.

"You look as if you have just seen a spectre, boy, you're shaking like a leaf," Estravai commented.

"It's so c-c-cold!" stuttered Grenfel. The young boy's response, however, seemed lost now on Estravai who now had fixed his gaze somewhere across the lake. Feeling like he should let his new friend be for the moment, Grenfel busied himself with trying to keep warm, and ignoring the harassing thought of how much longer he would have to be out here on the lake freezing.

As Grenfel was wondering if he would ever be warm again, Estravai began speaking. "I saw you serving at your uncle's castle as one of his armour bearers. You were groomed in all aspects of knightly protocol, groomed in fact to be the next commander of your father's army. You replenished the cups with ale and carted platters laden with exotic dishes of the likes of peacock, pheasant, and stuffed boar, always at the beck and call of your uncle and his guests. I saw you leaving your uncle's castle at Heathervane, where your father sent you to train as a knight at a young age. Your mother's stories swirled in your heart like the dust of a Sienna summer storm, tears falling from your eyes. You thought no one saw those tears, but He collected each one. He told me I would find you descending the slopes of the mountains, and that I should wait for you."

Snow began to fall gently from the sky, landing delicately upon Grenfel's face.

Undistracted, Estravai continued. "You heard your mother's stories, stories of the powerful ones of old, stories of how Zarel and Asan witnessed throughout Ascar through great works of healing, stories of how Naron stood up to the priests of Meldrock and spoke revelation to him by the instructed tongue he received from the Ancient of Days, though he were a simple woodworker. Stories of how Marcon called blindness upon the sorcerers of Meldrock and set a child free from the same one's spell. The Ancient of Days' anointed ones were like the ravenous birds of prey you and your father hunted with around the grounds of Castle Kreniston. What other things did the good Queen Julliet speak of? I know at least this much, for I myself shared stories with her many nights in the castle gardens, under the light of the moon. All before I was sent into exile."

Grenfel wiped a tear from the corner of his eye as he recalled how he had cherished those nights at Kreniston as he lay upon his bed listening for the sound of his mother's hand upon the latch of his door. He trembled with the vividness of his recollections. He recalled his mother's long emerald gown gliding along behind her as she seemed to float effortlessly to his bedside. Her glistening auburn hair had often been pulled back from her face with a jewelled hair comb. Her presence seemed to soothe any troubles of his mind and flood his soul with peace. Her voice captured his young heart, causing his adventurous spirit to soar beyond the castle's stone walls to the realms of heroes and quests and villains.

"Are you all right, boy?"

"Yes, I've just got snowflakes in my eyes." Grenfel replied while trying to maintain a brave face, but as the Revealer of Secrets was about to resume speaking, he blurted out, "She told me of Meldrock and his rebellion against the Ancient of Days, how he was thrown out of the throne room before the creation of Ascar. Mother spoke of how Meldrock's evil caused most people to forget the Ancient of Days, and that his power seduced even the priests that served the Holy One."

"Did Queen Julliet speak of the hawk-like nature of the powerful ones of old?" Estravai inquired. "Or of their keen vision to discern evil, their aggression and lightning-quick attacks against evil as the Ancient of Days directed and strengthened their hands?"

Grenfel shook his head. As Estravai went on speaking, Grenfel felt as though he were standing before the very throne of the Ancient of Days.

"Did your mother, the queen, mention that the last of the Ancient of Days' servants would be known as Hawkmen, and how before the Hawkmen came the Gatekeepers of the Fold, the Sowers of Seeds, the Instructors in the Way, and the Revealers of Secrets who would stand in the gap against the evil of Meldrock?"

"No," Grenfel whispered, staring at Estravai in wonderment.

Estravai's voice took on such a tone of authority that it seemed to Grenfel that the Ancient of Days Himself was using the Revealer of Secrets to share His pain. With a far-off look in his eye, Estravai spoke of the increase of darkness, and of the decline of those willing to replace those who had departed to be in the presence of the Ancient of Days. There had always been the strong and forgotten ones who through the generations responded to His voice. As a result, the Ancient of Days had been faithfully restoring certain mantles of authority back to His people. However, there was still a gap, and Meldrock's evil seemed to cover the land as the waters covered the sea. The cry of the Ancient of Days still sounded out, "Who will step into the gap?" He was looking for such ones night and day, continually and relentlessly, allowing Himself no sleep.

"Still, the last foretold key needs yet to be turned in order for Ascar to truly be freed from Meldrock's death grip," Estravai said forlornly. "His vow to be drunk with the blood of the Revealers of Secrets and all the courageous ones of the Ancient of Days kept those who chose to stand in the gap under his intimidating and ruthless shadow. If he could not seduce them with harlots, he loosed his priests to kill them. Their blood seemed to cry of things to come. They spoke of a portal that would open, and of two witnesses going to and fro throughout the kingdom working mighty deeds, even calling forth signs in the heavens. In those days, many would remember their love for the Ancient of Days."

Grenfel no longer took notice of the falling snow as he sat with his eyes wide, hanging on every word.

Noticing the awe reflected on Grenfel's face, Estravai reached into the leather satchel under his cloak and produced a small clay vial with a wooden stopper. Removing the stopper, Estravai poured the vial's fragrant contents upon Grenfel's head.

"What!" Grenfel cried, caught by surprise as the golden oil dripped down onto his linen shirt.

"The Hawkmen have arrived. I have waited my whole life to see this day," smiled Estravai.

As soon as the words left his tongue, a flash of brilliant light streaked across the sky.

"*You shall behold strange signs in the sky at the time the contents are poured from your flask*," Estravai whispered to himself as he sat alongside Grenfel in the raft, gazing into the heavens. "That shall be my sign that the portal has begun to open."

Ahead of the small raft, the water swelled.

"Leviathan!" the Revealer of Secrets cried.

"Who?" Grenfel inquired, his hand covering the dagger at his side. Rising to the surface of the lake was a huge grey coil with scales so tight a feather couldn't have been slipped between them.

"No doubt he saw the light in the heavens," yelled Estravai as the water churned.

Grenfel stood, paralyzed with fear, his dagger in his hand and his face as white as the fallen snow.

"See how his scales are tightly formed into rows of shields? Boy, you won't even scratch him with that bread knife," Estravai bellowed, though his voice was barely audible over the wind.

Grenfel's eyes widened and his every muscle tensed. He fully expected to be crushed under this mighty serpent's coil.

"Be not afraid. He's not here for us, boy," Estravai reassured him. "If his intentions were for our harm, we would not still be standing on this raft. Look! See how the water is settling down? No doubt this great serpent is already on its way back to his master, who has eyes and ears everywhere."

Without being told, Grenfel knew the identity of this great creature's master. He had seen with his own eyes the evil hidden beneath the surface of the water, just one of the many forces of Meldrock.

26

"You were snoring," Roxanne said as she nudged Tony with her elbow and pushed him onto his side.

"Sorry," replied Tony half-coherently. "Pin the tail on the donkey really wears me out."

"Well, be thankful we don't have twelve kids. So, who's Meldrock? Is she another one of those khaki-shorts-wearing, sun-tanned, my-mother-never-told-me-how-to-dress-properly fire girls on your crew?"

"No, no," he grunted, still half-asleep and struggling to open his eyes. "It's just a weird, never-ending nightmare. Now, can we get some sleep? Jordan gets up in a few hours."

"Can I have a kiss?" Roxanne asked, sounding like she had just drunk a whole glass of orange juice.

"Can I please get some sleep?" Tony mumbled, his face somewhat buried in his pillow.

"Hmm. I'll remember that next time you want a hug." Roxanne turned onto her side, facing away.

Tony rolled over only to find himself staring at his wife's back. He mumbled to himself as he fluffed up his pillow with his hands. "How can a guy get into trouble for wanting a little sleep?"

Tony's head soon met his pillow once more, and in no time, he succumbed to slumber.

CHAPTER FOUR

"Good morning, Tony," came the welcoming voice of Randy Foxworth in his easily distinguishable southern accent.

Tony smiled. "Good to see you again! You know I always enjoy dropping in on you, Randy."

Randy Foxworth was the senior pastor of the small but family-orientated Drummingsville Christian Centre. "What brings you all out before the hens in the hen-house?" asked the well-fed, short pastor who always dressed like was going to jump on a cutting horse and ride the pens.

Tony stared at the man sitting behind an old harvest-style desk that you purchase at a lumber store and finish yourself, who over the years had become more of a friend than a pastor. Tony took a moment, seemingly captivated by Randy's eyes. Every time Tony looked into Randy's eyes, they never seemed to lack compassion, though many found Randy a bit too straightforward. The compassion hadn't come cheap for Randy; as a veteran of the Vietnam War, he had developed it by walking daily amongst the wounded and lost.

It was not uncommon for people who met Randy to be reminded of Santa Claus, with his snowy white hair that receded back from his forehead and curled up around his ears and at the base of his neck. His bulging waistline and the jolly twinkle in his eye did little to correct others' perception of the pastor. Tony, however, never seemed any less overwhelmed by Randy's eyes—he knew they had witnessed much trauma.

"I know the light's on, but is anyone home?" inquired Randy. "I don't believe you all came out this morning to jus' stand like an ol' statue in front of my desk."

"S-s-orry, stuttered Tony, realizing he had drifted off in thought.

"No harm dun," smiled Randy. "How 'bout a swig of percolated coffee?"

"Don't make it just for me, Randy."

"Ain't nothin' to do with you, boy. I never pass up a chance to have a cup of percolated coffee in the morning for a kick of motivation. It's much like firing a twelve-gauge shotgun."

Tony spent the few minutes Randy used in getting coffee ready to wonder how his friend managed to work in an office that also served as the church kitchen/storage room. As big as the hearts of the pastor and congregation of the Drummingsville Christian Centre were, the space they occupied was much more concentrated. Consisting of the pastor's residence upstairs, a small sanctuary below it, and directly across from the sanctuary the small combination pastoral office/kitchen/storage room. Add the two small washrooms and the broom closet next to Randy's office and you had the whole blueprint of Drummingsville Christian Center.

Some, usually visitors, found the facility a little claustrophobic, but Tony was used to it as he found the church far more spacious than a heat-reflecting blanket.

The smell of fresh percolated coffee and Randy saying, "Give that a try, I believe it's black enough," brought Tony out of his mental tour of the church facility. Reaching out, Tony took the metal camping cup from Randy and proceeded to take a sip. Swallowing hard in hope of masking the bitter taste of the coffee grinds floating in his cup, Tony flashed a pasted-on smile at Randy who was now seated back behind his office desk.

"So, what's ailin, you, boy?" The directness of Randy's comment was all most as powerful as his coffee, and seemed to hit Tony with the same impact.

"It's just these meetings Roxanne and I have been attending," Tony explained, still feeling a little nervous about talking about apostles again so soon after coffee with Max. "Have you heard of them? The ones mentioned on the bulletin board down at Martha's Grocery Store. Being held at the community centre."

"Yeah! I reckon I heard wind of it." Randy crossed his arms as if to signify his stance. "Apostle Levi—I believe that's the old boy who hails out of Sarquis. I could show you a pile of papers on that there apostle so high it would make the tower of Babel seem like a wee little anthill."

"People are coming out to all his meetings."

"Yeah, that may be so, but mostly just from other flocks. The man's a sheep stealer and a zealot." Randy went on as if the very wrath of God was being declared through him. "He's led a rebellion against anything that smells like normal Christianity."

Tony was somewhat glad to hear this, since he'd been confused and frustrated with the apostle himself. However, deep down Tony still felt an impression to check things out before he threw his hat in with Randy. Out of respect for Randy's friendship, he stood silently and looked down at the floor, listening to his friend vent until he heard silence.

"I have questions," Tony said. "I guess that's really the crux of my being here. There's all kind of talk in these meetings about being free from religious spirits, of just getting into the river—not that I don't want to be in the river, assuming it means drawing closer to God and having God draw closer to me. I mean, I just don't know how to live that out. Do I just receive this teaching, no questions asked?"

"I'm just going to speak to you now out of love here, Tony." Randy paused to take a long sip. "The man is sowing seeds of disunity and rebellion, which my Bible equates to witchcraft. I'm not trying to put fear in your heart, but be warned. Sure would be a sad state to see either you or Roxanne get hurt. Pastor Devron of the First Baptist Church and Frank Lacomb, pastor of the Moravian Fellowship, attended some of Apostle Brandon's weekend seminars awhile back, just to see what all the fuss about apostles was. I remember when Frank got back he just shook his head and said, 'I still believe apostles ended with the early church. I tell you the man's deceived, Randy, best you and your congregation stay an arm's length away from his ministry.' It ain't just me. And it ain't a personal thing, you know?" declared Randy. "I meet with those two good ol' boys once every month for prayer. After all, we got the job of being the spiritual gatekeepers of our fine community here. I lean on those two good ol' boys hard in spiritual matters, so I've learned to highly regard their opinions."

"I just wish Apostle Brandon's team would be interested in whole family units," Tony said, letting his frustration show. "They just keep calling my wife, like if the apostle's team can't get me, they'll take whoever they can get. They're not fussy."

"Divide and conquer!" Randy said loudly and boldly, as if he were once again in the jungles of Nam. "If the enemy can split anything, be it ministries, marriages, or churches, he will. It's one of his favourite strategies. If he can weaken y'all, he can defeat y'all. The Amalekites came and attacked the Israelites' wounded, weary, and weak ones. But God said He would make war against the Amalekites from generation to generation. Here's some advice from someone who don't know a whole lot about everything but knows a lot about some things. It'd be best if you stayed out of the Amalekites' camp." Randy shook his head and smiled. "Shoot! I dun have got into sermonizin' with y'all!"

"It's okay," Tony insisted. "I think I needed to hear what you had to say. No, really, Randy, who wouldn't have the fear of God in their heart after such fine southern preaching? My ears may be screaming for you to stop sermonizing, but my heart thanks you for your concern for me and my family."

Tony scuffed his feet on the rough plank floor of the pastor's office until his embarrassment over being so transparent receded.

"I've been out to my father's ranch just outside Sarquis," Tony said. "It's about thirty miles out, I guess. I know what a good cutting horse can do in culling out the sick animals in a pen. Somehow, I can't help but feel that either I'm being culled out of my family or my wife is, and all by this so-called apostle and his ministry."

"I think you'll be all right, son. Y'all are seeking out the word of counsellors. There's a whole lot of wisdom in that, my friend," Randy said as he got up out of his wooden captain's chair.

"I'm encouraged by your faith in me."

"Well, I'll be praying for you," Randy said as he shook Tony's hand. "You and Roxanne and your son Jordan, is it?"

31

"Yeah, that's right. Jordan just had his fifth birthday."

"That's really fine," declared Randy.

"Sorry for dumping my whole life on you, Randy, but thank you for your ear."

"Ain't a worry boy, all you caught me doing this mornin' was messin' with a bunch of ribs out back the church on the barbecue anyway."

From the front porch of the church, Randy watched as Tony settled into his truck and when he saw that he was again looking out his front window he waved goodbye.

Tony looked admiringly at the pastor standing on the steps of his church. He was dressed in a down hunting vest, snakeskin boots, and two-tone plaid shirt.

Is this man really a pastor? Sensing the Lord rebuking him instantly, Tony remembered how God had chosen David not by his outward appearance, but by his heart.

"Forgive me for judging," Tony prayed as he shifted his truck into reverse and backed out of the church driveway.

As he sped away, Randy's words came back to mind like the surf crashing on the rocks of a shoreline: "Don't go into the Amalekites' camp."

Estravai sat calmly upon his muskox hide, chewing on a piece of venison as if this was a mere romantic outing. Grenfel, on the other hand, stood at the front of the raft gazing at the hazy outline of his horse grazing along the shoreline. In Grenfel's young mind Morgan still seemed so far away.

"He won't come any closer by you standing there watching him, boy. We're at the mercy of the wind and the waves." Estravai stretched out on the hide. "May as well get some rest."

"Rest!" Grenfel cried. "There are wild beasts to kill and evil lords to crush!"

Estravai chuckled. "You've got the same spirit as your mother, boy. That's good. But you'll be no match for the weakest of Meldrock's forces without rest."

Like a knight surrendering at the point of a sword, Grenfel yielded and sat down. He watched the water lap against the poplar logs in a rhythmic fashion. The sun was merciless and bore down upon them with the full force of its heat. Despite this, Grenfel drifted into sleep and began to dream.

In this dream, he saw a queen with long, raven-black hair tumbling down her shoulders like long-held captives released into the light of the sun. Her skin was beige, unlike his mother's fair complexion. She sat in front of her pavilion dressed in a dark velvet gown with a silver chain around her neck; a black spider dangled from the chain. It caused him to wonder if it was real or the clever work of a skilled silversmith. Her eyes seemed to melt anyone who gazed at them like wax dripping down a burning candle. Her lips were crimson, darker than any cranberry he'd ever seen on the Cabernish Mountains. She wore velvet gloves that extended to her elbows, and in one gloved hand she clutched a leather cord. With it, she kept a hawk enslaved high above her on a wooden perch. Her voice ensnared Grenfel with its seductive overtones.

"So, you represent the coming of the Hawkmen," she mocked. "Why, you're just a boy. Pray tell, is this the best the Creator can come against me with? How pathetic! He must be more desperate than I thought."

The queen appeared enflamed by the very thought of a weak Creator and broke out into shrill laughter.

"Who are you?" Grenfel asked, feeling afraid.

"I am known by many names, but you may remember me as the Queen of the Heavens." The queen leaned forward, lowering her voice to a whisper. "You like hawks, they can be useful. However, I much prefer serpents when I do my hunting." The queen smiled, sending a chill through his bones. Then, like a shark smelling blood, she sensed Grenfel's uneasiness.

"Funny," she said, pulling at the hawk's leash and drawing it from its perch. "You hunt using hawks and I hunt Hawkmen."

Feeling the tug of its leash, the hawk now descended upon the dark crystal surface of a high pedestal table with slender serpentine legs to the left of the queen. The magnificent bird no sooner had gathered in its wings, when the queen reached for a small gold case resting on the table in front of the bird's talons, and upon opening the case she withdrew a dagger. It had a slender blade shaped to resemble intertwined serpents and its handle was inlaid with blood-red rubies. Drawing the hawk close, the queen peered into Grenfel's eyes.

"Beautiful," she said.

"Wh—what is beautiful?" stuttered Grenfel. "The bird?"

With lightning quick speed, the queen plunged the dagger into the bird's heart.

"Not the bird, blood-red rubies," whispered the queen with a smile of satisfaction as she wiped the blood from her dagger.

"No!" cried Grenfel at the sight of the lifeless bird.

Awakened by the sound of his scream, Estravai sat up quickly and touched Grenfel's shoulder. "Easy, boy, you were sleeping."

The gentle voice was both reassuring and familiar. Feeling comforted, Grenfel opened his eyes. "A dream?" Grenfel asked, holding his groggy head.

"And from the looks of you, boy, not a good one," Estravai replied with a look of concern.

Noting how closely the raft had drifted back to the shore, and remembering how long it took for his young companion to get warm, Estravai said, "We'll have to jump in, but there's no need for us to both get wet."

Without waiting for Grenfel's response, in an instant Estravai was waist deep in water and pushing the raft towards the shore. At the water's edge, Morgan let out an excited whinny, prancing back and forth. It was hard to tell who had the least patience, horse or boy. When they were close enough, Grenfel sprang off the front of the raft like a coiled snake. He ran to Morgan and embraced his neck with both of his long arms. The Arabian nuzzled him.

"I missed you, old friend," Grenfel said.

"Come now, boy." Estravai smiled. "My company can't have been all that bad!"

CHAPTER FIVE

*D*imension, thought Tony to himself, *I feel like I've been in the fourth Dimension without reading this book about the apostolic church.* Tossing the book down upon his sleeping bag, Tony proceeded to unzip the nylon mesh door of his two-man assault tent and crawl out.

"Cabin fever already!" came an unfamiliar female voice.

Still down on his hands and knees and fumbling with the laces of his hiking boots, Tony wondered who his female caller might be. As he had not expected any visitors to be dropping in on him at the Blackhorn fire site, being that Dylan had just sent him out to do site assessment for camp construction.

"My name is Sue Henderson," came the female voice, again jarring Tony out of his thoughts. "Dylan sent me, thought I might be useful to you out here at the fire site if you ever emerged from hibernation."

"There's nothing like the smell of smoked campfire coffee," Tony said, inhaling deeply as he came to his feet in front of his tent. "I believe, though it hasn't been scientifically proven yet, that even a bear would give up hibernation for a stiff cup. My name's Tony Epson, as you probably already know if Dylan sent you."

Tony leaned over to finish tying up his laces, then stepped forward to shake Sue's hand.

"Oh. Didn't Dylan tell you about me? I'm an experienced faller, yeah I put down some pretty big trees at the last fire site with my saw."

Tony let go of Sue's hand like it was a cold fish.

"Is there a problem?" asked Sue.

"No!" Tony replied between sputters. "No, I just swallowed a black fly. They're bad out here."

"Try eating another one." Sue laughed. "Maybe the others will become afraid and fly away. Now, you probably thought I was one of those prissy office girls who just sat around and painted their nails while they talked on the phone all day. Well, am I right? Or did you think I was the camp nurse?"

Tony was speechless. He gazed blankly at the shapely blond dressed in a black Harley Davidson jumpsuit with a silver-plated Navajo belt hanging loosely around her slender waist.

Observing Sue, Tony could imagine Dylan hanging around the Drummingsville Forest Tech office, leaning back in his torn and over-stuffed office chair with his feet up on his desk. The short, bald-headed man with his thick, bushy, grey eyebrows was probably snorting like a farmhouse pig right about now. This was pure Dylan, one hundred per-cent classic Dylan. He was Forest Tech's executive manager and he could be as shrewd as a serpent or yet as gentle as a dove at times.

"Ground control to Major Tony, hello! Is anyone in there? I repeat, hello!"

"No," Tony said loudly, causing Sue to jump.

She was quick as a cat, however, to regain her composure. "No, what? No, there's no one in there? No, you didn't picture me as the camp nurse? Or were you simply venting stress?"

"No, it doesn't work," Tony said. "If you eat a blackfly, they still swarm around you, and yes to be honest with you I didn't picture you packing a chainsaw." He took a sip of coffee. "But I think I understand Dylan's choice in you. As a faller, you're easily an equal to Paul Bunyan—if not in brawn, then in brains."

"What did this temptress of Meldrock's tell you to call her?" Estravai asked as he swallowed a handful of large, luscious blueberries he had picked from a small bush.

"The Queen of the Heavens," Grenfel whispered, her very name causing him to feel lightheaded and his skin to become waxy. Estravai leapt up, spat the berries from his mouth, and caught Grenfel in his arms. Morgan had lifted his head from grazing, snorting uneasily as he watched his young master stretched across Estravai's arms like a sheaf of wheat.

"I tell you to get off this boy!" Estravai shouted at Grenfel's limp body. "Come out of him, spirit of death, in the name of the all-powerful one, the Ancient of Days! You cannot touch His anointed!"

The wind picked up to a near gale force, but the Revealer of Secrets stood unflinching, holding Grenfel in his arms with Morgan watching anxiously over his shoulder.

Without any announcement of his arrival, a large and muscular man appeared in front of the Revealer of Secrets. He had the head of a wolf. The Revealer of Secrets didn't cower in the ominous presence, but commanded boldly, "I send you back to Hades empty-handed, by the power and authority of the Ancient of Days."

As Estravai spoke, an invisible chain seemed to pull at the wolf-headed demon. It glared at Estravai through red eyes, then retreated, descending downward into the earth, as if it were suddenly summoned back by its master. Leaving Estravai now to simply stare into empty space.

~

In the mid-heavens, seated upon a throne of grotesque living forms, the queen reached for a silver chalice full of a foaming crimson liquid. Before her, two whirling demons hurled spells by the dark power of their sorcery upon the inhabitants of Ascar. The spells fell like raindrops, further binding the people in slavery to the Queen of the Heavens. The demons unleashed their Queen's wrath upon her every command. Saliva dripped from the demons' mouths as they anticipated that the moment might come for them, as it had for the spirit of Death, to be sent out.

"Go, my princes," whispered the queen as the demon princes spun ever faster, until they were nothing but a blur. They were set in motion by their Queen's words of freedom, and encouraged on by her sadistic laughter.

Grenfel sighed painfully. "What happened, Estravai? Did I fall off my horse?"

Morgan nuzzled his young master's face as if to say, *Good to have you back.*

"You were paid a visit by one of Meldrock's servants," Estravai said while trying to catch his breath. "He has managed to take many courageous ones before their time. I know this from experience. He may have taken their lives, but their hearts were faithful to the Ancient of Days. I am living proof of that, having been hunted every day, sent into exile, and at times fearing for my very life." Estravai took a metal flask out of the satchel hanging under his cloak and passed it to Grenfel. "Here, take a sip of this, boy."

Grenfel took the flask and saw that it contained a honey-coloured liquid. He sipped the warm fluid. "What is it?"

"Chamomile tea," Estravai replied. "It is good for relaxing the body."

"My mother always had sweet-smelling wild flowers in her bedchamber. This tea smells like them."

"How do you feel about those days, boy? Be honest. The Ancient of Days knows all things," Estravai said, speaking as though skilfully extracting poison from a festering wound. "Were you bitter towards your father? Were you angry at him for sending you away at such a young age?"

Grenfel, sitting upright, took another sip of tea. "How I miss my mother! I hated leaving Kreniston." A tear rolled down his cheek. "I never understood why I had to go. I cried, but my father only told me to be thankful, because most young men never have the chance to be groomed as commander to the troops."

"I fear this is the gate to your heart by which Meldrock's temptress was so quickly able to get a hold on you. Like bloodhounds, her servants are able to detect unloving attitudes of the heart. By the way Meldrock has shown such keen interest, it's pretty clear that the Ancient of Days has called you. For now, let's get some rest here, at the edge of the forest. It will be good for both of us. At the first light of dawn, we'll leave for the Sienna Desert." Estravai yawned. "There is one in the desert we must meet. He might be used by the Ancient of Days to prepare you. Now that the portal has begun to open, you will be enabled to fulfil the foretold word. Boy, you are one of the two witnesses. Do you understand any of what I've said?"

Turning towards Grenfel, Estravai saw that his young companion had leaned up against a tree, his velvet robe tucked behind his head, and was already fast asleep.

"No matter, boy. Understanding will soon come." He lifted his hands to the heavens. "Thank you, Ancient of Days, for releasing your hornets against our enemies today. It was not by our sword that they were turned back. Now, I ask that you send your horsemen to encircle our camp, your warriors with their flaming swords."

Estravai breathed deeply of the cool night air and fell back into the grass to sleep. Every last ounce of energy had been squeezed out of him like water from a sponge.

CHAPTER SIX

Tony burst through the front door of his condo like fireworks on the fourth of July.

"Roxanne! Jordan!" he yelled.

He made his way through the dark living room and to the kitchen. Turning on the light, he sat down at the table, still dressed in his orange coveralls and steel-toed boots. Dragging the phone across the table, Tony pushed the call display button in hopes of discovering where his family had gone. "Where are you, girl?" Tony muttered as the first call replayed. It was Max:

"Missed you at the Java Joint. Guess you left unexpectedly. When I didn't hear from you, I just figured you'd flown out to some fire site. Anyway, call me when you get back. The java is choice. It's java heaven— that ought to tempt you. Catch you later, dude."

"I could use an espresso right about now," Tony muttered as he hurried to the next message.

"Hi, honey!" Roxanne's voice said. "Didn't know when you would be back. Apostle Levi offered to take a group of us in his luxury coach to some meetings going on in Sarquis. If you get back before me, there's a supply of frozen dinners in the freezer. Oh, and don't worry, Jordan is spending a few days with the Philpots. Got to go now, because they're starting to sing around the payphone and I can't think. Love ya, hope you're all right, and see you when I get back."

The machine clicked off, but Tony just sat on his chair without responding to its signal. Roxanne knew better. She knew he didn't like her taking trips when he was out, because he could come back at any time and he liked her to be home when he got there. Their time together was so valuable to him.

He shook his head and got up from his chair, pacing the floor.

"This is not the sixties where everything is psychedelic and when you get a good vibe, you do something," he blurted out.

He became increasingly frustrated, anger pounding at his heart. He couldn't help but release what was churning deep within him.

"He calls himself an apostle. Ha! I call him a marriage separator! This Levi, he probably has a big pink neon flower painted on his bus, too."

He walked into the living room, still shaking his head in disbelief. *Roxanne, Roxanne. What am I going to do with you? Put you in a pumpkin shell?* He sat down in a wingback chair. Then, picking up the remote for his home theatre system, he clicked on the television to watch the news.

"A bizarre story having to do with a private abortion clinic made news today in regard to its controversial philosophy. It appears the doctors of the Belial Clinic are claiming the religious freedom to perform abortions anywhere geographically in the world in relation to the ancient practice of worshiping the Queen of the Heavens."

Tony clicked off the television, wondering if a smaller TV might make the news less disturbing. As he headed up the stairs to the master bedroom, dialogue from his dream swirled through his head: *"I fear this is the gate to your heart by which Meldrock's temptress was so quickly able to get a hold on you. Like bloodhounds, her servants are able to detect unloving attitudes of the heart."*

"Forgive me, Lord," Tony whispered as he reached the top of the stairs, feeling a wave of shame subside within him. "I opened myself to demonic attack by being angry in my heart towards Roxanne. I'm sorry, Lord, I'm weak. Perfect your strength in my weakness."

He took a deep breath as he walked into the bedroom. He hoped that this had all been nothing but a series of bad dreams, and that Roxanne would be home in the morning. As he climbed into bed and reached for the lamp on the nightstand, he thought about the big man with the wolf's head.

Chapter Seven

The landscape before the travellers entered the desert rose into large, cinnamon-coloured columns of sandstone. Atop a spiralled column sat a demon whose face was that of a bull, with eyes set deep into its skull. Its torso was covered in hair which writhed chaotically like a lair of snakes. Gigantic wings protruded from its back, giving it a grotesquely deformed look. High upon its sandstone perch. The demon remained undetected as it watched the travellers below as if they were mere insects through its bloodshot eyes.

"My queen will be pleased," the demon boasted. "She may reward me well this day."

It released its huge talons from the rock and lifted high into the mid-heavens.

Through squinted eyes, Grenfel peered at the never-ending mounds of red sand before him. "I doubt there's any living thing in this barren land."

Like dogs nipping at his heels, weariness and exhaustion shadowed his every step. Every one of his muscles ached, and seemed to silently scream for Mercy. All at once, he fell to his knees.

Estravai moved on, seemingly oblivious to his young companion's mental state. Holding the hood of his cloak with one hand for protection from the blowing sand, with the other he held fast to Morgan's halter. He staggered forward as if pushing through an invisible barrier of resistance, inching through the desert like a newborn turtle to the sea, for the moment lost miles away in his thoughts from his young companion's cries.

"I don't want to be a Hawkman! I don't even know if I believe in the Ancient of Days!" Grenfel knelt in the sand only to have his tearful cries smothered by the howling of an unsympathetic desert wind. In a state of delirium, he lifted handfuls of sand and dropped them again. He did this over and over again, overwhelmed with emotion. He even let loose an ear-piercing scream, which also went unheard by his traveling companion.

"I'm scared," Grenfel sobbed. "I'm scared…"

He felt chilled to the bone, feeling very much like a knight without his armour, naked in the face of his enemy. He grasped his own shoulders and tried to keep from shaking. His eyes stung as his tears mixed with blowing sand.

It was in this condition that a loving yet firm hand touched his back and pulled his head up from where it had been buried in his knees.

"You are afraid, and rightfully so," Estravai's familiar voice spoke in the midst of the howling wind. "Boy, look what was sitting on your back."

Estravai dangled a scorpion from his fingertips.

"Harmless enough now," Estravai assured him. "It's nothing but crystallized salt."

Grenfel let out a sigh of relief.

"Minutes ago, I felt an invisible hand touch my shoulder. A voice I recognized to be the Ancient of Days said, 'Stop!' As I stopped, so did Morgan, willingly, for his eyes and nostrils were encrusted with sand. I could scarcely see, since my own eyes were watering from the blowing sand. We were like the blind leading the blind, Morgan and I." Estravai stopped to sip from his flask before continuing. "Then, in the spirit realm, I saw a huge sea creature not unlike those I heard stories of from the Sea of Cercion. Its tentacles were wrapped tightly around your head. I cried in my spirit, 'Oh Ancient of Days, release your warriors to cut the cords of the wicked!' And instantly, two giant warriors with swords of fire touched the tentacles of the creature. As they did, the tentacles were severed and disintegrated. Then I saw one of the warriors touch the scorpion on your back, and a bolt of light flashed from his sword like a tongue of fire. This turned the deadly intruder into crystallized salt, thus rendering it powerless over you. A huge winged demon with the face of a bull then left you shrieking, its wings spiralling it high into the mid-heavens."

Feeling both enlightened and remorseful, Grenfel collapsed into Estravai's arms. His body heaved in time to the tears trickling down his cheeks.

Grenful wiped the sand from the corner of his eyes. "I'm sorry. My head hurt so much. I–I–I didn't—"

"You were in a confused state, boy."

"I do love Him," said Grenfel between sniffles, less embarrassed but still crying as he thought how his words might have caused the Ancient of Days to be hurt. "I've always loved Him, ever since I was small and listened to my mother's stories. When she would depart my bedchamber, I'd move over on my bed so that if any heavenly warriors were tired, they could lie down. How I longed to talk to the Ancient of Days, to see Him as I could see my mother, to be His friend. Oh, I longed for a friend! I used to pretend I was fighting His battles when I practiced with wooden swords at Heathervane. I so wanted the Ancient of Days to be pleased with me."

Estravai smiled, then lifted Grenfel's head to gaze into his young friend's watery eyes. "I believe the Ancient of Days is pleased with you, boy, for He has thought it important enough to deliver you from a life of enslavement to the sword."

In the distance, Grenfel detected a lone hooded figure walking towards them, carrying a staff in one hand. The wind gusted occasionally, yet the stranger seemed undaunted and continued on his course.

"Greetings!" Estravai shouted as the cloaked figure drew near. "Is it you, Morteque?"

After several seconds of silence, the stranger replied, "It is I."

"Then you saw the light in the heavens?"

"Yes," Morteque said. "The others are already gathering. We need to travel to Mirana, the place of the cliff dwellers."

"I had thought you would be the only one, Morteque, but the Ancient of Days is rewarding me with an unexpected reunion of many old friends," Estravai said as he embraced Morteque, suspending his friend several seconds in the air before returning him to the ground. "It's good to see you again, my brother."

After several moments, Estravai turned to face Grenfel. "Come, boy, bring Morgan. We shall continue on our journey."

⁓

"Rena Peterson here, for K7 News, with a special live news bulletin. We'll be switching to our camera in the sky as we continue to update our viewers on this story. Earlier today, a busload of mostly Drummingsville residents were hijacked when the bus driver pulled into a gas station just off Highway 97, heading to Sarquis. It appears a group of heavily armed men with a white van were waiting for the bus to arrive. When the driver started fuelling up, they took him at gunpoint onto the bus, and at that point took over the bus. It is not known at this time if the hijackers are connected to any known terrorist cells, however witnesses at the gas station said the group was heavily armed, and some of them spoke in foreign languages. We know there were at least five hijackers, but at this time the hijackers aboard the bus aren't giving any clue as to their intentions or destination. The service station attendant noted the bus pulled out onto Highway 97 and headed south, leaving the pump turned on and diesel spilling onto the ground at the gas station."

Tony stumbled into the living room with an egg flipper still in one hand.

"Oh Lord," Tony pleaded, still listening to the broadcast. "Not Roxanne's bus. There are ten righteous on that bus, Lord!" Tony cried aloud, his voice drowned out by the news story.

"For those of you just joining us, our top story is the hijacking of a bus. This is a full-size travel coach. We believe most of the passengers on the bus are from Drummingsville. Though we don't yet know the identity of the hijackers or their motives, we do know the bus is privately owned by an Apostle Levi Brandon. We'll follow all developments to this story as it unfolds."

Tony turned off the television and sat motionless, wondering what the hijackers wanted with their captives, and if Apostle Levi had had anything to do with this. Obviously, some people didn't agree with his religious views, but who would go so far as to put others in harm's way because of them?

That evening, a town meeting was called for those affected by the day's traumatic events.

"Just calm down now, folks," declared the voice of Sheriff Ryder. "I called this here town meeting due to the fact that you all are causing my phone to ring my ears off. Martha here has been kind enough to open her store tonight for us, so let's respect her by not helping ourselves to her stock. Martha has nicely donated coffee, but everything else comes out of your own pockets.

"Firstly I'd like to say, in regard to our missing loved ones, we have the initial direction the hijackers were headed. As well, our dispatch out of Princeton received a report of a sighting of the hijacked bus from a retired couple who had stopped their motorhome for a roadside picnic along the highway to Princeton. So we have reason to believe they're heading in the direction of Princeton, however we are still at the moment unsure of their motives or demands."

"Where's my Betty?" shouted a man dressed in a red plaid hunting cap, triggering other voices amongst those gathered.

"I want my Emily back!" yelled another voice.

Tony stood by the old potbellied stove silently sipping a cup of coffee.

"I know you're all upset here, but let's not be doing anything foolish," Sheriff Ryder reminded the crowd of approximately thirty people sitting in a horseshoe around the stove.

"You mean like grabbing our guns and jumping into our pickup trucks?" blurted Jim McFlurry, owner of the fishing tackle store called Men with Flies.

"Let me remind you all that this is Drummingsville, not Tombstone," Sheriff Ryder piped up. "There ain't gonna be any posse formed or vigilante justice served here."

Tony felt an urge to speak up and mediate the tension. "Come on, everyone, we all buy our groceries from the same store here. Let's just try to stay friends through this crisis and remain calm."

His words did little to defuse the tension in the room, which was starting to manifest at a slightly louder level through the deliberate sliding of chairs and loud coughing. This all had Tony wondering why he had spoken up at all.

"It's easy for you to be sympathetic," bellowed Fred Buehler, the neighbourhood handyman. "You were a friend of that there apostle!"

"I attended a few meetings," Tony replied, "but I wouldn't go so far as to say I was the man's friend."

"Yeah!" said Sharon Tillman, who ran a country craft and hobby store and occasionally went for coffee with Roxanne. "How do you explain the large sums of money you handed over in those meetings to a complete stranger?"

Sharon's question hit Tony with the same pain as Judas' kiss. Indeed, Roxanne might have contributed something to the apostle.

"So what?" Tony exclaimed. "I bet a lot of you men here don't slap your wives' hands when they're in *your* pocket."

His eyes started to tear up from all the memories flooding his mind as he thought of Roxanne. Didn't these people realize that he, too, had lost someone? He was just trying to help keep the peace.

Oh God, help! he prayed. Sweat started to form on his brow from the intensity of pouring out his soul to God. *Lord, how did you do it? How did you stand silently when they yelled Barabbas?*

The prayer was interrupted by an accusing voice in the crowd: "Look! He's unable to speak, just like the one he claims to follow."

There seemed to be no relief from this verbal lashing.

"I can't understand how a man with a luxury bus can't afford plane tickets for his own staff!" shouted another voice among the crowd.

"Excuse me, people!" Sheriff Ryder cleared his throat. "There will be no public hanging here today, so maybe we ought to all just go home and trust those in authority to do their jobs concerning the matter of our missing loved ones."

Tony shook his head and pushed open the general store's double glass doors.

"I can understand how Jesus must have felt being betrayed by Peter three times," Tony said to himself as he stormed out, letting the doors slam freely behind him.

CHAPTER EIGHT

"Mirana," Estravai said with a sigh, gazing at the towering limestone cliffs on either side of an almost undistinguishable trail used mostly by small animals and the occasional exiled holy one. These cliffs were riddled with caves, giving them the appearance of a giant honeycomb. "Mirana, Mirana, refuge to so many holy ones for so many years. Do not grow weary in your purpose, old friend. Do not grow weary," whispered Estravai in a subdued tone as he continued to gaze upon the limestone cliffs.

Morteque walked close to the base of one of the cliffs. He looked up at the large opening a hundred feet above their heads. He lifted his wooden staff into the air and shouted, "All glory be to the Ancient of Days, sustainer of His holy ones!"

A dark figure carrying a torch appeared at the opening of the largest cave, returning the cry: "Who displays His mighty power and reveals His secrets through His holy ones."

This new figure proceeded to turn a large handle on which a thick, braided rope was wrapped around a hand-carved spindle, supported on each side by wooden beams. On every crank of the handle, the spindle would turn and lower a woven basket to the waiting party below.

"You go first, boy," Estravai said to Grenfel. "Morteque will ride up with you. I'll follow once you're both safely up."

"I just can't leave Morgan down here alone," a troubled Grenfel expressed as he stood up in the basket.

"I'll wait with him while the two of you go up. Have a good ride." Estravai raised a hand in the air, which started the spindle-turning above. Grenfel reeled backwards onto his seat. "Hang on, boy!"

"Morgan!" screamed Grenfel from the basket.

"He'll be all right," Estravai assured him from below. "Though the grass is sparse compared to the forest, and coarser, he won't starve."

The basket rose higher and higher, out of the range of civil communication with Estravai.

The entrance to the cave was the product of nature's craftsmanship faithfully creating a masterpiece over a period of thousands of years. Grenfel felt a little nervous with so much rock hanging over him, but Morteque sensed Grenfel's fear and put his arm around the boy's shoulder.

"No need to fear," Morteque said. "Men have been using this entrance to go into the heart of these cliffs for centuries."

When Estravai arrived soon after, he turned to the figure who held the torch. "Is it really you, Benjael? Say it is true."

"It is true," came Benjael's tearful reply as he placed the torch back in its iron support, bolted to the cavern wall.

"I never thought I would live to see this day." Estravai lunged forward to embrace his old friend. "The Ancient of Days has shown great mercy to have allowed our paths to cross once again."

"So, the Queen of the Heavens has not found you yet, either," Benjael said, his face a picture of relief in the torchlight.

"I was punished. I felt the sting of her servant's whip more than once, but I still breathe this day."

"And what of you, Morteque?" Benjael asked, turning to another of his beloved companions from days of old.

"I travelled with Arnabe." Morteque's tone was hesitant. "We were fleeing the queen's threats when we came upon a small pool of water, where a young child was screaming for its life. Arnabe, exhausted as he was, didn't hesitate to run into the pool. He waded up to his shoulders. No sooner had he laid hands on the child than it transformed into one of the queen's dark princes, whose hands clasped Arnabe's throat and pulled him under the water. Arnabe was murdered in front of my eyes. As I lay in the sand, I was consumed with fear and an overwhelming sense of guilt for fearing for my life." Morteque shook his head, still in shock, his eyes beginning to grow watery from the memory of his lost companion. "I felt condemned for being on the run, so greatly that I failed to call on the Ancient of Days."

"We all hid," Estravai declared, "even though the Ancient of Days used us to speak such powerful truths at one time or another. No one here passes judgment on you, Morteque. We can little afford to fight one another and allow Meldrock to destroy us from within."

The three men hugged like family who had been separated for too many years. Then, taking his torch once again, Benjael beckoned his brothers to follow him. He held the torch to light a narrow passageway leading deeper into the heart of the cliffs.

"The others wait on us," Benjael said. Looking intently at both Estravai and Morteque, he added, "And my brothers, do not forget to bring our honoured guest."

"You need to hear about this. I'm very disturbed," said Flora Stevenson, a Drummingsville teacher, as she stood in the doorway to the principal's office nervously working the buttons on her white crocheted sweater.

Walking into the office of Jack Reeves, the newly appointed principal, one could imagine visiting the National Museum in Baghdad. There were shelves upon shelves of clay tablets, jewellery, and tiny miniatures depicting the Babylonian gods of Ishtar and Baal. The wall space that did not occupy shelves displayed Sumerian language translations and plaques from which hung rare Babylonian seals. The décor of Jack Reeves' office, however, was lost on Flora as she merely entered the room and silently stood before the faded wood desk, fidgeting with the buttons of her sweater.

"Oh? Why's that?" Reeves replied, his fingers moving along the expenditure column of the school's budget after several awkward moments of strained silence.

With one hand under her chin, Flora started to sway back and forth, as if to an unheard rhythm. She didn't respond immediately.

"Relax!" he said. "Sit down and we'll talk about it."

Flora fidgeted on the beige office chair, then cleared her throat. "When I'm out doing playground supervision, I hear kids talking about a new website geared for their age group. It encourages them to post pictures of themselves."

"What sort of pictures?" Reeves pushed up his gold wireframe glasses.

Flora grew uncomfortable and her face became flushed. "This website is called anythingbutstraight.com. It teaches children to experiment with sex in unnatural ways, and challenges them to post inappropriate pictures of themselves on the website."

Reeves loosened the knot on his wide tie and leaned forward in his chair. "I can understand your concern," he said as he punched up a spreadsheet on his computer. "Good. The figures show a surplus." He smiled to himself before looking up at Flora. "You know, I think I recall a similar report aired on the K7 News. Such internet websites are apparently being followed by children in elementary schools at most of the large neighbouring cities—Sarquis, Princeton, and West Georgia to name a few."

"It's not the big cities I'm worried about," expressed Flora, "but our own backyard."

"I can understand your strong feelings, Flora, but unfortunately the most we can do is monitor the use of computers in the school. Internet websites are hard to deal with, especially if children have access to home computers without parents present. These kinds of investigations fall more in line with the local police department."

"Oh! I see. Excuse me then," said Flora in some embarrassment. "I won't trouble you any further, Mr. Reeves." She rose from her chair and moved towards the door without looking back.

"Wait just another moment, please," implored the principal. "It's no trouble whatsoever. I always appreciate when staff members are concerned beyond the call of duty, especially when it has to do with students' welfare."

Flora turned to face him. "I will let you continue with the important task of the hour, Mr. Reeves."

With a final nod of her head, Flora turned and walked quietly back to her classroom, feeling no more at ease with her observations of the playground than when she had first walked into the principal's office.

⁓

In another part of Drummingsville later that evening, Tony sauntered over to his living room coffee table piled high with mail. Noticing all the unopened mail on the table, Tony swallowed hard as he remembered how efficient Roxanne had always been in processing their mail and tithes.

It was a bubble-wrapped envelope, however, that caught Tony's eye among all the unanswered bills, and upon picking up the envelope found himself wondering if he now held the remedy for a good night's sleep. If the envelope was his hope as a sleep remedy, reading the label, "Apostle John Bristane: School of the Apostles," did little to convince Tony of that fact with the absence of Roxanne. What should have been cause for festive celebration for Tony with the envelope from the apostolic school now in his hands, at the moment was barely able now to cause his heart but a faint flutter. It took the gentle calling of a child to finally jolt Tony out of his paralyzed state.

"Daddy!" came the persistent cry again from upstairs.

Tony gently put the package down and proceeded to run upstairs.

Jordan was bathed and tucked into bed when Tony came in to kiss him good night.

"I love you, little mister," Tony said.

Jordan whimpered softly and wiped his eyes. "I love you, big mister."

Tony sat down on the bed and embraced Jordan warmly. "Daddy's glad to have you back from the Philpots. They're nice people, but Daddy was sad in the house all by himself."

"When is Mommy coming home?"

Tony tried to hold back the tears forming in his eyes. "Soon, I hope."

"I miss Mommy," Jordan said with the honesty only a child can muster.

"I miss her, too," Tony replied. "Daddy misses Mommy big!"

"I bigger miss Mommy!"

"We can pray for Mommy. Would you like that?"

"Yes!"

"What should we say?"

"Thank you, Jesus, for food and a house, and beds to sleep on so we don't have to sleep on the floor, and make the mad men happy so they will bring Mommy home, and we don't have to eat burnt meat pies anymore."

Tony was touched to the core. "Amen," he whispered. "Bring my Roxanne back, Jesus. Bring her back."

He gave Jordan a final hug and shut off his light.

Well, your timing is perfect, Lord, Tony thought as he walked downstairs, scooping up the package from the School of the Apostles on his way to the wingback chair. Cradling the package in his lap, he reached forward in his chair and clicked on a nearby lamp. *You walk in the midst of our fiery trials, Lord. Maybe now as I open this package, a little more of your light will be shed on my bizarre dreams full of Revealers of Secrets, evil queens, and Hawkmen. Maybe now, Lord, I may understand a little more of the mystery of your ways.*

Tony opened the bubble-packed envelope and perused the contents. He pulled out one of the recommended books and read its title: *Everything You Wanted to Know About Apostles but Were Afraid to Ask!*

Sounds like God sent me a book of answers to my prayers, Tony thought as he opened the text and read the introductory paragraph:

Apostles are sent ones. They are sent by God. The very word in Greek means just that—sent ones. Apostles are ambassadors. They are like the ones a king would send to another land to establish his rule, and who were able to speak and act as if the king were visiting that land himself.

Tony paused from reading.

"Lord," he whispered, "I'd hoped that by reading this book tonight I'd gain peace in my heart about Roxanne's situation. I understand her situation is not just a fairy tale, where a wand gets waved and a pumpkin gets turned to a coach, but I had hoped maybe to get an impartation for her miracle. I can't say I feel any less lonely, though, reading about kings when my very queen is absent from her castle."

With his mind racing, Tony put the book down on his knee. Was there something to his dreams, as bizarre as they were? They were full of Revealers of Secrets, dark princes, Hawkmen, and evil queens. Just as the Hawkman in his dreams was important, was the apostle also a key to the solutions of his personal problems? And on a larger scale, were apostles key to Drummingsville's other problems?

Tony closed the book and glanced at his watch. It was almost midnight; he was surprised at how quickly the time had flown. He knew he'd better get some sleep, for Jordan would soon be shaking him awake for breakfast.

Placing his book on the coffee table, Tony stood up and stretched. He couldn't help but think there was more of the supernatural discussed on that one page of his textbook than he had witnessed at any meeting for a long time, Levi's included.

A brief yawn convinced him that he was still human and in need of sleep. He stumbled to the staircase and made his way upstairs.

High in the mid-heavens, the most powerful demon princes were gathered before their Queen's throne.

"My master and your lord has declared that time is short," roared the queen.

"Oh Queen, who there is none to compare in all the second heavens," spoke a demon prince, "is it not true that we have already laid siege to many of the minds of men in Drummingsville, including Tony's, by way of dreams and lies? We will rule Drummingsville as we rule Ascar, oh Queen, in the realm of men's dreams."

"Which of you princes believes he is able to speak in the presence of your Queen?" She laughed, her velvet-encased hand pointing a single finger into the faces of her trembling audience. "Do not forget your place, my princes, lest I demote you to the untouchables. Now declare yourself."

"It is I, the prince of Persia," came the trembling reply.

"Prince of Persia," said the queen. "Did not you need assistance in Daniel's day? And yet you address your Queen? You stand the fool before me. My master is not just interested in the minds of men. He demands the full harvest of souls, and the establishment of his kingdom in Drummingsville. He demands the destruction of the creator's rule wherever his servants attempt to establish it."

Prince Belial prostrated himself facedown. "Oh, Queen to whom there is none to compare in the second heaven, what is to be done for the one who does our lord's work?"

"Whichever of you, my princes, is able to gain the souls of the men of Drummingsville for your lord, and who causes my promotion in the eyes of my master, I shall have paraded on a dark horse throughout all the second heavens. He shall be declared the greatest prince among all my princes."

"Consider it done," replied Belial, his eyes still lowered to the ground.

"Tell me," inquired the queen, "how do you propose to accomplish the task?"

"I will attack the foundation of the building in the same way we attack the capstone. I will destroy the apostles and prophets in Drummingsville."

The queen laughed. "If I were you, my boastful prince, I would act quickly, for you have already been seen in Tony's dreams."

"That may be true, my Queen," Belial kept his eyes low, to avoid her terrible gaze, "but the mortal called Tony does not perceive my existence other than to be a bizarre dream. Our strategies in the second heaven the creator has not yet allowed him to hear."

"Nevertheless, you have been seen, as the creator has opened a portal in the heavens, by way of spiritual visions and dreams for the mortal Tony. You must act with haste and take Tony out before he connects your character to your name. I see you have already laid siege to Apostle Levi," smiled the queen, her crimson lips now seemingly in full bloom of evil and seduction. "Should you fail, though, to destroy Tony and my master not reap his harvest of souls in Drummingsville, I will personally see that my protective covering over you is removed, exposing you to the wrath of my master."

"I will destroy the foundations of the creator's house in Drummingsville, oh Queen," Belial proclaimed with his eyes still lowered from her gaze.

"Then rise, Belial!" smiled the queen as she unfastened a chain from around her neck from which dangled a metallic spider. Belial stepped forward. He was dressed in a black hooded robe trimmed in gold, and fastened at the waist by a belt inlaid with blood-red rubies. As he stood before the queen, he reached out to receive the chain in her gloved hand.

She smiled in delight to see the spider quiver in his hands. "Take care of my pet!"

"It is as you ask, my Queen. Your spider will spin its deceptive web in Drummingsville. You have my word as a high prince."

The queen pointed her gloved finger. "If you fail, know this, oh prince: I will not stand between you and Meldrock."

With his head still facing the ground, Belial turned and departed the queen's throne, the sound of her laughter ringing in his ears like a bell sounding out an insane funeral march.

Chapter Nine

Torches fastened to the limestone walls dimly lit the narrow passage. Water trickled continuously over the hand-carved stairs, making the going a bit slippery for the returning sons of Mirana. The air was musky, breathing a laborious task; Grenfel bore witness to this fact as he leaned against one of the damp walls, panting heavily.

"You're starting to remind me of your horse, boy, when we were in the desert." Estravai came alongside his young friend, laughing and offering his hand.

Grenfel pushed aside Estravai's outstretched hand. "I can stand by myself!"

Not wishing to add to his misery, Estravai decided to change the subject. "Ah, musty air. How one gets used to a few inconveniences when there's a price on your head, or to put it simply, when you're exiled. After a while, you even begin to take pleasure in the familiar sound of water dripping. Somehow it helps one not to feel so alone."

Benjael approached. "Tis not right that we keep Eltarz and the others waiting. We must keep moving."

Estravai well understood the look Benjael gave him, even in the dim light. "Yes, you're quite right. It's wrong to keep the others waiting. Forgive us for our insensitivity, old friend, and let us tarry no longer in idle chatter." With housekeeping matters now attended to, the group once more continued deeper into the heart of Mirana.

Shadows danced and stretched throughout the chamber ahead, its towering stone arches dwarfing the occupants below. People moved to and fro throughout this magnificent cathedral formed by nature's masons, a bustling anthill of festive merrymaking. In the centre of the chamber, far below the arches, stood roughhewn plank tables on which were set pewter jugs full of clear mineral water. Next to these awaited baskets of flatbreads and rustic clay vessels full of roast venison and pheasant. The meal's aroma wafted through the chamber as though a gift from the Ancient of Days Himself.

The loud blast of a shofar brought the jubilation to a sudden halt, however, and sent the room's occupants scurrying back to their crude wooden benches like rabbits evading the grasp of a hawk.

"Glory to the Ancient of Days!" Shouted Eltarz's escort, as he blew three short blasts on the ram's horn, paused, and blew three more.

"Glory to the Ancient of Days!" echoed the cries of the other Revealers of Secrets gathered around the tables.

The chamber fell into absolute silence.

"Be seated, brothers," declared the voice of Eltarz, whose cherished words resounded throughout the chamber.

The others all replied in unison: "Greetings, Eltarz, Revealer of Secrets to many kings."

"We are gathered as a great company," Eltarz said, speaking with the all-inclusive love of a father to his children. "Now after many years of hiding from the Queen of the Heavens, we are beginning to gain insight, as the foretold signs begin to unravel. Thus begins the process now of Ascar obtaining her freedom. Where there was no way for the two witnesses to come forth in power against the darkness of Meldrock, which permeates all Ascar, now a path has been laid for their emergence."

As the grey-bearded, weather-beaten, wrinkled man spoke, every ear savoured his words as if mesmerized. Grenfel felt an intense longing for home, reminded of the stories his mother had told him.

"I remember the first of His servants," Eltarz continued. "I was there when Marcon called blindness upon Meldrock's sorcerer. I witnessed Zarel's and Asan's powerful works of healing, and our united cry vocalized by our brothers' blood. We asked, 'How long, Ancient of Days, until the portal opens?' And now I have lived to declare to you, my brothers, that we are witnesses to the things foretold, for we have a young Hawkman in our midst."

With the pronouncement, the room swirled with excitement. All eyes fixed on Estravai and Grenfel, who began to make their way towards the front of the chamber where Eltarz stood.

"The blessings of the Ancient of Days be on you," Estravai greeted Eltarz, who embraced him.

"The presence of the Ancient of Days dwell with you." Eltarz walked over to study the tall, lanky boy. He looked into Grenfel's eyes. "So, this is our young Hawkman?"

Grenfel twitched nervously and his face began to turn red. He wanted to look everywhere but at Eltarz, who seemed oblivious at the moment to his discomfort. Reaching out a wrinkled, tanned hand, Eltarz placed it on Grenfel's trembling shoulders. "You remind me of a newborn deer just learning to stand on its long spindly legs," Eltarz said with a laugh. "You represent the coming of the two witnesses, young man, and the return of the hearts of Ascar back to their rightful master."

The chamber erupted into loud cheers, weeps of joy, and the most beautiful music Grenfel had ever heard. Eltarz led the brothers in spontaneous praise of the Ancient of Days. As the music poured over him like a mighty tsunami, Grenfel felt as if his arms and legs were made of jelly.

Eltarz lifted his hands to the heavens and cried out, "Oh Ancient of Days, we thank you for your gift of this young Hawkman." A tear trickled down Eltarz's face. "We ask that you stir up the gifting in this young Hawkman's life, as you have his mother, the queen. May your heavenly warriors protect him and may you empower him to stand against Meldrock's forces."

Grenfel lunged with a trembling arm for Eltarz, as the chamber started to spin and faces began to blur for him.

"What is it, boy?" Estravai asked, supporting the boy's weight from behind.

"I see a wall of thorns around a city, like a huge spiked collar worn by some giant, blood-red eyes, leathery wings, wet sticky stuff..." Grenfel recited his vision fearfully. "All is dark, dark!"

And as quickly as he had begun speaking, he fell silent and collapsed into Estravai's arms.

"I see a forest of giant thorns, the beating of many wings, and a woman wearing a stained garment, laughing." Eltarz lowered his hands. "My brothers, we have this day seen into the enemy's camp. The Ancient of Days has revealed to us one of the strongholds of the enemy, and it must be destroyed for Ascar to begin to be free of Meldrock's grasp."

Eltarz motioned for Estravai to carry Grenfel away.

"Let the boy now rest." Then, addressing again his children, Eltarz added, "Enjoy the Ancient of Days' goodness. Eat hearty, my brothers. I must go, and seek out His ways in the matter of these visions."

After turning to smile one last time at his brothers, Eltarz departed the chamber.

⌐

The phone rang for the third time, relentless as an impatient child wanting immediate attention.

"All right! Just one minute, don't have a fit!" Max yelled from the study.

Barbara knows I schedule Saturdays for personal reading, Max thought to himself as he ran to the kitchen and picked up the receiver.

Without as much as saying hello, Max began with, "Let me guess, Barbara, you flooded the car outside of Martha's store."

"No, no!" Loud and tearful sobs poured through the receiver. "I was inappropriately touched!"

Max was speechless. The voice on the line was a woman's, but not Barbara's. Caught off-guard, he turned to stare at the light coming out of his study, with its many academic works and personal computer. However, at the moment all this knowledge was lost to Max and out of the reach of his fingertips, and his mind simply went blank.

"Hello?" More sobbing. "Is anyone there?"

"Yeah—yeah, yes, sorry about that," stuttered Max. "The cat got my tongue for a moment."

"My name is Sue Henderson," the caller said.

Max listened silently, trying to assimilate facts. *How do I know this woman, Lord?*

"I'm a co-worker of Tony's," Sue said, then paused to cry. "It was Tony."

Max's thoughts began to race. The words jolted him. Tony would never do something like that... she had to have the wrong man!

"Are you sure it was Tony?" Max asked, shaking his head. "I've known Tony a long time, and this just doesn't sound like him."

"I know you're Tony's friend," replied Sue. "I've been so depressed lately since my encounter with Tony, barely able to get out of bed some days. I heard Tony mention your name out at camp. I was hoping you might convince him to settle with me without police involvement. That's really why I finally got the nerve to call you. One more thing, I do still have your friend's jacket. I grabbed it from him when he fled my tent. You might want to let your friend know I am open to discussion about the retrieval of his jacket. Please believe me!"

"How do I know Tony didn't just give you the jacket for some reason?"

"I have a recording of my encounter with Tony."

"Hold on," Max said, wiping his forehead. "Tell me about that jacket first."

"It's a grey leather bomber jacket with black duffel sleeves. On the back are the words 'Heli Firefighters Just Jump In,' in red letters. And there's a picture of a firefighter repelling down a rope from a chopper into a burning forest. On the right shoulder of the jacket are golden letters that say 'Roxanne/2003.'"

Max knew that was the year Tony and Roxanne had gotten married.

"I suppose you could know Tony's jacket just from having seen him wearing it."

"Oh no." She sniffled. "I have his jacket in my hands as we speak. And the whole thing was recorded on my cell phone."

"Your phone? Sue, I don't think—"

"Please, just listen."

Max heard static over the phone, and then a recording began to play. The voices were low, indistinguishable.

So far, Tony, you have nothing to worry about.

But his hope for his friend quickly deflated by what he heard next.

"Don't do this—please!"

"Don't worry, I'll treat you gently."

"I don't want to!"

"Well, there's only you and me. No one else is here."

"Ouch! You're too rough. I don't want to do this."

"You have no choice, lady. It'll be over quickly, I promise. You might even say it wasn't so bad when it's all said and done."

The recording ended, and after a moment of silence, Max let out a long, troubled sigh.

"Well, Sue, I'm really trying to understand the connection. All you've done is describe Tony's jacket and played a recording that could be about anything."

"It might seem that way to you, but if I present all this to Sheriff Ryder…" Her voice trailed off, and when she spoke again her tone had softened. "I'm afraid to go to work, and I know Forest Tech is going to want to know what's happening. I thought you and I could meet. That you, being Tony's friend, could inform him of my demands if he wants to avoid the courts in this matter."

"Ah. So now we get to the bottom of this," said Max. "Uh, just give me a minute to check my calendar."

"That's fine."

"Okay, it looks as if Tuesday at four o'clock is free. How would you like to meet at that Mexican deli next to Jim's tackle shop?"

"That's good for me. Is it the place with the patio?"

"Yes."

"Good. See you then."

With this, Sue hung up.

Max walked slowly back to his study. He sat in his brown leather office chair and shook his head in disbelief.

When the key turned in the lock of the front door, he looked up. In stepped Barbara.

"Hi, honey, I'm home. Did you miss me?" Barbara said all in one breathe. Her arms were loaded down with heavy grocery bags.

Max remained at his computer, staring blankly at the screensaver.

"I'm okay!" Barbara said, failing to mask her frustration. "No, really, I'll manage just fine."

She slammed the kitchen door loudly behind and dropped the plastic bags onto the kitchen counter. She silently reaffirmed her vow to just sit and watch a movie the next time Max wanted her attention.

Peeking into Max's study, Barbara observed him just sitting and staring trancelike at the screensaver seemingly oblivious to all external noise. Had he even heard her? Puzzled but knowing answers would come in due time, Barbara whispered a silent prayer for Max on her way back to the kitchen.

Lord, thought Max, *is this all just a big misunderstanding? I played hockey with Tony for years. He's not normally like this. But who knows what can happen to a person when tragedy comes like a thief in the night?*

Max leaned back in his chair, suddenly jarred out of his thoughts by the extra loud banging of groceries being put away in the kitchen.

"It looks as if my own henhouse needs some tending to," he muttered. "Better take care of that before I try to save the neighbour's farm."

Propelled by his thoughts into action, Max stood up from his office chair, gave his head a little shake, and tried to appear refreshed as he walked into the kitchen.

Elsewhere in Drummingsville, Sue remained in front of her phone, though she wasn't reliving her traumatic event. Rather, she busily sewed a charm onto the sleeve of her silk blouse. Her face mirrored the sadistic smile of one who sat in the mid-heavens, whose face was radiant with evil.

"My spider is spinning in Drummingsville," whispered the queen seductively.

"How long?" came the demonic cries before the queen's throne.

"Soon, soon. All of you will be sent. Belial, have you been faithful in your task?

Belial returned an evil smile. "It is as you say. Your spider still spins, oh Queen."

Far below the queen's throne in the second heaven, and beyond the edge of Tony's dreams in the realm of men, a large burgundy bus with tinted windows sat motionless in a forest, just before the mountains outside of the city of Princeton. The bus had been found tucked under camouflage netting in a grove of spruce trees. The ignition was still turned to the on position, though the last of the diesel had burned up days ago. The scene outside the bus resembled the aftermath of a hurricane. Bodies were propped up against the trees while others lay scattered in the underbrush. A few delusional passengers wandered about in a state of shock. Hypodermic needles littered the ground like a city parking lot after a rock concert. Remains of the makeshift camp could still be seen in the form of a few abandoned Yurts. Garbage had been strewn throughout the forest in every direction.

"In all my years as sheriff of Drummingsville, I've never run into anything like this," Sheriff Ryder said, shaking his head as a reporter from the K7 News team thrust a microphone in his face.

"Can you tell us how you came across this particular site, Sheriff?"

The sheriff pushed his dark sunglasses up his nose and smiled, soaking in the limelight. "Well, a couple of backwoods hikers came across individuals running through the woods in nothing but their underclothes. They said the people were cut up and scratched from all the thorns and branches but seemed completely oblivious to that fact. The hikers also mentioned that people were babbling on about giant, brightly coloured bugs that they thought were trying to eat them. Surprise would be an understatement in the minds of the hikers, when they discovered a camp instead of a crash-site. To say the least they were in shock when they stumbled into the main camp." Sheriff Ryder paused to take a breath, and smile one last time at the camera before stating, "That's all I can tell you at this point."

Paramedics scurried through the forest, preparing those who were propped up against trees or lying on the ground to be moved. Police officers from Norwood County and the Sarquis city police had responded quickly to Sheriff Ryder's call for assistance. They sealed off the camp with yellow tape, herding those still aimlessly walking around in the forest back to the main camp.

"This is Rena Peterson for K7 News with a special live bulletin from a forest just outside of Princeton. The scene resembles something out of a war movie, only there are no spent cartridges on the ground, just piles and piles of hypodermic needles. It appears the story of that hijacked bus ends here. We now know the armed men were not a terrorist cell but members of a militant group employed by drug lords, with possible connections to the mafia. The purpose for the hijacking is thought to have been to boost heroin sales. This, I'm sure, comes as an unexpected development for many families of Drummingsville tonight, who suddenly find the six o'clock news in their own backyard."

Rena paused for a moment of silence before continuing her report.

"It appears passengers of the hijacked bus were injected with heroin over the last few weeks, at gunpoint. The hijacking may have ended, but for many of these passengers the awful trip continues. The plan I'm hearing from the law enforcement people is that another bus is on its way from Princeton to take all the victims of this tragedy to a treatment center right in Princeton, where their vitals will be monitored for a short period. We'll keep you updated on future developments of this story. For now, I'm Rena Peterson for K7 News, saying goodnight to all our viewers."

The travel coach inbound from Princeton pulled up in front of Martha's general store. The sight of the bus arriving in Drummingsville this day had greatly being anticipated by many of the community's citizens, who had come out to stand along the boardwalk in front of the general store to wave their heart-shaped signs and to fly funky-shaped helium balloons. Their energy level was undeniable as it represented the bursting of many personal dams of pent up anger and pain which had accumulated over many sleepless nights for them. They were the ones left behind, victims in their own right, forced to live through the pain and injustice life seemingly had thrown at them. Now they stood unashamedly along the boardwalk expressing freely with their signs and balloons their love. Life had granted them a Kodak moment to finally laugh again with the arrival of the bus and the return of their loved ones.

Martha was a blur of color with her multi-colored patchwork waistcoat, yellow puddle boots, and the splash of rainbow color in her short spiky otherwise gray hair that one would expect to see in a free spirited soul's hair if they gave themselves a home dye job. She moved her willowy frame along the boardwalk, dashing in and out of the crowd distributing balloons to those just arriving and giving the "Welcome Home" banner she had just hung above the double glass doors of her general store another tweaking pull, like a bride adjusting her dress before entering the church.

The driver had released the air brakes, pulled open the front door of the bus, stood up from his driver's seat, and removed his gray uniform jacket from behind his seat and slipped it on. He then grabbed a pair of rawhide work gloves from the dash of the bus and stepped off the bus. Noticing the crowd gathered, he smiled and proceeded working through a series of stretches that looked like a warmup routine for a sprinter.

Looking like traumatized refugees who had fled a war-torn state with all their life possessions, the passengers began to disembark the bus, clutching at personal items, a sweater, magazine, the plant that had being in their room at the treatment center. As each new arrivee stepped of the bus, it was as if the energy level of the crowd became more subdued, to the point where it now resembled what one would expect to find if they had attended a wake. Those who had being standing along the boardwalk now rushed silently towards their loved ones like water does the banks of a river during flood season. There was the silent pats on backs and shoulders as they located their loved ones, the reassuring nods from those that had stood on the boardwalk to their loved ones that they were now safe, and amidst the emotional welcome, the sound of the driver tossing out boxes and bags from the cargo hold of the bus bringing to the moment a weird sense of normalcy.

Jordan now stood holding his folded paper heart card tied to his balloon in one hand and hanging onto his dad's hand with his other on the boardwalk out front of the general store. The morning at the Epson residence had being a little chaotic with Tony trying to get breakfast done while at the same time repeating to Jordan on more than one occasion throughout the morning that they needed to dress up today because Mommy was coming home.

He had rushed Jordan upstairs after they had finished their pancakes, telling him on the way to the bedroom, "We're not wearing our play clothes today, because today is a special day. Jordan had let go of his hand, rushed into his bedroom, and pulled open the bi-fold closet door.

"Dad, I want to wear my tie with the plastic things on it," Jordan had excitedly said when he had entered the room. Seeing a white short-sleeved shirt hanging in the closet, he had removed it from its hanger along with a pair of pleated dress pants. He had smiled momentarily when removing the dress pants from the hanger at the thought of Roxanne sharing the story with him of having got them from a free table at the community market. Carrying the clothing over to Jordan's bed, he had laid the items out for Jordan, telling him to get dressed.

"Okay Dad," came his son's soft reply.

Nodding at Jordan, he had walked back to the closet to look for the clip-on tie. He had found it scrunched up in a mega block in the bottom of the closet. Picking up the tie, he shook his head as he had said his son's name before turning to walk back towards the bed. Jordan had on the dress pants and shirt and also a pair mismatched socks he had found on his floor. He had knelt in front of Jordan an pressed the plastic tabs of the tie into the collar of his dress shirt, smoothed it with his hand, and told Jordan to play with his toys for a moment, then had rushed down the hall to the master bedroom to look for his dress clothes.

Pulling open the double doors of the master bedroom's only closet, he had pondered momentarily his small selection of hanging clothes that were pushed into the corner by his wife's ever evolving wardrobe. Deciding on the white tux he had bought for their wedding, he had pulled it from its hanger thinking *time to bring you out of retirement*. He had slipped the tux on hastily and then pulled on a pair of black dress-shoes he had found in the bottom of the closet. Feeling like a groom who wants to bypass the wedding practices just to get to the part of kissing the bride in front of the church, he had not wanted to spend forever getting ready. He had adjusted his burgundy bowtie, and then exited the bedroom.

Arriving at Jordan's room, he had peeked in and seen him sitting quietly on the floor in front of his bed flying his action figures through the air as if they were toy planes.

"Time to go get Mommy," he had said.

"Yeah!" Jordan had enthusiastically responded as he dropped his action figures and jumped to his feet. He had smiled at Jordan as he noticed that Jordan had just put on his sneakers from under his bed.

They would have to do, he thought, as he really didn't want to search through toys in the bottom of the closet for dress shoes. Taking Jordan's hand they went downstairs into the kitchen. He had grabbed the roses wrapped in green tissue paper that Martha had ordered in for this occasion for people off of the kitchen table, and then his truck keys from where they hung on a knob off one of the hanging kitchen cabinets above the sink.

Jordan was standing by the front door waiting with his heart-shaped card when he had come out of the kitchen. Jordan had said, "Dad, I wrote 'I luv you mom' on my card and that I am glad she is my mom," then he had looked up at him and asked if it was good.

Tony had taken Jordan's coat off of a peg hanging on the wall near the front door, and had set the roses down on the floor to kneel and help Jordan put his coat. "I'm sure Mommy will be very happy for your card."

They had arrived at Martha's general store forty-five minutes before the bus was due. He had parked down from the general store along the boardwalk, grabbed the roses of the dash, and then they had rushed towards the front of the general store like those at an airport do who are afraid they are late for a flight.

Martha had handed Jordan a balloon and a pack of M&M's, which he had put in his pant pocket, while he proceeded to tie his card to the balloon. As he was busy doing that, she had grabbed Tony's arm and enlisted him in helping her hang her "Welcome Home" banner above the door.

Jordan now stood with his heart-shaped card tied to his balloon in one hand and hanging onto his dad's with his other. The nervous waiting had ended for father and son with the arrival of the bus. Tony had spotted Roxanne nervously standing amongst a group of well-wishers, clutching her green tapestry bag to her chest with both of her hands. He had immediately whisked Jordan off the boardwalk, pulling him along like an engine does a rail car, excitedly waving the roses in his hand and calling Roxanne's name.

Expecting the warm smile he had received for roses in the past on date night, their arrival in front of her was only met with vacant eyes. They had come upon Roxanne with the excitement of those welcoming Jesus into Jerusalem as he entered the city riding on a donkey. He kissed Roxanne on the cheek, expecting her to say "I love you, my big fish" as she had whispered to him the last time he had worn his tux, when they had stood before the minister and she had lovingly looked in his eyes and whispered it. It was a word a prophet had given Roxanne before she had met Tony, to do with her love for fishing and that she was going to catch a big fish someday.

Tony swallowed hard as he realized the expected response to his kiss wasn't there. The look he remembered, the big fish look, was gone from Roxanne's eyes. A small tear formed in his eye as he whispered to Roxanne, "For better or worse. That's what I remember saying, my love."

He tucked the roses between Roxanne's bag and her chest. He was just hugging Roxanne when Jordan came running to join in the embrace of his mom. Seeing the roses tucked behind her bag, Jordan pressed his card behind her bag as well, saying he had made her a card and that he loved her.

Roxanne fidgeted nervously as they released their embrace of her. Then she lowered her bag from her chest and unemotionally said, "Can we get going?"

Jordan had stood paralyzed by the shock of seeing his mom just standing there with her bag as the helium balloon carried his heart for the moment out of his mother's hands.

Tony picked up the roses from the ground from where they had fallen when Roxanne had lowered her bag from her chest. Then he walked over to Jordan, wiped a tear from his cheek and said to Roxanne, "We can get going now."

The ride home was painfully awkward as Roxanne for the most part just fidgeted nervously on the truck seat and gazed out the side window. Jordan took the M&M's out and opened the pack. He had just put a handful in his mouth and started chewing when his mom turned towards him with a dark look on her face and grabbed the candy out of his hand, and then returned to her silent gazing out the window.

Jordan turned to look at Tony with eyes full of fear as he slid his body over in the seat belt towards Tony as far as he could go. Tony thought as he continued to drive, *God, we are a family that loves you, your word in Psalm 91 says you protect those that love you.* As Tony was silently crying out to God for help, they pulled up to the condo, parked, and exited the truck silently—like travelers arriving at a hotel late in the night, caring only about getting to their room. Roxanne spent what remained of the day pacing back and forth between the kitchen and living room.

Jordan for the most part had been Tony's shadow, and at the moment was sitting at the kitchen table playing with an action figure while Tony pulled the rustic vegetables and pot roast meal out of the oven, the same meal that had in the past had made him the apple of his wife's eye.

The evening meal at the Epson residence was monk-like and as loaded with tension as the plated food was with flavor. The sound of their cutlery scraping the china plates as they cut larger portions of food and Roxanne's water glass shaking in her trembling hand, Jordan sliding his wooden chair across the floor closer to Tony's, and their nervous breathing, proved to be the straw which would break the camel's back as Roxanne, unable to concentrate and becoming more agitated by the moment with the cutting of her food, threw down her cutlery, stood up trembling, pushed back her chair, turned from the table, and bolted out of the kitchen toward the stairs.

The sound of the bathroom door being slammed and water running from upstairs caused Tony to say to Jordan as they both sat in shock momentarily at the table, "Daddy has to check on Mommy. Are you okay with finishing your food later?"

"Yes Dad," Jordan replied as he had looked into his dad's sad eyes. "I love you, Dad."

Swallowing hard, Tony said, "I love you too," before taking Jordan by the hand and exiting the kitchen. They ascended the stairs together and he had walked Jordan to his room, telling him to play with some toys until he finished checking on Mommy.

"Okay," Jordan said as he knelt down by his bed and pulled out a Rubbermaid bin of mega blocks.

The door of the bathroom was closed and Tony could still hear water running when he arrived outside it. He called Roxanne's name, but hearing only gut-wrenching sobbing coming from within, he turned the doorknob and pushed the door open.

Roxanne was sitting on the floor by the toilet, leaning up against the wall as the water in the tub/shower unit continued to rise. Entering into the bathroom, Tony turned the faucet off, then softly speaking, he said, "I'm here for you, my love."

Dropping to his knees in front of his wife, Tony embraced her as he continued to whisper softly to her, "I'm here for you, my love."

"I'm a bad mother," she said tearfully. "I let Jordan's balloon go."

Tony lifted his wife's chin and gently wiped a tear from her cheek.

"I'm a bad wife," she had said between sobbing. "I dropped your roses, Tony. I have so much pain in my stomach, God," she cried out between sobbing, "I just want to die."

Tony wiped the sweat from his wife's head with a handtowel.

"Why can't God just let me die? I'm hurting people with my anger anyway. You guys would be better off without me." She continued to sob. "I feel so nauseous. Tony, you deserve way better than me. I just want to die, and I don't even know if I love you," she said, looking at him with vacant, tear-filled eyes. He had drawn her close to him, in a tight embrace.

Swallowing hard and struggling to see with his watery eyes, he whispered, "I need you still, my love, you are important. You are special to me and Jordan, it's all just lies from hell, Roxanne." He gently rocked with her. "Lies from hell," he whispered again, "you said the same thing as I did my love at the church, for better or worse."

Her sobbing became less desperate as he continued to rock with her in his arms, until she faintly said, "I'm just so tired, Tony."

He let her collapse on him, and simply lifted her gently to her feet as he stood. Then, placing one hand behind her head, he scooped up her feet with his other hand and carried her lovingly in his arms down the hall to the master bedroom. He gently placed Roxanne on his side of the bed, and reached across her to pull the covers back. Having done that, he rolled her over gently to her side of the bed. "I'm so tired," she muttered as she was rolling over.

He whispered, "I know, my love," covered her and kissed her on the cheek. Getting no response from her, he stood, smiled at her, and exited the bedroom to check in on Jordan.

Jordan had climbed up on his bed and was just lying there with an action figure of David with his sling under one arm, and Samson with a jawbone under his other arm.

"Hi little mister," Tony said with a smile as he entered his son's bedroom.

"Hi big mister," came a tearful response.

Sitting down on the bed beside Jordan, Tony said, "Daddy needs something really badly right now."

"What, Dad?" came another tearful reply.

"Daddy could really use a big hug."

Jordan threw himself at Tony without hesitation in an all-out embrace, like God answers our prayers before we even finish speaking.

Caught off guard by the suddenness of Jordan's response, Tony now found himself in a tight embrace with his son. He could feel his heart beating next to his, the wetness of his tears against his neck, the trembling and heaving of his small body against his with his sobs. His eyes had become watery again as he could relate to his young son's pain being expressed to him with his sobbing. He could do nothing but hang onto Jordan, and he felt so helpless, so unprepared for his family's pain, even with his faith and firefighting training. *I need your help God,* he thought as tears ran down his cheek. *Please, God, I don't know what to do for us. Don't let the enemy take us out like this, God, that others would look at our family, shake their head, and wonder if faith makes a difference. I call on the God of Elijah for help!*

Jordan softly said, "I'm scared of Mom, Dad."

"I know," he softly whispered as he continued to hug Jordan. "Mommy's scared right now, too."

Sensing a calmness in Jordan's breathing, Tony released his embrace and faced his son. "Remember when you had to get your appendix out? You were in a lot of pain."

"Yes Dad, I was really scared."

"I know, you were really worried. You kept asking Mommy if you were going to die. She smiled at you and said 'You're alive and I'm grateful to God for that.' Mommy is really sick right now and in a lot of pain like you were. The bad men that took her gave Mommy needles that made her sick. Mommy didn't need needles, she was healthy, so the stuff in the needles they put in Mommy made her sick."

"Is Mommy going to die?" Jordan asked with a look of fear in his eyes."

"Mommy is in a lot of pain like you were, but she is going to be okay," Tony said as he placed a reassuring hand on Jordan's shoulder.

I still love Mommy even though she let my balloon go."

"Daddy still loves Mommy even though she dropped his roses."

As he wiped a tear from Jordan's cheek, Jordan had softly asked, "Mommy's scared?"

"Yes," he nodded back at Jordan, "her sickness makes her scared. Remember your bad dream awhile back."

"It looked so real, Dad. There was a bull and this man stuck sharp sticks in its neck, and blood came out of the bull's neck. The bull got really angry and ran at the man. The man waved a red blanket at the bull. It got really mad at the man for that and stuck its sharp thing on its head into the man. The man was bent like he was doing up his shoe, blood was coming down his leg, he fell over and went to sleep. Then this old lady with a black hooded dress came and sat at the end of my bed. I got really scared, Dad, it was hard to get up, but I sat up. I jumped out of bed but it was so dark I was feeling the air. I got more scared because I couldn't find the bedroom door."

Tony nodded. "I remember how scared you were. You were so scared you ran into our bedroom to sleep with us. You know," he said, "Mommy's scared like you were when you couldn't find your way out of the bedroom in the dark."

Jordan reached out and pressed his hand into his and he felt at that moment a small surge of hope hit him like an electrical current with the joining of their hands. The feeling for Tony grew as Jordan said, "Dad I watched a DVD that showed Jesus touching a blind man's eyes and then he could see. We can just ask Jesus to get Mommy out of the dark, so she won't be scared."

Tony gave Jordan's hand a little squeeze, smiled at him, and said, "We can pray."

Jordan smiled back then prayed, "Jesus, please touch my mom's eyes so she's not in the dark anymore, please fix her body so she doesn't have to stay at the hospital by herself and eat gross food. God, send your biggest, strongest angels with the biggest swords to protect my mom. Thank you, Jesus. Amen."

"Amen," smiled Tony as he stood up from the bed. Noticing Jordan yawning, he said, "Maybe we should just go to bed now."

"Yes Dad," Jordan responded sleepily.

Reaching into the second drawer of an oak dresser beside Jordan's bed, Tony pulled out a pair of flannel pajamas with pictures of rocket ships on them and laid them on the bed beside Jordan. Standing to his feet, Jordan began to sleepily put his pajamas on, while Tony picked up a few of the stray blocks off of the floor and threw them back in the bin. After pushing the bin of blocks under the bed, he pulled Jordan's covers back and helped him into bed. Jordan closed his eyes as soon as his head hit this pillow, and was only partially awake when Tony covered him up.

"Goodnight little mister," Tony said as he kissed him on the forehead.

"Goodnight big mister," came a fading response, and then the sound of rhythmic breathing. He stood watching Jordan sleep for a few moments, thanking God silently for his life, then, taking a nightlight off of the top of the oak dresser, he walked over to the bedroom doorway and plugged it into an outlet next to the doorframe before exiting the room.

He found Roxanne still sleeping when he returned to the master bedroom. Other than her occasional muscle spasms in a leg or arm, things seemed stable, so he had laid down beside her on the bed, too exhausted even to undress, to even remember the happenings of the evening. He simply blacked out.

He was not sure how long it was until he felt the motion of being pulled back and forth like a rowboat on stormy seas. Someone was screaming, his name was being called, more shaking, he couldn't wake up, couldn't open his eyes, another scream—this one bone-chilling—and he sat up like a sprung mousetrap. He was breathing hard like a stallion running on a cold day. The room was dark other than the glow from the digital clock. He looked around.

Jordan was standing by the bed near him, pulling at his arm, screaming in shock, "Dad wake up, wake up, it's Mommy!"

He quickly pulled Jordan up on the bed by him and held him tightly as he whispered, "You're safe, Daddy's awake now, everything is going to be okay." Tony released Jordan to allow him to hide under the blanket as he turned to see Roxanne kneeling on the bed pointing at the wall across from the foot of the bed screaming and calling his name.

"Don't let them take me, Tony!" she screamed.

He knelt behind her on the bed, wrapped his arms around her, and whispered "It's okay, my love, I have you."

She dug her nails into his arms as she screamed, "They're coming out of the black diamond in the wall, seven groups, an army, Tony, that stretches up to the sky," she fearfully described as she dug her nails into his arm again in terror.

He hung on to her, trying to live through the pain of the moment to his arm, breathing like a boxer with an injury to his nose. He sat back on the bed, pulling Roxanne back into him, whispering gently again, "I have you, my love."

She pushed her body harder against him with her legs as she screamed his name, "Tony! There's one in front with a scroll, he's trying to give it to me, I don't want it Tony," she screamed, "they're trying to grab me, Tony, please help me, don't let them take the light from my eyes. Please Tony, help me," she sobbed, "help me God."

He held her tightly and felt her clammy skin on the back of her neck as he pressed his face into the hair on top of her head. He smelled her sweat in it as he kissed her gently on the top of the head and rocked her in his arms, continuing to whisper, "I have you, my love."

"Tony, I'm so scared, I'm so scared," she repeated as she turned her head and tucked it down lower. He continued to gently rock her in his arms, and like a wounded animal on the threshold of death ceases in its struggle to live, she eventually succumbed to sleep.

Supporting Roxanne with one arm and his body, he reached out his other arm to where Jordan had hid under the covers. He heard the sound of faint snoring as he gently pulled the covers back, and in the glow from the digital clock saw Jordan sleeping in a fetal position.

"It's all going to be okay," he whispered as he recovered Jordan. Sitting back up again, Tony once more held his sleeping wife with both of his arms, and as he sat there supporting her on the bed, in the quietness of the almost dark room he felt like a lone sentry on a city wall just waiting for the light of dawn. He wondered in those lonely night moments as he sat on the bed behind his wife how their family was going to survive. He cried out in his mind to God for wisdom and help, and then he just sat wondering if the little bit of loneliness he felt being the only one awake was similar in any way to what Jesus had felt on the cross, when the Father seemed distant to him.

They endured the night, and were as grateful for the new day before them as those who have lived through a tropical storm are grateful for its passing.

Roxanne sat silently in an overstuffed chair in the living room, her feet tucked up into the chair beside her, cradling a cup of coffee between her hands. Jordan sat on the sofa across from her still in his pajamas, playing quietly with his Samson and David action figures. Tony stood before the kitchen sink with his cellphone in hand, looking out the window above it. Each ray of sunlight that streamed through the window warming his face was like a little message to him from God reminding him of His goodness, and also that He had heard his thoughts from the previous night.

He smiled as he dialed Mrs. Philpots' number on his phone. He held the phone to his ear, listening for the sound of her familiar voice.

"Hello, who's this?"

"Tony—"

"Tony! Oh Tony, nice of you to call. How's Roxanne and Jordan doing?"

He tried to relay to her how good it was to see Roxanne, but halfway through his attempt he broke down as thoughts of Roxanne leaning against the bathroom wall, asking God to take her life, overwhelmed his mind.

"I understand your difficulty," she said in the silence when he couldn't talk. "The hearts of many in the community can relate to your pain, as they are suffering similar things with their loved ones this morning," she softly reminded him. Then before Tony could get to the purpose behind his call, she asked, "How would you like me to take Jordan for awhile? He seems to always enjoy creating wonders in my studio," she added before asking him if he would be okay with it.

"Mrs. Philpots, I believe you are a woman with an amazing sense of timing. I was just calling to see if you would mind taking Jordan."

"It's not a problem," she replied. "I'll be by shortly to collect Jordan."

Smiling, Tony clicked off his phone and silently thanked God for Mrs. Philpots' big heart on his way out of the kitchen to the living room.

Roxanne continued sipping her coffee as he entered the living room. He smiled at her and walked over to where Jordan was sitting on the sofa playing quietly with his action figures and sat down beside him.

"Good morning, little mister."

"Good morning, big mister," responded Jordan softly.

Noticing that Jordan seemed to continue to be engrossed in his play as if no one else was in the room, Tony just sat for a moment, nodding to himself as he stared at the floor in front of him and silently prayed: *God, I can understand this timidity I sense with Jordan. He's still scared. Please infuse his mind and heart with your peace.*

He turned to face Jordan. "Daddy needs to ask you something."

"What?" Jordan responded softly as he still focused his attention on manipulating the arms and legs of his action figures.

"Daddy asked Mrs. Philpots if you could stay with her while he helps Mommy get better. Would you be okay with that? You seem to have fun at her house," he added.

"Okay, Dad," Jordan responded while still focusing his attention on his toys.

"That's good. We need to go upstairs and put your pajamas in a suitcase," he said as he reached out a hand to Jordan.

Dropping his action figures on the sofa, Jordan took his dad's hand. Tony smiled across at Roxanne as Jordan waved at his mom. Roxanne's hands trembled as she hung on to her coffee cup, and she fidgeted about nervously in her chair, neglecting to return the wave and smile as she seemed preoccupied with looking over her shoulder to see if anyone was standing behind her.

Tony held on to Jordan's hand as they exited the living room and headed upstairs to Jordan's bedroom. Having entered his bedroom, Jordan let go of his dad's hand and went to sit on his bed, Tony walked over to oak dresser beside the bed and opened the top drawer. He withdrew a couple pairs of socks, underwear, and several t-shirts, then closed the drawer. Opening the second drawer, he took out a blue checkered flannel shirt, two pairs of jeans, and several name-brand hoodies. He carried the items over to Jordan's bed and asked Jordan to get dressed. As Jordan was dressing, he walked to the bi-fold closet, opened it, and reached up on the top shelf for a small suitcase. Turning from the closet with the suitcase, he saw Jordan had put on a pair of jeans and the blue flannel shirt. He approached the bed and placed the suitcase on it.

"Is your suitcase with Larry and Bob in their Jeep okay?"

"Yes Dad," Jordan answered as he helped place the items of clothing in the suitcase. Jordan had just placed a pair of socks in the suitcase when the doorbell rang.

"We need to hurry. Where's your shoes?"

"Under the bed, Dad."

Bending down, Tony pulled out a pair of Converse sneakers and helped Jordan put them on. "We don't want to keep Mrs. Philpots waiting," he explained as he stood upright and grabbed the suitcase off the bed. Smiling at Jordan, he said, "I think that's everything," and taking Jordan's hand they exited the bedroom and headed downstairs to greet Mrs. Philpots.

At the bottom of the stairs, Tony released Jordan's hand and dashed to the front door. Opening the door, he said, "I'm very sorry for making you wait, Mrs. Philpots."

"I understand, Tony," she answered as she shifted her beaver coat around on her dumpy frame. Seeing Mrs. Philpots standing on his porch in mid-summer wearing her fur coat and wrap brought to memory the time he was working on their condo's siding and inhaling liters of just about anything you would find in the cooler at Martha's general store that was drinkable. He had asked Mrs. Philpots how she could wear furs in the unbearable summer heat.

She had told him that she drank coffee in the hot sun as well. "It causes you to sweat, and what does sweat do?" she had asked him.

"Cools you down," he blurted out. "Oh, sorry Mrs. Philpots, a memory."

"So you remember," she smiled. "That's good."

Not wanting to waste any more of Mrs. Philpots' time, Tony said, "I really appreciate you taking Jordan on such short notice."

Mrs. Philpots smiled back and nodded. Excusing himself as Mrs. Philpots nodded at him again, Tony turned and headed to the living room to Roxanne and offered her his hand. Roxanne sat up in her chair, placed her coffee cup on the floor with trembling hands, and nervously stood to her feet and placed her hand in Tony's. Smiling at his wife, he whispered "I love you" before they slowly began walking to the front door.

Jordan was in the living room now. He had being standing in the doorway to the kitchen watching his dad. He walked over to the sofa and put his suitcase on it. Unclasping and opening his suitcase, Jordan collected Samson off of the sofa and put him on top of his clothes before closing the suitcase again. He picked up David with one hand and his suitcase with his other. Turning from the sofa, Jordan saw his dad standing by the front door holding his mom's hand, and so feeling a little less fearful he now made his way over and stood behind them.

Mrs. Philpots had told Roxanne it was nice to see her. Roxanne had stared at the floor and fidgeted nervously. Tony had squeezed her hand gently as if to say you're safe.

Noticing Jordan standing behind them, Tony squeezed Roxanne's hand gently once more and released it. "Time to go, little mister," he said as he turned to face Jordan. "Time to get your coat on."

"Okay dad," Jordan said as he approached Tony and set David and his suitcase down. Tony reached up on a peg near the front door and grabbed Jordan's coat. Kneeling down, he helped Jordan slip his coat on and do up the wooden buttons.

"Everything is going to be okay," Tony said, and then pulled Jordan close and hugged him. "I love you, little mister."

"I love you, big mister," Jordan said as he squeezed his dad's neck in a hug.

Roxanne was fidgeting nervously beside Tony as Jordan released his dad's neck and turned to embrace his mom. "I still love you, Mom. You're a good mom." It was as he said, "You will always be my mom," that a tear started to trickle down Roxanne's cheek.

Jordan let go of his mom and looked up into her face. "Guess what, Mom? We asked Jesus to take you out of the darkness like he did the blind man."

Tears continued to trickle down Roxanne's cheek, prompting Tony to reach out and gently brush them away with the sleeve of his shirt.

Jordan turned to pick up his David action figure, carried it over to his mom, and gently pushed it into her hand, starting to fold her fingers around it until she grabbed it.

"I'm leaving you David, Mom, so you're not so scared. He's really good at fighting giants, and you can sleep with him too."

Tony turned to look at Mrs. Philpots and nodded at her as if to say, "Okay, we're ready now."

Seeing his gesture, Mrs. Philpots reached out her hand for Jordan.

Tony took Jordan's hand again and walked him to Mrs. Philpots, then placed Jordan's hand in hers. Bending down, Tony kissed him on the cheek. "Have fun little mister, Daddy and Mommy love you."

Turning, Tony grabbed Jordan's suitcase and handed it to Mrs. Philpots. He then went and stood next to Roxanne and, with his arm around her waist, said, "Bye little mister."

Mrs. Philpots nodded and turned to lead Jordan out the door with one hand and his suitcase in the other. As they were going, Jordan said, "Bye Dad, bye Mom. I love you Mom, I love you Dad."

"I love you," Tony cried back as Mrs. Philpots helped Jordan into her car. She nodded once, waved, and then got in her car and they drove off.

Tony closed the condo door and wondered, as he stood in front of it momentarily with his arm around Roxanne's waist, if this was the easy part of her recovery and if it was now over just as quickly as he had closed their condo door.

CHAPTER TEN

The black cube vans rolled into Drummingsville in the dead of night and pulled up to a Victorian home with a "sold" sign on its front lawn. The sale of anything in Drummingsville, whether a car or cow, automatically became a matter of community interest. Rumours were already flying around town like a swarm of mosquitoes, especially around the coffee shops.

John, the most experienced coffee bean roaster at the Java Joint, had attempted to convince most of the regular lunch crowd that the kind of money needed to purchase the Victorian had to have come from out of town. Most likely, John had explained, it was some dynamic leader thinking he was Jesus and demanding all his followers sign their earthly belongings over to him for the glory of God. John's second theory was that the money had been collected through illegal trade in both drugs and sex. No one in the lunch crowd openly disputed John's theories, but then most of them never agreed on much anyway, except that they were sure John could roast a good coffee bean.

The light of the moon cast its eerie glow upon the caravan of now lifeless vehicles parked outside the Victorian. Exhaust settled around them like a fog, causing the vehicles to now resemble something from the undead with their engines now sitting idly rattling, like a great company of ghost machines.

"Careful with those crates!" yelled a thin man the others simply called Boss, whose authority seemed weightier than his body mass. He stood by a silver Porsche with the driver's door ajar, revealing a florescent orange instrument panel and all-leather interior. "I expect to see this place fully functional two nights from now when I return from picking up the clinic's doctors."

"No problem," grunted one of the men who was attached to the front of a crate going through the door of the house. The labourer's response, however, fell on deaf ears, as the Porsche's door had already slammed closed. The Porsche's spark plugs ignited as Boss turned the key and stepped down on the accelerator. Gravel spewed up as he peeled away from the house.

"Not really the sociable type," came the voice of another labourer at the other end of the crate in the house.

⟊

"I will accompany you," Morteque said to Estravai as they stood together at the base of the limestone cliffs.

"It is not necessary, my brother."

"I won't hear any reply other than that I may gladly continue with you. Besides, we haven't yet begun to delve into the tale-telling."

"Why the Ancient of Days would desire this upon me, I don't know," Estravai said. "That's another one of His great mysteries. I only hope my ears don't fall off from your continuous jabbering on our journey."

Benjael now joined his two old friends and handed Estravai a deer-skin sack. "Brothers, I don't want to dampen your spirits any, but rather pass on a little sustenance for your malnourished bones. Eltarz sends his blessing to your company, but I prefer to see you off in person."

With tearful eyes, Benjael grabbed both men and toppled them over. Estravai and Morteque lay sprawled on their backs, Benjael poised atop of them like a faithful hunting dog.

"Until we meet again, good friends," Benjael said.

Nearby, Grenfel stood aloof from his companions, getting reacquainted with Morgan, who nudged his young master with his nose. Grenfel stroked his neck and petted his long, full mane.

"Look!" said Estravai, pointing at Grenfel and Morgan. "They look like two young lovers, the way they're carrying on."

"How might you know about that?" asked Morteque.

Estravai's face turned a little red. "I read about it in the writings, I think."

"Yes, the holy writings." Morteque chuckled, snorting like a pig. "How could I have forgotten the writings?"

All three men broke out in unbridled laughter.

Estravai and Morteque then rose from the dust to bid Benjael farewell. Turning to Grenfel, the two Revealers of Secrets beckoned the boy and his horse to follow along.

The travellers were soon well out of sight of Benjael.

Before Estravai finally began to brush the dust from his cloak, Morteque said in a joking manner, "Don't forget to clean the sand out of your ears as well."

"I thought if I left it in, it could be a blessing from the Ancient of Days. That way, I wouldn't have to listen to your constant babbling. It's bad enough you snore most of the night." After noticing a look of dismay upon Morteque's face, Estravai reached out and patted his shoulder. "Just joking. It's good to walk by your side again, my brother."

After some time, Morteque asked, "Where might we be heading?"

"To Dremcon," Estravai replied.

"Dremcon?" Morteque looked puzzled. "The city of the mindless? Doesn't great evil lurk the streets of that city? Is it not like walking into a lair of snakes?"

"True, there are easier roads." Estravai glanced back at Grenfel and Morgan lazily following behind. "The right way, though, is that which is revealed by the Ancient of Days."

They continued on for many miles in much the same way, with Morteque and Estravai catching up for all the time they had been apart, and Grenfel walking with Morgan behind, listening.

The light of day turned to dusk and night fell, too soon for the travellers. Nevertheless, they settled on a place to rest and stopped to erect camp.

The night air was crisp and cool. Estravai sat around a small fire opposite Morteque. Grenfel lay a short distance away, propped up by a rock, his velvet gown cushioning his head. Morgan grazed nearby, as faithful as a sentry on first watch.

"Eltarz believes the leading of the Ancient of Days is for the purpose of the boy's preparation," Estravai commented as he sipped tea from his flask.

Morteque opened the deerskin sack Eltarz had provided and pulled out a few pieces of roast pheasant. After selecting the choicest cuts, Morteque handed the sack back to Estravai.

"Eltarz believes the Ancient of Days will disclose the time when the boy matures into his role as a Hawkman," Estravai said. "We will then return to Mirana, where Eltarz and others will lay hands on the boy. Grenfel will be separated from us and sent out to follow in the footsteps of Marcon, Zael, and Asan, the powerful ones of old. As for us, old friend, we'll continue on at Mirana, seeking for those who call on our understanding of dreams and visions. We may soon be competing with Eltarz for the longest beard amongst the brothers."

Both men sat staring into the fire, each lost in his own thoughts.

As the night wore on, Grenfel lay in a deep sleep due to the day's long journey. The others had drifted off into slumber as well and a hush covered the forest like a thick blanket.

In the world of dreams, Grenfel felt a warm and soothing hand upon his head. A familiar voice accompanied the touch: the voice of his mother. Her emerald gown draped over the side of the bed as she sat upon its edge, playing with his curly blond hair.

"It may not make sense right now, my son," she said, as her gentle words unlocked his young heart. "I've had visions since you were born. I see you lifting the hand of evil off many a heart, as if it were the very hand of the Ancient of Days. I have seen thorns grow up around you, fencing you in, my son; some of the thorns pierced your flesh." She struggled to continue as tears trickled out from the corner of her eyes.

The vision tore at her heart, but nevertheless she forced herself to disclose it.

"I saw you dressed in strange armour, with a strange head covering, and your hands held a spear which granted you the ability to walk amongst the thorns. You are special, my son. The Ancient of Days has His hand on your life. I don't want you to ever forget this, even when you're away from your true home at Kreniston. Never forget His hand

85

on your life. Promise me!" She rested her head against Grenfel's chest. "Promise me! Promise me, my son."

"I won't forget, Mother," Grenfel murmured, his head falling off the velvet gown he was using as a cushion. "I won't forget…"

He awoke, sat up, and shook off the lingering memory.

Grenfel took a deep breath of the cool air to calm his racing heart. Rubbing his sleep-coated eyes, he squinted in the darkness to try and distinguish something familiar in their surroundings. Moments passed— they seemed like an eternity—before Grenfel made out the dark forms of Estravai and Morteque curled in their cloaks beside the smouldering remains of a fire. Ever faithful as a watchman, Morgan looked up momentarily from his grazing to acknowledge his young master's presence. It was strangely silent, but Grenfel didn't mind. What seemed to elude the eyes of man, however, did not elude the Ancient of Days who alone watched as Grenfel feeling now more like a boy than a Hawkman in training, cried softly to himself, "I love you, Mother!"

The moment was too soon interrupted by a formidable force stealthily heading his way. A woman's silhouette appeared, her long hair tossed about in the wind, lashing at her shoulders like a cat o' nine tails.

Grenfel watched with eyes wide, trying to tell himself she was only a dream, as it had been while on the raft. Her black gown trailed behind her as she drifted like smoke past the sleeping sentries.

"Oh, but I'm not a dream," whispered the queen as she approached Grenfel, sipping from a chalice. "For behold, I come to you eating and drinking. You were crying! And the others thought only to sleep. Behold the guilty." She pointed an accusing finger at the motionless Estravai and Morteque. "I, however, have come to comfort you. Can you not tell who it is that truly loves you? Who loves you enough to care about your tears?"

Reaching out a gloved hand, the queen caught a tear from Grenfel's cheek. After drying his eyes with the sleeve of her gown, she leaned over and kissed him on the forehead. It felt cool and sticky to Grenfel, who was frozen in fear.

"I came to offer you greatness in the eyes of your father and all men," she whispered. "Worship me and someday I will set you as king beside me on a golden throne. You will know unlimited wealth and power, young Hawkman. Only forget this Hawkman business. It is a road of loneliness, poverty, and insignificance." She stroked his curly hair with one hand and pointed a gloved finger at Estravai and Morteque with the other. "What are they to you, Hawkman, these vermin who hide in dark caves and holes? Tell me you will worship me."

"I–I–I can't," Grenfel stuttered, icy chills piercing his body like a million sharp pins.

"Why?"

"I–I promised. I promised my mother I would never forget the Ancient of Days' hand on my life."

"What does your mother know about love? She laughed as the castle door closed behind you at Kreniston when you were taken off to serve your uncle at Heathervane."

"That's not true! Anyway, I promised," Grenfel repeated in a tearful voice.

Two brilliant warriors appeared with flaming swords and pointed them at the queen.

"You must tell her to leave!" one of the warriors said in a voice like a clap of thunder.

"I can't!" bellowed Grenfel. "Wake up Estravai, please! I don't know what to say, and he's better at speaking than I am."

"Young Hawkman, you have been gifted with authority from the Ancient of Days."

"Tell her to depart!"

These words hit Grenfel's heart with the force of a hammer.

"I'm so scared," he said, covering his face with his hands to avoid the brilliant warriors' eyes. As he cowered, one of the warriors touched the tip of his flaming sword to Grenfel's lips. At once, warmth penetrated Grenfel's body, instilling boldness in his heart.

Suddenly, the warmth exploded inside Grenfel and he shouted at the queen with unprecedented confidence. "Leave!"

The very word seemed to propel the warriors into action, as both now stood with flaming swords pointed towards the queen—who for the first time seemed to be trembling in Grenfel's eyes.

The warriors advanced on her, speaking in unity, their combined voices like the roar of a ferocious lion. "You have something that belongs to the Ancient of Days!"

The Queen of Heaven held aloft a single glistening tear. "If you mean this, there was no resistance on the boy's part, so I took it."

Tilting a slender glass vile suspended on a serpentine chain around her neck, the queen delicately dropped the tear into it. Glaring at the two warriors, the queen smiled a final mocking smile before vanishing into the darkness. For a minute, the two warriors remained with their flaming swords pointed into the night. At last, they turned and relaxed their stance. Acknowledging Grenfel, they too vanished.

Sue Henderson, dressed in a black leather jacket and leather skirt, weaved her way around the patio tables towards Max, who sat at the back wearing his blue pilot's cap. The sun seemed to be struggling to keep its head above the clouds, but the extra shadows did little to deter her; even with her dark glasses, her eyes were locked onto Max with the precision of a heat-seeking missile.

"Max," she said, waving.

Max gestured for her to join him. "I've taken the liberty of ordering the house appetizer, chips and salsa. I thought it might keep us from being interrupted by the waitress so often. Oh, and I also ordered a couple of bottles of mineral water, but if you'd prefer coffee, we can get it before we start." He tried to sound as obliging as possible, given the occasion.

"Mineral water is fine." Sue pulled out a chair and sat across the table. Placing the multi-colored fabric shopping bag she'd been carrying over her shoulder on the table, Sue reached inside and pulled out a man's crew jacket.

"I gather that's Tony's jacket," said Max as he dipped a chip into some salsa.

"Yes. I included a disc as well of Tony's conversation, the one I played for you on the phone."

Max cleared his throat. "I really don't understand what it is you want me to do for you."

"You're the man's closest friend," Sue said gloomily. "He took his liberty with me, and now I want something back. Or we could get the police involved."

"I'm not trying to sound naïve, Sue, but I need to hear all the details before I can understand where you're coming from. It's nothing personal, I've been this way since grade school." He took a sip of water. "Does Tony have something that caught your eye?"

"How about that expensive truck he proudly cruises the town in, for starters?"

Noticing the evil smile now on Sue's face, Max was momentarily brought to memory of Elijah's fear of Jezebel. He, however, was determined not to cower in a cave.

"Tony worked hard for that vehicle," Max said forcefully.

"I was hoping you could convince him of my serious intentions."

"Or what? You'll take his jacket to the police?"

"Well, I can see this meeting is going nowhere," she said coldly. "But I do mean to have Tony's vehicle. After all, he had his way with me, and there's the sound recording as well."

"That still doesn't connect Tony positively to you."

"Maybe not." Sue replied coldly as she glared back at Max through her dark glasses. "There are, however, other people I could talk to, if you're not up to the task of convincing Tony to sign his vehicle over to me. Maybe Dylan, or perhaps Roxanne. I hear she's pretty unstable right now. Then again, maybe a vehicle is more valuable than a relationship."

Sue got up quickly and drew out a leather wallet from the fabric bag. She pulled out a Forest Tech card with her cell number on the back, placing it on the table. "It's been a pleasure, Max. I'll be waiting for your decision. Don't keep me waiting too long!" She turned to leave, then added, "Oh, and there are many agencies that would rise to the occasion of rescuing a maiden in distress. There are many knights in shining armour."

Sue departed the patio with the coolness of a hitman. Leaving Max now sitting alone feeling like he had just been part of a mafia movie with what he was being asked to consider.

Chapter Eleven

Jim McFlurry pushed his white panama fishing hat a little further back on his forehead and off his nose that jutted from his face like a spinnaker sail full of the wind, allowing his light blue eyes to be finally seen like the sun emerging from behind a cloud. He pulled off his denim jacket, which was sun-bleached and reeked of Old Spice cologne and yesterday's catch, and hung it over the back of the chair in front of him. Rolling up the sleeves of his red turtleneck sweater to his elbows, Jim pulled out the chair and slid his matchstick frame into its seat.

Picking up the earthenware mug of coffee off the circular table, Jim took a sip and nodded across the table at Sharon Tillman, the outspoken but thoughtful owner and operator of Drummingsville's lone craft supply store.

Placing his mug back on the table, Jim pointed to his cheek and gave Sharon an inquisitive look.

"Oh!" smiled Sharon back at Jim. "You noticed my tattoo, and I thought we were going to spend the time playing Charades because you were out of fishing stories."

"That's what you call that thing," muttered Jim as he sipped his coffee. "Here I thought you went and tangled with a paint demon."

Sharon turned her head to the right to expose her cheek more fully to Jim. "It's a green dragon to match the label of dragon lady some in the community have chosen for me. Can't have them disappointed, Jim, now can I? I'm thinking of selling washable tattoos in my shop."

"Why on earth would Drummingsville need tattoos?" Jim had just muttered back when the loud ripping sound of cardboard being torn shifted the friends' attention to John, the owner and chief coffee roaster of Drummingsville's newest coffee shop called The Java Joint, who at the moment was down on his knees amongst a small fortress of boxes in the corner.

"What's with all the books?" Jim asked, asserting his small-town civilian right to know everything and everyone else's business.

"Oh," John muttered from the floor. "It's the latest market trend in all the big cities. The coffeehouse is the place where people come to sit down in a corner to read a magazine or book they're thinking of purchasing. Heck, in some of these coffeehouses you can even buy music."

"Sounds to me like some folks have their lines tied wrong," said Jim. "Next thing you know you'll be sitting behind the counter telling us all to be quiet. I mean, what's the world coming to? Books belong in a library. But just out of curiosity, let me see one of those there books anyway."

"My word!" Sharon cut in. "Don't tell me you're actually thinking of reading!"

"Well," spluttered Jim like a flooded outboard motor, "I do some sports fishing, if you remember. There might be something here my clients are interested in." Jim reached into a box and took out an oversized, soft-covered manual. "What's this, then? *Magic for the Everyday Witch: A Home User's Guide*."

"There you go, Jim, that's the perfect book for your business," Sharon remarked as she burst out laughing. "If fishing is slow, you can always put on a magic show for your clients. Or think of this, Jim: if your outboard cuts out on you, I'm sure you and your clients could fly back to shore on one of the oars."

"Excuse me, a word if I might," piped up John from where he stood dusting bookshelves. "Actually, books about magic, spells, witchcraft, and tarot cards equal big profits, just ask any book retailer. In fact, it's such a hot market that I plan to hire someone from outside on a full-time basis to read tarot cards right here in the Joint. A little live entertainment to promote the sale of soup, salads, and sandwiches."

Jim asked, "Why on earth would you want to waste your money doing a foolhardy thing like that?"

John scratched his bushy red beard and pushed up his sleeves. "It's about staying competitive, being current. At least I'm not using half-naked ladies to sell cars."

"You're just a step away," muttered Jim into his coffee.

"Hey! No guilt here." John scuffed his brown sandals on the wood-plank flooring. "I mean, if a prophet can set up shop to charge people for receiving a word from God, is my selling books in the coffee shop such a big deal? The prophet calls it a step of faith. For twenty-five dollars, you can get a CD with a word from God on it spoken just for you. I'm not doing anything different. People just want more for their money now, a big screen TV just to sell a cup of coffee. If I don't stay trendy, the Joint may eventually have to close its doors, and I'd rather try something to give the Joint a shot in the arm, if it means continuing to do business."

John kept taking the books out and vigorously setting them into the new wooden bookshelves, as if he had just taken one big step on behalf of all small business owners.

"It's really strange, don't you guys think?" Sharon said. "I mean, don't you wonder why our sleepy little town seems to be of interest to so many? I can't recall anything like this since the early frost three years ago had the neighbouring communities rallying to help the town's farmers get their squash off the fields."

John finished filling the shelf, then put his hand on the back of one of the chairs at their table. "I can take a break before the lunch crowd comes. Mind if I chat with you two for a few minutes?"

"What do you think, Jim?" Sharon asked.

"It's his place!"

John got comfortable and folded his hands on the table.

"All right then," Sharon said. "I was just telling Jim that I think it's strange. I mean, all the things happening with our community lately— that apostle and his meetings in town, the hijacking of that bus. Why has fate set its sights on Drummingsville?"

"Yeah, that sure was a shock," replied Jim. "Pretty sick, injecting all those people with heroin, if you ask me."

"What about the schoolchildren?" John asked as if he represented the town's moral conscience. "Sheriff Ryder mentioned the possibility that they were posting inappropriate pictures of themselves on adult websites." Jim shook his head. "That's disgusting. Glad I grew up with typewriters. We didn't have computers in school at all. Things were simple."

"Disgusting fails to even describe that new abortion clinic," Sharon said, trying to wash away the distaste with more coffee. "You know that Victorian house downtown? Well, it's in there. They put up posters advertising free services for women on their first visit to the clinic."

"What! Are we the new garbage dump for the neighbouring cities?" Jim crossed his arms. "Suddenly we've got abortion clinics, the children of the community using inappropriate websites, religious men charging fees to hear from God, and occult books for sale in the coffee shop!" He sighed, sounding exasperated with it all. "We need to return to the way it was when things didn't change much—like John's coffee. Ain't been hardly a problem with it over the last twenty years."

The chime at the door sounded as Roxanne walked into the coffee shop. John shrugged his shoulders, shaking off the awkward hush that filled the room. Excusing himself, he stood up and pushed his wooden chair into the table. He made his way behind the counter that held all the daily coffee decanters, managing to momentarily shield Roxanne from the rest of the customers.

Roxanne stood in a dream-like state, gazing at the multi-coloured chalkboard menu on the wall behind the counter.

"How can I help you?" John asked, trying to ease the tension. Roxanne just continued to stand there. "You're looking good. It sure is nice to see you again."

His comments seemed to bounce off Roxanne without fazing her in the least.

"Heard they're still going to try and pave the road from town out to the old Stillmore Mine," Jim said to Sharon, speaking louder than normal, as if she were wearing a hearing aid.

"That would be good for the town's economy," Sharon bellowed back. "If we're waiting to get rich solely off your fishing business, Jim, we may as well put up 'For Sale' signs in front of our shops."

"Hey! Slow down, woman. You can't be putting the sad state of the town's economy solely on my shoulders. It's not my fault the fishing isn't very good this year. All the rainbow trout want to do is feed on freshwater shrimp."

"You're right, Jim. Blame should go where it belongs," Sharon said, trying to keep a straight face. "So, let's blame the fish."

Meanwhile, Roxanne had finally made up her mind. "I'll take a pound of ground Colombian," she said in a quivering voice.

"Yeah, all right, I'll just get that then." John was glad for an opportunity to get away from the counter for a few minutes.

"Oh, there's Mrs. Philpot," Sharon said, pulling back the white lace curtain from the window as she got up from the table. "I'll go and open my shop. Knowing her, she'll want some more decoupage paste. It's been a pleasure, Jim."

With that, Sharon rushed out the front door.

"Will that be all?" John asked Roxanne as he placed a folded brown bag on the counter.

"Yes, I think that's all I was supposed to get." She fumbled through her purse, then handed John a crumpled bill. In the time it took John to get her change, Roxanne grabbed the bag of coffee and ran out the door.

"Here's your cha—Rox!"

John stood motionless, staring at the swinging front door.

"You got to feel for that family," Jim said, shaking his head. "They got themselves some major knots in their fishing lines. I heard their boy Jordan is messed up with some older kids with those adult websites. Guess that's the downside of having a small-town school, where the studies are self-paced and the whole schoolhouse consists of the principal's office, gym, and k-12 in two classrooms."

"I hadn't heard." John carried a tray of freshly washed mugs out of the kitchen. "Rumour has it Tony had an affair during the time Roxanne was missing."

"Well, I'll be. I never would have thought," Jim murmured. "Well, time to go hook a fish. Catch you later, John."

Chapter Twelve

The three travellers stood alongside Morgan atop a huge cliff composed mostly of large chunks of crystallized salt. They overlooked the flatlands surrounding the city known as Dremcon.

Estravai said, "One can always tell when Meldrock has travelled through a land. All the vegetation withers."

"They say his very shadow curses a land." Morteque looked out at seemingly endless rows of thorn trees encasing the city like a tightly fitted suit of armour.

The smell atop the cliffs was nauseating enough to cause Grenfel's eyes to water.

Seeing this, and realizing it wasn't the wind stinging his young friend's eyes, Estravai said, "The air doesn't get any less pungent down below. Come, boy, we best get down the cliffs before you faint."

Upon arriving at the bottom of the cliff, Grenfel's mind drifted to the giant thorn forest. He had heard the stories of it, but to actually see the forest of giant thorns caused a lump to form in his throat.

"We'll have to leave Morgan here," Estravai explained as he took a bundle of deerskin hides off Morgan's back and proceeded to untie them. "No one goes into Dremcon other than on foot, and all shed a few drops of blood to get there."

"What a wasteland," Grenfel uttered in disbelief as he watched Estravai and Morteque unfurling the deerskin packages in which they had stored equipment for their journey. Gazing over the equipment the Revealer of Secrets had begun to unfurl from the deerskin packages,

Grenfel asked, "Clothing? I've only seen hides used as blankets. What are those for?"

"Armour," Estravai replied.

"The armour I have seen at my uncle's castle is metal."

"For the wealthy it is, for others, well, perhaps you will best learn the value of the strange items lying before you by trying them on."

The two Revealers of Secrets looked like sculptors who had set about to turn a mere piece of stone into a masterpiece. Estravai picked up a thick strip of muskox hide and laced it up Grenfel's arm with strips of tanned deer hide. Morteque busily attached similar thick strips to Grenfel's legs, tying off the lashings with the skill of a weaver.

Estravai became preoccupied with unravelling another rolled deerskin. Contained within it were three wooden staves with pointed metal tips and razor-sharp edges and several metal helmets.

"It's amazing how the Ancient of Days has skilled certain brothers of Mirana to craft such wonders." Estravai picked up an iron helmet with four equally spaced bars to protect the region around the eyes and the bridge of the nose. "The Ancient of Days has given such knowledge to aid the brothers in hunting, especially larger animals. It seems there is never a shortage of bear or boar around Mirana these days."

Grenfel stumbled in an attempt to walk in his new protective covering. "It's too heavy and hot, and I'm itchy."

Morteque put a hand on Grenfel's chest to steady him. "Easy, boy. You'll wear yourself out. Save your energy for the thorns."

"But I feel like a caged bird."

Morteque smiled. "At least a caged bird is a protected bird. Be grateful, boy, for the wisdom of the Ancient of Days."

Estravai picked up one of the wooden staves and thrust it into Grenfel's hands. He could not contain his laughter. "You look like a ferocious knight with no equal to be found in all Ascar. When you're not slicing thorns, you may find the lance useful for maintaining your balance."

Like a charging bull, Grenfel began to slash his way through the thorns, making his way towards the city. Morteque and Estravai fell in behind him.

"Well, this is one less thing to be decided by meditation and prayer," Morteque said. "At least now we know who's breaking trail."

Grenfel looked behind him, scarcely able to see Morgan past the two men following him, yet he knew the beast remained at the base of the salt cliffs.

Having only ventured a few feet into the forest of thorns, Grenfel felt his arms and legs ache under the weight of his strange armour. He lowered his staff from the effort of wielding it.

The giant thorns were like unrelenting guardians loyal to Meldrock's cause. Inching ahead was tedious for the small party; every few steps, they became entangled by thorns that bit into their musk-ox armour and wrapped around their arms and legs. The travellers had to stop from time to time to dislodge thorns from their hairy armour, and each time they pulled one out, more of the thick hair was lost from their protective skins.

"It's hopeless," cried Grenfel in an exhausted voice from behind the bars of his iron mask.

With relentless blows, Estravai and Morteque attacked the thorns ensnaring their young friend. They were as madmen, hacking at the thorns in a trance-like state. Their blood trickled through their riddled skins, but the men were oblivious to the pain as they pressed on in the task of freeing their young friend.

At last, Grenfel was able to take another step forward, but his freedom came at a cost. Morteque and Estravai's blood now trickled from their many wounds.

~

High in the mid-heavens, the queen's raven-black hair uncoiled upon her shoulders like a serpent descending from a tree. She staggered in front of her throne, incensed with lust for the blood of the Revealers of Secrets and the Hawkman.

"I will have those drops and quench my thirst," laughed the queen sadistically as she threw her empty chalice at the heads of her demonic council. "Release the vultures! My obedient pets shall bring the blood to

---

me. Do it now or know my wrath," shrieked the queen at the heels of her fleeing council.

⁓

The travellers heard the beating of wings overhead, but only glimpsed the circling birds through the tangle of thorns.

"Our visitors are hoping we might seize from our struggling and rot here, helplessly impaled," Estravai said, feeling exhausted. "Even if we survive, they'll be content to retrieve drops of our blood and ferry it back to their Queen."

Grenfel found a surge of new strength as he peered through the last few thorn trees to Dremcon. The city was like a dark jewel inlaid in a setting of thorns. The ground was a dusty red and the smell nearly sucked the breath right out of him, like a million invisible leeches. "It's what I imagined Hades to be like," Grenfel said. "It's a natural dungeon."

"There's more truth to your words than you realize," said Morteque. "It seems when Meldrock finds an open door to a city, Hades ascends, plunders, and dwells there."

Estravai slowed to a snail's pace as the group approached the final entanglement of thorns. Just beyond, two enormous demons, their bull-like faces encased by spike collars, pounded the red dust with reptilian tails and spread their leathery wings across a small opening in the thorns that otherwise encased Dremcon.

"All who pass to and fro must contend with the city's gatekeepers," Morteque said. "Their very presence causes most who make it this far to have second thoughts and turn and run."

The demons glared out of red eyes sunk back into their skulls. They breathed noxious odours out of their bullish nostrils.

Estravai stepped closer to the demons and raised his hands to the heavens. With the same authoritative tone he had used before, Estravai commanded, "In the name of the all-powerful one, the Ancient of Days, stand aside!"

The demons glared before reluctantly stepping aside. Their glares carried the nonverbal message, "You are not welcome here!" Their demonic message pierced the backs of the trio of travellers like many tiny arrows of ice as they gingerly eased their way through the opening in the thorns.

The trio now found themselves knee deep in a wet, sticky substance. It smelled like raw sewage, causing Grenfel to feel nauseous, so he reluctantly shielded his nose with his itchy armour. The waterway in which the trio now stood might have at one time resembled a cobblestone street, though at present it appeared more like a shallow creek. Torches which lined the edge of the waterway mounted on high poles, cast their dim light upon the wet substance, revealing glimpses of red in the otherwise intense darkness which seemed to surround the trio like an assassin's cloak. On approaching the first torch, Estravai reached down to feel the water. He then pulled back and held his hand up to the torchlight.

"It's blood!" Estravai declared. "It appears we're travelling on death's highway."

"Truly this is Meldrock's signature of madness painted on this city," replied Morteque. "For it would take the greatest of massacres to produce this waterway."

At the word "blood," Grenfel suddenly felt faint and overwhelmed with grossness with the thought of having waded through a river of blood, more so than when he just had the noxious odour to deal with. It was in this state that Grenfel saw in the dim torchlight the outline of buildings, which seemed to follow the course of the macabre waterway like a forgotten dreary stone fence line. Squinting at the first structure, Grenfel saw it was a huge building with great iron bars over its windows.

He blinked, realizing his vision was getting blurry. He rubbed his eyes, thinking the light was playing tricks on him.

"What is it, boy?" Estravai inquired.

"My eyes! I think the fumes are getting to them." But then, as Estravai and Morteque looked on, he let out a surprised cry. "Oh! It's like a curtain has being lifted. I can see through the walls of that stone building without leaving this spot!"

"I believe you've been blessed with a vision. It has nothing to do with the fumes and everything to do with the Ancient of Days," Estravai said.

Grenfel nodded. "There's a room at the top of the stairs where a young child sits terrified, cowering upon an old bed. The child is being tormented relentlessly by shadow creatures." He stopped only to take a breath. "In another room, a woman stands upon a wooden chair, screaming as hundreds of mice scurry around her."

Then Grenfel suddenly reeled back.

"What is it, boy?" Estravai asked.

"I heard a voice in my head."

Estravai leaned in closer. "What did it say?"

"It said, why are you watching us? And the house is called fear." Grenfel trembled in the torchlight, as the visionary state seemed to pull him suddenly off again, like a wild horse whose tail he was desperately hanging onto, and he stuttered. "The next house is in a state of disrepair. There are frames but no windows, a door but no knob, a roof but no shingles. Inside, I see scantily clothed children who appear unwashed. Many of the children look as if they're mere skeletons covered in a thin veneer of skin. Each has a large clay bowl into which a hooded figure places a single grain of wheat. This only causes the children to reach out for more with desperate hands and pleading voices, all to no avail as the hooded figure mercilessly laughs and shouts back at the children, 'A grain of wheat for your souls.' When the children reach out again for a grain of wheat, the hooded figure pulls it away, saying, 'Not today, for we already own you.'"

He reeled back again, and Estravai and Morteque braced him from behind. "The voice in my head. It says, 'Why are you watching us? This house is called lack.'"

Grenfel clung onto his traveling companions like a child unwilling to part company with a pet.

"Easy boy," Estravai said in a soothing tone.

The vision caught Grenfel again. "I see the next building. It has more doors and windows than necessary. In fact, it's hard to make out any part of a wall that's not covered by a door or window. It also has more chimneys than hearths. Inside, a woman sits at a broken spinning wheel, her fingers bleeding, and around her are piles of spun wool. A hooded figure laughs at the woman as she tries to get the spinning wheel to work. The hooded figure taunts her saying. 'Just two more rooms to fill before you rest.'"

Grenfel leaned back, placing the full force of his weight on his heels.

"Voices in your head again, boy?" Morteque asked.

"Yes," replied Grenfel nervously. "They're asking why I'm watching them. They say this house is called greed."

As Grenfel rested momentarily in his companions' arms, they heard a clamouring from the direction of a bend in the river of blood. The sound increased in intensity as the trio stood motionless, listening. It was an eerie mixture of spoken threats, people crying, children arguing, women screaming, pleading cries, seductive invitations, bartering, foul cursing, and clanging swords—all to the rhythm of woeful moans whose individual notes comprised a demonic symphony.

"Truly this city is the heart of Hades," Morteque stated.

"I know not," replied Estravai. "Be it a nest of demons or the throne room of Meldrock himself, it matters little to us. We need to pass through as part of the boy's destiny."

Taking a half-coherent Grenfel under each arm, Estravai and Morteque proceeded to haul the boy towards the forlorn sounds. Estravai and Morteque walked silently along as Grenfel seemed to flip in and out of his visionary experience. On rounding the bend in the river, the trio came face to face with a hellish square lit on all sides by torchlight. Further adding to the madness were the towering ancient stone buildings that leaned over the square. Like great Titans betting on the evening's entertainment, and whose appearance seemed to suggest they were designed by a colour-blind architect. The noxious odour wafting from the bloody square did little to quicken the trio's steps through the city now, as they seemed paralyzed by the horrific sights being acted out in front of them as by a bizarre theatre group. The torchlight revealed children fighting, a merchant conducting business with broken scales, another being pierced by a sword in a duel, a woman screaming while being raped, another being beaten as she tried to prepare a meal for a man cursing at her in a drunken stupor. Others pleaded for food with hands outstretched while angry fists beat them for not investing their money wisely.

Estravai and Morteque supported Grenfel as they observed the unceasing acts of horror.

"Can you see them?" Grenfel cried out.

"See who, boy? The madmen before our eyes?" Estravai sounded confused.

"No. The others!"

"Others?" Estravai said. "Boy, if you're seeing others then you're looking into another realm!"

"By the children fighting," explained Grenfel. "I see warriors clad in black armour with iron helmets, shields, and lances. They're prodding the children. Near the merchant with the broken scales, I see one who looks no different in dress than my uncle, or like any lord; he's sitting on one side of the scales, a smile on his face. I see many other figures in the square, so many it would seem impossible for any more to enter. Some are human, and others half human and beast. Still others resemble creatures of the animal and insect realms. Swarms of flies cloud the air, stirred up by a sorcerer who calls them forth from the river of blood. Where you hear human cries, I hear demonic laughter."

Before Estravai had time to respond, a woman stepped out of the shadows and approached the trio. Her garments were stained with blood. Her hair was long, squeezed into thick dreadlocks matted with blood. She moved like a serpent towards Grenfell, who stood frozen in terror, not knowing if this was part of the vision or not.

"How about taking up company with me?" the woman asked, smiling as she ran a bloody finger through Grenfel's hair.

"I promised my mother I would never forget the Ancient of Days."

"The Ancient of Days!" She laughed. "Do you really think He would be found in this dark place? Stay with me, young Hawkman! Am I not the one offering you comfort?" The woman smiled as she again ran a bloody finger through Grenfel's hair.

"No!" Grenfel pulled away from the woman's touch.

"Pity! Had you chosen me, you would never again have known a lonely day in your life again." Her voice then shifted from seduction to a demonic growl. "So, you think you can see us, Hawkman?"

Grenfel was startled when her voice suddenly changed back to its seductive overtones as she said, "Oh well, I may never know the pleasure of your company. But your father's heart is ours!" growled the woman in a demonic voice once more. The woman stood before Grenfel for what seemed like an eternity. Her image only lost to him when a bright light flashed across his vision, and for a few seconds he thought he saw his father standing before him, his face twisted in an expression of agony, his royal robe tattered and bloody, his hands pinned behind him like one being led to the gallows.

"Do you see him?" Grenfel yelled.

"See who?" Morteque asked.

"My father, the king!"

"I've seen your father many times, boy," Estravai said, clearing his throat. "But that was before my exile. All I see standing before me now is this dirty woman."

A tear fell down Grenfel's cheek. "This cannot be my father! Please, Ancient of Days, I couldn't sleep knowing my father is to forever be a slave to Meldrock."

"Stand brave, Grenfel," Estravai whispered to him as the woman slunk back into the shadows of the square.

Her cries to entice people to join her in intimacy always ended in diabolical laughter, as she told them, "No you never have enough for my love!"

As the trio watched these horrific events being repeated over and over, they wondered if they would ever cease.

"Look!" Morteque shouted.

Estravai and Grenfel turned to him, then saw where he was looking—back in the direction they had just come. Grenfel saw two bright men walking towards them in clean garments. The newcomers were the same men who had fought the queen during the journey to Dremcon. The men came to a stop in front of them, speaking in voices that reminded him of a crashing waterfall.

"Due to the boy's cry for his father," they cried in unison, "the Ancient of Days has sent us to lead you out of this dark prison."

Within moments, the city's two menacing gatekeepers appeared to confront them. Grenfel suddenly realized he had been carried to the edge of the city by the men of light, his feet suspended in the air. Estravai and Morteque, too, had been spirited away from the square.

The bull-faced demons glared at their guests, drooling. Streams of blood fell from them, birthing a new river of coagulating blood at their feet such as existed in the city. The demons continued to glare, and Grenfel felt that had it not being for the presence of the two brilliant strangers, they all would have become the demonic gatekeepers' lunch. In a flash of light, the brilliant strangers pointed their flaming swords at the demons. Grenfel saw the blur of light from their swords arcing through the air, and he remembered the touch of their swords on his lips, before slipping once more into unconsciousness.

The demonic gatekeepers, recognizing a greater authority, still glared in defiance but reluctantly stepped aside and stood trembling in fear. With Estravai and Morteque following, the two brilliant strangers carried Grenfel past the incapacitated gatekeepers towards the forest of giant thorns. The brilliant strangers approached the giant thorns as if they were a mere grassy meadow. One of the strangers pointed his flaming sword at the chaotic mass; it groaned and creaked in protest at being untwisted against its will. He walked into the path between the massive towering walls of thorns and stood with his flaming sword pointed towards Heaven.

The other brilliant stranger carried Grenfel and led Estravai and Morteque along the path created by the invisible hand of the Ancient of Days through the thorns unscathed. As the brilliant stranger carried Grenfel, he glimpsed through unfocused eyes at Morgan standing in the opening between thorns at the end of the path. Fighting to stay conscious, it seemed like he had just closed his eyes when he felt the light touch of a hand on his head. Grenfel opened his eyes slowly and noticed he was still being supported by one of the smiling strangers. Looking around he saw the others standing next to Morgan. Behind them, one of the strangers stood amidst the forest of thorns, his flaming sword still outstretched towards the heavens, guarding the way.

Everyone and everything seemed so much more colourful and peaceful now that they were free of Dremcon and in the presence of these marvellous strangers. Grenfel no longer even noticed the putrid smell of the flatlands. He felt fresh and alive, like one feels in the cool morning air on the cabernish mountains. He wasn't sure why he felt so invigorated, but thought it must have something to do with the closeness he felt to the Ancient of Days while in the strangers' presence.

The stranger who had carried Grenfel now released him to stand on his own. Grenfel stood motionless for a moment, looking around at everything with the wonder of a child experiencing the outdoors for the first time. His state of awe drew a smile from the stranger and he handed Grenfel a flask and some bread.

"Let the boy eat and rest," the stranger instructed Estravai and Morteque. "Then head south. You know where to go."

With that, the stranger joined his companion amidst the forest of thorns. The same loud creaks and groans signalled the closing of the path, as had opened it when one of the two brilliant strangers had pointed his flaming sword at the thorns. Estravai, Morteque, and Grenfel stood motionless, overcome with amazement as the towering wall of thorns collapsed back into its chaotic entanglement, and a brilliant ball of blue light shot through the twisted mass of thorns and high into the heavens.

"There's no sense just standing around watching the sky!" declared Estravai as he began taking off his musk-ox armour.

Morteque did the same. "I don't know about you two, but I'm famished! Hand me some of that bread."

"What? Sick of your own cooking already!" Estravai laughed. "What do you say, boy, shall we take a break from Morteque's cooking this night?"

When Estravai turned to Grenfel, he saw that the boy had fallen asleep, without so much as bothering to unfasten his armour.

"Let the boy sleep," Estravai said. "His mother's not here to tuck him in anyhow."

"Pity!" Morteque sighed. "He'll miss the fine hospitality of our heavenly friends. Oh well. The more for us." He broke into a spontaneous outburst of laughter at the very thought of it.

"Looks to me like you better stick to the bread and leave the flask to me," Estravai advised.

❧

On a quiet night, Tony, Roxanne, and Jordan stood outside the Drummingsville general store awaiting the 11:45 p.m. bus to arrive from Sarquis. On the hour, it was scheduled to take them to the town of West Georgia.

"I'd feel better if you would at least let me drive you," Tony insisted to his wife as he buttoned his full-length coat.

"You've got enough on your mind," Roxanne said, sounding tired. "All those dreams about demons… I've got my own demons to deal with. Jordan and I will be at my mother's. If you find you're still interested in us."

Tony's lips quivered. He couldn't shake the feeling they might be leaving for good. "Nothing's changed between us, Roxanne, really. You believe that, don't you?"

The old green marine bus pulled up to the general store. Its tall, slim driver opened the door, put on his rawhide work gloves, and adjusted his stained gray uniform as he called out for tickets.

Roxanne buttoned the top of her brown suede jacket, then grabbed Jordan's hand. With her other hand, she reached down to pick up her green tapestry suitcase.

"Let me get that for you," Tony insisted, reaching for the suitcase. But Roxanne had already grabbed it.

"We'll manage just fine, thank you." Roxanne handed her tickets to the driver. With tear-filled eyes, she turned and looked at Tony one last time. "You know where we are if you decide you want us."

Tony knelt down and hugged Jordan.

"Bye, Dad!" Jordan responded between sniffles as he released Tony's neck from the hug.

"Bye, little mister," responded Tony in a tearful voice, practically shouting over the knocking the diesel engine. "Don't go!" Tony pleaded frantically, "I don't understand what's happening, Roxanne, but please stay. We can talk—"

But the bus doors were already closed. Before the words were out of Tony's mouth, the bus pulled out into the night destined for West Georgia.

Tony stood alone outside the general store, head bowed, silently vowing in his heart that he would get through this somehow, and that he would come for Roxanne and Jordan. That was his promise to them.

He walked towards his truck, unlocked the door, and jumped in. He pulled away, thinking in his heart, *I will not give up on you, my love. I will be relentless in my pursuit of you. I will not cease in this struggle until you're back in my arms.*

With a preoccupied mind, Tony drove aimlessly up and down the dark streets of Drummingsville into the late watches of the night. Every time Tony passed Martha's store in his truck, the moon in the sky seemed to become a little more out of focus for him and his head a little heavier. Finally he jerked his head upright and blinked his eyes in an attempt to clear his blurring vision and keep the road in focus. *Enough*, he thought, *time to head for home,* and he turned his truck right along a side street in the direction of his condo.

Arriving out front of his condo, he parked, opened the driver's door, and proceeded to step out of the cab of his truck. Standing still for a moment, he noticed the bigness of the moon and the quietness of the night. Usually he didn't mind the smallness of Drummingsville, but tonight he was feeling the smallness of the town. *Why couldn't somebody come out*, he thought *and at least throw a shoe at a cat,* but there was only the deafening silence of the moon watching him and he felt as lonely again as when Roxanne had departed.

"I miss you Roxanne," he whispered as he closed the door to truck and headed for the condo's front door.

Stepping inside the condo, he closed and locked the door behind him. Switching on the LCD light attached to his keychain, he navigated the stairs in the dark and headed to the master bedroom. Tony sat down on the bed next to his nightstand. Pulling open the drawer of the nightstand, he removed his Bible and closed the drawer again. Opening his Bible, he randomly began to thumb through its pages using his LCD light, hoping in his desperate searching to find a little solace for his troubled soul. *Why leave, Roxanne?* He thought as he continued flipping pages.

How does that help our family? We're only like a three strong cord when we're together, don't you understand that? By going you just give the devil a chance to unravel our family. As the painful issues of his heart passed through the corridors of his mind like shadow pictures on a wall, the light from his LCD flashlight fell on Isaiah 6. "Who will go for us?" he read as he fell back on the bed, letting his Bible rest on his chest as he repeated the prophet Isaiah's response, "Send me!" over and over, until he simply just closed his eyes, and then seemed to fall in a dream down a rabbit hole as Alice did on entry into Wonderland.

He was dressed in a black robe tied at the waist with an ordinary piece of rope, much like a novice would wear who was seeking to begin a career with a monastery. Looking around he saw others dressed like him standing in a long line which was moving through the center of a large, torch-lit chamber in single file between rows of long planked tables.

"Keep them moving, Estravai," instructed one of the robed figures standing behind a plank table at the front of the line. He felt the push of a hand on his shoulder from behind propel him forward towards the table.

"Say nothing unless Eltarz permits, novice," advised Estravai. Having being propelled forward, he now faced the daunting reality that every novice seeking admission into the Order of the Hawk at Mirana must face, and that was to stand before the eyes of the most sought after Revealer of Secrets in Ascar.

Eltarz's eyes fell on him like the all-seeing eyes of God. He trembled nervously under his gaze for what seemed an eternity before Eltarz asked Estravai for a name. Stepping beside him, Estravai repeated Eltarz's question. "So what do they call you?"

He stuttered back, "Gren."

"Well Gren, which castle has sent you, to be trained as a Revealer of Secrets?"

"Kreniston," he nervously answered.

Looking at Eltarz, Estravai declared the novice to be Gren of Kreniston.

Eltarz turned to a brother on his left holding a quill in his hand and said, "Morteque, enter the name Gren in the ledger under Kreniston."

Nodding in obedience at Eltarz, Morteque opened the heavy leather-bound ledger on the table before him and turned its pages to the one entitled Kreniston. With a puzzled expression on his face, Morteque looked up from the ledger at Eltarz and said, "It appears we have two novices to train as Revealers of Secrets to the King of Ascar's court."

Eltarz stroked his long blond beard momentarily before stating to Morteque, "Why should the king of Ascar not have double the Revealers of Secrets in his court than all other lords of Ascar. Enter Gren's name as well, Morteque."

Nodding in obedience, Morteque set to making the new entry.

Taking up his twisted staff from where it was leaning against the table beside him, Eltarz turned to face Estravai, "Collect the bow, quiver, and blindfolds."

Nodding at Eltarz, Estravai at once set off to tend to his request.

"Morteque," Eltarz called out as he again turned towards him, "continue to enter the novices in the ledger. I shall oversee the training of the king's novices personally."

Morteque nodded and then continued writing.

Turning to face Gren with his staff in hand, Eltarz beckoned him to follow. Gren walked along the table past Morteque on one side and Eltarz did likewise on the other. Clearing the end of the table, Eltarz led Gren towards a naturally formed archway which was supporting torches fastened to both sides of its opening. A lone novice stood waiting in the middle of the archway with his head bowed.

Noticing him as they approached, Eltarz said, "Levit."

The novice lifted his head just as they came to stand in front of him, and Gren saw the look of wonderment in his eye.

"You are to be joined by another from Kreniston," Eltarz explained to Levit. "A novice called Gren."

Levit smiled and Gren nodded back. Beckoning the novices to follow him, Eltarz led them through the archway out of the big chamber down a crude set of stone stairs along a natural tunnel lit sporadically by torches suspended from the tunnel's wall. The tunnel ended at another archway, with a round shield displaying a gold hawk's head in its center hanging above it.

"The king of Ascar's training chamber," Eltarz had explained as they had stood momentarily gazing at the shield. Eltarz beckoned once again and the novices followed him through the archway into another chamber half the size of the one they had just come from. The walls of the chamber supported lit torches. The chamber's floor was composed of large rounded paving stones. There was a large circle in the center of the room with the gold head of a Hawk in its center. Through the center of the circle the line of paving stones were dyed red up to the edge of the image of the gold hawk on both the left and right side of the image. The novices followed Eltarz to the circle. Gren counted ten red paving stones on both the left and right side outside the circle, and each line of red stones ended with a wooden post supporting a round, burlap-wrapped straw target which faced the center of the circle. As Gren studied the design of the dyed stones, Estravai approached with the requested equipment.

Eltarz nodded in acknowledgment of Estravai. "Prepare novice Levit."

Hearing Eltarz's instructions, Estravai proceeded with the equipment to Levit and beckoned him to follow him into the center of the circle adjacent to the red paving stones on either side of the golden Hawk's head. Handing Levit the bow, Estravai hung the quiver around his neck, and stepped behind him to secure a blindfold around his eyes. He then placed Levit's hands on the bow and made sure he was pointing it ahead of where he was standing.

"Now, take Gren and stand him behind Levit with his arms outstretched," instructed Eltarz. There was no time for Gren to wonder the meaning of this exercise before he felt the hand of Estravai on the back of his shoulder pushing him towards Levit where he was assisted by Estravai into the correct position behind Levit with his arms outstretched and looking directly at the center of the other novice's back, while Estravai remained at his side.

"Good, Estravai." Eltarz smiled as he observed the novices for a moment, then with staff in hand and a few large strides made his way to stand behind Gren. "To see for the king of Ascar is the high calling for a Revealer of Secrets. As novices who hope one day to serve in your king's court, you must find success first in his training chamber. However, success here will only come through unity in action. Gren, take this time to note the target's position mounted on the wooden poles, close your eyes, and see them in your mind. Do this several times until you are sure of their location with your eyes closed. When you are sure, raise your right arm and Estravai will secure a blindfold over your eyes."

Gren opened his eyes looked right, then left, closed his eyes, then after a moment he nodded and raised his right hand. Estravai quickly secured the blindfold over Gren's eyes and lowered Gren's right hand into its outstretched position.

Observing Gren now standing with his blindfold secured behind Levit with the bow, Eltarz continued to explain the training exercise. "Gren, I will touch one of your outstretched arms with my staff. When you feel it, and have noted the direction of the target in your mind, lean forward and speak it in Levit's ear. Levit, when you hear the direction, immediately turn that way and fire an arrow. Estravai will be moving from one wooden post to the other continually. He is hoping you trust each other."

Raising his staff, Eltarz nodded for Estravai to begin his circuits. Reaching out with his staff, he touched Gren's right arm. Seeing the target on the wooden post in his mind, Gren leaned forward and whispered the direction in Levit's ear, "turn right."

Levit, with his bow in position, arrow notched, began to turn in the suggested direction and then froze. "Are you sure you saw correctly, Gren?" Levit questioned as he lowered his bow.

Closing his eyes beneath his blindfold, Gren imagined the wooden posts and the targets again. "Yes, they look the same, fire the arrow!"

Levit raised the bow again, but again hesitated and lowered the bow. "I can't do it."

"Why?" asked Gren.

"What if Estravai is standing in front of the target?"

"Did you see him when you imagined the targets?"

"No," Gren replied, "I just saw the wood posts."

"I will not fire, Gren," Levit said as he dropped the bow. "A life is more valuable than a vision to me." Levit removed his blindfold and turned to face Gren. Gren removed his blindfold and saw the look of wonderment in Levit's eye as Levit shrugged his shoulders at him.

"It's okay. There's always tomorrows practice," Gren responded.

Eltarz banged the end of his staff on the paving stone, causing the novices to disengage their conversation and turn to face Eltarz. "Meldrock can easily fool the natural eye; he can put an image before you that you are familiar with but subtly change the small details, mixing the vision and bringing confusion into your mind. A true Revealer of Secrets, then, has to learn to see with his inner eye and heart. You did well, Levit realizing seeing involves one's heart as well. There is much time for the shooting of arrows and to learn the process of seeing what the Ancient of Days shows you for one's king, before you are sent out from Mirana."

"Before you are sent," muttered Tony as he sat up on the bed, knocking his Bible to the floor in the process. "It's only four a.m.," he muttered as he noticed the digital clock on the nightstand. Turning his head he saw the vacant space in the bed his wife normally occupied and he thought, *even my bizarre dreams God aren't enough to deaden the pain of my reality.* He fell back on the bed, not quite ready to face reality, yet his heart full of pain and his head of dreams.

Closing his eyes, Tony lay on the bed thinking and his mind once again took him far away for a moment from the pain of his heart, and he saw David on the battlefield facing Goliath and he wondered if God had a David for him and his family and for Drummingsville as well.

It was during these thoughts that he finally drifted off to sleep once more.

CHAPTER THIRTEEN

The phone rang in the kitchen. Tony jumped to his feet from the sofa, growling like a bear who had just been aroused early from hibernation.

"Isn't that the way it goes," he raved as he jammed another bite of pizza into his mouth, before reluctantly turning his head from the hockey game. "Just when a goal is about to be scored," Tony muttered as he walked past Max sprawled out in an overstuffed chair and on into the kitchen to take the call.

"Tony!" came the familiar voice of his boss, Dylan Cartwright, through the receiver.

"What?" Tony said. "Don't tell me I've got to catch a chopper in an hour."

"Not this time." He sounded upset. Tony had heard Dylan use that tone often, but never before with him.

"Let me guess," Tony said, hoping to bounce Dylan back into the practical joker mode he had through much endurance actually grown to love. "Is it a surprise staff party? Well, count me in for whatever you're collecting."

"That's not it."

Tony fell silent.

"I'm letting you go." Dylan's emotionless statement rang in Tony's ears.

"You're what?" Tony shouted, barely able to comprehend what he had just heard. "I've been Forest Tech's lead field hand for years."

"I know, but there have been complaints."

"So? What about it? There have been complaints before."

"I know," Dylan replied, "but as the executive manager, I have to make hard calls. And this is one of those. I believe Forest Tech's action to be justified in this case, though."

With Dylan hiding behind the company name, Tony knew his ticket had been as good as punched. He may as well clear out his locker and go.

"Fine then," Tony said, hanging up the receiver.

⸺

Dylan put down the receiver. "I hope you're satisfied," he said to the woman sitting on the other side of his desk. "I've just run off my lead hand."

"You're my knight in shining armour."

"You're Forest Tech's lead hand now." Dylan lit a cigar. "Tell your lawyer friends to leave me alone. And one more thing: don't let me down."

"You really know how to make a girl feel good." Sue smiled as she closed the office door behind her. Pausing momentarily, she pushed the door back open. "By the way, I've never let a man down yet."

⸺

Laughter echoed throughout the mid-heavens as demons fluttered jubilantly around the queen, who sat upon her grotesque throne. Her long raven hair sprawled upon her black velvet gown, like paint splashed on a canvas by a blind artist. Six tall princes encircled the throne as she drunkenly commended them for services rendered.

In a sudden burst of unrestrained madness, the queen threw her chalice at a small demon flying overhead. Upon observing the work of her hand, as the demon's flight path now took on a zig-zag pattern, she broke into a hysterical fit of laughter. This caused the lesser demons to work themselves into a frenzy.

"We're proving effective for our master once again. My spider continues to spin her web," she whispered. The whispers of the queen now further threatened madness on the demons' already frenzied state, like rabies affects a fox.

The mid-heavens couldn't contain the eruption of madness, and like a drunken rugby match some of the evil burst forth and fell like lightning upon the town of Drummingsville.

Tony walked back into the living room, looking like he'd just been hit by a freight train. He collapsed onto his overstuffed green sofa.

"I guess now's not a good time to ask if you want to know the score," Max said as he reached for another slice of pizza from the coffee table.

Tony sat silently, staring somewhere just beyond the screen of his television.

"Good pizza," Max said, searching for just the right icebreaker.

"I can't believe it!"

"It's only pizza."

"He actually let me go." Tony shook his head in disbelief.

Max decided not to say anything. For now, it seemed wise to just sit and listen to what his friend had to say.

"He actually let me go," Tony repeated. "Forest Tech's lead hand and team spirit logger for three years and now… Dylan, what's got into your head? You're usually so sure of yourself. I don't get it. So you got complaints about me. What kind of complaints?"

Max shifted uncomfortably and pulled his hat down a little lower over his eyes. "I've been wanting to talk with you, Tony," he said with some reluctance. He picked up a soda from the coffee table. "I wasn't sure just how to go about it."

"Well, if the roof of the house is going to cave in on me, I guess it may as well be the whole roof and not just a piece of it."

"Here goes, then. In all my years of playing hockey with you, Tony, I've never asked you anything like I'm about to. But friends should be able to discuss the hard issues, right?"

"What's on your heart, Max?" Tony asked, feeling no less frustrated than when he'd first returned from the kitchen.

"Did you touch Sue Henderson inappropriately in some way?" Max got to the point with the suddenness of a mountain lion leaping from its rocky perch onto an unsuspecting hare.

Tony stared at Max in horrified disbelief. "What?"

"W—well, Sue... she..." Max went on stuttering for a bit, then slowly picked up momentum. "Sue phoned me, and she was, well, she was crying. I met with her at a restaurant. She had your leather crew jacket, Tony."

Tony felt dumbfounded. The fact that Max was involved in all this made it all the more difficult to take in.

"Sue played me a recording over the phone, Tony, with your voice on it. I have to admit, it sounded pretty bad."

"What recording?" Tony asked with a look of astonishment.

"I wrote down the main points. It begins with you laughing. Then you say, 'Don't worry, I'll treat you gently.' Then Sue says, 'I don't want to,' and she's crying." Max sighed heavily and hung his head.

Tony stared. "Well, what else? Did she say anything else?"

"Yeah, there's more. You said, 'There's only you and me, no one else is here.' Sue then tells you you're being too rough, that she doesn't want to do this. Now I don't understand this, Tony, but you tell her that she has no choice and it'll be over quickly. The last comment I heard you make was, 'You might even say it wasn't too bad.'"

Tony sat wide-eyed and in shock. "Sue probably played the recording for Dylan," he said with dawning realization. "That would explain his decision."

Tony covered his face with both hands, overwhelmed with emotion. He sniffled faintly, then wiped the corners of his eyes.

"This is my story," Tony said, sitting up straight. "We had finished clearing the site and had a little time to kill before the expected rendezvous with our chopper."

Max handed him a box of tissues.

Tony took a tissue from the box and held it loosely in his hand, saying, "Really, Max. I'm okay!" He sat forward. "Sue asked if I could take her up to Blackhorn Peak, as the rest of the fire crew just wanted to sit around camp and read. She wanted to take a few shots of the mountain with her new camera before our ride home. As I recall, we were climbing a steep face on our way to the summit when her jacket came undone from around her waist. I was ahead of her, so all I could really do was watch her jacket float down for what seemed like an eternity. We continued on and were closing on the summit, working our way over jagged rocks, when Sue's foot got jammed in a crevice. Her ankle turned under her weight. Well, I helped support her with the rope, and we crawled the rest of the way to the summit. It was such a beautiful day."

He paused briefly, continuing his explanation as if he were a witness recalling the events of a crime in a courtroom.

"We sat for a short time marvelling at the other peaks in the area. Sue shot a few pictures, but I suppose her film has conveniently disappeared by now."

Tony laughed and looked out the window blankly. He found it hard to believe so much had happened to him in such a short time. He wanted dearly to make it all go away, to have Roxanne back at home and get his job back. He closed his eyes and imagined that when he opened them, everything would be back to normal. But this was his reality now, and all he had was the hope that he could convince his friend to believe him.

"I finally told her that we had to begin making our way back to camp if we had any chance of connecting with the chopper. Sue kind of hemmed and hawed and didn't seem to want to be on her feet anymore that day. I guess I was laughing to try and take her mind off her foot, and that's when I told her not to worry, that I'd treat her gently. I had Sue under one arm to try and take the weight off her injured foot, but when we got to the edge of the cliff, where our rope still hung down, she became a bit nervous and started to cry. She just plain didn't want to go down the mountain. She was stubborn as a mule and didn't budge.

"I didn't know what to do at that point, because we had to get back to camp. I thought a reality check might help her get past her pain, and that's when I said, 'Well, there's only you and me out here and no one else.' Sue kind of nodded at me and placed one hand on the rope. I was now climbing below her, so she could lean most of her weight back on me. I guess I started descending a little too fast, because I remember her saying, 'Ouch! You're too rough.' That wasn't the only time I heard those words from her on our way down the mountain.

"I didn't think she wanted to go through the agony of hobbling back to camp at all. I figured she hoped we would be reported missing and swept off the mountain by a search-and-rescue helicopter. I knew it was now just a matter of a few hours before our chopper would arrive, and we were responsible to be there if we didn't want to wait another two weeks for the next flight out. I guess I was kind of thinking about Roxanne and becoming a little short in my patience. I wasn't about to let anything stop me from catching my flight out, so I told her she didn't have a choice and that it would be over quickly. Finding creative ways to keep her mind off the pain was stressful, and that's when I said, 'When we get down off this mountain, you'll probably look back up and say it wasn't all that bad.' Or something like that.

"It seemed to take forever, but we made it off the mountain finally. I noticed Sue was shivering, so I took off my crew jacket and gave it to her. She nodded and thanked me, but I don't suppose that made it onto the recording. Anyhow, we dragged ourselves back to camp like a couple of shot-up desperadoes walking in out of the desert. Now it was only a matter of waiting, so we collapsed around the remains of a fire and did just that.

"Funny! Now that I think of it, Sue wasn't crying about me touching her in anyway inappropriately to the rest of the fire-team, or for that matter crying at all. In fact, she was laughing by the end of the ordeal. She raved about how relieved she was to be going home. I doubt I'll get my jacket back now." He looked at Max. "So, Sue recorded our adventure, did she? I can't believe it. This is how I get repaid for being willing to show her Blackhorn Peak."

"That's what I told her!" said Max, feeling rejuvenated by his friend's story, relieved to hear he had been right about Tony. "I said the recording could be about anything, but Sue insisted that combined with your crew jacket it would be enough to persuade you to sign your truck over to her."

Tony stared at the floor, taking a sip of soda. "I tell you, that woman may have my jacket, but she won't get my truck. If I were the last man standing in the face of a thousand enemies, they'd have to get through me to take one piece of what I own."

Max smiled. "Now you're sounding more like the guy I went into the corners with at hockey practice."

"It's like my dreams."

"How's that?"

"I've been having a series of dreams for quite a while now, and they're unbelievably graphic. From my studies, I think the main characters are a couple of prophets and a young immature apostle. Anyway, in the last dream they were in a very demonic city. The boy saw that there are individuals exhibiting bizarre behaviour, but because they dwell mostly in darkness they don't notice a lot. It's like everyone's consciences are seared. I think there are a lot of people around Drummingsville lately with seared consciences, or if not, at least they're walking in great darkness. That includes Dylan and perhaps even Roxanne."

"Could be you're on to something," Max said, standing up. "Although I tend to think you might be under some stress from all you've been through. Maybe you should get out of town for a while. Take a break and let the dust settle for a bit."

"Thanks, Max. I appreciate you."

Tony got up and gave his friend a big bear hug. Max quickly composed himself, then smiled and stepped out the front door.

Tony turned on his porch light and called after his friend. "I hope you won't be in too much trouble with Barb!"

"No!" Max said as he unlocked his car. "Barb will be all right. She knows I'm watching the game with you."

"Yeah, but it's pretty late."

"That's okay. Barb's probably asleep with a book by now. If not, I can always tell her the game went into three periods of overtime." Tony laughed heartily, probably for the first time all night. "Oh, one more thing!"

"What?"

"Let's not make this hugging thing a habit," Max joked. "I only like body contact when it's running at me from centre ice. Anyway, goodnight. I'm standing with you all the way, just like we did for the divisional cup."

Max smiled as he closed his driver's door and drove onto the street.

"I know you are, Max," Tony whispered to himself as he waved from the porch. He stood alone for a moment, content to just watch his friend's taillights be swallowed by the darkness like one might stand and watch a beautiful sunset.

Chapter Fourteen

Tony turned his truck right onto the pavement of Highway 97 from the gravel, pot-hole-infested road he had being traveling on for the last hour out of Drummingsville. He passed the big green sign informing that Drummingsville was 50 miles back in the direction he had just come. Traveling north now in the direction of the city of Sarquis, he spotted the rusted-out steam shovel marking the turnoff for the tourist information board. Figuring that he may as well start his trip the same as other tourists usually do, he signalled left and pulled his truck into the picnic area. He parked by the log restrooms, which were painted in the usual park colours of dark brown and green.

Tony opened his driver's door and stepped out of his truck. Closing it behind him, he headed over to a log display with a map and essential facts tourists usually found helpful. Tony noticed the large arrow with the red letters declaring, "You are here." Norwood County. A vast wilderness area, composed of many rugged mountains, white-water rivers, and trout-filled lakes, and Drummingsville was located right in the middle hemmed in by the mountains, rightfully earning by its foreign visitors the title "Little Switzerland."

Yeah, I can bear witness to the wilderness facts, thought Tony, *as I have personally rescued many stranded adrenaline junkies who challenged Mother Nature a little too hard.* Scanning the map further, Tony saw where the gravel road from Drummingsville met the highway heading north to Sarquis and south to Princeton.

Tony noticed the info board had the usual facts one would expect a tourist would want to know, such as whether the area was suitable for camping, fishing, or off-roading. Under the list of services he noticed Martha's store, Mrs. Philpots' video rental, Crester's cave, but no Forest Tech. *Well that's probably good,* he thought, *one less thing to give Dylan a big head.*

A graphic of a miner on horseback with various other first nation images around it, including one image of Chief Issack, caught Tony's eye. He read the heading near the images: "History and Legends." *This should be enlightening,* he thought. The display explained that the original people to the area of Drummingsville were a first nation people called the wolf people. They used the area of Drummingsville as a summer hunting and fishing camp. *That's interesting,* thought Tony, *I remember seeing the remains of old wooden fish traps when I was out in the bush a while back.* Tony continued reading. The wolf people thought of the mountains around Drummingsville as sacred; having found shiny gems within them, they thought that somewhere in the mountains was a pathway to the stars. A prospector named William Kade happened on an opening in one of the mountains when seeking shelter, and stumbled on a few shiny gems when searching the cavern in the mountain for burnable material. His excited cries in the nearby towns erupted into the great 1800s mining boom in the Drummingsville area, and in July 1802 the Stillmore mine was created.

Tony continued to read the notes on the info board regarding the history of Drummingsville, and learned that Chief Issack moved his people from the area because of the influx of miners, who he thought would corrupt his people and they would forget their ways. He could not understand how the miners could kill each other over the shiny gems and steal each other's women. The legend said that the night Chief Issack and his people departed, he danced in the town graveyard and cursed the Stillmore mine because of the miners' blatant disregard for his people and their sacred land.

Tony read the word curse. *No wonder,* he thought, *the population of Drummingsville is only 400 if they put stuff like this on their tourist board.*

Turning to walk back to his truck, he thought of all the old mining stories he had heard regarding accidents, many of them due to greed he surmised, although some would probably have been described as acts of

God. *Do I really need any more negative news?* Tony thought as he closed his truck door, started the engine, and pulled back out on the highway heading once again for Sarquis. He drove for some time just rehashing in his mind as he travelled the idea of the Stillmore mine being cursed. Feeling a little more refreshed by the thought of finally pursuing some answers to the chaos of his life of late, he picked up his travel mug from its holder and took a cautious sip of coffee. His brain snapped alert, like sentries on the walls of a sleepy city, sending a silent message to rest of his body; even his fingers tightened against the steering wheel.

Through widened eyes, he beheld a silver flash speeding around the corner towards him on the wrong side of the road. His heart skipped a beat and he dropped his coffee, grabbing the steering wheel with both hands.

Seeing that he was about to cross paths possibly with a drunk driver, Tony thought, *what more could happen to me?* He cried out, "God, please forgive my rebellion, don't let me be cursed, please God…oh Lord," he continued to pray. "Jesus, what can separate—"

Thud! The silver Porsche clipped his front left headlight. Glass flew everywhere. Resolutely, Tony kept praying through gritted teeth as he came to a stop on the shoulder.

"—us from the love of God."

The phantom Porsche had careened by as if in slow motion. As it passed, Tony was able to read the back plate: "BELIAL." He watched its taillights rush around an S-curve and disappear down the road.

Alone in his vehicle and gasping for air, Tony managed to smile through gritted teeth out his driver's side window and wave off the occasional slowing motorist. It took several moments before he was able to release his white knuckles from the steering wheel, and even longer for Tony to reach for the keys with his trembling hand to shut off the ignition. The sound of a semi blowing its horn was enough to snap Tony out of his state of shock. Waving the trucker by with a smile, Tony finally climbed out of his truck. He walked around to the front and saw a dent on the left fender, alongside the broken light. He supposed he would have to put his truck in a body shop and have the fender pounded out and painted. The fender pounding would be a future project, however if time permitted he might stop in Ruston on his way to Sarquis to have the light repaired. On the positive side, he knew it was a silver Porsche that had hit him. He also knew the speeding car's license plate, and that it had been heading towards Drummingsville. There weren't many cars like that in Drummingsville, increasing the chances of Sheriff Ryder being able to locate the car. Or maybe not; one just couldn't be sure of anyone or anything lately.

Tony jumped back into the cab of his truck, closed the door, and put it into gear. All this would have to wait, as he was on a personal quest to discover the nature of apostles, and more specifically on his way to visit Apostle John Bristane at The School of the Apostles.

～

Grenfel walked with his head down due to the brightness of the sun. Estravai and Morteque strolled in front of Grenfel and his horse, sharing pieces of dried venison. They travelled over the ice fields of Ascar as though they were on an afternoon sightseeing trip. The sun reflecting on the ice beneath the travellers' feet glistened like jewels.

Grenfel lifted his head only to have his eyes begin to water again.

"Everything's happening to you at once, boy," Estravai said as Grenfel rubbed his eyes. "You're like an unrestrained river, but be of good cheer. Though I can't fix the heart—only the Ancient of Days can do that—I can help your eyes."

Estravai pulled loose a deerskin bag from amongst the other equipment Morgan was carrying, so far without complaint. He then patted the horse, as if to thank him for his considerable loyalty during their journey.

"The man I mentioned who gave me the muskox hide also blessed me with several pairs of snow goggles made from bone." Estravai handed a pair of the goggles to Grenfel and helped his young friend adjust them.

"They only have tiny slits," complained Grenfel. "I don't want to wear these."

Morteque came alongside Grenfel so the boy could hear him, even if he couldn't see him well. "Better to see a little and walk with your head up than to be squinting because of the sun, or bowing your head because of the issues of your heart. Besides, your lack of vision is more than made up for by the Ancient of Days."

The journey was starting to feel eternal. Each step Grenfel took seemed only to bring more of the same barren land all the way to the horizon. Walking had become a cursed ritual; with the sun causing the snow to waver in the distance much like heat did in the desert, his eyes often played tricks on him.

Grenfel stopped walking long enough to pull the goggles up onto his forehead, for he thought he had seen shadows on the horizon. Shadows of what, though? There was nothing out there. He rubbed his eyes and looked at Estravai and Morteque in bewilderment.

"Is that an illusion?" asked Grenfel. Morgan suddenly reared back, refusing to move on. "What is it, Morgan? What do you sense?"

"No doubt he smells evil," Estravai replied. "Every hair on my neck is standing up."

"It is so," Morteque explained. "The presence of great wickedness is ahead, just like it was at the pool where Arnabe was murdered."

Two whirlwinds spun ahead at such a speed that they were nothing but a blur. Then, without slowing, they just stopped to reveal two dark princes dressed in black. The princes wore turbans made of silk with single rubies in their centres. Tiny gems glittered in the sunlight from where they hung suspended on the prince's dark silk garments, causing them to seemingly be enshrouded by their own little universe. Their capes were fastened at their necks by tiny metallic spiders and danced around them like worshippers in the throes of a religious ritual though there was no wind. In one of the dark prince's hands, Grenfel noticed with horror the same jewelled dagger the queen had slain the hawk with.

"No!" Grenfel cried out as he clutched at Estravai's arm.

"So, you remember the queen's dagger?" one of the princes asked.

Morteque raised his staff in the air to call on the Ancient of Days, but the other dark prince spoke out. "You were a cowering fool when I dragged Arnabe under the water that day. I presented his blood to the Queen of the Heavens. She savoured every drop. So, put your hands down."

Intimidation seemed to exert a force on Morteque's staff, forcing his trembling hands down until he cowered in their shadows. Estravai, too, was about to call on the Ancient of Days.

"You who cursed the day of your birth in the damp caves of Mirana, what will you now say?" the prince interrupted.

Estravai recoiled in shame.

The two princes turned to Grenfel and addressed him in unison: "And you, young Hawkman, as you enjoy being called."

Grenfel suddenly remembered the excitement that had rushed over his heart that day on the raft as the oil trickled down onto his linen shirt.

"Your father, King Ulrich, is just one of Meldrock's pawns," the first dark prince said. "His heart is bound with Ascar. Meldrock owns his soul, for the king exchanged it for the unchallenged reign of his throne in Kreniston. Meldrock's priests have their way with the people and the king has no voice. There is blood on your father's hands as he turns a blind eye to the poverty, murder, and rape that goes on in his kingdom every day. He traded his people for the right to continue to sit on the throne, and Meldrock is collecting villages soul by soul."

The second dark prince smiled. "The king puts on a show with feasts and tournaments, but that's all it is—a show. He is truly powerless. He plays the defender of Ascar, but Meldrock has his way unchallenged day after day. If Meldrock was to lose his grip on Ascar, your father's heart would be collected in exchange, and we would greatly love to be chosen by our master for such a task."

A tear trickled down Grenfel's cheek; it felt icy and cold. He stiffened in rage.

"Your mother couldn't wait for the day your father decided it was time for you to train at Heathervane," the prince continued. "As soon as the castle door clanged shut, she let down her auburn hair and took off her emerald green gown, singing like she had never sung before. Such tones of freedom she produced that night! Don't you see? You come from a house of blood. You are no Hawkman; you're guilty of what you saw in Dremcon. There's blood on your hands."

Grenfel fell to his knees. He could no longer see out of his watery eyes. "No! It's not so! No, no!"

"Your mother sleeps soundly at night, no longer burdened by the laborious task of telling tales after the court's endless demands. She exhausted herself for your pleasure, but no more. She is truly free now." The princes exchanged a glance and broke into mocking laughter.

Another sound now reverberated across the ice fields above the mocking laughter of the demon princes and Grenfel's heartfelt cries. It was that of a song, "There is no one like the Ancient of Days who rides on the heavens to help us. He drives out our enemy, saying, 'Destroy them!'"

The chorus repeated louder and louder. The dark princes shook, their tongues flicking outward in serpentine fashion. Its effect on the travellers was different; the chorus caused joy and strength to massage their hearts, as though the Ancient of Days himself cradled their hearts in His hand. The song seemed to draw the travellers into itself and like a mighty company of minstrels, they sang loudly and joyfully, caught up in the song.

"There is no one like the Ancient of Days who rides on the heavens to help us. He drives out our enemy, saying, 'Destroy them!'"

Dancing light surrounded the party as the princes transformed into two huge snakes. Out of that light, two brilliant warriors appeared, moving as silently and fluently as the light itself, their flaming swords held aloft. As Grenfel sang the words, the warriors struck the snakes on their heads, inflicting deadly wounds upon them. In the place where they had stood, two piles of grey ash fell to the frozen ground.

The warriors vanished, the singing stopped, and the lights phased out like fireworks in the night, once again giving way to the bright sun above Ascar's icefields. "Hello," cried the voice of a stranger. When he appeared, Grenfel saw that his clothing was made of caribou skin. The stranger stopped momentarily to kick one of the piles of ash with his sealskin shoes, which extended up to his knees.

Estravai approached the stranger. "Omri, old friend, is it you?"

"The very one who fashioned the goggles you now wear," replied Omri.

Estravai gave his old friend a hug. "Tell me, how do you come to be here?"

"This barren land has been my refuge for many years. How strange to encounter my old companions amongst these hunting grounds. And you, Estravai?"

"We were led to Dremcon from Mirana by way of Eltarz's vision." His mention of Mirana, the beloved refuge to so many Revealers of Secrets, brought a small tear to Omri's eye. "Two strangers brought us out of that dark dungeon, giving us nourishment. They then told us to head south, explaining that I would know where to go."

"Truly only the hand of the Ancient of Days could cause an encounter with old friends such as this. I, too, encountered two strangers in brilliant armour. They told me to walk out across the ice fields singing the Ancient One's song of deliverance." Omri paused, looking down at the two piles of ash. "So, you've done battle with the queen, I see."

Grenfel looked at Morteque in amazement as if to ask, *how does he know?*

"The ash on the ground could only mean one thing," Omri said. "A battle and not a fire, for there is no wood here to build a fire. And a battle such as that must mean you, my friends, are most likely hungry and weary. Come, follow me; this land is not as desolate as it appears. The Ancient of Days has been good to me. He led me to a people who are mostly unaffected by Meldrock's priests—perhaps it's too cold for them," laughed Omri, before beckoning his friends to follow him once again. "Come, we will go to them and you will be my honoured guests amongst a wondrous smiling people."

Chapter Fifteen

Tony walked up to the glass door of the School of Apostles, which slid apart on his approach like the Red Sea parted for Moses and the Israelites. Stepping through, Tony walked into a lobby complete with tall leafy palm trees, Aztec print sofas, and a spinning book rack. Soft music played in the background. Tony made his way to the receptionist's counter, his eye drawn to its long marble countertop.

"Hello, can I help you?" the receptionist asked.

"Oh, yes. Sorry, everything is just all so breathtaking."

The receptionist smiled warmly.

"I'd like to meet with Apostle John Bristane," Tony said nervously.

"Is he expecting you?"

"No, uh, not really...I..."

"Well, you'll have to book an appointment to meet with the apostle. I'm sorry, sir."

Tony started to explain himself, only to be interrupted by the receptionist clarifying their office procedures. He fidgeted uneasily. "But I—I—I'm taking one of... one of the apostle's correspondence courses."

"You and a thousand others. That doesn't give you VIP privileges. The apostle is a busy man."

"I've come too far to be turned back. Don't make me go back to my vehicle and get my chains, I've done the whole save the tree thing, and I don't imagine your school door much different to be chained to than a tree." Tony said, working up his courage. "I'm having strange dreams lately. My life has become something like those glass globes you turn upside down at Christmas to watch the snow fall. I need to talk to the man today."

"Okay, I'll try buzzing him," the receptionist said, sensing the frustration and desperation in Tony's voice. "One moment, sir."

"Yes, what is it?" a voice boomed out of the speakerphone a moment later, like God speaking to Moses from the burning bush.

"There's a man at the front desk who's been taking your correspondence courses. He seems tense and has travelled a long way to see you. He also said that if you don't see him today, he'll chain himself to the front door."

"What's his name?" asked the apostle.

"Tony!" Tony said abruptly, without giving the receptionist an opportunity to answer.

"Uh, I don't know a Tony. Give him one of my books and tell him it's impossible for me to see him today. I'm catching up on some work."

The receptionist pressed a button and disconnected the line. "Excuse me, sir," she said to Tony. "Apostle John is really busy today, but he says to help yourself to one of his books." She pointed to the book rack.

Tony sighed, feeling deflated. "Well, I guess I'll go get my chains."

"I'll try asking the apostle again, sir," said the receptionist, trying to avoid further conflict. "Hello, Apostle John?"

"Yes!"

"I informed Tony of your generous offer, but I really don't think he's going to leave without seeing you. If you don't come down fairly quickly, I think you'll find an addition to the school's architecture… chained to the front door!"

"All right. Thank you, Nancy. Tell him to have some coffee."

"There's coffee in the corner by the sofa," said the receptionist as she turned off the speaker phone. "Feel free to help yourself. It looks like the apostle will be right down to see you after all."

Tony smiled a little sheepishly. "Sorry I was such a pain."

The receptionist just smiled back, as if to say, *No problem, I deal with people like you every day.*

The gym in the Drummingsville School was packed with locals and a few guests from out of town. The K7 News crew had come from West Georgia to shoot live footage of the public forum, which could have big league repercussions in the surrounding areas.

Mayor Thomas opened the meeting by welcoming all the locals, praising their attendance as a positive sign of a healthy community spirit. He then asked the audience to warmly welcome the special guests who had graciously juggled their schedules to be in Drummingsville on this day. As he glanced down at his podium notes, he announced that the first item on the agenda was the reopening of the old Stillmore Mine.

"I know that reopening the mine is a sensitive issue to many here tonight. Some of you still hold memories of loved ones lost to untimely accidents through the ravenous hunger of that old mine. Still, we need to be open and unafraid of discussing new ways to develop our community's lagging economy. If we have any hope of seeing Drummingsville avoid becoming a ghost town and all our young people fleeing to larger cities to find jobs, we need to change! A few vegetables and fish aren't going to sustain our community. We need to discuss other potential sources of revenue. At this point, I'm pleased to invite Grant Timmons, chief engineer for Belial Enterprises, to speak. Grant!"

The mayor stepped aside to allow Mr. Timmons to come forward.

"Thanks, Mayor Thomas," said the short man dressed in a blue-striped shirt and a burgundy tie. His hair receded from his forehead, but the loss was balanced by a bushy handlebar moustache. He looked out at the audience from behind the plexiglass podium. "Howdy, folks. It's real exciting to be able to discuss with you tonight the future prospects of your Stillmore Mine. The field studies my company has recently completed, and the core samples retrieved from the old mine, have caused Belial Enterprises to believe there are a few productive years left in the old mine. We believe the mine, when in full production, could be a major competitor on the world market for diamonds, and it's our desire at Belial Enterprise to see the mine active once again."

Grant stopped speaking long enough to smile at the audience and give them a few seconds to mull over some of what he had already said.

He continued, "The community of Drummingsville stands to profit. We can create jobs both in the mine itself and also in our new cutting and polishing plant. Many of you have concerns about safety, but let me reassure you that mining technology has come a long way since the 1800s. The equipment is more automated now. Belial Enterprise, however, understands your hesitation and fears, so as a further safety precaution we would offer an introductory course on diamond-cutting and mining out of the school. The idea has already been put forth to your mayor, as well as to the school principal. They have been most obliging and supportive."

Grant paused, taking a minute to survey the audience's expressions. "No longer will you have to see your young people leave Drummingsville to seek employment. Most college students coming to Drummingsville for the usual parks and forestry jobs will now have the option to work for Belial Enterprises if they go through the diamond cutting and polishing course. I'm looking forward to not only doing business here, but also getting to know you people. Thanks for listening."

"Thank you, Grant," said Mayor Thomas as he returned to the podium. "We would now like to open the floor for questions."

"Am I to understand there is no downside to what Belial Enterprises proposes?" asked Randy Foxworth as he stood in front of a microphone in the centre aisle. "While in Nam, I saw enough of man's capabilities to abuse God's creation all in the name of getting the job done."

"Really, Randy," said Phil Devon, the First Baptist minister, from the front row. "Drummingsville is hardly at war! Furthermore, I believe the Lord has given the citizens of Drummingsville a number of talents, and He expects us to make the most of them."

"Say goodbye to canoeing on our many pristine rivers and lakes," Randy muttered as he returned to his seat.

Sensing the meeting was starting to derail, Mayor Thomas tapped on the podium microphone. "Folks! Mr. Timmons has assured me that the trade-off of new revenue will far exceed what little damage might be incurred to the wilderness around our community. Now, if I may direct your attention back to the agenda, we need to move on. We still have a full evening ahead of us. The second item this evening is far more controversial, as it deals with issues of morality. It has being brought to my attention that young children have started to experiment in certain deviant sexual practices." He stepped back from the microphone momentarily to cough before approaching it again. "The invasion of Drummingsville by perverted sexual practices has blossomed because of the easy access children have to computers and the large number of adult websites they can visit in the comfort of their homes. These websites encourage children to post inappropriate pictures of themselves, stealing their innocence right from under our noses."

Mayor Thomas took a sip of ice water and cleared his throat before announcing another guest speaker.

Stephen Drakeo was a tall, clean-shaven man dressed in a navy-blue trench coat, whose wavy blond hair seemed perfectly held in place by an exotic brand of moulding paste. "I'm Stephen Drakeo. I've been graciously permitted to speak tonight by the law firm I represent. That's Leviathan Law, for those who have not heard of us. I believe the capacity crowd at this meeting tonight to be evidence of the belief that some among you have, that the reputation of your wholesome community of Drummingsville is being tarnished by a few children viewing adult websites.

"This may be news to many, but morality laws are changing. Same-sex couples have many of the same rights now as those of the opposite sex. They will paint your crosswalks their bright rainbow colours, fly their flags in your communities. You can no longer speak out in public against their sexual preference, even if you believe your Bible tells you it's a sin. Prayer is no longer mandatory in schools. Groups are lobbying daily to have books describing same-sex relationships in your school's library. Children are growing up with either two moms or dads. What was considered normal family structure is being challenged daily somewhere in the world. The masses are relentless in their effort to force the hands of lawmakers by their continual cry for open-mindedness and equal representation of an individual's rights.

"You may think websites teaching your children to be open-minded are perverse, but you have to remember that those of the Victorian era thought any kind of sex was dirty. Were they right or wrong? For the sake of making you think, and for those of you who sometimes attend church, I might ask this question: can something the Creator designed for pleasure be called dirty or evil? Can you see that it's not so black and white? It's about different perspectives. For example, as a parent, do you have the right to spank your children if they're misbehaving in public? Some would say no, but others with a more religious background would shout, 'Spare not the rod!'

"As parents, do you have the right to tell your child that they're perverted for being interested in the same sex instead of the opposite? Even classroom teachers aren't allowed to condemn students' interests in alternative sexual lifestyles, especially with all the literature bombarding the schools and the constant revamping of the law.

"Tell me, why do many parents feel they can play God when it comes to directing their children's preference in sexual partners when they no longer even have the freedom to spank them in public? Think about it. As a representative of Leviathan Law, I hope to work hand in hand with Sheriff Ryder to help sort through all your confusion over these matters of morality, to help you determine what might be a different sexual perspective and what is criminal, all from within the safe boundaries of the law. Thank you."

With this, Stephen turned to walk back to his seat behind the podium.

"When a community such as ours experiences a tragedy," Mayor Thomas said, "like the hijacking we just went through, we elevate everything to crisis level. But maybe it's really a question of being more open-minded. Having said that, we really need to move on to the next item on the agenda." He momentarily studied his notes before continuing. "The next issue to be discussed is also one of morality. It has to do with the new abortion clinic in town. I would like to call Dr. Anderson of the Belial Abortion Clinic to come speak to us. Remember, just listen with an open mind."

"Thank you," said Dr. Anderson as he stepped forward. He seemed to be more of a mountain man than a doctor, with his grey hair tied in a ponytail at the back of his oilskin hat. He wore a bomber-style jacket and a pair of faded blue jeans. "I suppose everyone here was expecting a doctor wearing either a suit or a white lab coat with a stethoscope sticking out of its pocket. Sorry to disappoint you, but I hope my appearance won't prevent you from hearing what I have to share as a trained physician.

"We at the Belial Abortion Clinic are firm believers in an individual's rights. That's why the size of a community doesn't have any bearing on whether we offer services to it. I know that many of you find the idea of abortion horrifying, but just think of earlier civilizations that excelled in science, math, engineering, and even to some extent extreme medicine. Yet the major kingdoms of that day also offered their children as human sacrifices to various gods all in the name of religion. This was an accepted practice for the times. We at the clinic believe highly in our vision of respecting an individual's rights. Who of you here would say that people who gave up their children for sacrifice were wrong to do so, when it was part of the accepted culture of the day? And who sitting among us is to say a woman has no right to the services of an abortion clinic if it's connected to her religious beliefs? Our doctors are all practitioners of ancient religious systems, and we believe in the practice of abortion.

"What if a woman's religious beliefs permit her an abortion? Would any here dare to tell a holy man that the religious food he eats is against the law? Does the declared teaching of a holy man ever allow him to transcend the law? Think about it, you who are so quick to throw stones. Is the issue of abortion also a question of differing perspectives? I'll leave you to think about that."

The mayor approached the podium as Dr. Anderson picked up his notes. "Thank you, Dr. Anderson. And thanks to all the special guests who participated tonight. At this time, since this is a public forum, we would like to open the floor to field a few more brief questions."

A little grey-haired lady with cat-eye glasses stood on her toes to reach the microphone. Flora Stevenson spoke with the boldness of one representing the Lord, as David went against Goliath not only with a sling, but also with the presence of God resting upon him. "I'm greatly troubled that as experienced as these young men are, their words haven't been life-producing but full of the very breath of Satan himself. They are speaking words of death into our hearts, as well as that of our young people. I am shocked that we've just sat back here tonight and let these seeming angels of light, these ambassadors of Satan himself, assault our minds with his poison. Satan is telling us to accept immorality with an open mind, to allow ourselves to listen to their seductive messages. I will not be silent. I will not simply cast a blind eye to it. I will resist the devil as long as I have breath."

Sue Henderson stood up next, dressed in a black leather jacket and tight leather skirt. She glared angrily at the elderly woman. "We need to come out of the dark ages, people, and quit cowering behind the skirt of religion. If my parents had governed strictly everything I could or couldn't do, I would have done it anyway. I am in support of the changes talked about so far tonight. I think it's good to have qualified professionals leading us as generals in our community's quest for future development. And I agree that we need to be a lot more open-minded about things in town, other than just each other's business. That's my point of view, anyway."

"I agree with Sue," Phil Devon said. "I think God is interested in us as individuals in making correct choices on our own. Praise God that the Crusades have long past. I thank God that the pen is mightier than the sword, and I thank God for the open-minded lawmakers in our country. We as a community do not have to fear change, for only by stepping through the door of change will we see our community truly grow."

Mayor Thomas approached the podium once more. "We'll have to close the floor to questions at this point. We still have one item on our agenda to mention, that being the construction of a new super mall in our community. I know many of you here tonight are merchants and you may feel your business will be smothered by such a development. I ask you now to think things through.

"If the Stillmore Mine is approved to begin production, more people will be coming to our community. It's not unreasonable to think Drummingsville could boom. People will come from all over—West Georgia, Sarquis, and other towns, drawn to our community as though by a giant magnet. Representatives from Behemoth Construction, a division of Belial Enterprises, have told me that if production is approved for the mine, they'll be willing to sink four and a half million dollars into the development of the mall. For once we may be the ones not to see our youth leave, as they have always done so in the past, seduced by attractions the bigger cities have to offer. Personally, I think the reports I have heard tonight to be among some of the best news our community has heard in a long while."

Jim McFlurry jumped to his feet. "What happens if a store like Big Hooks moves into that there super mall? What do you think will happen to my fly-tying shop? I can't buy in bulk like they can, so they'll always undersell me."

Mayor Thomas took a sip of water. "The developers have assured me they won't allow any similar businesses to the local shops here in town."

"Yeah! And I just stepped off the boat yesterday." Jim shook his head and sat back down.

"Folks, I think we've heard a lot of exciting proposals tonight," Mayor Thomas said as he tried to restore order again. "Let's break for the evening, as our guests need to get some rest. Many of them will be getting up early to catch flights. I'd like to thank you all for coming out and participating in our forum. I'd ask that you give a big hand to our guest speakers for taking the time to be here tonight."

The mayor smiled, said goodnight, and proceeded to mingle with the guest speakers.

Outside the building, the media was preparing to go live with the results of the evening's meeting. "This is Rena Peterson for K7 News, live from Drummingsville School. Tonight, the town heard from several out-of-town guests in a public forum to discuss future development. In reality, it turned out to be at times very emotional. If you consider the evening's proceedings, it poses an interesting case study to other developing communities, and even larger cities both locally and regionally. We'll keep our eyes on the community of Drummingsville over the next few months and make our viewers aware of any new developments. For now, I'm Rena Peterson for K7 News, saying goodnight from Drummingsville, now thought of by some of its residents as the little town that could."

CHAPTER SIXTEEN

The dark-skinned man with wavy, coffee-coloured hair approached Tony as he was perusing one of the books from the lobby's book rack.

"Brother Tony, is it?" boomed the brassy voice of Apostle John Bristane.

Tony jumped up from the sofa. "Yes."

"So, you're the one who's responsible for dragging me away from my day's work."

Tony's eyes widened as he beheld the apostle's short but muscular build, which seemed to be testing the seams of his double-breasted navy-blue suit jacket, and he suddenly felt like Samson when his hair was cut, or Popeye before ingesting spinach. "Can I still just pick a book and go? I'm really sorry to have bothered you, sir. I think the book will be very helpful."

A smile spread across the apostle's face. "Don't sweat it, Brother Tony! God's got you covered. You're looking at two hundred and eighty pounds of solid sanctified muscle. People always react to me this way, and I must admit, it's good for recruiting for the school's choir. The real fear of God, though, has nothing to do with muscle, but who am I to remind people?"

Tony saw the smile on Apostle Bristane's face and knew him to be jesting. Apostles are human, Tony thought, as he felt a gentle tug at his arm, and once again the booming voice he had first heard through the speaker phone.

"So, my desperate brother, shall we go to my study to talk?"

"I could really use some coffee about now."

"Not a problem, my friend. I have a cappuccino machine in my office, if you'd like to follow me."

The stairs leading up to the office were covered in a rich purple carpet. Apostle Bristane ascended the final step and led Tony past a table under a window with a huge antique Bible on it. Opening the door to his study, he beckoned Tony inside and casually told him to make himself at home.

Tony walked into the office with the amazement of Alice walking into Wonderland. He stopped to drink in the rich décor with his thirsty eyes, as the apostle closed his office door behind them. Approaching a luxurious wingback chair covered in Burgundy leather with studded piping, Tony took a seat. Apostle Bristane sat opposite him, facing a stone fireplace hemmed in by bookshelves that towered up to the ceiling. Tony sat momentarily and just brushed the forest green carpet with his foot, watching the spot change colour from light to dark like a young child conducting a science experiment.

"What's happening, then?" boomed the apostle's voice.

"I'm not sure. My whole life has started to slide into the cellar since I started taking your course. Have you ever done any winter driving? Well anyway, it's the same feeling you get when you hit some black ice and your brakes lock up. Things are happening to you which you have no control over." He looked down at the carpet again, waves of emotion seeming to push their way up inside him like a geyser about to blow.

"This might be a good time to have a cup of cappuccino. I'll get it. Just relax."

The apostle stood and headed across his study towards a stained-glass window with a beautiful French provincial sofa table supporting a stainless-steel cappuccino maker. As the man fetched the coffee, Tony noticed that the walls had been painted to resemble marble.

Why would anyone go through all that trouble for the walls only to display a single wooden picture frame on them? thought Tony as he rose from his chair and walked over to the lone picture.

"A quote!" he exclaimed.

"Yes, and quite a work of inspiration," answered Apostle Bristane. "You should read it."

Tony turned his eyes back to the quote and read:

In this point could never our enemies cause us to faint, for our first petition was that the reverend face of the primitive and apostolic church should be brought back again to the eyes and knowledge of men.
— John Knox on the Reformation in Scotland.

"That's an unbelievable statement," Tony said after a moment.

"I think so," replied Apostle Bristane as he pulled a lever down on his cappuccino machine that released a shot of steam.

Tony said, "It's hard to believe anybody so far back in church history prayed like that. I mean, I'm just beginning to recognize the importance of apostles. I guess I can understand why you framed it."

"Chocolate or cinnamon?" asked the apostle as he smiled from across the room.

"Uh, chocolate. I think of it as my Delilah."

"How's that?"

"I have a passion for it," said Tony. "Give me enough of it and I'll tell you all my secrets."

"I think you were about to anyway." Apostle Bristane handed a cup to Tony.

Having reseated himself, Tony took a moment to sip his coffee through its rich, creamy topping. "My wife and I started going to these meetings held in Drummingsville by Apostle Levi Brandon. I can't say much for his ministry. I never witnessed any signs and wonders at his meetings."

"I know Levi," Apostle Bristane admitted. "I can bear witness to my brother's calling, for it was confirmed on his life by way of a seasoned prophet's word. We need to be careful that we don't put ourselves under God's judgment by attacking his anointed."

"But did you know that Apostle Levi took a bunch of people from Drummingsville on his luxury bus? And that they were hijacked by members of an extreme militant faction working for the mafia, who were hoping to get a hold on Norwood county through the drug trade?"

"Yes," replied Apostle Bristane. "I watched the news coverage."

"My wife Roxanne was on that bus," Tony said, his voice trembling from emotion. Thinking about his wife triggered a dull ache in his heart. "They hooked all the passengers on heroin. Now Roxanne has taken my son to her mother's in West Georgia, saying things about me that didn't make much sense. Things like, 'I have my own demons to deal with.' I didn't understand her at the time, but I think I can understand a little better now, after talking with my best friend Max. He told me a female colleague I just started to work with is saying I touched her inappropriately. I think she may have also gotten me fired. She's the woman of my worst nightmares, and now she's trying to blackmail me into signing over my truck to her.

"If that wasn't enough, on my way here I was hit by a silver Porsche whose back plate had the word Belial on it. On top of all that, I'm having a series of graphic dreams that have Max convinced I'm suffering from stress and in need of a vacation."

"I can't speak to your need of a vacation, but how about another cup of cappuccino?" asked the apostle, noticing Tony's near-empty cup.

"Yeah! That would be great." Tony felt like a great weight had lifted off his shoulders. "I've been feeling like I'm being wrapped up in a spider's web. It's really good to just breathe again."

Apostle Bristane smiled and handed him another tall cup of coffee. "I'm inclined to believe that what's happening to you isn't a result of stress but simply the Lord giving you discernment, or a revelation. Have you stopped to consider that the Lord may be trying to speak to you through your dreams?"

"Too many things have been going on for me to even think about that."

"You need to understand that the language of the spirit is different from the natural. Visions and dreams are a big way God speaks to us. Sometimes he speaks to us when we're inactive, such as at bedtime. You aren't the first to have experienced graphic dreams. The Bible is full of examples of God's prophets receiving visions and dreams. For that matter, even heathen kings had visions or dreams once in a while."

"Well then!" Tony said, feeling much less foolish about his dreams. "Here's the condensed version. There's a place called Ascar, which is under the evil grip of Meldrock, who has an endless army of demon-ic forces. Some of these forces include demons of higher ranks, such as princes. There's also this queen who rules along with the higher-ranking demons in the mid-heavens, and she likes to be called the Queen of the Heavens. Some of the high-ranking princes who periodically appear in my dreams go by names such as Belial, and another is a great sea serpent called Leviathan. It appears there are three main characters the dreams relay information about. Two appear to be prophets, but in my dreams they're called Revealers of Secrets. Traveling with them is a young boy and his horse. The boy seems to have a divine calling, but I'm not sure what it is. He's often referred to as a Hawkman."

Apostle Bristane rubbed one hand against his chin. "Brother Tony, these names—Leviathan, Belial, the Queen of the Heavens—are actual names of ancient principalities and end-time spirits. They're the ruling class of demons, the generals and princes in the enemy's dark army. I believe there's a connection between your dreams and reality, and I don't think it was by chance that your vehicle was hit by the silver Porsche with the name of Belial on its back plate. In fact, I'm convinced it was an at-tempt to take you out, just like the pharaoh drowning all the male babies back in Egypt. The enemy always tries to get rid of the Lord's deliverers."

Tony sat in awe, listening to the apostle like a child listening to his mother's bedtime stories. In one afternoon, this man had been able to explain all that had perplexed him for so long.

"You said you felt like a spider was wrapping you in its web," the apostle said, then sipped his own cappuccino. "This was probably truer than you realize, my brother. Also, did you know that the hawk is a pro-phetic symbol of the apostle?"

"No. I'm only on the fourth video of your correspondence course. I still have twenty-six to go."

"Don't get hung up on that," laughed the apostle. "I think the Lord is accelerating you through His own training program. You're not just dipping your toe in the water. You're in the deep end, swimming in shark-infested waters. But be of good cheer, for the Lord drives away all your enemies before you. Your Lord is a warrior. If you're going to tan-gle with the heavyweight demons, you best not forget that. The dreams themselves don't surprise me, for it is a realm I've seen into on more than one occasion. I'm not free to speak or write about some of the things I've seen, but I believe the young Hawkman in your dreams is what we would think of as an apostle who's in the process of maturing into that office."

Tony felt very excited. "That's interesting, because in one of my recent dreams the main characters came upon two powerful dark princes who virtually paralyzed them through intimidation. The Ancient of Days, as God is known in my dreams, sent a stranger singing a song of deliverance, saying, 'Destroy them! Destroy them!' When the young boy, Grenfel, started singing the chorus, two brilliant warriors with flaming swords struck the dark princes, reducing them to ashes."

Apostle Bristane sat forward, deep in thought. "Excuse me for a moment. I'll be right back."

He set his coffee cup down on an oak end table and rose from his chair. He made his way to one of his towering bookshelves, scanning the many volumes. He soon found what he was looking for.

"Ah! Here it is." He took a thin book from the shelf and opened it to a particular page. "Every servant of God, Brother Tony, is sent by God. However, the very word for 'apostle' in the original language means 'sent one.'" Smiling, he passed the book to Tony. "I think you should take a look at page twenty-seven."

"Apostles are pioneers," Tony read aloud when he found the spot. "They are pathfinders, commander of the troops equal to Joab fighting battles on David's' behalf. They are spiritual explorers equal to their natural representatives for charting and mapping new territory on the behalf of the children who would follow in their footsteps. Overall, apostles are representatives of their King, commanding the same respect as if He were present. Those who come face to face with an apostle could testify to witnessing the King's own authority."

Tony transitioned from reading to thinking aloud. All this talk of apostles caused him to catch the scent of enlightenment.

"My wife Roxanne gets hijacked, people are saying I inappropriately touched a co-worker, my boss lets me go, my wife and son go and stay at her mother's in West Georgia, a Porsche with an end-time spirit's name on its back plate clips my truck… I even have dreams about prophets and spirits, and now I believe apostles. Why me, though?" Tony looked across the room at Apostle Bristane with bewildered eyes. "I was just Forest Tech's lead hand in the field, and that's what I want to be again. I just want my normal life back—my job, my wife, and my son. I never asked to tangle with end-time spirits."

"Didn't you?" asked the apostle. "Let me ask you a question, Tony. Why did you take up studying my correspondence course, and why have you travelled so far to talk with me today?"

"I'm not sure," remarked Tony honestly. "When someone showed up in town claiming to be an apostle, I wasn't convinced. I wanted to check it out. I thought checking it out would only involve a few good word studies. But I'm telling you, God is turning my whole life up-side-down. I mean, His classroom even extends into my dreams, and I'm truly at the point of feeling hemmed in. I'm really overwhelmed with it all. I just really need some peace and my normal life back again. Coming to visit you hasn't been a waste of time, though. It's been most revealing. Actually, talking with an apostle has made me feel a little less crazy." Tony laughed a bit deliriously.

The apostle nodded, his expression serious. "I can understand that, but saying you didn't ask to tangle with end-time spirits is the same as trying to keep God in a box. You said you only meant to learn about apostles, but in the process of showing us things, God sometimes shows us the big picture. Do you, like Jonah, have a right to complain if the leaf withers on the vine, causing you to feel the heat of the sun, when he's trying to draw your attention from the withered leaf to Nineveh?

"Listen! I believe God has His hand on your life. Instead of fighting back, you could save yourself a lot of hardship by saying, 'Okay, Father, work in me this day what you will, what is pleasing to you.' What rights do you really have, Tony? Can the pot tell the potter what it wants to be? You say, 'I just want to be a Forest Tech worker; I was happy.' But were you really? It appears to me you were searching for more of God, and nothing makes the Father's heart happier than that. I also believe you have the calling of a prophet on your life, and that God desires you to serve Him to this extent. This might be God's highest purpose for your life, and you may need to rethink your desires." He took a final sip of coffee. "I apologize. Time has quickly passed by, my brother, and I should be letting you get on with your other business."

Apostle Bristane got up and walked Tony to the door of his study.

"You haven't kept me from anything," Tony said as he left the room. "You were my business—"

"One more thing, Brother Tony, before you depart," the Apostle interjected.

"What is it?"

"Would you please pray for Apostle Levi? I'm praying for him, too. I believe that the devil desires to sift him. I'm only asking because I know you won't disappoint me in this matter."

Tony smiled at the apostle from the hallway.

"Oh!" the Apostle added, "and watch out for vehicles with the names of end-time spirits on their plates."

Tony laughed as he turned and made his way down the staircase into the school's lobby. His heart was full and his mind raced. He knew there would be some changes in his life; nothing was the same anymore. *He* wasn't the same anymore, and he couldn't help but walk differently to reflect his newfound self.

CHAPTER SEVENTEEN

The instruments on Tony's dash radiated florescent green as he sat in the otherwise dark cab of his truck.

Your dreams might be connected to your reality. The thought ran through Tony's mind like a song on a CD set to continuous play. He hadn't had much time to think lately, considering the whirlwind of events he'd been caught up in.

Flashing red lights and an eerie police siren behind him jolted him out of his thoughts and slammed him back into the driver's seat of reality.

It must be the headlight, he thought nervously. *I should have taken the time to have it repaired.* Driving now with one eye on his speedometer and the other on his side mirror, he saw the police cruiser gaining on him and wondered if he should pull over. Maybe he was caught in the middle of some high-speed chase. *I better get out of his way. Heaven knows, the last thing I need right now is another dent.*

The cruiser pulled up alongside Tony with its interior light on, and the officer signalled Tony to pull over to the shoulder. He then manoeuvred his cruiser in front of Tony and guided him to a stop. It only seemed to take a few seconds before the officer stepped out of the cruiser, turned on a long-handled flashlight, and walked to the back of Tony's vehicle to check his plate number. Scrawling the number down, the officer looked up to peer into Tony's vehicle. The flashing police lights made Tony feel a little nauseous as he waited, regretting that he'd consumed so many cappuccinos. Tony heard the officer call his plate numbers in over his cruiser's radio.

I'd really like to get home tonight, Tony thought as he toyed with his keychain dangling from the ignition. He felt a little like a mouse in the dark, expecting to be pounced on by a cat at any moment.

The officer finally stepped up to Tony's window, which he'd already rolled down in anticipation of the moment.

"Where are you going tonight, sir?" the officer asked.

"I'm just on my way back to Drummingsville from Sarquis."

"Are you Tony Epson, and are you the owner of this vehicle?"

"Yes," Tony replied again, trying to mask his nervousness with politeness.

"May I see your driver's license and vehicle registration, please?"

"Of course." Tony unfastened his seatbelt and popped open the glove compartment. Maps and garbage spilled out all over the floor. "I knew I forgot to hang the maid service sign out today," joked Tony as he fumbled through his personal papers. Spotting what he was looking for, relief appeared on his face. "Here it is."

He handed the officer a plastic folder containing his registration papers. Tony then slipped one of his hands into his back pocket and produced a tattered black leather wallet.

"You'll find everything checks out, officer."

The officer took Tony's license and looked at it for a minute, then at Tony. "I saw you pass me five miles back. I was sitting on an access road waiting to make a right-hand turn onto the highway. Your vehicle, from what I observed, seemed to match a vehicle description reported in a hit-and-run accident to the Drummingsville sheriff's office earlier today. Now I see the name matches up, too. It appears a Doctor Anderson reported that you crossed over the centre line at a fairly high speed, clipping the front of his Porsche, and then sped off in your truck. The poor doctor, from what I heard, was an emotional mess when he filed his complaint, and he kept complaining of a sore neck. So if I were you, I wouldn't be surprised by a summons to court. However, to prove I'm a professional, I actually took the time to call in your plate number. Can't have you feeling like you're a victim of police harassment."

"I feel so much more relieved now, thanks," Tony muttered.

"Not a problem." The officer smiled. "But I'm going to have to ask you to follow me into Drummingsville, sir."

"Why?" replied Tony anxiously. "The doctor's lying! I didn't do—"

"I'm sorry, sir. The courts will have to decide that. It appears that the doctor is taking you to court."

"What? This is so absurd!"

"The courts will decide the degree of absurdity in the matter," the officer repeated, shining his light on the front of the truck. "But I know one thing. The damage to your vehicle matches the doctor's accident report."

"I can't believe this is happening!"

"Well, sir, I'm going to ask you again to follow me into Drummingsville, where your vehicle will be impounded by the sheriff's office and held as evidence."

"Well, at least Sue Henderson isn't going to get it," Tony muttered under his breath.

"Pardon?"

"Nothing, officer, I'll follow you back." *How much can any normal human being take?*

The officer turned back to his cruiser.

Tony pulled back out onto the highway, proceeding to follow the police cruiser, It seemed he had only just gotten back onto the highway when he found himself breaking into laughter, over the thought of receiving the same type of police escort foreign VIPs get on visiting the country. *So, this is how the president and the pope feel,* he thought as he watched the cruiser with its flashing lights speed along in front of him like a greyhound just bred to run.

❧

Several kayaks were towing a small white whale to shore in the Nevron Strait, the passage of icy black water separating the southwest coast of Ascar from the shores of Tarmaze.

Grenfel shouted in excitement as the group approached the coastal whaling camp known as A Goul Eak Bictok. Omri translated this as "to face the storm."

"Look, houses of snow!" Grenfel shouted.

"Igloos," said Omri. "Ascar's ice field castles."

Children dressed in caribou skins peeked out of the igloos in wide-eyed wonder at the sight of the strangers walking through their camp. Women looked up from fleshing muskox hides to offer toothless, wrinkled smiles. As they grinned, their dark eyes seemed to laugh and twinkle with the very life of the ice fields themselves. A few of the village's brave children ventured out with their dogs to follow the strangers. The children stared at Grenfel and his companions, whereas the dogs sniffed at Morgan's heels. They quickly retreated, though, when Morgan turned to face them.

"Here it is. Kutek's house!" Omri pointed to an igloo larger than the others, with dry fish hanging on racks outside. Standing at the entrance was a short man with long black hair and brown leathery skin, whose wrinkles made him appear to be laughing, and he too offered a big, toothless smile.

"Kunna it pit?" Kutek said.

"Na goo yak quana a ne lo mik," replied Omri. Turning to his travelling companions, Omri explained, "Kutek asked how I was doing. I told him I was well and thanked him for opening his house to us. Kutek is the head elder of A Goul Eak Bictok."

Omri turned his attention back to Kutek, who motioned them to come inside. "Da ge."

"He would like us to go in," Omri said to his companions as he turned from Kutek to see that they were already moving towards the entrance of the igloo, having understood Kutek's body language.

The travellers bent down and crawled inside.

Grenfel laughed in amazement. "It's like being inside a big frozen beehive." Along the inside walls, he noticed ledges made from ice blocks and piled high with muskox hides. They looked as inviting to Grenfel as any bedchamber in his father's or uncle's castles.

Kutek pointed to his stomach. "Ney ya inn."

The travellers looked at one another, puzzled.

"What's he talking about?" Grenfel whispered. "His words are full of tones I've never heard before."

"Kutek is wondering if we've eaten," Omri patiently explained. "I told him we have not."

A woman dressed in an amauti-style parka rose up from where she was sitting upon the muskox hides and stood by Kutek. A young child smiled, peeking out the back of the woman's parka at Grenfel. The boy's mouth dropped from the surprise of seeing two people in the same garment.

Kutek whispered in the woman's ear, and she then crawled out of the igloo only to return shortly with several frozen fish. She placed them in front of Kutek, who sat on the floor of the igloo facing his guests.

Picking up a small half-moon knife with a whalebone handle, Kutek began to cut pieces of frozen fish flesh. He handed them to Omri, saying, "Ne ga wit."

"Kutek would like us to eat," Omri said for the benefit of his companions. He took the frozen fish from Kutek. "Quana ne lo mik."

Kutek nodded, smiling. Omri then passed the frozen fish to Estravai and Morteque, who took it gratefully.

"Well, at least if the food is in this state, I can't complain about your cooking, Morteque," Estravai said.

"Such words from one who seldom sets anything over a fire, but prefers to chew dry deer flesh," said Morteque. "This must be to your liking. Another uncooked food source!"

Omri passed around the pieces of frozen fish. He was about to hand a piece to Grenfel when the boy shook his head and turned his eyes away.

Kutek looked puzzled. "A key tok kin?"

Omri didn't wish his friend to feel insulted, so spoke quickly on Grenfel's behalf. "Ee nun nuk hin nick."

Kutek pointed to the ice block ledges around the interior of the igloo.

Omri leaned over to Grenfel. "Kutek says you may go and lie down. He asked if you were full, but I told him you were tired."

Grenfel felt relieved to be excused from the meal and was excited about warming up in one of the thick muskox hides; one of those would keep him warm as adequately as a fire upon any castle's hearth. He lay down on one of the hides and pulled another thick hide over him, feeling as content as when the gentle hands of his mother used to push the hair back on his forehead until he succumbed to sleep. His eyes seemed as heavy now as some of the swords he had trained with at his uncle's castle, and he fought off sleep as long as he could, but Grenfel's eyelids soon dropped closed and he found himself caught instantly in the grips of a dream.

Cutting another piece of frozen fish flesh for himself, Kutek talked with his friends as long as they would listen, and listen they did, with one ear open to Kutek's speech and the other to Omri's translation. Thus, they engaged in conversation with merriment as the seal oil in the lamp burned on into the night. Kutek was an experienced storyteller and easily captivated his listeners not merely with words, but equally with the tone of his voice. Images seemed to form from the fluctuating tones of his speech, swirling in the minds of his guests like the wind tossing snow about the icefields. It was in such a fashion Estravai and Morteque learned of the sudden departure of those who had come to the village before them, fleeing the queen. They'd disappeared into a storm one day, never to be heard from or seen by the villagers again.

The night passed quickly for the relaxed travellers, mesmerized by Kutek's animated storytelling. They heard how the Ancient of Days had informed Kutek of spiritual seasons through dreams, and how he and his people had been waiting for a Hawkman to visit their village, as the others had come to the village before. Then the elder fell silent, simply gazing at his visitors' faces in the lamp's flickering light.

"He's studying our faces like he reads the land," said Omri, "to see if one of us may be the expected Hawkman."

"Tell Kutek that we receive dreams as he does," Estravai said, "and that we are not the one sent out in his dreams to liberate Ascar but simply those who come before the Hawkman."

When Omri explained this to Kutek, they waited in a silence that seemed to stretch on for an eternity. Then they observed a small tear trickle down Kutek's cheek.

Estravai said, "Please explain to Kutek that Grenfel is the one he and his people are waiting for."

Rising before the burning oil lamp, Omri walked over to Kutek and stretched out a hand to where Grenfel lay asleep.

"Behold the Hawkman," declared Omri. Kutek smiled and then spoke in an emotional voice. Omri translated. "He is thankful for being introduced to the Hawkman, but as he and his people let others walk off into the storm last time, this time he and his people want to follow the Hawkman into the storm."

Estravai nodded his head in encouragement as Kutek's tears continued to trickle down his cheek.

~

Long, crimson velvet curtains blew in the wind, rags now only suitable for scullery work, shredded mindlessly as if their very colour had incensed the castle's unscheduled visitor. The gold-embroidered quilt of the royal bed lay strewn in a pile on the marble floor, tossed aside with the ease of a bucket of waste thrown out a window.

Queen Julliet lay face down on the floor, sobbing, her long auburn hair torn out in places. Blood dripped from claw marks on her arms and legs, and her beautiful Emerald green dress, the one she so often wore upon bidding Grenfel goodnight, was torn in places and stained with blood. Lamenting from the floor the queen's hand was outstretched, as if she were still trying to grasp the intruder's heel. All was for naught, though, as the wooden entrance door of the castle could be heard in the distance sadly swinging on its hinges in the wind.

"He's gone!" she cried weakly. "They took him, my husband! King Ulrich is gone."

Grenfel sat up screaming. Tears flooded his eyes as he broke out into loud sobs. Morgan whinnied in the cold outside, sensing his young master's distress. Kutek stood paralyzed, knife in hand, unsure what was happening. Estravai jumped up and ran to Grenfel's side, sitting beside him with his arm under Grenfel's neck.

"What is it, boy?" Estravai whispered.

"My father," Grenfel said, weeping. "He's gone!"

"Gone?"

"Taken! The King of Ascar, my father, has been taken!"

"This smells of Meldrock," interjected Morteque, standing by Estravai's side.

"The time has come," Estravai replied resolutely. "It is time to journey back to Mirana."

CHAPTER EIGHTEEN

In her black silk dress, Roxanne held back her curly orange hair and placed a hairclip firmly on each side. She practiced balancing on a pair of stilettos in front of the antique full-length mirror that had hung in the foyer of her mother's house since she was a young girl trying on oversized shoes in front of it.

Well, you're shaky enough just working on your recovery without trying to balance on a pair of heels, she thought to herself. *Not to mention following through on a foolish idea like going to dinner with another man.*

Thoughts of possibly being unfaithful to Tony caused Roxanne to smile nervously back at the mirror. Glancing through the stained-glass windows bracketing the door, Roxanne noticed a taxi pulling up to the curb in front of the house. Not long after, she found herself speeding towards West Georgia's downtown core.

As the cab weaved through the bustling night traffic, Roxanne used the time to check her makeup in a small compact mirror. Only the sound of the cabby's voice, calling out for fifteen dollars, made her look up and drop the mirror into her purse. Fumbling through the contents, she pulled out twenty dollars.

Stepping out of the cab, she adjusted her bag on her shoulder and took a deep breath before finding the courage to cross the street to Bernie's jazz club, one of the hottest spots in the city.

"It's now or never, girl," Roxanne whispered from where she stood paralyzed at the club's front door. *It's okay, you're in control.* With that thought and a nervous smile, Roxanne finally stepped forward and pushed the glass door open.

The rich full tones of a saxophone spilled out of the club like a cresting wave when she entered, and now threatened to carry her into a sea of moving people. *Great. Just when a girl gets the courage to live a bit, she gets held up in traffic,* she thought to herself. *Oh well, surely, I can cross a crowded dance floor.*

She inched her way through the crowd, stepping on more than a few toes with her spiked heels.

"Sorry!" Roxanne said to a man wincing in pain.

"Get those things registered! They're lethal weapons!"

Noticing her plight, another man—the man she had come to see—called to her from the edge of the dance floor. "Shall I throw a life preserver?"

"I am in control," shouted Roxanne as the crowd seemed to carry her closer to the man like a surging wave, and possibly to the first of many forbidden moments.

"Glad you had the courage to come, Roxanne." The man reached out a hand to pluck her from the crowd, like Jesus pulling Peter from the sea.

"I wouldn't have missed it for the world, Dr. Michaels." She tried to steady herself on her heels. Like a high-wire artist checking her balance, Roxanne momentarily paused to check her thoughts, wondering if she had really just said what she did.

"Come now. Let's drop the formality. Just call me Robert." He took her by the hand and led her up a flight of winding stairs to a balcony lit with Japanese lanterns.

Robert Michaels was a tall, muscular man with short black hair and plastic frame glasses. This evening, he was oddly dressed in a wrinkled blue suit. He looked more like Clark Kent than Superman, and he certainly didn't look like an addictions counsellor. Roxanne walked silently alongside him, thinking this must be how he dressed outside of work.

"My, you look outstanding," Robert commented, hoping to break the awkward silence as they walked to a table midway across the balcony.

"Thank you!" Roxanne hoped her tone wasn't too desperate. Even with the subdued light of the paper lanterns, she was sure she was blushing, and that Robert had noticed. She muttered a prayer under her breath with the hope of not missing the chair Robert had just pulled out for her. She managed a quick and silent amen as her backside made contact with the polished wood.

"To be honest with you, I wasn't sure if you would show," Robert said candidly as he sat across from her. "It just shows that even with all my years in the field, a client can still surprise me."

"I almost didn't come," she replied. "No offense meant or anything. I know we've been through a lot of sessions together, but my mother is the one who suggested it might be nice for me to get out. I can still hear her voice. My mother, God bless her, said to me, 'I'll watch Jordan. Don't worry about a thing! Just go out and blow the cobwebs off. You never know, it might do you a world of good.'"

"My praise to your mother, then." Robert's big green eyes watched her cheerily.

The waiter's arrival saved her from drowning in a sea of green. Dressed in a black tuxedo, he brandished a tray supporting two large crystal glasses and a pitcher of ice water.

"I'm Fredrico," he informed them, balancing the tray on one hand. "I'll be your host for this evening."

The thought of being served by an eloquent penguin caused Roxanne to spontaneously giggle.

"Is everything all right, my lady?" inquired Fredrico.

"Oh, I'm sorry," Roxanne responded, a little embarrassed. "I just get a little giddy when I'm tired."

"There is no need to explain." Fredrico spoke as if he were conversing with dignitaries at a royal dinner party. Without missing a beat, he turned his attention to Robert. "Would you like to choose an appetizer, sir?"

"Yes!" Robert glanced at Roxanne before taking the liberty of ordering for both of them. "We'll have the tiger prawns and some pita bread."

"Anything to drink, sir?"

"Just bring us two cups of coffee for now."

"Very well, sir. I'll be back with your coffee in a few moments." And Fredrico strutted off to fill their order.

"I was complimenting your mother, if I remember correctly," Robert said as he leaned over the table towards Roxanne. "I believe your mother is right—not simply because I enjoy the company of beautiful women, because I do indeed, but also because it's important to consider Tony's unfaithfulness to you. After all you've been through, his behaviour hasn't been encouraging. The effort you've been making to put your life in order is commendable. You deserve to let your hair down a bit."

"How do you know about Tony's unfaithfulness?" Roxanne asked, feeling uncomfortable.

"Sorry. I had no intention of upsetting you. I only shared what is common knowledge."

She looked to the floor in silence, then looked up at Robert and smiled with a flushed face. "I know. I just have these moments when I get so tense. For now, I'd still like to believe the rumours of Tony's unfaithfulness to be idle chatter of bored small-town folk."

Robert paused to allow Fredrico to set down a huge platter of mouth-watering prawns and a basket of warm pita bread.

"Thank you," he told the waiter.

"Will that be everything, then?" asked Fredrico as he set a coffee urn onto the table, along with two cups.

"Yes."

"Fine, then, but feel free to let me know if you require anything else." With a nod, Fredrico politely excused himself.

"I don't want to sound like a nagging housewife," said Robert as he poured Roxanne a cup of coffee, "but the fact of the matter is that I've been giving counsel to a very distraught young woman from Drummingsville over the phone. This woman is quite insistent that there's more truth to the local rumours than some would like to acknowledge. She has called me on more than one occasion, painting a very bleak picture of Tony." He paused to take a sip of his coffee. "I mean, the whole situation is so volatile. I heard that Tony has been let go from Forest Tech."

"I hadn't heard," Roxanne said in a shaky voice, struggling to keep her eyes from tearing up.

Robert helped himself to a couple of fat tiger prawns. "I'm only trying to say that you are important, Roxanne. As I've said in our sessions, your personal health matters. You need to take steps to get on with your life, even if that means leaving Tony to figure out his own. I'm just trying to be honest with you. If you don't get on with your life, you could quite possibly relapse into heroin, and even lose your rights to your own son. I know you're probably thinking, 'What fun is it to go out to dinner with a prophet of doom,' but please, bear with me."

Roxanne took a moment to take it in, then reluctantly surrendered. "Go on."

"I'll try to make it as painless as possible. One of my colleagues, Dr. Andrews, is starting a clinic in Drummingsville. He asked me to augment the clinic with my counselling practice, and I have agreed. The clinic has purchased a large heritage house for their office and residence." He spoke carefully, as if not to cut the wrong wire and cause everything to explode in his face. "However, since most of the doctors, including myself, are often out of town, working in the neighbouring counties, we thought it would be helpful to have a permanent resident in the house to keep it running smoothly. You know, keep the plants watered and the tropical fish fed. It might be something for you to consider, Roxanne." He finished the last prawn on the platter. "I know it can't be easy staying with your mother indefinitely."

"It's not so bad," Roxanne said, looking down at the table and shrugging.

"Would you like some more coffee?"

Roxanne covered her cup with her hand. "It's okay, I'm fine."

"Look, Roxanne, I know you're still a bit mixed up about life in Drummingsville, and possibly a little afraid even, but think about it. Even though you're staying at your mother's, you're on your own with a young child. If you take me up on the offer, you'll be in a positive environment, where monitored drugs such as methadone and naltrexone would be available to ensure you don't relapse. As well, you would receive encouragement from trained medical staff during your stay at the clinic. That can only help you continue to walk in recovery."

"I'm not sure about much right now, but thank you for the evening." Roxanne's smile back across the table at Robert was more personal, as it seemed to say to her, *Girl, you're doing good. you're still in control.*

"I understand. There's no pressure here, just a friend wanting to share a good opportunity with someone he's concerned about."

"I really do appreciate all you've done for me." Roxanne blushed at Robert's attempt to mask his intimacy.

He glanced at his Rolex, realizing it was getting late. "If you decide you're interested, you know my office number. For now, how about I just drop you off at your mom's place? You'll be able to think more clearly after a good night's rest."

"That's sweet of you, Robert, but I can find my own way home."

Robert reached for the cheque, which Fredrico had discretely slipped onto the table. "Please, I wouldn't hear of it. It's really no trouble."

Roxanne finally agreed, thinking that by doing so she would get back to her mother's place faster, as she now had the overwhelming sensation she had spent the whole evening being charmed by a snake.

～

The telephone rang in the main office of the Drummingsville School. The short receptionist, in a white-pleated skirt and athletic shoes, answered with a merry tone.

"Hello, Drummingsville School… One moment, I'll check!" She pushed a button on her phone and buzzed the office of Principal Reeves.

"Yes?" Reeves answered.

"Mayor Thomas is on the line."

"Thank you, Marlene. Have the call put through to my office." After a moment, he picked up the receiver and leaned back in his chair. "Hello, Mayor Thomas. This is a pleasant surprise."

"I wish that were so," Mayor Thomas said on the other end of the line. "I don't like to be the bearer of bad news, but quite frankly my job as mayor calls for me to voice my concerns occasionally. Jack you remember the last town meeting, don't you?"

"How could I forget? When one of my staff members was pretty vocal, to say the least. As the school principal, I was more than a little embarrassed."

"Well, Jack, that's exactly how I felt. Now, we can't have prospective business investors treated in such an embarrassing and shameful fashion, can we?"

"No, of course not."

"And we can't have our own paid professionals publicly labelling these investors as ministers of Satan, can we?"

"No, we can't."

"Well, I think it's easier to replace one teacher than go looking for more investors."

Reeves hesitated. "I get what you're saying, but it won't be easy. Flora is a very gifted teacher."

"I know, but I have full confidence that you can make the right decision for Drummingsville and for our community," the mayor said.

The line went quiet.

"Hello? Are you still there, Jack?"

"Yes, Mayor Thomas," Reeves said, feeling troubled.

"Now, don't be condemning yourself, Jack. Think about it. You're just helping the woman, by all rights. She should have retired a few years ago anyhow. Am I right?"

"Yes, I guess so."

"Now, Jack, I'm going to make this easy for you. Just listen to what I'm about to say. I'd like you to plant a file with some photographs taken from a school camping trip, of students swimming in their shorts. Don't forget to include the students' names and emails, along with a few inappropriate pictures of children from the adult site along with the website's email address. Put the file in Flora's classroom, Jack. Then I want you to convince one or two of the children supposedly involved with the adult website to accuse Flora of promoting the perversion amongst the children at school. Are you still with me, Jack?"

"Yeah."

"I need to know if you're able to do the job. Well, are you up to it?" Mayor Thomas paused, eagerly awaiting Jack's reply.

"I can handle it," Reeves said nervously, "but the school must continue to function. Who will teach in Flora's place? I mean, Drummingsville doesn't exactly have a great reserve of school teachers."

"I understand your hesitation. After all, you're responsible for making sure the school runs smoothly. But not to worry, my friend; we have a suitable individual for the position. She's currently working here in town as a tarot card reader."

Reeves sighed. "That's all I need. Another fanatical teacher on staff."

"She's hardly that, I guarantee you," the mayor assured. "Miss Starr holds a teaching degree and is a very gifted educator. Trust me. The alternative is to know that you stand in the way of Drummingsville's development. You do understand the importance of what I'm asking of you, don't you, Jack?"

"Yes." Jack paused for a moment to exhale. "It's as good as done."

"Excellent!" Mayor Thomas said with satisfaction. "I knew you were capable of making the correct decision for all involved. Believe me, my friend, it will be a very prosperous decision for you. You might finally be able to get a few of those rare Babylonian pieces for your collection. Well, I've got to let you go now. I have to tend to other crucial matters of my office. It's been a pleasure talking!"

"Good day, Mayor," Jack replied and hung up. A smile twisted onto his face as he thought about adding those precious Babylonian pieces to his collection.

This may not be a big deal at all, he thought. *Certainly nothing to take issue with.*

⸜

High in the mid-heavens, the queen's crimson lips mirrored the principal's twisted smile. Her raven hair tossed insanely upon her shoulders like many miniature whips, as she stood imitating a spider spinning a web with her slender, gloved fingers.

"My spider still spins," she said, laughing in a drunken frenzy, "and it shall yet bring me the souls of men, for I am none other than the Queen of the Heavens!"

Upon hearing this loud proclamation, the mid-heavens erupted into a frenzy of demonic worship, superseding any festive gathering ever thrown by a mortal.

CHAPTER NINETEEN

The banging on the front door of Drummingsville's Christian Centre was as relentless as a leaky tap.

"Y'all wanna ease up on that door?" yelled Randy Foxworth from an upstairs window. "I'm on my way down!"

Randy descended the last of the stairs from his apartment above the sanctuary.

"It's not enough that you got a fax machine, a phone number, and a message answering service," he muttered as he arrived at the front door. "People are still determined to punch holes in your front door. Technology is for the birds."

Pulling the door open, Randy instinctively ducked Tony's fist which now beat the air zealously above his head, having altogether missed the door.

"Sorry, Randy," said Tony sheepishly.

"No harm done to these old bones." Randy straightened up. "Was the punch brought on by my preaching or just a wake-up call from the Lord? No matter. I believe in your innocence. The Lord just used you, Tony."

Randy closed his eyes. *Forgive me, Lord,* he said to himself. *Your word really hasn't been in me.*

"Randy!"

"Forgive me, boy." Randy snapped back like a parent caught by their child sleeping through a movie. "Looks like I dun forgot my manners. Here I am carrying on a conversation with the Lord and you're lookin' like a cat that's been dragged through a wringer washer. Well, no sense jawin' out here. It's late. Come on in. You can be the first to taste a new homestyle barbecue sauce I'm trying."

"Thanks, Randy. I really mean it."

Tony followed Randy up a set of wooden stairs with a wide banister. Randy led him into a very lived-in living room. Tony thought it resembled a museum for used furniture of various eras. There was a green leather recliner which sported a few tears, a 1920s-style sofa with a faded brown damask pattern, several Queen Ann chairs, and a colonial coffee table. Books were scattered everywhere upon the orange shag rug, and various pictures hung on the walls, ranging from black-and-white sketches of horse-drawn farm implements to a black velvet painting of a Spanish galleon, all highlighted by the glow of a hanging Tiffany lamp. Music from an eight-track player cranking out MT fresh fiddle tunes affected Tony like a pail of cold water thrown in his face. It served to remind him that he was not hallucinating about Randy's choice in décor.

"Sit yourself down, boy!" Randy yelled from the kitchen. "I just need to give an eye to my barbecue sauce."

I'm really too tired to be fussy, Tony said to himself, as if his body needed convincing. He flopped down into the green recliner like a man whose meter on life had just expired.

"Well, I do declare," said Randy, entering the living room holding a wooden spoon, "this here barbecue sauce would downright do my momma proud! Haven't seen y'all for a spell, boy. I make it to be about the time I was smokin' ribs out back of the church here."

Randy paused to get comfortable on his old sofa. Noticing Randy settling in, Tony seized the opportunity to explain himself.

"I've been out of town," Tony replied in a groggy voice, "taking a bit of time away from things."

"Well, I can't say it's done you a heap of good. You sure look all tuckered out to me."

"That's why I love you, Randy." Tony chuckled as he propped himself up. "You're so encouraging. I drove on through Ruston to Sarquis to visit the school I'm taking correspondence courses from."

Tony paused to lean back and allow the footrest to come up. He stretched out his feet, sighing like a contented cat.

"As I was driving," he continued, "my truck was hit by a silver Porsche with the word BELIAL inscribed on its back plate." He then tried to paint a picture for Randy of why he now seemed to be almost a complete wreck.

Randy giggled a bit as he sat, still holding the wooden spoon.

"What's so funny?" Tony asked, not really wanting to be laughed at.

"I was just thinking. If a fellow's car is going to get hit, a Porsche is about as fine as they come to get hit by. Sorry, I'm not making light of what you've been through. Please don't give me no mindin' to," smiled Randy, "I get a lot of creative thoughts late at night, living by myself. Go on then, boy, continue."

"I learned from Apostle John—he's the one I'm taking the courses from—well, he told me that Belial is the name of an end-time spirit."

Randy put up his feet and stretched out, listening to Tony's story.

"Oh, I'm really sorry, Randy!" Tony said suddenly. "It's late and you probably want to sleep. I should be leaving."

"Sit back down, boy," said Randy, waving the spoon in the air. "I ain't in bed usually till much after one. There's always something around here that keeps me fussin' late into the night. And tonight, I reckon it's babysittin' that there barbecue sauce. Besides, I don't reckon that either of us would get any sleep tonight without a little jawin' first."

"In that case, I won't disappoint you." Tony unravelled the threads of his recent experiences. "Roxanne took Jordan to her mother's in West Georgia, my truck was hit on the way to Sarquis. A police officer stopped me on the way back to Drummingsville, saying my truck was going to be impounded and that a Dr. Anderson was taking me to court. I've been having a series of recurring and very graphic dreams. The apostle of the school I just visited thinks my dreams are related to what's happening in my everyday life. He also said apostles are like pioneers. I don't know why I'm telling you that. I really must be overtired. I'm starting to ramble now." Tony yawned.

"That's interesting!" Randy crowed like a rooster calling in the day. "Cuz a vision came upon me lately like a big ol' twister. I thought my heart was gonna pop out of my chest. I've had some flashbacks from the war, but they ain't nothing compared to a vision from God. The vision took hold of me like an ol' gator and images started a-swirlin' around my mind like a hound dog chasing its tail. Images of soldiers crawling on their bellies, just a-hidin' in the dark from the enemy. They were all trying to sneak up on the enemy's stronghold and mark it on their maps.

"Lo and behold, a huge spotlight shines right on one of 'em good ol' boys and then I saw a hundred flashes of light and a dark body slump to the ground like a deer felled by a crossbow. I reckon I had me one of them their ladder experiences with God just a short spell back, just like Jacob sleeping on that their big ol' stone a-dreamin'. I heard as I lay on my bed the voice of God. It caused my bones to tremble. I thought my ol' bed would shake apart at the sound of the Lord; it was like a great freight train rushing by.

"As I struggled to catch my breath, I heard the Lord say, 'Touch not my anointed one!' I sprung up from where I lay asleep like an ol' jack-in-the-box, and I stood in the darkness of my room sweatin' like a groom waiting for his bride at the front of the church. The good Lord, I believe, would have us all to pray for His faithful ones on the frontline of battle. Or the enemy just might snatch 'em from our midst like he did a third of the stars in the heavens. Even gossip!"

Randy kept on going, like an old Quaker reformist. "The unbridled tongue of a brother might be the arrow to fell one of his good ol' boys. Sure, wouldn't wanna have to answer to the Lord for that, but I guess I've been rambling on long enough here that a hen could have dun laid an egg by now. But you mentioning pioneers set me to thinking the soldiers in my dream were like pioneers before the main forces moved into an area. It seems God is definitely trying to get a message through, but I'm just too darn thick-skulled to grasp the revelation this late at night. You just rest your bones for a spell. I'll be right back." Randy got up off the sofa. "That there barbecue sauce in the kitchen has been keepin' warm on the stove long enough. A little movement might be good for it."

Where are your frontline soldiers, your mapmakers, and target markers for Drummingsville? Tony thought as he closed his eyes and began to relax in the recliner. *Who are they, Lord?*

A few minutes later, Randy returned carrying two tall glasses of iced tea. He handed one to Tony, then sat back down on the sofa. "You know, come to think of it, Drummingsville reminds me of a military camp right now, one that's gettin' ready for battle. I mean, with all the construction going on all over town, it's strange! They all dun started to work on that there new super mall, and that big diamond processing plant. There's an army of hardhats on the streets these days, I declare. It's like we've been invaded!"

"Maybe we have been," said a sleepy-sounding Tony. "But not by hardhats. By demon princes who aren't fortifying Drummingsville. They're laying siege to our town."

"I do declare! We all might be of His specialty troops, keeping surveillance on the enemy's movement in Drummingsville."

Randy looked over at Tony for a response, but he saw his guest's half-drunk glass of iced tea resting on an end table, and Tony sprawled out in the recliner, already fast asleep.

Sharon Tillman lifted the cup of hot coffee to her lips and sipped it like an alert deer drinking from a brook. She set her cup back down on the table. "You're awfully quiet today. What's the matter, Jim? Cat got your tongue?"

"Ain't much to get all worked up about," Jim replied as he straightened his white fishing hat, then gave his coffee a slow methodical stir.

They were meeting again at the Java Joint. John approached and put down a plate of food in front of his friend. "Here you go, Jim. One combo burger with fries." He bustled off to clear another table.

The ever-wrathful Sharon sat across from Jim in a hot pink tank top that read like an ad for a site to meet singles. Bored! Call a craftsperson, they create conversation. Her short blond hair was perfectly feathered back and her eyes were once again accented with the bold green eyeshadow that complemented the green dragon tattoo on her right cheek that she had taken up wearing due to her earned reputation of being the town's dragon lady. Like a huge-winged dragon leaving its perch, Sharon spewed out her wrath at Jim. "How can you be so blind as to say something like that? The future of Drummingsville is now!"

"It's easy for you to be so jubilant now that your pockets are lined with gold," Jim replied in a bitter tone. "You sold out for thirty pieces of silver. Whatever happened to the sticking together as the merchants of Drummingsville?"

"Oh, quit being such a grumpy old man," she said with as much compassion as a crocodile whose jaw was closing on its lunch. "You had the same option as I did—or any store owner, for that matter!"

"Why should I have to sell, especially when at a public forum we were promised no duplicate businesses were going to be offered space in the mall? Well, so much for promises!" Jim said, pausing only long enough to sip his coffee. "I hear Big Hooks is opening a store in the new mall. Why should I have to sell my family business to go work for another company simply because they're bigger? I for one will not trade the McFlurry inheritance for a lucrative employment package. As merchants, I thought we agreed to support each other and act together."

"I see. So, you're going to let my business deal come between us as friends?"

Jim silently stared down at his plate as he shifted fries back and forth with his fork.

Sharon shifted in her chair and pulled her denim jacket around her shoulders. Throwing back her head and brushing a tear from her eye, her dragon's tail struck like white lightning. "Remember this, Jim, when I'm lying in the hot white sand at some exotic island resort this winter, and you're tying flies late into the winter night just to break even. You'll wish you had done the same thing I did."

Jim still wouldn't look up at her. She sniffed and got up from the table, walking towards the door.

John, from his perch behind the counter pouring freshly roasted coffee beans into a glass jar, tried to keep the communication alive between the two old friends. "Don't forget our special pizza night! Buy a large and get a free beverage." But John's words seemed unable to bring any lightness back into the air.

Sharon hesitated in front of the door momentarily, as if it represented change to the community of Drummingsville. Knowing some friendships might not survive, she sniffled, pushed open the door, and stepped out

⌒

The sound and smell of bacon sizzling in a hot cast-iron pan aroused Tony's senses like a bear coming out of hibernation. He stood up and stretched the knots out of the muscles in his lower back, squinting at the bright orange shag rug. It was too harsh a reality to face without having had a cup of coffee.

He stumbled into the kitchen like he'd just completed a marathon.

"Mornin', friend!" came Randy's energetic welcome. "Sit yourself on down and try some of my homestyle pan-fried potatoes."

Randy shovelled a trucker's portion of potatoes, bacon, and fried eggs onto Tony's plate.

"I really didn't mean to spend the night," Tony said as he picked up a glass of orange juice.

"No harm done!" said Randy, laughing. "I didn't have the recliner rented out last night anyway."

Randy put a couple of eggs atop his potatoes, threw a handful of bacon on the pile, and covered it all with table syrup.

"Mind if I join you? I can't seem to find another table," smiled Randy as he set his plate down on the table across from Tony and sat down. "So, what are your plans now?"

"I'm not sure at the moment."

"Pardon my intrusive curiosity," Randy said as he burped down a bite of eggs.

"No offense taken," Tony sputtered back with a mouthful of toast. "After all, I'm the one who was making the racket at your door last night. Anyway, I was thinking I'd find out who's managing the construction projects in town and see if I can't land myself a job. There should be no shortage of work for the willing."

"I just might have something of interest to you." Randy got up from the table and walked over to his kitchen counter, where he pulled open an ivory drawer and fumbled through some papers. "Didn't think I used it to start my barbecue…"

"At last!" muttered Randy as he pulled a recent edition of the Drummingsville Star out of the drawer and handed it to Tony. The front page captured Tony's attention like a bird in a snare. It read: *Local Resident Becomes Millionaire.* He stared in disbelief at the black-and-white photo of Dylan Cartwright beside the column.

Tony read aloud:

Cartwright quit as executive manager for Forest Tech to be the foreman over the construction of the mine's new diamond-processing plant, and also the super mall. Replacing Cartwright as executive manager is Susan Henderson, a well-seasoned woman who was the lead field hand for Forest Tech.

"Oh well," Tony said as he put the paper down on the table. He shook his head in disbelief. "I guess getting my old job back is out of the question now. And I can forget about trying to land a construction job. Sue can buy her own vehicle now and take her eyes off my vineyard; my name isn't Naboth, you know."

"How about a shot of fresh coffee?" offered Randy.

"Yeah. I could sure use one now!"

Randy grabbed the percolated coffee off the stove and poured Tony a cup. "There you go, boy, just like the cowboys drink it on TV."

"Thanks."

"Nothin' beats the smell of percolated coffee to get your ol' nostrils flaring like a stallion running in the wind."

"I guess," answered Tony blankly. "You know, I just remembered something Apostle John said. He asked me to pray for Apostle Levi because the devil desires to sift him. I'm starting to think the whole town is the devil's sandbox, that he's sifting people at his own pleasure, like a kid playing with a pail and shovel in the sand. I'm not trying to set you off or anything, Randy. I know how strongly you voiced your opinion concerning Apostle Levi's ministry, but do you know if he's still around town?"

"Yeah," Randy replied after a minute of silence. "The ol' boy is still around, but I hear he ain't farin' too well. Heard he's holed up at Crester's Cave."

"That place is a real dive."

"Yeah, I know, but the ol' boy near lost his kingdom, all his assets, his TV and radio show. Most of his followers dropped him after the hijackin' and forced drug inducement of his bus passengers."

"That's bizarre! What happened was a tragedy no one could've foreseen."

"I reckon that might be so, but there are plenty of ol' wolves out there who only see one thing, and that's sheep! They were just lickin' their ol' chops the minute the fiery darts started hittin' that ol' boy, and seeing dollar signs in their eyes, they led his small flock away. You know how it all is. Where there's a carcass, the vultures gather."

Tony took a sip of coffee. "Is that a tone of sympathy I detect in you, Randy?"

"I guess I've kind of been like an ol' mule in the past in regard to supporting Levi," Randy confessed. "But I've been thinkin' since you came poundin' on my door that the ol' boy has been having a hard time at the plough. And I reckon some of the difficulty falls on me from all the negative words I spoke about him. The Lord's been tellin' me lately that if I ain't lovin' my brother, I ain't any better than an ol' cheat or murderer. I think the good Lord takes great displeasure when we take pleasure in another's suffering, and if I don't get these things straight in my heart, He'd find another shepherd after His own heart for the Drummingsville Christian Centre."

"Only the footprints of the Lord could have gone ahead of me on that ground," said Tony, "because I was going to ask you for a ride to visit Levi. I just wasn't sure how to do it."

Reflecting on heaven's approval of a changed heart, Tony flashed a smile in Randy's direction.

"One of the ways the Lord worked on my heart concerning Levi was a dream I had," Randy said. "I can relate to that prophet Ezekiel being grabbed up by his hair and taken away in the spirit, cuz I done found myself in that there dream from the Lord set down in a desert just crawlin' across the sand like a caterpillar on hot asphalt. Before I could blink, this here ol' soldier pops up in front of me in full combat gear, just out of the sand. Got me thinkin' about Adam comin' out of the dust. And then it happened again. A huge hand just pulled me high up into the heavens and, I declare, them ol' soldiers was poppin' up all over the earth. Just clamourin' out of their caves and poppin' out of the woodwork ready for battle. The spirit of the Lord seemed to be impressing on me that He has servants. Though they may appear a-hidin' to the naked eye, they will arise in their season by His Spirit and not by power or might. Call me Peter, but I just got to figurin', who am I to judge who the Lord's anointed are?"

"That's exciting!" Tony said. "Maybe there's a connection between your dream and our visit to Levi. Maybe God is about to reveal to us one of His hidden soldiers." Tony burst out laughing.

"What's tickled your funny bone, boy?"

"I don't mean anything by it," Tony said, "but I find it hard to picture you as a Joseph-like dreamer."

"I admit, I ain't no Joseph, but lately it could be said that I, too, am among the dreamers."

"Don't tell me that everybody is walking among the dreamers now."

"I don't reckon that is the case." Randy finished his coffee and set his cup down. "In my Bible, anyway, it's the old men who dream dreams."

"What was that?" Tony said, smiling. "I forgot where I put my hearing aid."

CHAPTER TWENTY

The dark underground pit of the newly resurrected Stillmore Mine was a beehive of activity, but oblivious to the men of the deep with their headlamps were the two bull-faced demons walking unseen amongst them, their eagle-like talons clutching a huge anchor chain from an ocean liner. The demons' putrid smell turned neither a head as the miners continued to push the envelope—in their laborious toiling under the merciless taskmaster known as production, as if nothing out of the ordinary was transpiring on their shift.

Looking around, the two demons smiled boastfully at their ability to go undetected as they slipped into the company elevator to ascend to the surface with several miners. Their putrid smell eventually broke the silence of the elevator, in that several men began wheezing and coughing uncontrollably. Observing the miners' discomfort only served to cause the elevator's undetected demonic passengers to smile, as they were well aware it was their presence causing the miners discomfort.

Like penitentiary gates being rolled back for a convict's release, the elevator doors opened at the surface. The two demons walked out, smiling along with the miners. A tall demon prince in a long black duster, his hair combed back and held in a ponytail by a blood-red ruby, looked out through dark sunglasses at the two approaching demons. He grinned as the two bull-faced demons walked towards him with their heads down in respect, passing through both miners and gravel trucks on the way to where their prince stood. The two demons finally came to stand before their prince, who was positioned next to the guard at the gate checking in vehicles. Unfazed by the mine's procedures, the two demons wasted no time in falling at their prince's feet, who seemed to have another purpose in his visit to the mine than that of being grovelled.

⌒

Jim McFlurry never said a word as he closed the door of the Java Joint behind him, effectively shutting out John's silent stares as if it were a pay-for-view sporting event. As Jim stepped out of the Java Joint, the demonic prince from the mine met him, and seemed to hasten his steps along the boardwalk of Drummingsville's main street. The demonic prince parted the sea of hardhat workers before Jim as if he were a defensive lineman protecting his quarterback.

Jim suddenly and silently stopped, as did the demon prince, before a shop door with a closed sign displayed in its window. Jim fumbled through the pockets of his blue denim jacket for his keys. Finally, he withdrew a shaky hand, only to struggle like an inebriated man to get the key in the lock. To the delight of the demon prince, Jim soon turned the key and pushed open the shop door.

Stepping inside, Jim flipped the light switch, revealing a fly fisherman's fantasy. Hundreds of brightly coloured flies hung on boards covering the walls like wallpaper. This small family business had been a tribute to the sport of fly fishing for generations amongst the McFlurry clan. A workbench stood in the centre of the shop, cluttered with feathers, tools, and flies in various stages of completion.

Like water channelled through a canal, Jim seemed to be guided by the dark prince over to his workbench. Jim stood over the workbench, gazing at all the barbs and tools he had fondly handled so many times. For a few second, he reminisced of less complicated times.

The dark prince grew impatient and reached out his leather-gloved hands, placing them against both sides of Jim's head. Jim pulled open the old cherry-stained drawer and fumbled through its contents like a blind man. He clutched his grandfather's old service revolver and set it on the workbench. He fumbled through the drawer again for a partly torn carton of bullets, which he grabbed with no more thought than a farmer off to shoot a field gopher.

Why couldn't we be happy with our small town? Jim wondered as his head pounded with a severe migraine. Nevertheless, he mindlessly jammed bullets into the open cylinder of his grandfather's revolver. The entire time, the prince kept one of his gloved hands on Jim's head, and the other he placed on Jim's hand. Two hands picked up an old rag to muffle the revolver, and two hands now held the gun to Jim's head.

The sound of his heartbeat seemed now to fill his head, and he yelled.

"I won't sell! I'll close with my shop!"

A single finger pulled the trigger. Instantly, Jim's body slumped forward and slammed into the workbench.

The prince smiled in satisfaction, then stepped away from Jim's fallen form and walked to the shop door, pausing momentarily to observe Jim's terrified face. The demonic prince then exhaled a breath, causing the lights to go out before stepping outside. In his wake, the two bull-faced demons appeared to shackle Jim around the neck with a massive iron chain. They dragged his spirit from his shop screaming, right through Sharon Tillman as they followed in the steps of their master.

～

Tony walked alongside Randy, eating roasted peanuts out of a can and enjoying the simple pleasure of a good conversation between friends. At a snail's pace, they made their way along the boardwalk of Drummingsville's main street.

Suddenly, as if hit by the blast of a cold morning shower, Tony's eyes widened and he began to tremble. His mouth locked in an open position and his outstretched hand froze to the can of peanuts.

"I knew I should have taken first aid," Randy muttered. "Don't tell me you're having an allergic reaction to peanuts. Can you hear me, buddy?"

Randy waved his hand in front of Tony's eyes frantically. People pushed by them on the sidewalk from all directions, ever so slowly, as if trying to appease the hunger of their curiosity.

"Well, don't just stand there gawking like a bunch of barn owls!" Randy bellowed to the crowd. "Call 911! My buddy's in serious trouble!" He took Tony by the shoulders and looked him in the eyes. "It's going to be okay. Don't worry. Ol' Randy here ain't ever left a man behind."

Soon a siren could be heard working its way up Main Street. With the precision of an elite group of Navy seals, the paramedics moved through the crowd gathered on the sidewalk.

"What happened?" one of the paramedics asked Randy while the other approached Tony.

Noticing the look of terror in Tony's eyes, the paramedic crouched and said, "I'm here to help you, sir. I'm a paramedic. Can you hear me okay?" Receiving no response from Tony, the paramedic explained he was going to take him to the ambulance to check his vitals. Still getting no response, the paramedic assisted Tony in walking to the ambulance, opened the side door, and helped him in.

"I think it might be that the boy is allergic to peanuts," Randy said, gasping to catch his breath. "All I know is that we were just walkin' on down the boardwalk eating peanuts and my buddy froze and fell."

Considering all the intensity of the situation, Randy began to have a flashback. Burning jungle, intense heat, white light, the sound of rockets screaming through the darkness… like the demon-possessed man running through tombs, like unrelenting rockets pounding the ground like Thor's hammer, like a cry for help amidst a symphony of terror. Then a Samaritan's response: "I ain't leaving you here, I ain't leaving you!"

"Are you all right?" the paramedic asked.

"What? Oh, yeah, sorry." Randy shook his head. "I must have drifted off a bit. You know, one of those nasty lingering side effects of war."

"Your friend's suffering from shock. We're going to take him in and get him checked out at the clinic. Was he a comrade in arms with you?"

"Not in a previous war, but in this one he sure is!"

The paramedic looked a bit confused. "Well, we need to get your friend to the clinic. Would you like to ride along?"

"No sense standing here jawin' about it," said Randy as he jumped into the ambulance beside Tony. "I got a man to bring in."

The paramedic smiled as he closed the back door of the ambulance, saluting to him.

It was normally a ten-minute drive from Main Street to the hospital, but with all the construction detours it rounded out at twenty-five minutes.

"It appears your friend is just suffering mental shock," said Dr. Norman Wiebe as he stood beside Randy in the examination room. "His breathing rate has increased, and his eyes are dilated. I think the worst-case scenario is that he'll be very thirsty when he comes out of shock."

"That's a relief!" remarked Randy. "I thought for sure Tony was one of those people who have allergic reactions to peanuts."

"Well, you can rest easy on that point," the doctor said.

"No!" Tony abruptly shouted as he suddenly sat up on the examination table.

"Mr. Epson, you're suffering from shock, but you're going to be okay," reassured the doctor. "I'm Dr. Wiebe, and you're in the examination room of the Drummingsville Hospital."

Tony didn't seem to hear Dr. Wiebe. In a rasping voice he said, "I'm really thirsty."

Randy smiled. "Thanks, doc, but I think I can supply the cure for that." He positioned himself under Tony's arm, taking his friend's weight on his shoulders. "Time to go home, soldier. Ol' Randy's got you. You're going to be okay, because I make a mean lemonade."

Randy thanked Dr. Wiebe again, then proceeded to carry Tony out the front door like a shepherd returning a wounded sheep to the fold.

The queen's hair thrashed upon her naked shoulders like ocean surf breaking upon rocks. She glided in her velvet gown amongst the tall, dark princes who knew her as the Queen of the Heavens.

"My spider is spinning! With its precision and skill, its web grows tighter." She raised her chalice to her crimson lips, delighted by her strategy. "The first of many of the souls of Drummingsville has been caught in its web."

⌐

Sharon paused to shiver as though stepping over a fresh grave, then continued her journey to Jim's shop. As she walked, she mulled over what she might say to Jim to convince him that they had known each other too long to stop talking altogether, no matter their differences. The town was too small for that.

She walked along, unaware of the demon prince keeping pace beside her. His hand rested on the back of her neck, causing her to walk along in a slumped fashion.

When she approached the front steps of Jim's shop, she saw the door ajar.

That's strange, she thought to herself. Jim's keys were dangling from the lock. *I've never known Jim to be this careless.*

Cautiously, Sharon pushed the door open and reached for the light switch. She held the switch for a moment as if it were a detonator, hesitating to flip it. Her heart raced.

I don't know. Something strange is going on. Do I really want to be here? What if...

Stopping herself form thinking the worst, she flipped the switch.

⌐

"Horror. Unimaginable horror!" Tony said as he sat still trembling from his ordeal on the edge of Randy's sofa, whereas Randy sat perched on the edge of his leather recliner, soaking in every syllable Tony uttered. "They had bull-like faces and there were two of them."

Tony stopped speaking to swallow the growing lump in his throat.

Taking a pitcher of lemonade off the colonial-style end table beside him, Randy poured a tall glass of lemonade and handed it to Tony. "Here, take a sip of this. Momma's cure for just about everything that ails you!"

"Thanks." Tony reached out to take the glass. "The demons had a huge chain they were dragging along behind them. Attached to the end of the chain was Jim McFlurry. His face a picture of sheer terror, as the demons pulled him along the boardwalk through us heading in the direction of the old Stillmore Mine. I can still hear his screams." Tony felt his throat closing. He got a little choked up at the thought of what he had seen.

Tony pushed on. "Behind Jim walked a tall demon prince dressed in a black duster with dark glasses." Tony paused momentarily to take a methodical sip of his lemonade. "He had long black hair fastened behind his head with a ruby. I've seen a ruby like that before, but where? Was it in a mafia film? Did my great-grandma have a ruby like that? Did I see one in a documentary about the lives of the royal family? Or was it on a wax figure at the museum?" In complete mental exhaustion now, Tony collapsed back on the sofa.

"Careful, boy!" Randy said. "You look as contorted as one of them Chinese acrobats. You remind me of my ol' kettle just before it's going to blow."

Tony stared blankly ahead without even acknowledging Randy. "Blood-red rubies... blood-red rubies..." Tony put his hands on his forehead. "Oh Lord, quicken my memory!"

Like a lit flare exploding in her face, the graphic image of Jim slumped over his wooden bench in a pool of blood burned itself into Sharon's mind. She made a motion to turn and run back outside, but she felt consumed with nausea. She thought she was going to vomit or black out, but with a gloved hand the demon prince turned her head again to Jim.

Jim! What foolish thing have you gone and done?

Pain pierced her heart like a knife twisting deep. Grief enveloped her.

The prince led Sharon with one hand to Jim's side, where she stood shaking. With the hand of evil now upon her shoulder, Sharon managed to miraculously compose herself and wipe the tears from her eyes.

"There, that's my girl," the demon prince seemed to say.

Instantly, as if a huge python had constricted away all her compassion, Sharon stood up straight. "Well, I'm not going to end up like this. You were a fool not to take the money, Jim, but that's your loss now. I'm going to get what I can from this town before I turn into an old maid!" She turned from Jim's fallen body and walked towards the door. "This just means one less postcard to send from my winter resort."

The prince stood smiling in the doorway as Sharon passed through him, like a duellist who thinks the victim deserving of their fate.

High in the mid-heavens, the queen reflected the prince's smile. She lifted her chalice to her lips and drank deep. The demon princes followed suit.

"To the high prince!" toasted the queen.

"Victory is his!" shouted the demon princes back.

CHAPTER TWENTY-ONE

"A serpentine blade with a blood-red ruby embedded in its handle," Tony shouted as he turned the key in the lock of his condo door. "It's the queen in my dreams!"

"Well, slap the rooster and crow all the louder," replied Randy from the porch behind Tony.

"The queen in my dreams!" shouted Tony excitedly as he pushed the front door open and rushed to the kitchen to check the call display on his phone. Randy disappeared to the living room.

"Yes, two new calls!" Tony said, doing a silent victory dance before pushing the button to replay his calls.

Two new calls, Tony thought, *and just maybe one of them is from Roxanne*. The beep before the message played intensified the moment, making him feel momentarily like a contestant on a game show. His heart fluttered when he heard that the first caller was a woman.

The ecstasy was short-lived as he recognized the voice of Flora Stevenson, the teacher whose voice was usually bursting with all the sweetness of a freshly baked pecan pie. How very sad she sounded now. She was embroiled in some kind of personal crisis and wanted to talk with him, but what could be troubling her?

The booming voice of Apostle John jarred Tony out of his thoughts. Even the recording of the apostle's voice caused Tony to sense the power and anointing on his life. "Brother Tony, God bless you! You recall the story in the Bible relating to the demon from Gadara? Well, in that story is a significant word for you and your community, my brother. This word is on the forefront of my mind. Siege. It's a picture of possession, the final state of the enemy laying siege to an individual, nation, or community. I believe the Lord would have me share that word with you, Tony, to give you a greater understanding of what you may be up against. Remember, though: no matter where you are, even if it's the valley of the shadow of death, God is with you. He never forsakes you. The Lord is a warrior who enables you to destroy your enemies, and He gives you His shield of victory. One more thing, brother. If you're still going to visit Apostle Levi, will you mention to him that there's a general anointing on him? I have full confidence that you will do what I ask and more, my brother. God bless you and keep you!"

When the message ended, Tony murmured, "Thanks, Apostle."

He got up from where he had been sitting at the kitchen table, overwhelmed with feelings of ambivalence. He was sad because Roxanne hadn't called, and happy to hear from Apostle John.

A loud belly laugh lured Tony into the living room.

"I just can't get enough of these old silent films," Randy said, his eyes twinkling as if he were cherishing personal memories from a family photo album. With the reappearance of Tony from the kitchen, Randy now corrected his slouching position in the overstuffed chair. Diverting his eyes from the TV to Tony, he gave him his full attention.

Tony said, "Sorry for leaving you to entertain yourself." He let out a sigh as he sat down on the sofa. "It just shows who the real host in our house was. That was one of Roxanne's strengths. She was always so thoughtful and considerate about others' comfort."

"Well, ain't anyone waitin' on me hand and foot, boy. Ain't like I've grown accustomed to maid service. Besides, these here old silent films kept me silently entertained."

"Blood-red rubies!" Tony said randomly, as he just stared at the TV as if in a trance.

"Now, just put things on hold here for a minute, boy. You're not gonna do that peanut thing you did on the street again, now are you? 'Cause if that's the case, maybe I ought to just be takin' my leave and let you rest."

"No, wait, please!" Tony held his hand in the air like a traffic cop. "I saw the ruby in my dreams. It belonged to the queen I told you about!"

"Yeah, what of her?"

"On one occasion, the queen killed a hawk with her serpentine dagger. The dagger's handle was inlaid with blood-red rubies, the same type of ruby I saw on the demon prince who was walking down the street behind Jim McFlurry. I think my dreams are starting to spill over into my reality." Tony sounded a little nervous at the prospect. "Not only do I dream about the spirit realm, but I can also see into it. I don't know. What do you think, Randy? Is being able to see into the spirit realm a blessing or a curse?"

"Can't say I personally had the experience in all my years of walking with the Lord," replied Randy. "About the closest I ever came to seeing somethin' invisible with the naked eye was when I was in grade school. A few of us here boys ordered a pair of x-ray glasses out the back of a comic book. They were supposed to enable us to see through people's clothes, but they only succeeded in giving us headaches and eyestrain when we put 'em on. I can only truly speak as a war veteran. In combat situations, I always appreciated the ability to see the enemy."

"Yeah," said Tony aloud as he pondered Apostle John's phone message. "The demons from Gadara…"

Phil Devron approached the pulpit at the First Baptist church like he was greeting an age-old friend, completely unaware of the dark visitor sitting behind him on the stage. Phil pushed the double Windsor knot on his burgundy tie tighter against his neck and played with his navy-blue suit jacket that always seemed two sizes too big. As it was befitting for a minister to wear a suit, Phil had endured the custom, though he always felt like David in Saul's armour. Glancing at his watch to see how much time remained before the start of their Sunday morning service, Phil's instinct was confirmed. It was time. Phil took a quick sip of water from a bottle under the podium and began to address his congregation, gathered for what they expected to be another predictable Sunday morning service.

"In the twenty-some years that I've been your pastor here at First Baptist, I have never used the morning worship service to talk to you as a father to his children." Phil stared momentarily at the beautiful stained-glass windows in the sanctuary before continuing. "But as the shepherd over this flock and a father figure to you all, I must confess I'm troubled in my spirit this morning. I want to give warning to you all. First, though, I'd like to introduce a beloved brother who we are so blessed to have working in our community. His name is Shane Carvon, and he's a gifted prophet."

A tall man with stringy blond hair approached wearing a white T-shirt with a picture of the astronauts planting the American flag on the moon. Next to it read, "Man has taken one giant step to walk on one of His lights, but struggles to take small steps each day to walk in His light."

Shane smiled at Pastor Phil and took the microphone from his hand. He walked to the centre of the stage and smiled at the congregation. "I'm really excited to be alive in what is called by some the third day. I believe it to be the day of the Lord now, and I'm excited about the supernatural manifestations God will work through His people, His church. To demonstrate to the nations His kingdom rule and power, God is saying much, but we need to listen to what the Spirit is saying to the church. I'm also grateful for your pastor, who has given to my ministry. Indeed, He shall receive a prophet's reward! I encourage you not to put God in a box by failing to support your pastor's leadership. Be faithful armour-bearers to him!"

With that, Shane handed the microphone back to Phil and made his way to his seat.

"Thank you, Shane, for your encouraging words," Pastor Phil said. "I now want to say something, and I'm going to be frank. Most of you already know that many brethren from mainstream churches have criticized Shane because he charges twenty-five dollars to receive a personal word from God. Let me just say I support this young prophet and have received from him a word from God for my life. As your pastor, I can tell you that he is a prophet."

The quietness of the congregation didn't help make Phil's speech any easier. He stepped out from behind the pulpit. He lifted his head, and faced the congregation again.

"I'm concerned," he remarked with a shaky hand pointing towards the heavens. "I'm concerned about another minister, and part of the word I received from Shane convinced me to speak out this morning."

"Thank God," came a reply from a zealous member of the congregation.

"I believe Randy Foxworth is doing his congregation a great injustice by supporting Tony Epson," Phil continued. "That man is said to have touched one of our church members inappropriately. How would you feel if it were your daughter? I think Pastor Foxworth should call out this sin instead of befriending it. Cast the immoral brother out if there are no signs of repentance! This doesn't seem to be the case with Pastor Foxworth."

Phil shuffled a few papers into his Bible behind the podium, before risking his next statement. "At this point, I sadly cannot recognize Randy as a fellow pastor, nor can I have fellowship with him any longer. I suggest you all protect yourselves by avoiding his spiritual council or friendship until his relationship with Tony Epson is made clear." He finished, drawing a deep breath. "Well! Time is slipping away this morning and we don't want any burned pot roasts for lunch. So, let us close in prayer."

After a short prayer, Phil dismissed the congregation.

Afterward, Sue Henderson, wearing a tight leather skirt and black jacket, made her way through the crowd towards the pulpit.

Up close, Sue smiled at Pastor Phil. "I just wanted to thank you for your boldness to speak out, Pastor, concerning the issues the Lord has put on your heart."

"I appreciate that," Phil replied. "You can never tell when you speak as frankly as I did this morning if an angry mob will rise up and drag you outside to be stoned."

"Excuse me, Pastor. I just saw someone I need to catch before they leave." Sue dismissed herself politely.

Phil smiled as she left, then continued to greet the other parishioners who came up to see him. The dark prince stood beside him now as he shook their hands; he watched the congregation milling about, talking, collecting coats, and rushing children out the front door. None of them were aware of the slimy coating that had settled over them with the exchange of a handshake.

⌒

"Dylan, could I talk to you for a moment?" Came the sound of a feminine voice across the church foyer. Recognizing Sue's voice, and now feeling her gentle touch on his shoulder, was more than enough to turn Dylan's head.

"What's on the mind of Forest Tech's new executive manager?" Dylan asked, enjoying the attention he was getting from such a beautiful woman.

"Do you feel up to rescuing a maiden in distress? I haven't gotten my new vehicle yet and I sure could use a lift home."

Dylan was surprised to hear that. "Strange that someone with your high-paying position wouldn't have a car."

She laughed. "I'd rather take someone else's car by blackmailing them before actually purchasing one for myself."

"Ah. A girl after my own heart," he said. "It would be a very special honour to drive you home, but I have a few things to do first. I won't be long! Wait for me by the door."

"Don't keep a girl waiting too long now," Sue answered as she returned Dylan's smile.

⌒

The weary party of travellers stood at the base of the towering limestone cliffs known to many a prophet and bird of prey as Mirana.

"Allow me, my brother," Morteque said to Estravai. "You may not have enough strength to sound the call."

"The Ancient of Days has kept me all these years from the Queen of the Heavens," said Estravai. "I'll be sounding the call long after the younger brothers start following you around. But feel free to sound the call on this day."

Morteque murmured something inaudible to himself, then cleared his throat and bellowed, "All glory to the Ancient of Days, sustainer of His holy ones!"

High up in a cavern set in the limestone cliffs came the return cry: "…who works His mighty power and reveals His secrets through His holy ones!"

They then heard the squeaking of the reed basket being lowered down the side of the cliffs, sounding out its old familiar welcome for them as it had for so many brothers before them. Reaching up and grabbing the woven basket, Estravai guided it the final distance and set it in front of the group.

"Women and children first!" he joked to Morteque.

"You may make sport of me…" Morteque trailed off as he helped Estravai haul a sleepy Grenfel into the basket. Grenfel collapsed onto its woven floor like a sack of grain.

"Heads up!" said Estravai, laughing. He flung several pieces of muskox meat off Morgan's back, then gave the signal. The old Revealer of Secrets stepped away as the basket began to rise, carrying Mortque and Grenfel up the cliffs.

Morteque righted himself like a cat fallen from a tree. As he peered over its edge at Estravai, he yelled, "I was saying you may make sport of me, Estravai, but I may tell Bajeel just to leave you down there. Then we'll see who laughs last, brother! I'll send the basket for you in the morning."

Estravai was still standing at the base of the cliffs considering Morteque's brotherly competitiveness when his thoughts were interrupted by the sound of the basket making its decent from above. Smiling at the basket descending, he light-heartedly said to himself, "So I see I am missed after all."

CHAPTER TWENTY-TWO

"Good evening, I'm Rena Peterson for K7 News, broadcasting live from outside the Drummingsville School. It's a little chilly out here this evening, but I'm not sure how much warmer it'll be inside the school, as we await the start of a second highly publicized forum to hit the little community since its founding. Once again, the issues of the hour are related to community development through large corporations. Until recently, you might have honestly said you've never heard of Drummingsville. Such is not the case tonight as neighbouring communities are watching to see if these efforts will succeed or fail. Even if the country seems to be watching through a mirror darkly, they are nevertheless watching."

A chilly wind blew through, and Rena pulled up the collar of her full-length raincoat. She closed it around her neck with one hand.

I've seen worse, she thought. *Monsoons in Africa, the icy winds of the Arctic...*

"It appears the mayor and town council are beginning to arrive. We'll take a short station break now to relocate our equipment inside the gymnasium and resume our live broadcast momentarily. For now, this has been Rena Peterson with K7 News. See you shortly."

She smiled at the camera as the live feed ended. Motioning at a cameraman with a portable video unit to follow, she bolted for the gymnasium door like an athlete competing against the clock.

Inside the gymnasium, Mayor Thomas was speaking to several of the evening's guest speakers seated on the stage. Most of the gym's four hundred seats were already occupied by the time the K7 News team rushed in to begin setting up. The crew had just set their video camera in place and barely managed to get the power button turned on before Mayor Thomas rose from his seat and approached the podium.

After taking a sip of water, Mayor Thomas began speaking. "I want to thank everybody for coming out tonight. I should also like to thank our special guests for showing their support by once again taking the time to schedule our town meeting into their already busy lives."

The audience applauded.

"Thanks also to those of other communities who are watching this meeting by way of television, those who have an interest in our small town's business. And it is our business as a community that has once again ushered us onto the world stage." Like any great statesman, the mayor felt at home with this public environment, so he didn't rush matters; he took another sip of water before moving on with the agenda. Only when he was assured by the silence of the room that he had one hundred percent of the crowd's attention did he continue.

"I think perhaps it would be fitting to start with a few encouraging reports. Once again, we're privileged to have with us Mr. Grant Timmons, chief engineer for Belial Enterprise. Grant, if you'd like to come and speak at this time…"

The mayor stepped to the side of the podium.

Grant Timmons played with the ends of his handlebar moustache for a few seconds. Two dark princes looked out at the crowded auditorium through dark glasses, standing on either side of Grant.

He pushed the sleeves of his blue shirt up to his elbows and cleared his throat. "It's a pleasure to be here again, and an honour to report on the progress of the Stillmore Mine. As I speak, diamonds are being mined in the honeycomb caverns deep beneath the quiet, relatively unchanging streets of your community. There are three major jewellery chains interested in buying Drummingsville diamonds. The potential for Drummingsville to compete in the world markets looks very promising. The main setback, as I foresee, is that our cutting and polishing plant is only half-built, and we're not yet reaching our peak production. Be encouraged, though! Belial Enterprise is considering all avenues for speeding up completion of the new processing plant. We are very excited about the Stillmore Mine. Thank you!"

Grant turned to make his way back to his seat.

Like the ringmaster of a circus, Mayor Thomas once again took control of the podium. "Thank you for your encouraging update. I would now like to call on Dr. Robert Michaels, who recently joined the staff of the Belial Abortion Clinic, to come and speak to us."

"Thank you, Mayor Thomas," said Dr. Michaels as he pushed his plastic-framed glasses further up the bridge of his nose. He flashed a Colgate smile. "I must say I'm extremely delighted to be a resident of your beautiful community. My report tonight isn't about reopening the old can of worms of debating the issue of abortion. Rather, I want to talk about another essential service the Belial Abortion Clinic will soon be offering to Drummingsville's citizens. The doctors of the Belial clinic were so grieved by the tragedy of the bus hijacking that, in a unanimous decision, they decided to open their new clinic in the Victorian house to those seeking to overcome substance addictions. I'm really excited to be able to contribute my services as a counsellor, and to support the clinic's vision."

Dr. Michaels paused to listen to the audience. There were awkward coughs, the sound of nervous fidgeting, and a mixture of both negative and positive remarks.

"We need more services!"

"About time we got something rather than just the bigger communities!"

"God alone has the right to take a life!"

Smiling, Dr. Michaels tried to soothe the people's anxiety. "It appears there's a diversity of opinions in the room. That's okay. Arriving at change is often a process of taking many steps over a long period of time to mature into a new pattern. On the other hand, getting back to my report, the Victorian house the doctors have recently purchased for their clinic is currently housing one female client in its upstairs apartment. She and her young son are taking advantage of the clinic's highly qualified medical and counselling staff. Indeed, I believe the Belial clinic has already caused many good things to happen for the community of

Drummingsville. At our clinic, individuals suffering from drug addiction can gain the ability to choose and enjoy a healthier lifestyle."

On that positive note, he concluded his presentation. He picked up his notes and walked back to his seat.

"We are very grateful tonight for these reports," said Mayor Thomas as he resumed his position in the podium. "They enable us further as a community to come out of the dark ages in our thinking. Now, I'd like to draw attention to what the locals in Drummingsville have dubbed the 'big one.' That is, the colossal construction project that was recently completed in our community. For those of you watching by television, I'm referencing the new pride and joy of Drummingsville: our super mall!"

Brief applause followed. Some were excited for this change in the community. Still others were uneasy; with stony expressions, they sat with their arms crossed and leaned back in their chairs.

"I want to put to rest any fear or doubt that might linger in some of your hearts. In regards to a community the size of Drummingsville supporting such a mall, it's important to remember that this is a productive mining town now. Secondly, I'd ask each of you to do what I have done, and that is to walk through the mall and just observe. Let its endless maze of waterslides overwhelm you, its international cuisine seduce your appetite, its unlimited specialty shops take your breath away. Let the mall's numerous aquariums, full of exotic and colourful sea life, soothe your troubled minds. And let its amazing, mind-bending rides cause your head to swirl. I can assure you, even when you pinch yourself it will remain a reality. As residents of Drummingsville, you can now enjoy the mall experience on a daily basis, if you so choose—a shopping extravaganza undreamed of by our town forefathers.

"I will go further to say that the fruit of this money tree is already being reaped by our citizens. People from all over are flying in because we took a step of faith as a small community and built the 'big one.' Yes, we built it! People are coming, getting into the sales lines of our mall's many specialty shops. They're coming to hand over their hard-earned money to our merchants, to make our cash registers ring for once, a sound many a local merchant can tell you was almost forgotten. People come to give us hope, to add excitement to the discussion groups of our local coffeehouses. The people come to fill our streets with laughter. The people come because we had the faith to take action, and now our dreams are our reality!"

With this inspired message and passionate decree, the mayor resolutely braced the edges of the podium and leaned forward. He looked intently at the audience and waited for their response, which he assumed would be stirred to action. He felt his performance had been quite convincing, and with satisfaction he saw his constituents nod with agreement.

Yet some of the audience appeared to need further nudging. Mayor Thomas smiled and resumed speaking.

"Enough, though, about the mall. I trust that most who make Drummingsville their home have had their faith rejuvenated, aroused as if from a long sleep! It's been a long time since many have had anything to cheer about, and I say to you that your hour has come! And now, having said all that, I'd like to open the floor to questions."

"Excuse me," Randy said as he made his way from a row of seats near the back. Scuffing the toe of his snakeskin boot on the floor, he looked up towards the front of the gym. "I hate to be the one to pop the balloon here, but in my thinking, when a man—I should say an ol' friend like Jim McFlurry—is driven to take his life 'cause of all the pressure to be part of this uncontrollable monster we're creating, I get real concerned! Because the monster may turn and eat us as well, just like it ate Jim. It ain't all a picture of roses!"

"You're just like Jim!" Sharon Tillman jumped up from her front row seat. A dark prince standing beside her duplicated her every gesture, his gloved finger pointing right at Randy. "It's pig-headed people like you, Randy, who will end up dragging Drummingsville right back into the dark ages. I knew Jim, too! I, for one, would rather be riding on the steamroller of progress than standing in front of it!"

Randy shook his head. "I don't see the Sharon I've talked to on more than one occasion over coffee. The Sharon I knew had the patience to teach beginners how to cross-stitch. No, sadly, the woman I see here tonight is just the shell of that girl."

Mayor Thomas started to get up to re-establish order, but Grant put his hand on the mayor's wrist and forced him to sit back down. No sooner had the mayor's backside made contact with his chair than Phil Devon jumped to his feet.

"I'm appalled!" Phil's face was bright red. "I'm sickened by your comments tonight, Randy, being a minister of the gospel! That you would even think of passing judgment on a person's character, and to do it in a public forum, is absolute foolishness. I thought you had more wisdom than that, that you were more sensitive to others. I see tonight I was wrong in my assessment of you." His nostrils flared like an enraged stallion. "What right do you have to give your opinion on community affairs, or people's lives for that matter, when you choose to befriend the likes of one who's being charged with a hit-and-run, and who also most likely has touched a fine young lady from our community inappropriately? Go home, you prophet of doom!"

A loud crack reverberated through the gym like wood being split on a cold winter's day. Randy winced and grabbed his left arm with his right hand; it quickly reddened, a growing circle of blood saturating the left sleeve of his flannel shirt.

Several dark princes were walking amidst the rows like mafia hit men; instead of brandishing guns, they waved their hands in the air, seeming to create a panic. Women began screaming, chairs were knocked over, and Sheriff Ryder stood in the midst of the chaos getting more exasperated by the minute like a misunderstood mime.

It seemed to Randy, in his state of shock, that everyone in the room was moving in slow motion. Then he saw an individual in the crowd wearing a black balaclava and waving a gun in the air. Distracted, he failed to see the K7 News team being bowled over by the gunman. Their camera flew into the air. The gunman then stopped and fired several shots before kicking some chairs out of his path.

At the sound of shots being fired, several dark princes again moved through the auditorium, causing people to trip and push each other in a frenzied state.

Still waving his gun in the air, the gunman slammed into Flora Stevenson by the gym door. For what seemed like an eternity, she seemed to fall. In horror, Randy watched her head bounce several times off the hardwood floor like a rubber ball.

"No!" he cried out in vain as his compassionate pleas fell on deaf ears, amidst all the screaming, crashing of chairs, and reverberations from the gym door being slammed closed. Adding to the chaotic noise in the gymnasium was the dark princes' laughter, which seemed to bring up the volume in the room to a crescendo. Noticing the extreme panic they were now causing in the room, the dark princes smiled at each other and stepped over Flora's unconscious body and out the door to follow in the footsteps of the lone gunman.

Laughter rang throughout the mid-heavens as the dark princes approached the Queen of the Heavens, smiling with great satisfaction. She tossed her black hair with one hand and clasped her chalice in the other.

"So, my spider is slowly sucking the blood out of its prey," she whispered, "but I shall have the blood of the apostles and prophets in Drummingsville, just as I have tasted in Ascar." The thought of the slowness of her diabolical plan now darkened the queen's expression, and she threw her chalice where her princely council had just recently vacated, having sensed a change in her mood.

Chapter Twenty-Three

G renfel yawned and rubbed his eyes, afraid that if he fell asleep his head would hit the wooden plank table, which was less festively set now than when he had first visited the grand chamber.

Morteque turned to Estravai. "I would have left you the whole night to keep Morgan company had not Eltarz suggested that your presence at this meeting would be highly beneficial to all."

"Too bad you didn't leave me," Estravai said. "I would have preferred the company of Morgan over you. It would have been a welcomed change. Morgan's breath may be bad, but at least he doesn't snore."

Estravai just had time to smile at Morteque before the room succumbed to complete silence as Eltarz entered the chamber.

Eltarz waved off the formality of announcing his entrance with a ram's horn. His countenance seemed far from festive this night.

"Brothers, I greet you in the name of the Ancient of Days." Eltarz picked up a clay goblet from the end of the table, as all the brothers did likewise. "The cup from which we drink this night is a mixture of both sorrow and joy, of laughter and tears. We are highly jubilant upon the return of our brothers Estravai and Morteque, along with the boy Grenfel, who the Ancient of Days is maturing as a Hawkman. On the other hand, they have informed me that King Ulrich has been taken. That is the reason for the great sadness in our hearts tonight."

Whispers filled the chamber, sounding like a forest of chattering ground squirrels.

"Tis the work of the queen!" shouted one of the younger brothers.

"No doubt the queen had her hand in King Ulrich's removal from Castle Kreniston," Eltarz said. "The visions we have received from the Ancient of Days reveal that the price of Ascar's freedom from Meldrock's grip is the collection of the king's soul itself." The news swept through the chamber like a silent wind. Many of the brothers' spirits seemed on the verge of failing as they wept for their king.

Eltarz chose his next words carefully so as to infuse courage into their heavy hearts. "Remember the prophecy! The anointing of the Hawkman signifies the beginning of a portal being opened, of the two witnesses powerfully declaring the name of the Ancient of Days, and of many powerful works being done by their hands. Meldrock's power will diminish! Though it seems like a dark hour now, the morning comes." He paused, looking across the assembled faces. "Estravai and Morteque, come forward!"

The very sound of his name caused Estravai to smile at his beloved mentor.

Morteque pushed a sleeping Grenfel off his shoulder as both he and Estravai made their way along the table.

"I knew we should have returned after Dremcon," Morteque whispered to Estravai, "but you thought we should venture south. Now we're probably going to be told we were away too long."

"The place and length of time we tarried was not of my doing," Estravai said to him just before they came to stand before Eltarz.

"Estravai!" Eltarz spoke. "Did you not empty the contents of your flask upon the boy Grenfel's head due to the sign of the shooting star in the sky, and as a witness to the foretold key to the return of the Hawkman?"

"Yes," Estravai said, wondering what road Eltarz's questions were leading him down.

"Likewise, when your party encountered two dark princes en route to the ice fields, is it not true that they were in the process of overwhelming you with lies, until you heard a song being sung by our beloved brother Omri as he faithfully journeyed across the ice fields in response to the Ancient of Days' command? What effect did the boy Grenfel's singing have on the two demon princes?"

"The princes were burned up by the Ancient of Days' fire." Estravai thought he saw a twinkle in Eltarz's eyes. Were these questions perhaps for the benefit of the others?

"How was it that you come again to us at this season, Estravai?" Eltarz asked.

"It happened by way of the boy's dream."

"Go on." Eltarz motioned as his hand once again came to rest under his grey-bearded chin.

"As it has already been told, our good brother Omri's song came upon us shortly after he arrived and led us to the ice house inhabited by a close friend of his—the very ice house where other servants of the Ancient of Days also fled to the frozen land to hide. Late one night, the boy departed from our company to take a rest. After a period of time, he awoke crying out in great distress and fear. I ran immediately to where Grenfel lay, and through his tears I heard him say that the king was gone. In Grenfel's dream, he saw the act just after it was committed and heard his mother's words as she lay on the floor of the royal bedchamber. She whispered, 'The king's gone.' I bear witness to all that I have spoken, and I stake my honour upon it."

"Estravai, Morteque, listen carefully, and then answer." Eltarz spoke now with the authority invested in him by the Ancient of Days. "Do you bear witness of the boy Grenfel being a vessel of the Ancient of Days, such that he speaks His very words against Meldrock's dark forces? As well, do you believe the boy Grenfel is being used by the Ancient of Days in disclosing the enemy's movement, and his dark deeds, by way of dreams and visions? Answer to the fellowship."

"We do," responded Estravai and Morteque in unison, facing the brothers.

"Good!" Eltarz smiled, lifting his hands in thanksgiving to the Ancient of Days. "I suggest before you all, my brothers, that the time has come to release the hawk!"

"Release the hawk!" Tony said aloud as he banged on Randy's door. "Release the—"

The door flew open. "I ain't keepin' any hawks and I don't figure you're the town's wildlife officer neither," Randy said.

"Oh, sorry. It's just a thought that came from my dreams."

"You sure your real name ain't Joseph?" Randy laughed as Tony followed him up the stairs and into the kitchen.

"How's the arm?" Tony asked as he straddled one of the kitchen chairs.

"It hurt me a whole lot less at the meeting than my heart, and that's the simple truth of the matter. I've had me a few other scratches like the one on this here arm of mine. This one ain't so special and appears to be mendin' just fine. Coffee?"

"Sounds good." Tony picked up a block of wood off the table, noticing the outline of a spoon etched into its surface, and the handle already partially carved.

Randy put down two cups of coffee and sat. "Been doing a bit of whittling' again."

"Looks pretty serious to me."

"Ain't all that special. Just another trinket I can't take to heaven with me." Randy stirred his coffee slowly.

"Sounds like it was a wild town meeting," Tony commented as he took a sip.

"Yeah, it was a strange one." Randy shook his head at the very memory of the previous night's activity.

"I was planning to go, but I lay in bed just for a minute and fell asleep with my boots on. I missed the whole meeting. Guess I was more burned out from my trip than I thought. And to think I went away to rest!" Tony finished his coffee and paused to consider how to say what was really on · his mind. "I kind of need a ride, Randy, if you're not too busy. Since my truck was impounded, I find myself without transportation."

Randy grinned. "I guess my whittlin' can wait. Can't have you wearin' out your shoes on account of me, now can I, boy?"

"Well, I really want to go visit Apostle Levi. My dream the other night ended with the words I was muttering on your doorstep. I believe the Lord wants us to go see Apostle Levi, and that if we go, God will be faithful to release His hawk. I mean, you do still feel compassionate towards our brother since we last talked, right? Maybe I presumed that."

Randy stared down at the red and white checkered tablecloth for a moment. "Ain't nothin' you presumed. I was just sittin' here thinkin' how much more I can relate to ol' Levi now. Strange things are happening. People I thought I knew seem different. An ol' prayer partner calls me a 'prophet of doom' at a town meeting. I get all shot up in the arm. It's like a big ol' dragon tail coming out of nowhere to hit you when you have your head turned, and afterwards you don't even know what hit you. No, I think I can relate to that there ol' boy a bit more now that I've walked in the same shoes of adversity he has. Just sit tight, Tony, and let me fetch my truck keys."

"Can I use your phone for a minute?" Tony asked as Randy stepped into the hall.

"Yeah! The thing's gotta earn its keep."

Tony dialled his friend Max and listened as the answering machine relayed its greeting, then the beep. "Hey Max, it's Tony. Randy and I are heading out to Crester's Cave to see Apostle Levi. I was hoping you could join us."

Still holding the receiver to his ear, Tony whispered a quick prayer.

"Lord, you know I don't like leaving messages, but please help Max hear this in time."

With the sound of Randy's returning footsteps, Tony hung up the receiver.

"All right, then," Randy said. "We best be getting' ourselves into the gap now. Maybe the Good Shepherd will let us assist Him in bringin' a lost sheep back into the fold."

Randy's beat-up but much-loved truck pulled up under the burnt-out neon motel sign and parked.

"So, this is Crester's Cave." Tony surveyed the water-stained stucco motel with its dark wooden doors and Christmas lights still hanging from its eaves. He saw the "No Vacancy" sign in the office window and thought, *I find that hard to believe.* He pushed the truck door open, causing it to groan on its rusty hinges. Motorcycles were parked in a long row out front like horses tied up outside a saloon. Pushing the truck door closed, Tony stood in disbelief at the "No Vacancy" sign. He whispered a silent prayer thanking God for his river view condominium.

Randy's familiar voice punctuated the end of Tony's prayer. "No sense poking around out here, boy. Come on, let's get on with things."

Making their way to the door with the gold star painted on it, Tony now read the word "office" which had being painted in black letters through the star.

Randy said, "Go on, boy. Give it a knock. Let's see if the sheriff's in."

"The door's open!" came a gruff reply from within.

Tony cautiously pushed the office door open and walked into its stale-smelling air. A little old lady chewing gum and reading the *Drummingsville Star* stood behind an old brown arborite counter.

"There's no vacancy!" she growled. "Just like the sign says."

"I'm not looking for a room," said Tony.

"Well then, it will cost you two dollars to wash and another two dollars to dry a load."

"That's not it, either," said Tony. "I heard you might have a Levi Brandon staying here."

"Number forty-one. Go out the door and all the way down to the end." The manager snapped her gum and continued to read the paper, not once looking up at either man.

"Thanks, I guess," Tony said as they left.

"Ain't nothin' like these five-star hotels for their service."

Their attention was diverted by the blast of a horn. Tony's face lit up with a big smile at the sight of the blue station wagon parked beside Randy's old truck.

"Max!" shouted Tony as he approached the station wagon. "Good to see you!"

Max leaned out his open window and pushed up his pilot's cap. "Good to see you, too, dude! It's been a while."

"I was afraid you wouldn't get my message."

"I got it, all right! I was just praying I wouldn't be too late."

"Your timing, or I'll say His timing, is always perfect." Tony smiled at his friend and noticed Randy approach. "By the way, do you know Randy Foxworth, the pastor of Drummingsville Christian Centre?"

"Yeah, we know each other," Max said. "We've done coffee a few times. Good to see you again, Randy!"

"Good to see you again, too. A fella can never have too many friendly faces in his day, but I'm afraid if I stand here too long I'll get to reminiscing about days past and the sun will dun set on us."

Tony nodded. "We should check and see if Levi's in. I mean, isn't that why we're here?"

"Come on, boys!" said Randy as Max stepped out of his car. "In our pride, we walked by the wounded on the Jericho Road once too often. The time has come to be good Samaritans, long as we expect Samaritans to ever give mendin' to our wounds."

"It's time, indeed," said Tony. "Time to see a hawk released."

"What?" Max asked.

"Dreams!" Randy said. "It appears we have a Joseph in our midst."

Max grinned. "That's not a problem with me—I'm not a baker."

Chapter Twenty-Four

"I'm unable to come to the door right now," a disgruntled voice called out of the room. "Go away or leave a message at the motel office!"

The blue glow of the television screen flashed through the motel room curtains as the channels kept changing. Like a federal agent glancing at his stakeout partners, Tony peered at Randy and Max.

"Just keep bangin'," Randy said.

"Go away!" Levi growled.

If Randy felt frustrated, he didn't show it. "You best answer! You don't want to be gettin' the other motel occupants mad, because we're gonna stick here a-bangin' on your door like barnacles on a ship."

"Can't a normal human being have a bit of privacy?" muttered Levi as he shut the television off.

"A bit's fine!" shouted Randy. "But you're turnin' into an ol' hermit crab."

"All right, give me a minute!" This was followed by the loud banging of bottles being tossed in the garbage.

The motel door opened a moment later and there stood Levi dressed in a white tank top that fit him like a tent. He wore green and yellow plaid boxer shorts that hung below the knees, and what used to be white athletic socks were a dirty grey colour. With the stubble on his unshaven face, Levi looked like a human porcupine. He offered no apologies for his appearance. Sadly, Tony also noticed the look of wonderment absent from his eyes from the first time he had seen the apostle.

"I suppose you've all come to fire deadly arrows with your tongues," Levi said as he looked at the group standing at the door. "Well, go ahead and get it over with so I can get back to watching TV. I can't fall much further from here, anyway."

Randy stepped out from the others. "I need to ask you to forgive me, Levi. I was one of the people who used his tongue like a sword to strike at you and your ministry."

Levi stared at the ground for a minute. "I got knocked right off my high horse after the hijacking, bombarded with accusations from both the church and the media. It's gotten to the point that I don't expect anything different now. The attacks that hurt most, though, were the ones from those who lifted their cup with me. My financial support took a dive into the cellar. I lost my ministry and personal assets, so I declared bankruptcy."

Like a boxer with all his wounds exposed, Levi faced them courageously.

There's got to be a thousand voices screaming out within him to run back into the motel room again, like all the other times, and slam the door in our faces, Tony thought.

"It's a bit draughty out here," Levi said. "Why don't we go on inside?"

The invitation brought Tony out of his thoughts. "Um! Sorry," responded Tony like a parent who had fallen asleep while their child was reading to them. "Yes! Inside would be great," Tony repeated enthusiastically.

Not surprised by their friend's behaviour, Randy and Max smiled at Tony before following Levi into his motel room. The overpowering stench of old fish cans and week-old garbage combined with the smell of stale socks to nearly suck the breath right out of them. Even Randy, who had endured much discomfort on the battlefield, was relieved when Levi offered them a chair. Levi then pulled out a metal kitchen chair with an unscrewed seat and sat in it.

Tony sat beside Levi silently composing his thoughts. There were a few awkward moments of staring at the condiments on the table experienced before Tony said, "Forgive us, Levi. You probably don't even know who you're sitting with."

"I've seen your faces around," Levi said, "though I wasn't too worried about who you were. Talking to anybody is better than talking to my TV. I don't get many visitors anymore, not even the angry ones."

"Well, all the same, I'm Tony Epson, ex-smoke-jumper, and sitting next to me is the pastor of the Drummingsville Christian Centre, Randy Foxworth. Next to him is Max Lumstrom. Max and his wife do mission work."

Levi chuckled. "A battered apostle, a pastor, and a missionary. We can have a church council meeting, and a safe one, too, with our fire fighter here. No fear of revival flames burning down the place." But then Levi stopped chuckling, and a faraway look appeared in his eyes along with an intense expression of longing for days gone by.

Tony cleared his throat and explained that they weren't in the habit of dropping in on folks just to make them feel uncomfortable.

"Well, y'all could have fooled me!" Randy said, smiling.

Tony's face turned red. "I bring greetings to you from Apostle John Bristane."

"John!" Levi exclaimed, shaking his head. His face brightened and a small tear glistened in the corner of his eye.

"Apostle John told me to tell you that there's a general's anointing on you," Tony said. "He believes the enemy's plan was to sift you, but John also wanted you to know he's praying for you."

Levi sat back in his chair, reminiscing. "Never could hide anything from John. He'd always expose the snares of the enemy in my life, and speak the word of God to my situations. It seemed like the hammer hit the nail every time, even now. John's got it right again, and from so far away. Though I didn't always enjoy when John spoke the word of God over my life, cuz sometimes it was like God grabbing me by my shirt collar and saying, 'Now you listen to me, Levi!' But I gotta admit, I appreciate John, though the dimension of anointing he walks in as an apostle caused the fear of God to come on me at times. I'm afraid reality is a crueller taskmaster than John's anointed words of correction, though." Levi shook his head. "Got some instant coffee if you're interested."

"Yeah," said Max. "I'm starting to get a headache. I must be suffering from withdrawals already. Just kidding! But I never say no to a good cup of coffee."

"Great. I'll put the kettle on." Levi got up and filled the kettle with water. "Come to think of it, you boys look as if you've all seen better days yourselves."

Randy smiled. "Yeah, we're just your regular garden variety wounded soldiers."

"I had a dream about you, Levi," Tony finally said. "Actually, two dreams."

Randy smiled again, this time at Tony. "Oh, I forgot to add dreamers."

"Well, you sound just like my kind of people." Levi looked like he was enjoying himself for the first time in quite a while.

"I'd like to explain the dreams," Tony said. "In the first dream, Levi, I saw us at Miranna—that's the dwelling place of these prophet dudes called Revealers of Secrets in my dreams, whose job it is to see on behalf of their king. In my dream, you and I were at Miranna, both of us novices to be trained to be Revealers of Secrets for the king of Ascar."

Both men listened as Tony described in detail the tense training exercise with the blindfolds and bow and arrow. Finally, Tony said, "I guess the dream was pointing out the fact that when apostles and prophets work together in unity, they can effectively do damage to demonic strongholds over an individual, city, or nation."

"This is better than TV," Levi chimed in as he poured hot water into a cup of instant coffee and stirred it around.

"I'm glad y'all think so," Randy said. "I know another dreamer whose brothers were less than tickled with his dreams. But you're playing to a better crowd today, Tony!"

"Thank the Lord," Tony said. "Now, the second dream is based on the story of David and Goliath. I saw a battlefield with the army of Israel forming a line along its edge. The field was empty of any soldiers representing the Lord for a season. The single occupant on the battlefield was consistently Goliath, for what seemed to be a humiliating time for God's army. However, God is sovereign, and soon His chosen vessel in the boy David appeared and stepped out of rank with the army of Israel. He crossed the threshold of the battlefield to face this giant who thoughtlessly defied the living God. David knew His God was with him and that His Lord was a warrior.

"As a result of David's faith and obedience, Goliath fell. The main point is that most of the church is standing on the sidelines of the battlefield, for whatever reason. But God is raising up those who are able to see into the enemy's camp and who aren't afraid to come out of the ranks and onto the battlefield against disease and end-time spirits. They're able to accurately discern the evil they face and speak the words of God against the demonic strongholds over their towns, cities, and nations. These anointed ambassadors won't just see natural walls fall, like the walls of Jericho, but also walls in the spirit realm."

Levi watched him closely. "I get the feeling there's more purpose to your visit than flaunting your coat of many colours."

"That's one way to say it," Randy said. "The hijacking of your bus, the framing of a school teacher in a sex scandal, the reopening of the Stillmore Mine, the construction of a new super mall, the death of Jim McFlurry, the false rumours that Tony inappropriately touched a co-worker, Tony's truck getting hit and his upcoming court date, as well as the numerous physical and verbal attacks all over town... they all point to the fact that an enemy force is laying siege to Drummingsville and destroying it stone by stone. Tony says it's all the work of end-time spirits. I reckon I never saw one personally in my dreams, but it looks to me like you got tangled with something demonic, Levi, and it's been swinging its tail at us. But I can say one thing for sure, as a veteran combatant: I know the signs of war."

"End-time spirits," Levi muttered. "I sure wasn't looking out for them up on my high horse."

"Tony here's been havin' a series of continual dreams," Randy went on. "But why don't I just clam on up and let the boy speak for himself."

Tony swallowed. "I feel as if I added fuel to the fire of adversity that came against you, Levi, and I want you to know I'm ashamed of that. However, because of my initial persecution of your ministry, God led me to study the apostles, and I started having graphic recurring dreams whose cast would be the envy of any stage play, with the likes of a Hawkman, Revealers of Secrets, Belial, Leviathan, and the Queen of the Heavens. Paralleling the beginning of these dreams, my reality began to fall apart, as I'm sure you can understand. You of all people are familiar with rumours. Well, it's been said I touched a co-worker inappropriately, my truck was hit by a Porsche with the name of an end-time spirit on its back plate, I now have an upcoming court date related to me supposedly hitting a Dr. Anderson, my wife was on your hijacked bus, I got let go from my job, and my wife and son left me to go live with her mother in West Georgia. As a further bizarre twist, Randy and I were walking down the street shortly after Jim McFlurry shot himself, and I saw demons dragging him down the street in chains toward the Stillmore Mine, as clear as I see you sitting in your chair. The frightening thing was the demon prince following Jim McFlurry up the street. He had a blood-red ruby in his hair, the same as I've seen in my dreams. It's like the characters in my dreams are spilling out into my reality."

Levi sat forward, wide-eyed in his chair. "What ever happened to safe religion, where you just come to church with your family on Sunday morning all dressed up and sing a few hymns that make you feel warm and tingly?"

"I'm afraid the enemy dun got into our camp, cuz we were all having one too many potluck dinners," Randy said. "Not that I don't appreciate a good piece of chicken myself. But now God's placed His watchman on the walls of the church. No longer will the thief be able steal into the camp of God's people without detection, nor our cities and towns for that matter. Not as long as the likes of Joseph walk among us. Those who just sit in the boat singing warm tingly hymns in a time of war, saying 'Peace! Peace!' may find themselves passed over by the one who walks upon the waves."

Tears erupted from Levi's eyes. "I'm all washed up, though, boys!"

"I don't believe that," Tony said, "though I can understand why you feel that way. The gifts of God are irrevocable. Think of David as a young boy who got anointed with oil by a prophet, then told he would be king. It didn't happen until later in his life. First he learned to tangle with the lion and bear, and let's not forget Goliath. You're a hawk, Levi.

You received a prophetic word about the headship ministry of an apostle, but I believe you haven't yet really understood what it's all about, even though you've used the title. I believe God is going to release you as a mature apostle and send you forth with power."

"I really would like to encourage you, Levi," said Max as he stretched out his legs under the table. "How we say it in the world of hockey is it's time to put your game jersey on again!"

CHAPTER TWENTY-FIVE

Tony felt a cold chill run down his spine as he spotted the silver Porsche parked with its engine running outside the Drummingsville General Store. Seeing the car with its unforgettable plate right here on the streets of Drummingsville felt like an invasion of his personal privacy. Tony couldn't make out the driver through the tinted windows, but he suddenly felt nauseous and afraid. He tried to turn and continue on to the store, but the Porsche's very presence set his nerves on edge.

The door of the general store flung open and Roxanne rushed out carrying a plastic bag full of groceries in one hand, and dragging Jordan along with her other.

"Roxanne!" Tony yelled. "When did…"

But Roxanne whisked herself and Jordan past him like tumbleweed down an empty street. Tony walked into the store, his eyes tearing up as he heard Jordan crying.

"Daddy!"

Everything looked blurry as Tony felt his way around the shelves, grabbing blindly at boxes, then stopping at the back of the store to wipe his eyes and practice smiling in the mirrors used to show off the fresh vegetables.

"Is this all?" Martha asked at the checkout. "Just five packages of diet pudding?"

"Yes, that's it. Did Roxanne say anything?" Tony couldn't help asking as he looked up at the owner of the general store.

Martha simply handed Tony his plastic bag.

"Thanks anyway, Martha," Tony said, struggling to keep it together long enough to get outside and inhale a big breath of fresh air.

⌇

"I'm here to talk with Principal Reeves," said Michelle Starr, a lanky woman with long black hair. She looked like she'd be more at home on the set of a fashion shoot than as a teacher at a school.

"Go right in," the secretary said. "I believe he's expecting you."

"Thanks." Michelle walked towards Principal Reeves' door. "You must let me read your cards sometime, Marlene."

Her knock on the office door aroused a business-like growl from within, which had served him in the past in gaining a few extra moments of solitude needed to check through some of his often neglected files.

"Come in!" he finally bellowed, realizing with this caller he would get none of the solitude he sought. "Oh, Ms. Starr! I apologize. I was just trying to type my final remarks on a report. I seem to be always pressed for time. Just sit down, please. I'll only be a moment."

"Thank you." Michelle gazed at the rich Babylonian décor.

"Does my taste in art meet with your approval, Ms. Starr?" Reeves inquired, looking over the top of his laptop computer.

"I had no idea you were a collector," Michelle said. "I never dreamed of seeing such extravagant pieces in a principal's office."

"You collect, I assume, Ms. Starr?"

"No! Just an admirer. But one who's consumed with studying what she can about ancient civilizations in her spare time, specifically Egyptian and Babylonian."

"Well, that is most interesting." Reeves picked up a folder off his desk and deposited it in one of his desk drawers. Brushing his hands together, he looked right at Michelle. "How do you like your students?"

She crossed her right leg and leaned forward to ensure she was the centre of Principal Reeves' attention. "I think they're typical children for their age."

"No outstanding concerns, then?"

"Not that I've encountered."

"That's good. I think you're doing a fine job. Tell me, though, if a boy comes up and tells you when he grows up he'd like to marry another boy, what would you say to that student?"

"I would affirm his choice."

"You wouldn't be troubled?" Principal Reeves asked. "Some of your students might be involved with adult websites."

"Nothing shocks me all that much. After studying ancient civilizations with their systems full of promiscuity, orgies, and violent rituals, what new things could a few young kids discover?"

Principal Reeves broke into a grin. "Well, I must say, I'm very glad to have you on the team here. As much as I liked Flora, she had a hard time not imposing her religious beliefs on her students, as well as other staff members. Is hearing about Flora upsetting? I know she's still in her coma."

"Not in the least. Her situation is not relevant to my life."

"Well, you're doing an excellent job." He glanced at his watch. "I really shouldn't delay you any longer. After all, you have to prepare for your class. Just one more thing, though, if you might spare me another moment of your time—"

"Oh, I might be persuaded for the right incentive."

"Good! Because I would be greatly honoured to have you view my private collection of ancient artefacts at home. I have an excellent miniature statue of Ishtar."

Michelle beamed at him. "How unexpected and exciting. As it turns out, I'm greatly intrigued with Ishtar."

"Well, then, you really must join us," said the principal. "I host a group of affluent community members who gather because of their mutual interest in Ishtar. I believe you'll find the gatherings most enjoyable, Ms. Starr.

Michelle smiled. "Yes! I believe I would as well."

Reeves stood up behind his desk. "I also want to say that I look forward to showing you some of the more prominent pieces in my collection, and perhaps discussing them with you over a good cup of coffee."

"Is this a date, then?" Michelle turned to look back at the principal.

Principal Reeves tried to keep from blushing. "I hadn't thought of it that way!"

Nonetheless, he chuckled with enjoyment at the idea.

～

Giant teeth ripped into the rock walls of the main cavern of the Stillmore Mine. The lights atop the cab of the frontend loader searched the black rock walls of the mine for precious gems, like a mechanical dinosaur with a relentless hunger.

"Roger, Belial," the operator said into his radio. "Control, this is Kyle Morris, operator of the Hades IV loader. Can you have Dylan come down into the main cavern? I've stumbled onto something strange, over."

Kyle placed the handheld radio back into its clips on the cab roof.

Before him, broken lanterns were clutched in bony hands, and pieces of tattered fabric clung to the protruding bones of a rib cage. Skeletal fingers clutched rusted picks and shiny stones. Empty eye sockets looked out from under rusted mining helmets, as though to say, *"Stay away. Let us rest in peace."*

Dylan walked into the cavern, turning his flashlight on to see heaps of rocks, strewn bones, and rotting timber. The scene resembled the aftermath of a bomb blast.

"Poor fellows!" Kyle whispered in a solemn voice.

"You saw nothing here tonight," Dylan replied in an authoritative tone. "We don't want to get the good people of the town worked up over nothing, then find ourselves out of a job, now do we?"

"No, I need this job," Kyle said. "I have a family."

"Good! Then we understand each other. Get this cavern sealed back up, quickly. It never existed as far as we're concerned. Do you understand what I'm saying?"

"Yes, sir," answered Kyle as he climbed back into the loader, now wishing he had never agreed to work the overtime. The light of Dylan's flashlight shone towards the elevator shaft as he proceeded hastily towards it, accompanied unknowingly by a tall, dark prince.

211

Torches fastened high on the limestone walls lit the chamber.

"Arouse the boy!" Eltarz declared as he turned from the brothers to stare at the now empty space where Estravai had stood. Shaking his head and returning his gaze once more to the brothers, Eltarz detected Estravai now halfway back to his seat. "Truly a gifted Revealer of Secrets among so many," he whispered. Estravai's hand firmly but lovingly pushed Grenfel's arm where he sat sleeping with his head on the table.

"Stop it, Morgan," said a groggy Grenfel.

"It's not your horse that bids your attention, boy, but Eltarz himself."

Grenfel sat up and rubbed his eyes. "Who?"

"Eltarz," repeated Estravai. "Come. Let's not keep him waiting."

"Okay! I'm coming," Grenfel replied sharply as he rubbed sleep from his eyes, and stood to his feet.

"I might suggest," said Estravai, gesturing to the side of his face, "that you wipe the porridge off your face first."

Grenfel wiped his face with his sleeve. "Sorry for falling asleep."

"Be thankful for the shadows the torches cast, for they may hide your red face from the eyes of all present." Estravai turned to lead Grenfel along the plank tables to the front of the great chamber, where Eltarz waited.

"Time is of the essence, for Meldrock has already taken prisoners," Eltarz said. "The time for the sending out of the hawk has fallen upon us. Estravai, Morteque, join me now around young Grenfel. Let us seek to know the Ancient of Days' purpose concerning his Hawkman."

Music swirled around the high arches of the chamber like snow falling on a winter's day, as one of the brothers began to play on a flute-like instrument. As Grenfel now stood in the middle of a circle formed by the Revealer of Secrets at the front of the chamber, Eltarz laid one hand upon his shoulder and raised his other to the Heavens.

"I see a city with unnatural walls composed of giant thorns," said Eltarz. "A lone rider on a white horse riding to the edge of the cliffs. I recognize this place as Dremcon. The queen's hand outstretched, a white dove with a crimson breast falling from the sky. Talons glistening, a bird of prey rising, darkness fleeing, and captives beginning to be set free." Eltarz opened his eyes. "We of the Revealers of Secrets witness the calling of the Hawkman upon you, Grenfel, and we send you from our midst. Go in the power of the Ancient of Days."

All the gathered brothers stood and lifted their cups, saying, "May he who rides on the heavens help you!"

⌒

"Send them out, Lord," Max prayed, his face buried in his living room carpet and his body stretched prone before the Lord. "Raise up your apostles and prophets and send them into the harvest field of Drummingsville."

Tony sat up in his rocking chair and opened his eyes; he almost expected to see Eltarz in Max's living room. The cry of Max's heart seemed to echo the vision still swirling around in his head.

"Mercy, Lord, mercy!" Tony cried out, a tear trickling down his cheek. "Oh Lord, listen! Oh Lord, forgive us, for we have shamed you and been unfaithful to you."

Randy joined in from the green loveseat. "Yes, Lord! You have been patient with us, not treating us as our sins deserve, even though we have continued to wallow in our rebellion like pigs in the mud."

"Do not reject us, Lord," Levi prayed, kneeling on the carpet with his face buried in his hands. "Send your light and truth to guide us to your holy mountain, to the place where you dwell, and let us worship you before your holy altar. May you be our joy and delight." Weeping now, Levi lifted his head towards the heavens. "Lord, I'm asking for another chance. I'm placing myself in the gap, Lord, between you and the citizens of Drummingsville. Stay your hand of judgment on this community! Cause us to bend a bow of bronze to destroy our enemies, to shackle kings—or if not, then take my life."

There was now the sound of repentant weeping in the room, as if the Spirit of God had once again returned to the threshold of the temple.

Chapter Twenty-Six

With one hand, Dr. Michaels fumbled for the doorknob, at the same time juggling an armful of magazines; he finally succeeded in opening the door without so much as dropping a single issue of his subscription to The Family Counsellor. Backing into residence, Dr. Michaels managed to close the door and lean against it, and was in the process of catching a short breath when he happened to peer over his armload of magazines at Roxanne sitting in the living room.

She sat on the edge of a leopard print sofa, sipping her café mocha while Jordan played with a few blocks on the honey-coloured hardwood floor. Dr. Michaels stood motionless, just leaning against the door with his armload of magazines, staring at Roxanne. The gears of his mind turned like a grandfather clock as he pondered what verbal kiss could be offered to awaken his sleeping princess.

Finally settling in his mind, he decided to break the ice by asking, "So, how's our princess today?"

Roxanne didn't so much as flinch an eyelid. Dr. Michaels shrugged off his disappointment and occupied himself with unloading his portable library onto the table by the door. When he finished, he once more glanced at Roxanne.

"Well, then," he said, shuffling papers and magazines around on the table, "maybe it's time for another therapeutic massage, followed perhaps by a session of hypnotherapy?"

"Robert, I saw Tony today." Roxanne spoke with little life in her voice. "It happened when Dr. Anderson took us shopping."

Dr. Michaels walked into the kitchen and opened the fridge door. "Oh? How do you feel?"

"I'm not sure." Roxanne brushed the hair out of her eyes. "I feel so confused. My shoulders are tense and my heart has been racing."

"I think that what you really need to do for your health, Roxanne, is get involved with other men. Cast off restraint, as Tony has probably done by now. Who are you saving yourself for anyhow?" He took out a carton of orange juice, poured himself a glass of juice, then walked back into the living room. "You knew things back here in Drummingsville could trigger painful memories, but to progress with your recovery you chose to leave your mother's place in West Georgia. Unless you start to live your life independent of Tony, even the thought of him, you'll always have his act of unfaithfulness staring you in the face. You need to start pursuing romantic encounters again, Roxanne." Thinking of an even better solution, he added, "You know, a good way to start might be to attend one of our gatherings at Principal Reeves' home. Oh, and Jordan is welcome as well. Just think about it. It might do you a world of good."

"I can't be unfaithful, Robert," Roxanne said in a trembling voice. "My conscience would give me no rest."

Dr. Michaels polished off his glass of orange juice. "You have the right to seek romance in other places, and I believe God will excuse you from your marriage vows. What is your alternative?"

"I don't know. I haven't thought about it."

"Most likely, the thought of Tony's unfaithfulness will eat away at you, possibly pushing you over the edge of sanity or causing you to relapse. Just think about it, princess." He glanced at his watch. "I have to run downstairs to the clinic to do a session. Perhaps we can discuss your thoughts on what I've said later."

Grabbing a CD player off the table, he smiled once more at Roxanne and waved before dashing out, leaving her once again to watch her son playing on the floor.

A phone rang loudly in the plush outer room of Mayor Thomas' office. His secretary answered, "The mayor's office. Yes, Mr. Cartwright. One moment, I'll transfer your call." She turned to the mayor. "It's for you, sir. Dylan Cartwright on the line."

"Fine. Thanks, Selena. I'll take it in my office."

"Yes, sir, right away."

He picked up the phone receiver and leaned back in his leather chair. "Dylan! How are things in the construction business?"

"Excellent, overall," Dylan said. "Except I was called down into the main cavern of the mine last night."

"Technical problems?"

"No. Our frontend loader punched through a rock wall and found the site of an early mine accident."

"Really?"

"Yeah! About five to six miners still clutching at stones beneath a pile of rock and rotting timber."

"Who knows about this?" Mayor Thomas asked.

"Just another operator named Kyle Morris, and myself."

"Have you taken any action on this matter?"

"I immediately had the chamber sealed back up."

"Excellent! Dylan, we want a tight web, as Grant always puts it. We can't have this pile of old bones causing people to reconsider the need for the mine. The discovery of a past tragedy would cause Drummingsville's web of development to come undone, and neither of us would prosper from that, now would we?"

"I hear you," Dylan said. "I'll monitor the situation at the mine daily."

"Good! Always a pleasure to hear from you, Dylan."

"Yeah, likewise."

Mayor Thomas hung up the phone, sitting for a moment with his hands folded on his desk. With a sigh and a shake of his head, he picked up the phone and made a call.

"Belial Enterprises," Sharon answered.

"Hello, Sharon. How's the town's new mall manager?"

She laughed. "To tell you the truth, I'm a little overwhelmed."

"Well, I'm sure it's nothing your enthusiasm and drive can't overcome."

"I'm glad to hear you say that! I'm beginning to feel a bit like a hamster on a treadmill."

The mayor's voice suddenly took on a business-like tone. "Sharon, there are a couple of things on my mind."

"Oh? I can't imagine what."

"The higher ups of Belial Enterprises," Thomas explained, "feel that the mall's main grocery store should drop its prices for an indefinite period of time."

"I don't understand. The store is already undercutting all its competitors—"

"Yes, I realize that, but the brass don't want to just have the lowest prices in town. They want to eliminate *all* the competition."

"That means Martha will have to close the general store," Sharon said, a lump forming in her throat.

"Unfortunately, change has a price, and those who won't change will be the losers." Thomas paused for a moment, listening to Sharon's nervous breathing. "You're not getting soft on me now, are you?"

"No, no! You don't have to worry about that. I'm this town's original ice queen, if you hadn't heard." Without detection, a tall demon prince placed his hands against the sides of Sharon's head. "Martha had opportunity to sell."

"Exactly! Now you sound more like the Sharon I've gotten to know, and the girl who stopped crying long ago for others' weaknesses."

"Well, after all, business is business, isn't it?" Sharon said coldly.

"Yes, indeed it is."

The line was awkwardly silent, so Thomas fired off another volley of questions. "How's the infiltration of consumers going? Have you received any complaints? As the new mall manager, are you aware of Belial Enterprises' desire for the new mall they are financing? As they are the main financial backers to the mall project, Belial Enterprises believes it's their right to proselytize the patrons of the mall. In the minds of Belial

Enterprises, this means giving every consumer who passes through the doors of the mall a free spiritual word for their lives."

"Are you referring to the three-step WEB program? You know, Welcome/Evangelise/Blind? It appears to be going smoothly. The cashiers place a computerized fortune in every customer's bag. The security guards hand out flyers with a fortune inserted into them as well. Most of these flyers offer a free session of tarot card reading with Michelle Starr, or a personal word from God by Prophet Carvon. John from the Java Joint reports an increase in sales of occult books in the second location he's opened in the mall. John has even allowed Michelle to give tarot card readings to the lunch crowd on weekends. He can't book her for any more days since she's preoccupied with classes during the week." Sharon continued speaking, the whole time gaining strength from the presence of the dark prince beside her. "For those who would never think of having their fortunes told, Prophet Carvon sets up shop by the religious section of Pages, the mall's main bookstore, and offers his free service. According to our in-store merchant survey, a large percentage of the Christian community shops there."

The mayor appeared satisfied. "Clearly, I need not stand in the way of progress. We as a community are blessed to have such a successful woman as yourself for our mall manager. You have a wonderful day now, Sharon. I'm sure Belial Enterprises will be pleased with your work thus far."

"Thank you," said Sharon proudly. As she hung up, the demon prince, his hands still clutched to the sides of her head, flashed a smile.

～

The red pickup pulled out from where it had been parked in front of Jim's old shop and out onto the street in front of Randy. Randy hit the brakes and the horn at the same time.

"Come on, Frank, don't be so heavenly minded," he shouted out the window, slowing down to avoid rear-ending the Moravian church pastor, Frank Lacomb. "Now get your mind off your Sunday morning sermon and onto your driving. I declare! Some of these people drive as well as they sing on Sunday morning."

Randy came to a full stop and watched Lacomb's red pickup from the shoulder of the road as it pulled over a few feet ahead of him.

"What now?" Randy let out a chuckle as he watched Frank, his old prayer partner, get out of his truck.

I suppose he'll want to be takin' this matter to the street now with duelin' pistols. Well, I'm up for the ol' boy.

Frank walked up to Randy's driver's-side window.

"Howdy, Frank!" Randy greeted him.

"Where did you ever get your license to drive?" Frank asked, shaking his head. "Out of the same magazine you got your license to pastor? I don't know why I ever thought we were running for the same prize."

At a loss for words, Randy sat silently. Dumbfounded.

"Why couldn't you have just gotten yourself some real revelation?" Frank continued, raising his voice. "Like the revelation I've received from Prophet Carvon. You need to hang around those who walk in the five-fold ministry, Randy, instead of getting a reputation for eating with sinners. Surely then your fellowship would prosper. Our church's attendance is up, just as it is up at the Baptist church. We should have our building's mortgage completely paid off by summer. If I were you, I would repent! Get some vision before God's judgment falls on you."

Without waiting for a reply, Frank turned to walk back to his truck. A tall demon prince walked alongside him, then turned and pointed a gloved finger at Randy's head; he raised his finger to his lips and blew on it as though it were a smoking gun. The demon prince then broke out into bone-chilling laughter as Frank slammed his door and drove away.

Randy sat shivering in the cab of his truck as he watched Frank accelerate up the street. Several moments passed before he was finally able to pull back onto the street and continue on towards his destination.

～

Tony stepped out of his kitchen carrying a large bag of kettle chips and a container of dip. He placed them on the coffee table in front of Levi and Max. "Sorry, guys. It's not as fancy as Roxanne would do it. I didn't spend all morning preparing vegetables."

"We'll forgive you this time," Max said. "But don't let it happen again!"

Tony laughed. "I'll try to keep that in mind."

A loud bang at the front door interrupted them. Tony made his way to answer the door.

"Lord, let it be the pizza man," Levi said. "Who is it?"

"It's Randy!" Tony called back.

"Does he have food?"

"I'm not sure. Do you have food, Randy? Max wants to know."

"Yeah," Randy said as he slipped his shoes off. "I picked up a party pack of donut holes."

"He's got donut holes," Tony relayed loudly.

"Well, don't stand in the man's way," came Max's reply.

Randy entered the living room and sat on the sofa next to Levi and Max. "I'd feel a little nervous about my choice in prayer partners tonight, if I didn't know you all so well, seeing as y'all are more concerned about your bellies more than getting the counsel of the Lord."

"Glad you made it, Randy," Tony said as he sat in a wingback chair. "It's been a real trial for me of late. The other day, while at the general store I encountered the same silver Porsche that tangled with me on the way to Sarquis. If that weren't enough of a shock, Roxanne came out of the store with Jordan and passed right by me like I was invisible. The whole time they were getting into the Porsche, I could hear Jordan calling for me. That was the toughest part of it all." He wiped away a tear. "Here I go again, getting all teary-eyed. Next thing you know, I'll be going to the store for all kind of things I don't need, just on the chance of running into my family. I ended up buying five boxes of diet pudding I didn't want or need. I just know Roxanne is caught in this evil web that seems stretched over Drummingsville, but I'm not sure to what extent."

"A web of evil might explain the struggle Barbara and I have come up against in trying to maintain any sort of prayer life, or even in carrying on our daily devotions," said Max.

"It could also be the reason I've suddenly been told to vacate Crester's Cave," Levi added. "All they told me was that someone lodged a complaint. Who knows? Maybe I switched channels on the TV too loudly."

"I'm a little in shock myself!" Randy shared. "Earlier, as I was driving over here, Frank Lacomb pulled out in front of me in his big ol' red pickup. I had to brake so suddenly it near sent my fried chicken for a loop in my stomach. Then the ol' boy gets out of his truck, and I'm a thinkin' he's gonna apologize to me, but to my surprise he tells me he didn't know why he thought we were running for the same prize, that I should quit hanging out with sinners, and that he has got himself a mess of that there revelation from Prophet Carvon. I'm a-thinkin' if I hadn't heard of these end-time spirits, I might be a-wonderin' if John's elevator were a little shy of grain. He's tellin' me I spend too much time in the company of sinners. I wonder what he thinks Jesus did. He says I'm going to perish if I don't get me some of Carvon's revelation and repent. You know, the kind of revelation you get if you grease the palm of the prophet's hand a little."

"I find this all very interesting," said Tony. "The plate of the silver Porsche that clipped my truck had Belial's name on it, the very name of an end-time spirit, and the abortion clinic that recently opened in town has the same name. I've seen a giant sea serpent in one of my dreams that was called Leviathan. It is also interesting that the lawyer defending Dr. Andrew, who works for the Belial Clinic and who also hit my truck, works for the Leviathan Law Firm. The construction company that built the mall was called Behemoth Construction. Now, my guess is that the name of their company is the name of another end-time spirit. Also, have you ever noticed the trucks going in and out of Stillmore Mine? They have decals on their doors that depict a man with the head of a wolf. I realized when I was shaving the other day that I've seen the same thing before—and again it was in my dreams. In the dream, it was connected to death and Hades."

"Flora, God bless her, has been replaced in her teaching position," Max said. "Word has it that she was fired for influencing young children with adult websites. Her replacement is Michelle Starr, who I hear is also a tarot card reader. Isn't it interesting that this woman, who is steeped very much in the pagan beliefs of ancient Egypt and Babylon, is now a school teacher?" Max reached out to grab a handful of chips. "Remember the K7 News story about the abortion clinic's doctors also being practitioners of ancient religious systems? They used it to justify performing abortions. And why are all these huge corporations descending on our town? What is Drummingsville compared to the super nations of the world?"

"I'm not sure why these so-called end time spirits have picked Drummingsville," Tony said sombrely. "But the fact of the matter is they have, and we better wake up to that reality before they take us all out."

"Sea serpents!" Levi leaned forward on the sofa. "Kind of sounds like one of them old black-and-white monster films where you've got your giant prehistoric dinosaur devastating all the infrastructure of some major city. Forgive me if I sound a bit sceptical, but I've watched a lot of television lately. Tony, you don't need TV. You've got something better; you have dreams."

"What say ye to all your brothers now?" Randy asked, smiling. "If all we ever needed a vision or a dream, now would be a good time!"

Tony got up and walked into the kitchen. He removed a six-pack of cola from the refrigerator, then walked back into the living room and placed it on the coffee table. "I learned one thing from Apostle John. Some spirits are more powerful than others. He explained to me that Belial's mandate is to lure the people of the world into sin, causing them to become candidates of God's judgement. Sin camped at Cain's door and he did not manage it. Belial causes many to not manage sin and become marked or cursed by God."

"That's starting to make a whole lot of sense to me," Randy said. "Just maybe there was a demonic prince who lured Jim McFlurry to his tragic end."

"Belial was in my dreams!" Tony felt excited as he recalled the details. "He was always dressed in black, and now that I think of it, I believe he was the prince who was walking behind the demons that dragged Jim McFlurry away. My eyes were opened in broad daylight to see into the enemy's camp. I saw a queen in my dreams also, and she's known as the Queen of the Heavens. On more than one occasion, she mentioned that her spider was spinning."

"A web of evil over Drummingsville that's demonic in nature," Max suggested, like a trial lawyer presenting his case. "Satan ensnaring the souls of men through deception, unbelief, luring them into temptation by degrees, blinding their eyes, hindering prayer by the hands of his princes. And if that isn't enough, the accuser of the brethren contesting for their souls. Brothers, we need to pray!" He paused for breath before setting down his can of cola. "Oh Lord, we place our hope in your unfailing love. Our eyes are on you, Lord. Release our feet from the fowler's snare."

"Bend and string your bow, Lord," Levi wept. "Prepare your deadly weapons and make ready your flaming arrows, for you, Lord, are a warrior! I shackle Belial with my praise and I bind him with the word of God that says if I bind something here it is bound in Heaven. Oh God, let your kingdom come and your will be done in the earthly realm of Drummingsville as it is in heaven."

Tony covered his ears as Levi interceded. His ears had picked up a high-pitched shriek in the mid-heavens—the shriek of the queen writhing in agony. As Levi violently came against the evil powers, Tony saw in his mind an image of the queen. Her black hair tossed about like unrestrained darkness on the last light of day. Drops of foaming crimson liquid spilled from her chalice. "I will have the blood of the apostles and prophets," laughed the queen wickedly, "and I will still have the souls of the men of Drummingsville." The very thought of possessing the men's souls combined with the queen's insane laughter caused the mid-heavens to erupt into a crescendo of shrieking, the music of death, a demonic symphony.

"Lord," cried Randy, breaking Tony out of his vision, "we don't know why these end-time spirits have the right to stay. We ask that you cause the scales to fall from our eyes."

"I see bones, but I'm not sure what it means," Tony said. "I believe they're connected with what we've been talking about—Belial and the other end-time spirits, including the Queen of the Heavens' web of deceit over Drummingsville, to capture souls."

Randy nodded. "It appears to me that these end-time spirits have been quite busy, and we've all just been perishin' over the years for lack of knowledge."

Max suddenly got up off the sofa. "Sorry, guys, I'm going to have to call it a night. If I don't get going, I might be perishing prematurely. I promised Barbara I'd help her with something if I wasn't too late."

He proceeded towards the front door. When he reached for the doorknob, he paused and turned to face the others.

"I do have one final thought," Max said. "We need to be pleading the blood of Jesus over our families, and our homes, and cover each other in prayer unceasingly."

"Yeah," Randy agreed. "I should probably be leavin' as well if I aim to get any sleep. I got one of those clocks that a little birdie comes out of every morning to greet me with its cheerful racket. Educated folks call it a coo-coo clock, but I call it a thief. I think maybe one day I'm just gonna shoot the thing and sleep like a baby, without so much as a troubled conscience. Say, Levi, as I was sittin' here tonight, I was thinkin' that you might want to bunk out at my place. I know it ain't all that much to look at, but you're welcome to it."

"I'm not fussy." Levi smiled at Randy. "After all, it's not like I can afford to be."

"Well, all right then. I'll just go and fire up the truck."

"Wait, guys, one moment!" Tony interjected as he got up out of his wingback chair. "Mirana!"

"What's that?" inquired Max.

"I just remembered. In my last dream, these prophet guys laid hands on the boy named Grenfel. He was being sent out against the enemy's strongholds in hopes of rescuing his father, the king. I think God's shifting our wrestling match with these end-time spirits to a more aggressive stage. The Hawkman was being released just like in Isaiah, when he mentions the Lord sending a ravenous bird out, a man to execute His purpose. I believe this is happening right here in Drummingsville. The Lord is sending out His ravenous bird, his hawk, against the evil forces laying siege to our community, and I think the Lord's just released His net over Drummingsville. This time, He's not making us fishers of men but the net in His hands."

"No wonder Joseph's brothers were always unhappy," Max said. "He probably wore them out explaining his dreams all the time."

"Sorry, guys," Tony said, a little embarrassed now about his lengthy speech. "I guess it's getting late."

Max sighed. "No problem. We'll just be on our way and leave Joseph here to his dreams."

"Yeah!" added Randy as he walked out the door. "Try to get some sleep, Joseph. I mean, that is when you're not all preoccupied with dreamin'!"

Chapter Twenty-Seven

G renfel stood in the woven basket, ready to be lowered down the lime-stone cliffs. "Why can't you come?" he asked Estravai, nearly crying.

"Eltarz's vision was of a bird of prey rising," Estravai answered as he stood alongside Morteque beside the winch.

"I can't go by myself," exclaimed Grenfel. "Not back to Dremcon!"

He trembled as he recalled his conversation with the girl wearing the blood-stained clothes. He could feel the lump in his throat from when she had told him that his father's heart was Meldrock's. Then there had been the pungent smell of the cliffs above the city itself, and the giant forest of thorns. How would he get through it a second time?

"No! I'm too young! I'm just a boy! And without armour, I'll never get through the thorns. I'll pass out on the cliffs from the smell. I'm afraid to go alone." Grenfel's rushed words ran together. "You go, Estravai— you're older and braver."

Without waiting for Estravai to agree, Grenfel began to climb out of the basket. He then felt Estravai's reassuring but firm hand on his shoulder.

"No, Grenfel. As much as my heart would will it to continue our travels together, it is the season for me and Morteque to remain here at Mirana." Estravai paused to smile. "I'm sure of that. However, if Eltarz was given a vision from the Ancient of Days, you can be assured of His help. His protection, His strength, and His guidance are with you. That's more than two ornery Revealers of Secrets could ever give you."

Grenfel looked down at the ground and nodded. He had always trusted Estravai and Morteque, but now he began to doubt in his heart whether they truly understood the danger of his mission. Perhaps they had put their hope in him too soon.

If only there was more time, he thought.

Estravai smiled in an effort to de-escalate the storm clouds forming in his young friend's mind. "Remember when we encountered the demon princes on our way to the Asar's Icefields? You sang the song of deliverance and the demon princes were reduced to ashes. Remember, boy."

Grenfel's trembling levelled off as he recalled the triumph. Detecting this, Estravai raised his hand and Morteque lowered the basket on its journey.

"Estravai!" cried Grenfel, wiping his wet face.

"You must lean on the Ancient of Day as you have his servants, Grenfel!" Estravai yelled down. "Until we meet again, young Hawkman, farewell!"

"Farewell," Grenfel whispered as the basket took him down the cliffs. "Farewell, my father!"

⁓

Tony straightened the knot in his tie. It had been a long time since he'd tied a double Windsor knot, as there wasn't much call for ties when he was out fighting fires. Then, pushing aside the living room drapes, he watched Max's blue station wagon pull up in front of his condo.

Well, it looks like it's showtime, Tony thought as he shifted his grey suit jacket before walking out the front door.

"Looking good, guy!" Max said from the car. "The judges give you tens across the board for style."

Tony opened a rear passenger door and slid in beside Levi. "Earning style points isn't my goal at the moment. I'd rather score points with the judge."

The station wagon made its way along the street towards Drummingsville's courthouse.

"I'm really glad you're all going to be in the audience today," Tony said in the midst of silence.

"Well, you all know how it is, boy." Randy turned around to face Levi and Tony. "We never leave one of our own behind."

And thank God for that, Tony thought, smiling.

∼

"Good to see you again, old friend," Grenfel said to Morgan as he stroked his nose. Morgan whinnied in contentment. "I love you, too, boy."

With one hand on his halter, Grenfel pulled himself up on the Arabian's back.

He leaned forward on Morgan's soft, full mane and placed his head on the horse's neck. "I'm asking you to carry me into the face of death, boy, but I know you have a brave heart. I need you to carry me with the swiftness of a hawk to Dremcon."

At the sound of the forsaken city's name, Morgan whinnied a few times.

"For the Ancient of Days and the king!" Grenfel shouted, as he gently nudged Morgan with his heels, causing Morgan to speed off in the direction of Dremcon with Grenfel hanging onto his horse's mane for all he was worth.

Estravai and Morteque watched silently from their high perch in the cliffs. They followed with their eyes as Grenfel sped off towards the horizon.

"Ride, young Hawkman," Estravai whispered. "Ride like the wind, and may the Ancient of Days give you a brave heart!"

∼

"Rena Peterson here for K7 News, coming to you once again from the tiny community of Drummingsville. We're outside the town courthouse. In just a short time, long-time resident Tony Epson will defend himself against Dr. Andrews of the Belial Clinic, who's represented by Stephen Drakeo of the prestigious Leviathan law firm. Charges include vehicular assault against Dr. Andrews.

"Our coverage of this small town and their decision to allow major developers free rein in their community has brought our news team back on more than one occasion, and it's becoming clear that the effects of development on this community haven't all been prosperous. By way of a quick recap, the town's last meeting was anything but productive. In fact, it ended up with a local pastor being shot in the arm, and I also understand another local shop owner took his life rather than conform to the changes happening in Drummingsville. The question of the hour is, should major corporations be given free rein in such a community as this? Is economic success really success if the change seems to impact the locals negatively? This all seems connected, as the lawyer Stephen Drakeo also spoke at both local meetings regarding Drummingsville's future, and the doctor he represents works at the Belial Abortion clinic, one of the new companies bringing change to Drummingsville.

"We at K-7 News felt the trial today might shed some light on whether large companies have a negative effect on a community. Is the community of Drummingsville a transferable model of success or failure for your community?

"This has been a live broadcast from outside Drummingsville's courthouse, where we're waiting for the trial of Tony Epson to begin. I'm Rena Peterson for K7 News, saying goodbye for now."

~

As the station wagon came into view of the courthouse, Tony saw the large crowd gathering outside.

Looks like everyone is expecting some big celebrity, Tony thought, feeling nervous. *I hope they won't be too disappointed when they see it's me...*

"Give him a brave heart," Tony murmured under his breath.

"What was that?" Max asked as he pulled the car to a stop outside the front of the courthouse.

"Just something from a prayer a prophet dude prayed in one of my dreams," Tony replied.

"Sounds like good encouragement," Randy replied. "What's the worst thing that could happen to me, compared to the absence of my family? I mean really! What?" Inquired Tony as he looked at Levi's face, hoping for a sympathetic response. Just as he said this, the station wagon was swarmed by the crowd like bees around a hive.

"You could lose your vehicle and be suspended from driving," Max pointed out.

"I'm not afraid to walk," Tony said. "After all, Jesus did enough of it."

Max hesitated. "You could be facing jail time, too."

Tony laughed nervously. "Well, I hope the comparisons you guys keeping making between me and Joseph don't end with me being sent to the dungeons."

"We're all applying the word of the Lord to your situation in warfare prayer," Randy said. "The Lord gives you His shield of victory, and we're all believing He's gonna release your feet right out of the enemy's old snares because…"

Randy trailed off as Sheriff Ryder pushed his way through the crowd, stooping down and motioning through the passenger window for Tony to get out of the car. Tony opened his door and just managed to straighten up when Sheriff Ryder yelled to be heard above the jeering crowd, "Tony Epson! I'm going to ask you to follow me into the courthouse."

Tony nodded at his friends, exhaled, then proceeded to follow the sheriff. The noise of the crowd buzzed around him with sounds of accusation and judgment. As he was led through the crowd by Sheriff Ryder, Tony looked back at his friends and shouted, "I'll see you inside I guess!"

The pungent smell atop the cliffs overlooking Drencon caused Morgan to turn his head back the way they had come.

"I know," Grenfel said, gasping for a breath of fresh air. "If it were up to me, I would have stayed in Mirana, as cool and damp as it is there."

His mother's words pushed their way to the front of his mind. Grenfel could still picture his mother in her emerald dress, saying, "Promise me you'll never forget the Ancient of Days' hand on your life." He gasped in a whispering tone as he turned Morgan's head towards the narrow trail leading down to the wasteland below.

Grenfel closed his eyes and rested his head on Morgan's neck. Partially overcome by the odour, he whispered in Morgan's ear, "You have to carry me on, boy, I'm too weak! We must keep going, Take me down the cliffs, old friend. We have to save my father."

Blackness overcame Grenfel and he fell silent, with only Morgan's hooves to be heard, as they created a hollow sound on the hard-crystalized salt path. With his young master now solely at his mercy, Morgan faithfully carried Grenfel to the barren wasteland below.

⁓

"Hang on, son!" Tony muttered to himself.

Sheriff Ryder glanced back at him through dark sunglasses as they walked through the front door of the courthouse

"You talkin' to me?" the sheriff asked.

"No."

Shaking his head, the sheriff led Tony down a long hallway with red carpet. Police officers stood all along the walls like enormous potted plants. A few moments later, they stopped outside a pair of large double doors. The officer guarding the entrance to the courtroom glared at Tony with a contorted expression on his face, like a chained bulldog that spotted a kitten. The guard's look went unnoticed by Sheriff Ryder who simply pulled open the courtroom door with one hand.

At the sight of the courtroom doors, Tony was suddenly seized by panic over the thought that he might just start speaking random things from his dreams before the judge, so he whispered a prayer. "Lord, restrain my vision while I am in the courtroom…"

⁓

Morgan stood at the base of the salt cliffs waiting for Grenfel to come to, whinnying softly as he tossed his head from side to side.

"What's the matter, boy?" asked a groggy Grenfel. "Oh, we're down! I knew you would get me here."

Grateful to his horse for carrying him down from the cliffs, Grenfel rewarded Morgan with a gentle pat on his mane. However, the excitement of being out of the putrid smell at the top of the cliffs was short lived as Grenfel now found himself staring at a massive tangle of thorns directly ahead. Unable to process the surge of hopelessness that came with seeing the thorns again, Grenfel simply dropped his head.

"I don't know why I asked you to bring me down the cliffs only to come face to face with this forest of thorns. Forgive me, my friend."

Morgan let out another whinny, trying to jar his young master out of his hopelessness. He pranced from side to side to lift Grenfel's spirit, but to no avail, as hopelessness now encased his young master's heart like a plaster mould, leaving Grenfel thinking it was just no use to try to get through the thorns. Oblivious to his master's feelings, Morgan continued in his excited whinnying, as if to say I'm not listening to you. It was his horse's excited whinnying that now triggered his mother's words in his mind: *Remember, the Ancient of Days has His hand on you.*

Grenfel lifted his head and began to speak. "Oh, Ancient of Days, you gave Eltarz a vision in which I rode towards Dremcon. I need your help to go on. My mother told me to remember your hand was on my life. Please help us get through these thorns to save my father, the king." Then, in his next breath, he shouted, "I curse these thorns!"

All was silent for a few minutes. The forest of thorns appeared unchanged, still as sharp and deadly and tangled as ever. He thought to turn Morgan back, but at the moment of his utter lapse of faith in the Ancient of Days, a wind rose up. Grenfel listened as the sky came alive with the beating of wings.

"Hawks!" Grenfel cried. "Just like my father and I would use for hunting."

Grenfel and Morgan watched as a veritable cloud of hawks flew towards the thorns, confronting there a line of vultures sent to retrieve the drops of blood to be spilled by the unfortunate wayfarer. The hawks set to assaulting the thorns with their razor sharp talons.

"Look, Morgan!" Grenfel shouted. "They're clearing a path through the thorns."

⌒

"Excuse us," Sheriff Ryder said as he cleared a path through the crowded courtroom. "Nothing like a full house to make victory all the sweeter."

"No, not again," muttered Tony. Surveying the room, he saw a dark prince walking beside the sheriff with matching dark glasses.

"You talkin' to me?" Sheriff Ryder asked as he stared coldly at Tony.

"No, sorry."

"Good, then. You sit over there." The sheriff pointed to a long wooden table with a single chair at the left side of the courtroom. "Just you and your invisible friends."

Sheriff Ryder chuckled to himself as he turned away.

Tony sat in the wooden chair and loosened the knot in his tie. On the opposite side of the courtroom sat Dr. Andrew and his lawyer. The courtroom was a sea of strangers, but after a few seconds Tony managed to pick out a few familiar faces. The cold, unsympathetic looks from Sue Henderson and Sharon Tillman made it hard for him to relax. Theirs were looks of death. Tony turned away from the crowd, trying to draw encouragement now from those in the crowd who he knew supported him.

The bailiff came into the room through a side door from the judge's private chamber. He commanded everyone to rise in respect of Judge Bruce Whitiner.

The spectators clambered to their feet as the judge entered and sat on his throne-like chair. When Whitiner spoke, his tone was both grandfatherly and kingly. Many in the community knew him in both modes: outside the courthouse as a grandfather figure and inside as the king whose word held final authority.

Leaning forward, he motioned for all in attendance to sit.

Clearing his voice, Judge Whitiner looked towards Tony. "Is the defendant ready?"

"Yes, your honour!" Tony said as he stood up.

"Good," the judge said. "Is the prosecutor ready?"

Stephen Drakeo pushed his chair back and came to his feet. "Yes, we are, your Honour."

"We will then proceed with today's case—Mr. Andrews versus Mr. Epson."

Chapter Twenty-Eight

"Okay, Morgan, the hawks have cleared a path through the thorns." The horse needed far less convincing than his young master and had already started along the trail that twisted through the chaos.

"Steady, boy!" Grenfel whispered as a vulture tried to get at them where the trail was clear from above. Just as it dove at them, its screeches were cut short, as its lifeless body fell to be impaled by the thorns.

Pressing forward was gruelling work for both horse and boy. Their muscles grew weak and tired from the continuous tension. From this weary state, Grenfel whispered to Morgan, hoping to keep his faithful horse encouraged in the task at hand.

An eternity seemed to pass before they emerged from this forest of thorns to catch a glimpse of the city: Dremcon, one of Meldrock's dark jewels. Grenfel felt his skin turn to goose bumps. Where were the bull-faced guardians to greet the unfortunate travellers? The city seemed unusually peaceful compared to their first visit to this nest of demons.

Despite the lack of apparent danger, Morgan drew to a halt.

"What is it, boy?" Grenfel asked. "What do you sense?"

And then Grenfel saw her, floating toward them in silence. The queen's black velvet gown trailed behind her, her hair tossed about as if it had a will of its own. Her red lips called to him like a siren to a ship's crew. In one of her gloves, she clutched the serpentine dagger inlaid with blood-red rubies.

Rooted to the spot, neither Grenfel nor Morgan seemed able to do anything, least of all flee. Their arms and legs had locked up, and now they stood paralyzed like a rat about to be eaten by a snake.

"If it isn't my little Hawkman and his faithful nag," the queen's sultry voice called to them across the distance. "It's been a long time since our first meeting, and I've so longed to see you again."

When she arrived, the queen stroked Grenfel's curly hair and motioned with her hand for him to be still.

"I have something of yours," she whispered in his ear. "I've kept it as a priceless treasure for so long."

Reaching for the vial suspended by a chain around her neck, the queen gently poured its contents into the palm of her gloved hand. A single glistening tear dropped out.

"You do remember crying for your mother while your companions slept, do you not? But your mother didn't stop your father from sending you to your uncle's. Where's the love in that? I kept your tears. I've carried them with me always! Now, by what name did I instruct you to remember me?"

Grenfel struggled to speak, but stuttered finally, "Y—y—you're the Queen of—of—of the Heavens."

❧

"She's here," Tony yelled out. "The Queen of the Heavens!"

Judge Whitiner banged his wooden gavel. "Mr. Epson! Would you please answer Mr. Drakeo's question?"

"She's just like she appears in my dreams. Her long hair, crimson lips, and black velvet gown... can't you see her?" Tony stared right into Stephen Drakeo's face. "She's right over there—the Queen of the Heavens!" He pointed to the centre front row, near Sue Henderson.

Drakeo looked at Judge Whitiner, completely mystified.

"Mr. Epson, if I could so kindly have your attention," the judge said firmly, again banging his gavel.

Tony turned his attention away from Sue.

"Thank you!" Whitiner said. "Now, if you don't mind, you were asked to explain how you incurred the damage to your vehicle."

"Pervert!" Sue burst out, jumping to her feet. Judge Whitiner banged his gavel again, but Sue continued to yell. "Lock up the pervert!"

Rolf Peterson spun the news camera around on his shoulder at the back of the courtroom like he was part cyborg.

"Make sure you get that last bit of activity," instructed Rena. "For once maybe we'll give *People's Court* a run for their money."

"Order!" said the silver-haired judge, looking out at the crowded courtroom over bifocal glasses. The room returned to a quiet hush. "That's better. Now, Tony, do you think you might now be able to share your side of the story?"

The calming effect of his question had helped ease Tony's anxiety. "I was leaving Drummingsville and was driving along in my lane when—"

Suddenly, he covered his eyes with both hands.

~

"Come, young Hawkman," said the queen, smiling seductively. "Here, take my hand."

Grenfel shuddered, making no move to do what she said.

"Don't be afraid. Here, I brought you a gift." She held out the serpentine dagger, grasping it by the blade. "I want you to have it. Every prince is worthy of such a dagger."

Slowly, Grenfel stretched out his trembling hand, the glint of dagger capturing his eye like the eye of the groom for his bride.

"Take the handle," the queen pressed. "Would I give you a dagger if I wanted to harm you?"

"N–n–no," stuttered Grenfel.

"Good, then. As friends, I would like to show you something. Come along."

The queen placed Grenfel's free hand in hers and led him toward Dremcon, with Morgan following close behind.

"Mr. Epson. Mr. Epson!" Judge Whitiner repeated. "Is everything all right?"

Tony shook his head to try to clear his mind of the vision. "Yeah. Sorry about that."

"That's fine, but if you're ready, please continue."

"Sure." Tony replied as he loosened the knot in his tie a bit more. "I noticed up ahead a silver Porsche speeding toward me on the wrong side of the road."

Don't choose the wrong side. The thought pounded in Grenfel's head as a feeling of uneasiness settled in the pit of his stomach. Nevertheless, he continued walking hand-in-hand with the queen.

Standing ahead of them he saw the two huge, bull-faced demons, each holding a massive chain whose end was fastened to one of the arms of his father, King Ulrich. When the demons pulled the chains in opposite directions, Ulrich winced in pain.

"Father!" Grenfel yelled, causing the slumping king to lift his head.

"My son," Ulrich whispered, slipping in and out of consciousness.

Grenfel turned to the queen with hot tears running down his face. "Tell them to let him go!"

"We need to talk first." She wiped the tears from Grenfel's cheeks.

"I'll not talk to you! You're a murderer!" Grenfel raised his hand and pointed the ruby-encrusted dagger at the queen. "I'll make you let my father go! He's the king, which is more than you are."

"A pathetic excuse for royalty," she said with a laugh.

Without warning, the grey coils of a massive sea serpent wrapped around Grenfel's waist. As his breath became restricted, Grenfel frantically stabbed at the serpent's impenetrable scales. His futile efforts only seemed to fuel the queen's laughter like brush added to a fire.

"Leviathan!" Grenfel gasped.

"Leviathan!" Tony yelled.

"Your Honour," Drakeo interjected, "I fail to see what my law firm has to do with Mr. Epson hitting Dr. Andrews and fleeing the scene."

Judge Whitiner turned to Tony with pleading eyes. "Order! Mr. Epson, would you stick to the facts leading to your involvement with Dr. Andrews?"

"Not your law firm." Tony stood and leaned over the table to lock eyes with Drakeo. "The great sea serpent, described in the book of Job and which appears in my dreams… it's here!"

Drakeo paced in front of Tony momentarily, then turned. "Just for the sake of curiosity, and on behalf of those unable to see this great sea serpent in the courtroom, where is it?"

Judge Whitiner sat silently and observed the proceedings with interest.

"I see a grey coil wrapping itself around your head, Mr. Drakeo." Tony looked across the spectators and saw the two pastors, Phil Devon and Frank Lacomb. "Other coils are beginning to tighten around both Phil Devon and Frank Lacomb."

Overcome with rage, a dark prince triggered Phil's emotions, pushing the minister to his feet. Phil pointed at Tony from across the courtroom, shaking with anger. "This man is a raving lunatic, as well as a pervert!"

No sooner had the accusations spewed from Phil's mouth when he suddenly grabbed his throat as if he were choking. A dark prince smiled at Phil as he continued to squeeze his throat. Leviathan continued to squeeze Phil's head like an iron band, as the demon prince continued to restrict his breathing. With his heart now threatening to explode like an overinflated balloon, Phil unleashed his anger with the fury of a tornado at Tony. "The man's possessed with demons. I'm glad I'm not an immoral, deceived sinner like he is!"

The sound of Judge Whitiner's gravel striking the oak table echoed through the courtroom like an iron spike driven into a rail line.

"Order! Order!"

Several police officers, including Sheriff Ryder, moved through the crowd, busily reseating people.

"I want to make it clear to all in the courtroom today that the case being tried is not to determine whether Mr. Epson is abusive, but rather if he is at fault in a vehicle collision," Whitiner said. "Please hear me on this matter. If anyone insists on disrupting the proceedings, I will have them thrown out. As for you, Mr. Epson, I would advise you to tell your story while you still have my patience. Continue!"

"Yes, your Honour. I'll try." Tony took a deep breath, attempting to focus amidst the chaos. "The silver Porsche came speeding around the corner ahead of me, on the wrong side of the road, as it collided with my vehicle on its way past me I was able to read the word BELIAL on its back plate."

———

Belial appeared beside Grenfel now with his hand grasping Grenfel's wrist, forcing him to continue his stabbing motion, even though his energy was spent. The queen observed Grenfel, thoroughly entertained.

"As I told you, I hunt Hawkmen," the queen said. "As you use hawks in hunting, I use snakes, such as Python or the great serpent Leviathan to squeeze the life out of my prey. You come to save the king, and you can't even save yourself! How pitiful that the Revealers of Secrets cower in their caves, sending a mere boy up against the wisdom and sorcery of the Queen of the Heavens! Meldrock has his price, and I have mine. It's no secret that the portal has been opened. I may not be able to prevent it, but I can kill the two witnesses—and you are one of them." The queen smiled with feigned compassion. "However, there might be a way I might be persuaded not to kill one of the Ancient of Days' witnesses today, and that is if you, young Hawkman, were to worship me. Nothing would delight me more. Perhaps it would even save your life."

"I promised my mother!" Grenfel gasped, as Leviathan's coils tightened a little more around his waist. However, his struggling against Leviathan's coils only seemed to intensify, as he witnessed Morgan lose a little more of his zeal, as Belial forced the great horse to submit to a muzzle.

The queen's gaze intensified. "Listen. Many people in Dremcon are held in the grasp of Meldrock. I may be able to secure their freedom, and you may live, in return for you, Hawkman of the Ancient of Days, worshipping me." The queen paused to relish the thought. "And now, to further aid your decision, observe!"

Grenfel gasped for air as Leviathan momentarily relaxed its coil around him. A loud scrape filled the air as he saw a fissure start to form in the ground in front of the two bull-like demons. The fissure widened, and inky black smoke now seeped out as if it had intelligence of its own.

"What is your choice?" said the queen coldly.

"I promised my mother I would never forget the Ancient of Days' hand on my life."

"Well! You have already failed in that promise, for you accepted my gift. And behold, you have also failed to save your father."

At her signal, the bull-like demons tore out King Ulrich's heart and pushed his quivering body into the smoky fissure. Holding the king's heart in their hands, the demons committed it Meldrock.

Grenfel cried out with his whole being. "No! My father, my father!"

The loud scraping sound filled the air again and the fissure closed up, swallowing the king.

"Meldrock has just collected his price," smiled the queen wickedly as she took a triumphant drink from a chalice Belial presented to her. "Foolish Hawkman, with your weak attempt to free the king. Be sure that I will collect my price as well—the blood of the Revealers of Secrets and the souls of the men of Ascar."

～

The window of the royal bedchamber in Kreniston castle was open, its shutter swinging helplessly in the wind. Queen Julliet lay sprawled over the window sill in her torn emerald dress, her arm outstretched as if attempting to grab something before it could slip away.

The sound of her cries echoed through the castle. "My lover has fallen! My white dove from the sky, his breast as crimson as a pomegranate.

The king is not coming back. Farewell, my lover! Farewell!" Lamented the queen.

∽

"I heard a loud scraping sound, metal grinding on metal, causing sparks to fly," Tony explained. "The silver Porsche struck my truck, then sped off. I pulled over. My heart was in my throat, having just seen my life flash before my eyes. I sat trembling in the cab of my vehicle, thanking the Lord for sparing my life. It was several moments before I could start my vehicle and pull back onto the highway."

Drakeo strutted like a peacock in front of Judge Whitiner before stopping in front of Tony. "Would it be more appropriate to say, Mr. Epson, that you crossed over the centre line in a dream-like state, striking Dr. Andrews' vehicle as he was en route to perform a crucial medical procedure at his clinic? Did you then proceed to speed off, leaving the poor doctor sitting in his car fearing for *his* life?"

Through these accusations, Tony could feel the powerful jaws of Leviathan coming against him.

Father, be the protective covering over me, he prayed.

"Isn't that the more accurate picture of what transpired between Dr. Andrews and yourself?" Drakeo insisted.

"No! I already described what happened to the court!"

"Mr. Epson, given your tendency to hallucinate, as we've all witnessed here today, I would say the events as I portrayed them are probably more accurate." Turning to face the audience, Drakeo smiled and pointed to Tony. "Behold, the man who sees invisible creatures! Would you want to drive with your family when he's on the road?"

"God allows me to see things," Tony said. "I never asked for it, but I describe what He shows me. Call me delusional or a dreamer, it doesn't change the fact that I see one of Leviathan's coils around you, Mr. Drakeo."

Tony lowered his eyes momentarily as he whispered a prayer to God, "Okay, God, I have no wisdom on my own, but I'm willing to be faithful to what I sense you're saying to me!" Lifting his eyes to Drakeo, Tony placed his hands on the edge of the table and leaned over it.

"The Lord rebukes you, Leviathan!" Tony shouted.

Drakeo grabbed at his neck. Stiffness and pain seemed to encase his neck and shoulders like an iron mask. Then, unable to stop himself, his backbone rippled like a snake slithering across a rock.

With the calmness that Jesus silenced the storm, Tony prayed: "I ask, Lord, that you pierce Leviathan's jaw with a hook right now." At the sound of his words, Drakeo become even more incapacitated. He struggled to compose himself, but to no avail.

Seeing the state of Mr. Drakeo, Tony pressed on in prayer. "I bind you, Leviathan, in the name of Jesus. I plead the blood of Jesus over Mr. Drakeo, and I tell you to leave him!" At the sound of Jesus's name, Mr. Drakeo started to groan loudly.

"I see a figure dressed in a black robe with gold trim walking away from you, Mr.Drakeo!"

⌒

Tears and sweat trickled down Grenfel's face as Leviathan held him by the waist.

"Oh, Ancient of Days," he wept, "I'm sorry I took the Queen of the Heavens' gift, and that I forgot the promise I made to my mother."

The thoughts of his failures seemed more crushing to Grenfel's spirit than having his breath sucked out by Leviathan's coils. It seemed that if he weren't crushed by Leviathan, he would be overwhelmed by hopelessness, shame, and embarrassment.

The queen continued to laugh in enjoyment. "It's too late, young Hawkman. It's no use struggling. You're mine now!"

"No!" Grenfel cried out. "I see something!"

"What is it, boy?"

"I see my mother sitting on her bed in her emerald green dress, combing her long hair with her ivory comb. She's singing. Yes! A melody is arising that could only be meant for the high courts of the Ancient of Days. I hear the music. It's a song of deliverance."

The queen's face twitched as Grenfel became strengthened by the Ancient of Days' love.

"The Lord rebukes you, Leviathan," Grenfel declared. "The Ancient of Days puts His hook through your jaw."

Upon hearing Grenfel's confession, Belial's hold was broken on his wrist and the boy dropped the dagger. It hit the ground and vanished in a wisp of smoke. Surprised, Belial retreated hastily, then vanished just as suddenly.

The air filled with the sound of mighty wings beating it. The razor-sharp talons of a swarm of hawks flashed, ripping at Leviathan's closely-knit scales.

"Hawks!" Grenfel exclaimed.

Leviathan hissed loudly as the hawks forced it to release its grip on Grenfel. The creature slithered away from the battlefield to report to its master, Meldrock.

A brawny warrior materialized, shining with light, and appeared to lift Grenfel from the ground. The warrior placed a hand on the boy's shoulder, as if to say that the Ancient of Days had forgiven him. A tear trickled down Grenfel's cheek as the warrior seemed to infuse him with the Ancient of Days' love. The brilliant warrior turned and pointed his flaming sword at the queen, who writhed in agony.

"Speak, young Hawkman!" the warrior thundered.

"You're no queen," Grenfel said, gathering still more strength. "You called my beloved horse a nag, but you're the old nag."

Grenfel's eyes widened in amazement as he spoke, for the queen shrunk away from him like a wax figurine melting from the heat of his words. Her seductive, youthful beauty fled and Grenfel saw before him a little wrinkled old lady bent at the waist. Her velvet dress was replaced with the tattered rags of a scullery maid. She let out a bone-chilling shriek that caused Grenfel's skin to break out in goose bumps, then turned her wrinkled face and disappeared before his very eyes.

~

Tony now dashed past the disabled Drakeo towards the middle of the courtroom, toward where Sue Henderson sat. From his seat near the back, Max broke into prayer with Levi and Randy beside him.

With a direct visual line now on Sue, Tony positioned himself midway across the courtroom and prayed. "Father, we ask right now that your will be done in this place. We plead the blood of Jesus over this courtroom and ask that you, Lord, release your heavenly warriors to restrain the enemy's vessels from hindering your true purpose here today. In Jesus' name we ask this, amen."

Max, Levi, and Randy continued to pray in tongues, listening as Tony confronted the Queen of the Heavens over Sue's life.

"Jezebel, you're no queen! You're no virgin, but rather the mother of harlots. This day, both widowhood and loss of children shall overcome you. Go down. Sit in the dust, daughter of Babylon. Sit on the ground without a throne. No more will you be called tender and delicate! I see your beauty and seductiveness being stripped away. I see only a wrinkled old whore."

Sue let out a prolonged scream as Tony pressed on.

"I see a huge silver spider with a large egg sack crawling away from you, Sue!"

With this statement, Sue became overwhelmed with the joy of being released from the enemy's shackles. She collapsed to the floor, sobbing loudly.

Judge Whitiner seemed mesmerized by all the goings-on and didn't seem able to halt any of it. Two angels were flanking him, keeping him in check.

On the other side of the unusually loud room, the K7 News team didn't miss a frame of the action.

"Take it to them, Joseph!" Max called out in support.

"I see bones!" Tony said as the crescendo of sound crashed, leaving the room in absolute silence. "And skulls wearing miners' helmets. I see rusty, broken lanterns still holding their candles, stiff bony fingers reaching for diamonds, rotting timber, and a cavern in the mine sealed off from natural eyes."

Dylan leapt to his feet from the audience. "Enough! I've worked too hard for a fox like you to snatch away my golden egg!"

In his hands, Dylan clutched a revolver, aiming it directly at Tony's head. Two dark princes controlled him like a puppet. One had his hands on the sides of Dylan's head while the other placed his hand atop Dylan's trigger finger. "I will not lose this chance!" screamed Dylan.

"It's me, Dylan," Tony said. "Your lead hand, remember? I don't see the Dylan I worked for standing before me today. This isn't you."

Dylan snarled. "Yeah, well, he was weak. I've become a more able, successful, and powerful version of myself!"

"Don't let Belial and these other end-time spirits push you over the edge, Dylan," Tony pleaded. "Not like Jim McFlurry."

Sensing a train about to derail, Randy jumped up from praying and bolted towards Dylan.

"Say goodbye!" screamed Dylan.

Randy lunged.

Dylan pulled the trigger.

The pastor took the bullet in the chest, and Tony screamed.

"No, Randy!" Tony watched his friend hit the floor. Everything appeared to move in slow motion. Almost without thinking, Tony found himself at Randy's side, just a few moments before Max and Levi came running to their fallen friend with red watery eyes. The bailiff grabbed Dylan and forced the gun out of his hand. As he fell to the floor, the bailiff handcuffed him.

"Hang on, old soldier," Tony cried as he knelt beside Randy.

"This is the one," Randy whispered.

Tears blurred Tony's vision. "You're going to be okay."

"No," said Randy, his voice calm. "For the first time in my life, I see things the way you do all the time, Joseph. I see a heavenly warrior with a golden breastplate walking across the sky towards me. I'm going to be carried into glory, boys, in the arms of a heavenly commander, like the good shepherd bringing in the stray lamb."

A peaceful expression crossed his face as he let out a final sigh and fell silent.

"I see an angel of the Lord," Tony cried from his knees. "I see Randy in his arms, just a-smilin' as they step upward into glory. Farewell, old soldier. Farewell."

CHAPTER TWENTY-NINE

"Rena Peterson, live for the K7 News. I'm standing inside the Drummingsville courtroom where we've been covering the proceedings live concerning Mr. Epson versus Dr. Andrews. The case has been far from ordinary. It hasn't been so much about court proceedings as wrestling in the supernatural—a brawl between two unseen superpowers. Today's events have been simply unbelievable, resulting in the death of one local pastor, Randy Foxworth. Most of the people now in the courtroom are in a state of shock and confusion. Many are weeping. Paramedics are rushing to the side of the fallen pastor. One would almost believe our news coverage was coming from the frontlines of a war zone, but—excuse me one moment!"

Rena held her hand to her ear.

"I'm receiving a word now... I've just been told that Judge Whitiner has used a sua sponte dismissal to end the day's proceeding. In light of the irregular court activity. I believe most watching or listening to the events would agree with the judge's decision, particularly in light of the murder of a pastor."

Again Rena paused to listen to the voicing coming to her through her headset.

"We're going to take a short break to bring you closer coverage. We'll be back momentarily."

Rena rushed with her cameraman to the place where Tony was standing over Randy's body, covered and lying on a stretcher. As the paramedics wheeled the deceased out of the courtroom, Rena took her cue to approach Tony with her microphone and gently get his attention.

"Excuse me, Mr. Epson. I don't want to appear insensitive to your loss. I can understand how the judge's decision would seem bittersweet, considering the loss of a close friend, but would you be able to comment on today's events?"

"I'm saddened," Tony said as the curious and compassionate crowd pressed in around him. "I feel sad for the loss of my friend, Randy Foxworth. He was a faithful soldier, never willing to leave one of his own behind. However, I also rejoice. Not because of the judge's dismissal today, but because I know my friend is with the Lord."

Tony paused to wipe his moist eyes. He sighed and finally just closed them. It was several agonizing moments before he felt composed enough to open his eyes and continue.

"I'd like to add that in our haste to develop this community, we've laid its stones over the blood of our own—and their blood cries out to God for justice." Like a biblical prophet relaying God's vision to a king, Tony now declared what he was seeing in the spirit realm. "I see a web of deception over our community, held in place by one corner. That corner has allowed our community to become a nest for end-time spirits who have pushed many of us to a place of God's judgment. Through the works of the flesh, these ruling spirits have gained control over many of our lives. Some of you have changed in character so much I hardly recognize you. The Queen of the Heavens and the great host of spirits may have let you think you were prospering, but that was only part of their deceptive web. They have ensnared your souls.

"Only the Father above truly gives good gifts. For many, your newly acquired wealth wasn't enough to satisfy your greed. Nor could you climb high enough on the management ladder to satisfy your lust for power. The gold trickled through your fingers like water, and in the end, it fell back into the hands of the Queen of the Heavens. It was an insignificant trophy to this queen. She and her spirits don't lust after gold. Their mission is to reap a harvest of souls. They hate apostles and prophets, because they expose their plans. These ruling spirits are the ones truly responsible for the death of my friend today."

"There you have it," said Rena as she withdrew her microphone. "A summary of all Drummingsville's concerns and questions in one statement. As Mr. Epson puts it, they are called demons. Whether it's fate, luck, or the work of ruling spirits, you decide. However, one thing can be said for sure. The normally unheard-of community of Drummingsville has made for a lot of front-page news."

All eyes turned from Rena to Tony, who was beginning to stutter as he fought to say one more thing. "I see the Queen of the Heavens writhing in pain, her black hair whipping about her shoulders. Her face appears paralyzed in pain, as if all her facial muscles were composed of stone. I hear her continuous shrieks, which cause the other ruling spirits to stay at a distance. It appears the cup in her hand is empty of blood. The reveal of her spider's web by the Creator's light seems to be driving her into madness." He paused, his eyes widening in amazement. "I see something beginning to happen. Her face is changing from a look of pain to a mocking smile, and her shrieks have transformed into laughter."

Tony hesitated, trying to see what the Lord was showing him.

"Lord, cause the scales to be removed from my eyes," he prayed aloud. "I see a steel door, and a huge open pit with a stone bridge spanning it, with hooded figures chanting."

"What is it?" asked Max. "Tony, tell me!"

Tony's face turned a sickly white. "It's Roxanne! Oh, God, have mercy on her!"

Dr. Andrews pushed his chair back and ran for the door of the courtroom, leaving his briefcase open upon the table.

Realizing what was happening, Tony shook his head to regain his focus on reality. "Excuse me!" he yelled as he pushed his way through the crowd, stopping only to look behind to search for his friends. Noticing them pushing their way through the crowd towards him, Tony yelled, "Head for the mine, Levi! Max, follow me! The time has come to crush the head of a serpent."

A blur of red carpet flashed by as Tony vaulted down the hallways of the courthouse, finally bursting through the front doors to see a silver Porsche speeding away from the curb and up the street.

Max rushed through the front door several seconds later like an escaped elephant from the zoo, praying the whole time. "Lord, we ask that you release angels around Roxanne and Jordan, and that you would be a protective covering over them!"

Standing on the courthouse's front steps, Max spotted Tony pacing back and forth on the sidewalk.

"Heads up, Tony!" Max yelled as he tossed him his car keys.

Tony caught the keys, pivoted around a lamp post, and ran to Max's blue station wagon. With the speed of a professional carjacker, Tony had the door open in seconds. He started the motor, jammed the shifter into gear, and was just about to pull away from the curb when Max yanked the passenger door open and collapsed into the seat, panting heavily as he closed his door behind him.

Tony stomped on the brakes as he observed Sheriff Ryder exiting the courthouse with Dylan in handcuffs. From the top of the steps, Dylan spotted Tony sitting in Max's car. He flashed a big smile at him as Sheriff Ryder prodded him with his nightstick.

"Pay no attention to him," Max said to Tony. "God's watching your back."

Tony nodded and punched the accelerator to the floor, speeding up the street after the elusive silver Porsche. They searched down one backstreet and up another for who knows how long before finally spotting the car.

"Just as I figured," Tony said as he pulled up behind the Porsche, now sitting empty with its driver's door ajar. It had been left deserted in front of the Victorian house, also home to the Belial abortion clinic. Tony pushed open the driver's door and ran towards the front door.

Max followed closely behind, with less grace but a full cup of loyalty.

"It's the same steel door I saw in my vision back at the courthouse," Tony hurriedly explained as he pummelled the door. "Oh God, I hope we're not too late!"

Max and Tony now threw themselves at the steel door like two drugged patients of an asylum who were immune to pain, unaware that help had now arrived and stood behind them on the front steps.

Restrained from another burst of energy, Tony felt a strong grip on his shoulder. He turned and looked with vacant eyes into the face of the K7 News cameraman.

"Let me have a go at it," said the tall, muscular saint with flaming red hair, brandishing a crowbar in one hand. "Be a good mate and stand aside."

The man's effort sounded like nails being pulled out of plank flooring. He showed the clinic's door no mercy. Like a trap tripped prematurely, the lock popped and the door sprang open.

In an irrational moment, Tony grabbed the crowbar from the cameraman and ran through the clinic's front door only to stop in the living room, frozen by the sight of Roxanne's handbag on a leopard print sofa.

"Roxanne," he whispered in a fearful voice.

Max came alongside him. "That's her bag, isn't it?"

Tony nodded and wiped his eyes with his shirt sleeve. "My eyes got a little bit blurry for a minute there."

"Hey, it's okay. You don't have to pretend to be dignified for my sake. We've known each other too long for that."

Rena appeared behind them, giving the cameraman direction. "Let me see. Okay, Rolf, I definitely want a shot of the handbag on the sofa. And another shot of the blocks scattered about on the floor."

I've got to collect my thoughts, Tony said to himself, stunned by the impact this day was having on him.

"Okay," he said slowly after some time had passed. "I'm fine."

"You sure?" asked Max. "We can take a moment."

"Yeah, I'm fine." Tony wore a look of determination. "Search upstairs, Max, and I'll take the main floor. Yell if you see her. We'll meet back here in the living room when we're done."

Max nodded in agreement, then dashed toward the spiralling staircase that led to the second floor.

Tony walked out of the living room, leaving Rena and Rolf alone to go about their business. He explored the main hallway, pushing open every door and looking into each room. He found no sign of Roxanne.

He stood in front of the final door, hoping Roxanne was sleeping just behind it. He turned the antique ivory doorknob and pushed it open only to lose hope. No Roxanne. What had he expected, a perfect ending?

Tony chided himself, but then his eyes moved from the empty bed to the oval mirror hanging on the wall. In its reflection, he saw a green tapestry bag sitting on the top of an oak dresser in the corner, behind the door he had just pushed open. He recognized Roxanne's luggage right away.

The sight of Roxanne's bag triggered the courtroom vision in his head again, and he thought of the huge open pit with the stone bridge spanning it, and he heard in his mind the hooded figures chanting. "I know you're here, Roxanne," he whispered as he staggered back towards the living room.

Max was already waiting with Rena and Rolf.

"If I didn't know you better," Max said, "I'd say you're drunk."

"That's how I feel when these visions come on me so strongly," Tony explained, weaving slightly.

"That's a relief." Max pushed his cap up on his forehead. "I thought maybe you looked that way because you found Roxanne's body."

"No, thank God for that! But I did find her luggage, and it triggered the vision of the pit with the stone bridge. Strange, though. I didn't find any actual people. What about you, Max?"

"Just offices and operating rooms," Max replied, wishing he had better news.

"What about a basement?" Rolf asked.

Rena thought about it. "Did either of you find a basement door?"

Tony shook his head. "The only room I didn't search yet is the kitchen."

"We're running out of rooms," Max pointed out. "I've played Clue enough to know we should be looking for a secret passageway. You know, behind a false fireplace or a revolving bookshelf."

Tony smiled. It was a good idea. "Roxanne's handbag on the sofa, her luggage in one of the bedrooms, the Porsche outside, the absence of people inside... it all seems to point to two possibilities. Either everyone was raptured or there's a concealed door somewhere in the house."

"I put my money on a concealed door," Max said. "Could the doctor have tipped off everyone in the house, allowing them enough time to get away?"

"Only God knows," answered Tony. "I only know that I need to find Roxanne—and fast."

Tony tightened his grip on the crowbar as they walked from the living room into the kitchen. The stove was quite ordinary, and the table in the centre of the room was built from rustic planks.

I expected something a bit more modern, Tony thought as he scanned the room, locking his eyes on the doors of a towering pantry to his right. Its doors were stencilled with decorative leaves. The door handles were more of a mystery; there were two, each fashioned from antique silver and featuring a gothic "B."

"'B' stands for Belial," Tony said. "Quick, Max, help me push the pantry out from the wall. I think I'm onto something."

The resulting thud of Max and Tony throwing their shoulders against the pantry was like that of a bird hitting a pane of glass.

Rolf shouldered them aside. "I believe this is how we first met, eh, mates? Stand aside."

Wiping perspiration from their foreheads, Max and Tony leaned against the wall, breathing heavily. Rolf backed into the pantry and began to push. Slowly, it slid like the stone of a tomb, revealing a cavern. Dim light shone from its depths.

"It's an old mineshaft," Tony said, peering down. "The light is probably coming from torches in the mine passages."

Tony stepped into the cavern opening, finding himself atop a crude set of stairs, leading downward.

"I sense shades of Mirana here," Tony whispered.

"Shades of what?" Rolf asked, following him in.

"Just a place from one of Tony's dreams," Max explained. "Somebody's gone through a lot of trouble to revamp this old shaft."

Water trickled down the crude steps. The cold and lifeless tunnel's air smelled of mould. The distant torches were their only source of light as they began their descent.

Rena grazed the wall with her fingers, balancing herself. "It feels like we're walking into hell."

"The passage seems to be straightening now," Tony called from ahead. "Seems to be widening, too, unless my eyes are playing tricks on me."

The passageway abruptly opened into a series of honeycomb caverns. Tony was about to press on when he stopped in his tracks.

"It's him!" Tony cried.

Max looked across the empty cavern. "Who?"

"The dark prince I saw walking behind Jim McFlurry!"

"Though I walk through the valley of the shadow of death, I will fear no evil," Max prayed. Tony joined in.

In the dim light, Tony made out the shape of the same dark prince he'd seen on the boardwalk. The demon seemed determined to confront them.

Tony pointed right at him. "Lord, I ask that the angel of the Lord draw his sword and drive our enemy back to the pit like chaff in the wind."

He heard the beating of wings in the darkness, growing louder, then suddenly the dark prince just blew away.

"What's happening?" asked Max.

"God!" replied Tony in amazement.

A smile broke out on his friend's face as Tony explained what he'd heard. Together, they marched across the cavern to the spot where the dark prince had stood.

"Listen, did you hear that?" Tony asked.

Max looked confused. "What, the same beating of wings?"

"Listen! There it is again." Tony paused, cocking his ear. "Do you hear it?

"Sounds like muted chanting to me," Rena said as she caught up to them. "Do you think we should go on? That sound sends chills up my spine."

Rolf shivered. "I've got a genuine case of goose bumps myself."

"It's supernatural," Tony said. "The events of the courtroom, the evil presence causing you to fear now… our struggles aren't being waged in the flesh but in the spirit, with spiritual weapons. The effects and attacks of the enemy are different from those we face in the flesh. Those who live for the Lord call it spiritual warfare, and the Bible says the enemy comes as a thief bent on destroying God's children. I'm not trying to alarm you. After all, the One who resides in the believer is greater than the one in the world. He gives us His shield of victory."

Tony began to pray. "Lord, I bind the spirits of fear, mind control, and death from this place. I command these spirits to leave now in the name of Jesus. I plead the blood of Jesus over this place, and over our body, soul, and spirit gates. Lord, walk with us. Prepare your deadly weapons, God. The battle is yours, Lord, be a protective shield over us in Jesus' name, amen."

Breathing a sigh of relief, Rena wiped a tear from her eye. "I feel like Rahab under the protection of Israel when Jericho was destroyed. Tony, my instincts as a reporter tell me we should move on."

Rolf looked sideways at Rena, surprised by her Biblical reference. "Turning over a new leaf, are you girl?"

"Not really," Rena said, shrugging. "Just some of my mother's influences—her prayers and preaching—that until now I'd managed to suppress."

With a final smile at her cameraman, the two co-workers once again re-joined the others making their way deeper into the caverns. As they passed through a stone archway, the muted chanting erupted into frenzied shrieks, as if a hornet's nest had just been disturbed. At the sight of Rolf's camera, a mass of hooded figures scurried into the adjoining caverns to avoid detection.

"That's it," Tony said as he pointed at a circular pit in the centre of the cavern, spanned by a bridge with a statue of Ishtar in the middle. "It's just like my vision. And he's back."

"Who?" inquired Max.

"The dark prince," exclaimed Tony, franticly. "He's standing in the middle of the stone bridge spanning the open pit. There's a robed figure in front of him holding Jordan with one hand and Roxanne with his other. I see the dark prince has his hands on the robed figure's head."

"Roxanne!" Tony yelled, sprinting towards the bridge. "Jordan!"

But with the feverish wailing echoing through the cavern, his cries were drowned out. Noticing Tony bolting towards the bridge, the robed figure leaned over to whisper something into Roxanne's ear. Roxanne trembled like a leaf now in response to what was being asked of her. Tear-streaked mascara had painted her cheeks and now her white gown as she tried to wipe her watery eyes with her sleeve. Helplessly Roxanne looked into the robed figure's eyes for a sign of mercy, but her eyes were only met by his stone-cold stare. The dark prince laughed at Tony's effort to reach the bridge to save his family, but Tony blocked out the demonic laughter and pressed on with everything in him.

He looked up just as the robed figure, guided by the dark prince's hands, placed Roxanne's hands around Jordan in a tight grip.

Tony strode on towards the end of the bridge fuelled by adrenaline and desperation. "Don't do it Roxanne!" he screamed, as he stumbled onto the bridge.

Again the chanting drowned him out, increasing in tempo: "Do it! It will make you tender and delicate."

The rhythm of the demonic chanting seemed to get into Tony's head. He struggled to move forward but his muscles wavered, his inner ear seemed out of whack, and he felt nauseous as if he were about to lose his lunch. The sickening chant swirled around him.

Staggering ahead, Tony lunged at the robed figure standing behind Roxanne and Jordan with the dark prince's hands still on his head. The robed figure easily sidestepped Tony's attack with his demonic assistance. Then with the strength of a demon the robed figure ripped Jordan out of Roxanne's arms, lifted him high over his head, and flung him into the pit.

"Daddy!"

Fluttering and flailing through the air like a newborn bird's first attempt at flight, Jordan screamed out for Tony over and over again. The huge pit seemed to swallow Jordan alive, and the greyish smoke seeping out of it seemed to effectively muffle his final fading cry of, "Daddy!"

Lying face down on the bridge, Tony's blood trickled from a gash on his forehead. It collected in a small pool atop the porous stone.

Tony felt like he had been struck by the talon of a demon. He heard Morteque's voice crying from the shore of the pool, "Arnabe, no!" He saw the same dark prince that had stood behind the robed figure, his hands now on Arnabe's throat. He felt himself suddenly choking as the grip around his throat tightened. He saw the plate of the silver Porsche

flash across his memory. The name Belial pounded against his brain like
a hammer striking an anvil. He struggled to breathe as the grip tightened around his throat. He opened his eyes and managed to look over his
shoulder. He saw the robed figure atop him, the dark prince's hands now
shadowing the hands locked in a death grip around his throat.

"Belial!" Tony gasped as he noticed the blood-red ruby in the dark
prince's ponytail before things went black.

Having watched the events on the bridge through the viewfinder of
his camera, Rolf quickly handed the camera to Rena and charged for one
end of the bridge while Max made his way to the other. The demonic
chanting in the cavern seemed to impede Rolf and Max as if they were
running with weights on. They pushed on in determination.

Arriving at one end of the bridge, Rolf ran to where Roxanne lay
weeping on the bridge a few feet away from Tony. In the time it took
Rolf to check her pulse, Max ran onto the bridge from the other end
towards Tony.

Seeing Max approaching, the robed figure standing over Tony released a hand from his neck to push down on a circular stone on top of
a statue of Ishtar. The centre of the stone bridge now suddenly began to
descend, as if carrying Tony and the robed figure to hell. Max looked
down over the edge, where Tony descended, as if he were searching for
climbers who had suddenly fallen into a crevice. The thick grey smoke
seeping upward impeded Max's vision and unable to see anything he
cried out to the Lord in despair.

"Oh Lord, take up your deadly weapons. Father, I ask that you pluck
Tony like a brand out of the fire. Deliver him from the fowler's snare. See
my weeping and let my cry for mercy come up into your temple and into
your ear, God, please answer my prayer. Cause Tony's enemies this moment to be turned back in flight, and save your anointed, Lord."

Max fell to his knees, his face bowed to the ground, weeping. When
he opened his eyes, they were drawn to the pit again. His heart leaped into
his throat as the faint outline of the bridge rose back out of the smoky
pit. After what seemed like an eternity, the bridge clicked back into place.
There stood Tony, like one of the three Hebrew friends who had stepped
out of the furnace, with the robed figure now trembling at his feet.

Max smiled. "This is why I believe in the resurrection."

"I feel a bit like Daniel coming out of the lion's den," Tony said as he grabbed the robed figure by the neck and hauled him to his feet.

"What happened down there, dude?" asked Max.

"Tell you later. Do you still have that extra harness rig in the back of your car? The one we use for weekend climbs?"

"Yeah."

"Can you go up and bring it down here?"

"You know it!" Max headed off the bridge towards the archway that formed the cavern's only exit.

"Do you mind if we exchange partners for a moment?" Tony said, smiling at Rolf. "Could you escort Roxanne off the bridge when you're taking your robed friend, to wait near the exit for the sheriff who I'm sure is on his way?"

Rolf gently let go of Roxanne. "It would be a pleasure, mate."

"I don't believe he'll give you any trouble now," Tony said as he looked at the robed figure, now a shadow of his former self.

With great enthusiasm and longing, Tony embraced his wife. "I blame none of what has happened to us—none of this—on you, Roxanne," he whispered in her ear. "It's not your fault!"

He held her tightly, thanking God for her return. As Heaven wept.

CHAPTER THIRTY

From the shadows of the cavern, a lone figure hastily slipped off her hooded cloak and let it drop to the ground. Her slender hands admired the priceless dagger with its inlaid blood-red rubies and serpentine blade.

"So, my little beauty is real," smiled the woman to herself, as she wrapped the dagger in a silk scarf. "The dagger *does* exist outside of legends, and now it's mine!"

She shoved the dagger into her black leather shoulder bag, and like a wisp of smoke she passed through the stone archway, exiting the cavern, oblivious to all cries for help behind her.

Max hurtled through the open front door of the Victorian house at breakneck speed, wasting precious little time in retrieving the rope and the ring of pitons and carabiners out the back of the station wagon. He was in the process of coiling the rope around his arm when Sheriff Ryder and his men pulled up in their police cruisers.

Jumping out of the cruiser with the gold star on the door, Sheriff Ryder approached Max.

"I'm looking for Mr. Epson!" the sheriff said.

Max hastily continued to pull out the climbing harness. "He's behind the pantry in the kitchen."

Sheriff Ryder stared at Max silently for a moment, and then a smile appeared on his face. As he noticed the ponytail protruding out of the back of Max's cap, he said, "Behind the pantry? Okay, Alice! Lead us to Wonderland."

Max quietly asked the Lord for patience as he finished his check of the climbing harness. He had no time for foolish debates.

"The climbing harness and axe seem fine," Max said, grabbing the equipment and bolting towards the front door.

"Don't lose sight of that white rabbit!" Sheriff Ryder's mocking laughter seemed to nip at Max's heels as he entered the house.

Spurred on, Max moved through the passageway behind the pantry as quickly as he could. A few minutes later, he arrived at Tony's side in the middle of the stone bridge.

"I feel like a window washer on this thing," Max said, brandishing the harness and climbing gear.

Tony nodded in appreciation, then leaned over and pushed the circular stone that would lower them into the smoky pit. Max coughed as the smoke thickened around him. He pulled out a handkerchief to keep from inhaling too much of it.

Tony wiped tears from the corner of his eyes and coughed. "You would be unemployed very fast today, for hell has no windows," he said hoarsely.

The stone platform came to an abrupt stop and clicked into place, suspended like an elevator caught between floors.

"End of the line!" Tony took the harness from Max and began the process of slipping into it.

"Here, take this." Max threw Tony his handkerchief. "The smoke looks thicker down below."

Tony caught it in one hand and smiled at his friend. "You're the kind of dude I'd love to have on my fire crew."

Max returned Tony's smile, then dropped to his knees and drove a piton in between two stones on the bridge's deck with the climbing axe. He then screwed a carabiner to it, and threaded one end of the climbing rope through it, tying it off like an expert woodsman.

"Okay, Max!" Tony signalled the thumbs up. "We'll do it just like we used to on our weekend climbs."

Max handed the other end of the rope to Tony, who threaded it through the carabiner screwed to the climbing harness. Tony sat down on the edge of the stone bridge with his feet dangling into empty space in preparation to be lowered down into the smoky pit.

He pushed off from the edge of the bridge, sinking lower into the greyish smoke and the top of Tony's head quickly vanished from Max's sight. Tony now hung suspended in the air by his climbing rope, like a spider on its silken thread. Max listened intently for signs of life, to make sure Tony was okay—a gasp of air, a cough echoing from the depths below, the shifting of the rope through his hands.

Suddenly, the rope stopped moving.

"Oh God!" Max cried out. "Lift my buddy from this miry pit, set his feet upon a rock, enable his feet to walk on the high places, and deliver him from death."

Max wiped the perspiration from his forehead and then felt a slight tinge of movement in the rope.

"Thank you, Father!" he whispered.

～

Tony's feet came down on something solid, jarring him to the bone. With little time to react to the pain, Tony quickly felt the knotted rope connected to his harness and untied it. The darkness forced him to rely on other senses rather than sight. He cautiously slid his feet along the rocky ground until he bumped into a large stone. Finding the stone's edge, he felt a small crack and then another stone. These two stones were fit together so precisely that Tony thought they couldn't possibly be the work of Mother Nature. He felt the joint between the stones again to confirm it. At the edge of the second stone, Tony's hand encountered a third, bulging stone. He slowly ran his hand up its side.

A pillar. Tony breathed a short prayer out in the darkness. "Lord, please don't let this be the ruins of some ancient temple where they made sacrifices to other gods."

Letting go of the pillar, Tony stepped into empty space and inched forward in the dark. When his knee abruptly hit another solid mass, he realized it was a second pillar. Feeling along, Tony came across two more large stones identical to the ones he'd found by the first pillar. He worked his way back to the empty space, wondering what these objects were for.

Standing in the gap between the two pillars, he considered whether he should continue forward in the darkness. He had never been afraid to step into danger before, no matter how hot the fire, yet now he had second thoughts.

Shaking his head and resolving to act quickly, as he always had, Tony shrugged off his insecurities. His pace gradually increased, as did his confidence, until minutes later his foot came down with nothing to support it. His knees buckled and his entire body propelled forward—and downward.

With a sickening thud, Tony's head made contact with a huge overhanging rock. Pain like hundreds of tiny pins pierced his brain. He felt around and came across the short set of stairs that had caused his fall.

The tumble seemed to awaken him again to the difficulty of breathing in the smoky abyss into which he had descended. He wiped the blood trickling from his forehead to keep it from his eyes and ducked through the stone archway he had just hit with his head.

The nagging thought of where the staircase would lead troubled him. He took another cautious step only to have his foot come down on something he knew was not of an earthy nature. He lifted his foot slowly off the object, then gingerly lowered his body so as to avoid any further unnecessary stumbles.

He scooped a hand down to retrieve the object that had been under his foot. Feeling its shape, it dawned on Tony that he was holding a skull. This hypothesis was confirmed as he stuck his fingers through two empty eye sockets.

Tony coughed as a particularly thick cloud of dark smoke enveloped him. Worse, the skull led him to a morbid thought: had other children been tossed off the bridge? Did this skull belong to a child not unlike his son? He knew he had to get beyond his worries; every moment he wasted would make it that much more difficult to rescue Jordan, assuming he wasn't already dead.

Sulphuric fumes burned his nostrils. Tony wiped his watery eyes with the handkerchief Max had thrown to him.

I've got to press forward, he thought. *Jordan needs me.*

With each step, an eerie orange glow became more visible through the darkness. It felt to Tony that he was descending into hell.

Suddenly, the stairs ended.

Tony stood gazing in bewilderment like an explorer who found a lost tribe in the jungle at the huge altar surrounded by circular paving stones. The altar had four large bronze horns, one at each corner, and almost seemed to be alive; flames shot forth from its top, sending endless plumes of black smoke spiralling upward out of the pit.

The heat was unbearable. The paving stones surrounding the altar all glowed a fiery red.

I'm in hell. Tony raised an arm to shield his eyes from the glare of the blazing altar. In the process, he managed to make out small piles of bones scattered overtop the paving stones. If this wasn't ghastly enough, he then saw Jordan, lying on his back, surrounded by the bones of a rib cage. Other skulls stared at him with hollow sockets. The sight seemed to suck away a little more of Tony's breath as if he were being restricted by a python.

"Jordan!" Tony yelled in a hoarse voice between gasps of air. Hoping for a miracle, he ran to his motionless son's side. "Jordan, my son. Daddy's here."

He felt for a pulse—and located one. "Thank you, Jesus!" he gasped.

He prudently continued his assessment of Jordan's condition, finding what seemed like a shallow wound, a broken arm, a few cracked ribs, and a broken left ankle.

"Think!" he said aloud, struggling to maintain his focus.

A stream of hot air emanated from the ground, and with it a strong stench assaulted his nostrils. The smell was getting to him, and with it came an onslaught of terrified thoughts:

Can't call 911.

God, I hope he lives.

What is that sloshing sound?

I need to get out of here.

Just keep moving.

Operating solely on much-practiced rescue procedures, Tony gently lifted Jordan and, cradling the boy's unconscious body, stumbled back towards the stone staircase. All the gasping and coughing threatened to bring him a little closer to losing consciousness. Only the continued whispering of his son's name induced him to find the inner strength to propel himself up the stairs and into the space between the pillars. When he was finally in position, Tony reached out for the climbing rope. Feeling it in his fingers, he quickly arced the rope over Jordan's body and reattached it to the climbing harness. He then pulled three times.

~

"I got a bite! Well, glory to God!" Max coughed as he wrapped the rope around his thick arms and started to pull it through the carabiner. The rope strained in his hands as he laboured inch by inch to pull up his friend. "God, give me the strength of Samson."

Several long moments later, the head of a child appeared through the smoke, and then a huge hand grasped the side of the bridge deck. Hearing once again the familiar sound of his friend's cough, Max tied off the rope and hurried to assist Tony in rolling Jordan onto the bridge. Max grabbed Tony by the arm and hauled both man and boy onto the bridge deck. Drenched in sweat and standing with the lifeless rope in his bloody hands, Max pushed the circular stone.

Compared to the slow progress of hauling Tony up from the depths, the bridge seemed to now propel upwards as though by rocket boosters. It seemed that Max had only just taken his hand off the circular stone when the bridge was already clicking back into place.

Through bloodshot eyes, Tony made out Max's hazy form and managed a weak smile before his eyes closed once more, from where he and Jordan lay sprawled on the bridge.

As everyone stood still, the cavern seemed to take on the half-hour hush of heaven. All eyes were directed towards the centre of the bridge. Only the sight of paramedics bolting into the chamber with oxygen tanks served to permit the activity and noise to resume.

The paramedics rushed to Tony, who sat up beside his still motionless son.

Max glanced at Roxanne, who was still trembling from her ordeal and being comforted by Rolf as they watched the paramedics work. Fatigue beginning to consume him, Max collapsed by the statue of Ishtar, a single tear trickling down his cheek on behalf of Tony's family, the type of prayer that is quickly carried on angel wings to the very throne of God.

Sheriff Ryder and his men released dogs into the network of mine tunnels to search for the many robed figures seeking sanctuary in the shadows. Seeing the action, Rena motioned to Rolf to pick up his camera.

Rolf walked Roxanne to an officer. He then picked up the camera, turned it on, and aimed it at the reporter.

"Rena Peterson for K7 News, broadcasting from caverns deep under the property in Drummingsville known as the Belial Abortion clinic, or by the locals simply as the Victorian house. A few weeks ago, we aired a story about the clinic doctors practicing abortions in the name of religious freedom."

Rolf panned the camera around the cavern bustling with robed figures being cuffed and paramedics running. Then he focused on the huge pit with the stone bridge.

"Bureaucratic red tape may have permitted the doctors the freedom of their beliefs and the continual operation of the Belial clinic," Rena explained, "but the clinic doors are likely to be barred and locked after the discovery today that the clinic doctors appear to be involved in human sacrifice. We've also just learned that Tony Epson, whose young son was thrown into the smoking pit just hours ago, is starting to make a recovery."

Tony shook the grogginess from his head as Rena approached him.

"I know this is a difficult time," Rena said, "but I recently heard you used to be a firefighter."

"Yeah." Tony paused to take a breath of air. "I used to be a smoke jumper. I was lowered by chopper into a fire site to build helipads before the main crew arrived."

"Sounds dangerous!"

"It can be tense at times," Tony explained. "With a wall of fire close by, you have to keep your head on your shoulders. But as much as risking my life on behalf of saving a few trees is a worthy cause, this is one fire I willingly went into."

Tony smiled at Rena, thanked her for the interview, then mustered his strength to push his weak body up into a standing position. He walked towards Max and Roxanne.

Rena spotted Sheriff Ryder, who flashed a big smile for the camera.

"Can you explain what's going on here, Sheriff?" she asked, pointing the microphone at him.

"Just a little mop-up operation. We've been aware of this group's activities for some time, through our stakeouts of both the clinic and Principal Reeves' residence. Our activity today was a planned raid, executed with superb skill. From our surveillance, we suspected they were practicing human sacrifice. As you can see from the open pit and the altar below, these meetings weren't casual affairs."

"Did you find anything substantiating your suspicion of human sacrifice?"

"I haven't personally been down into the pit at this point, but from the comments Mr. Epson shared, I think I'll be calling a forensic team to examine the bones he described. We've already found evidence of drug use and pornographic material in the cavern. I also think we have enough evidence to proceed with a few convictions in court, on kidnapping charges and the intent to inflict bodily harm. It's just a matter of time. I call it a gut feeling, but murder will likely be added to the charges. That can't be proven until I get the forensic results."

"From what you've told us, Sheriff, it sounds like there will be a few vacancies in high-profile jobs in Drummingsville."

"It appears that may be likely," replied Sheriff Ryder. "My men are still rounding up members of the group, but the identity of several members is already known to us. The robed figure who threw the Epson boy into the pit from the bridge, now standing between two of my officers, is a Dr. Michaels."

Rolf panned the camera to the doctor, who appeared pathetic, tortured, and panicked.

"We also have Mr. Reeves and Dr. Andrews," the sheriff continued. "My men have just informed me that our dogs have cornered Mayor Thomas as well."

"Our sources have suggested Ms. Michelle Starr may be involved," Rena said. "Any sign of her?"

"At this point, we cannot confirm if she was a member of this group, but as we speak my men are bringing in the stragglers. That said, one of my men did take note of a tall woman with long black hair leaving the building. She was carrying a Sarquis Times press card with the name Nikita Summers on it. That's all I've got for now."

Rena smiled at him. "I suppose your name will make history in the Drummingsville Police Department."

"Well, I don't know about that, but I might get the popular vote for sheriff for another term."

"I'd like to thank you for your time. I know you need to get back to taking charge of the situation."

Sheriff Ryder flashed one more smile for the camera. "It's been a pleasure!"

"I'm Rena Peterson and this has been a K7 News broadcast."

﹌

As the buzz calmed around them, Tony embraced his wife and with tear-filled eyes. He kissed her gently on the cheek.

"Welcome home, my wife," he whispered in her ear.

Like summer rain, tears streamed down Roxanne's cheeks. Though she still trembled, she had a smile on her face for the first time in a long while.

Tony looked his wife in the eyes. "For better or worse, whether rich or poor, until death do us part—that's the commitment I've made to you, my love!" Next, he turned to Max. "God has shown me favour this day.

My wife, who was dead to me, has come back to life! Watch her for me, Max. There's something I still need to do."

Tony turned his attention back to Roxanne and kissed her on the lips.

"Remember this," he whispered. "I promise we'll talk more when I return."

Letting go, Tony looked up.

"Your youth has failed you!" he shouted to the mid-heavens. "Your walls are broken down, Jezebel! You are no queen, just an old nag, and you'll not get my wife's soul or my son's, or any other souls from Drummingsville!"

High in the mid-heavens, the smile on the queen's face transformed into an expression of agony as two more souls escaped her grasp.

CHAPTER THIRTY-ONE

Levi walked out of the mine's garage through the employee door. Kyle, one of the Hades IV loader operators, walked alongside him. Kyle was a short, wiry man with dirty brown curls and a welcoming smile that stretched across his face like a circus clown.

"So, you were sent here? Um," muttered Kyle. "I'm guessing control told you I was at the garage working overtime tonight. Since we haven't been officially introduced, the name is Kyle Morris, by the way."

Levi reached out to shake Kyle's hand. "Oh, I'm sorry. I'm Levi Brandon but folks have taken to calling me Levi."

"No offense taken, I hope, if I pass on the handshaking for now." Kyle wiped some grease from his hands onto his bright orange coveralls. "Follow me then. I can take you down to the mine's main cavern in the employee elevator."

The creaking of the elevator as it descended into the depths of the mine sent a chill up Levi's spine. He thought about the martyred souls beneath the altar crying out for vindication.

The bell sounded and the elevator door laboriously opened.

"Here it is." Kyle shone his flashlight on a massive pile of rocks protruding out of the cavern's wall. "I guess Dylan told you about it?"

"No, actually."

Kyle looked at Levi with a puzzled expression. "Dylan did send you, didn't he?"

"Not really."

"Then how did you learn about the sealed cavern?"

"A prophet had a vision from God," said Levi matter-of-factly.

"A who had a what?"

Levi repeated himself, a little slower this time.

Kyle wiped his forehead with his handkerchief. "I think just maybe I ought to take you back up to the surface. I'm sorry, but I'm going to have to give Dylan a call. Come with me."

"I'm afraid Dylan's a little tied up at the moment," Levi said. "And as far as going up to the surface, more people will be coming down soon, so we may as well just wait."

"This here's a mine, not a museum giving guided tours."

"It's not too late to start!"

The elevator doors opened and out walked Tony, Max, the K7 News crew, and a few members of the town council.

Tony walked up to the pile of rocks. "A terrifying vision!" he cried out, his face contorted. "I see demons, some of which look like animals, others like people, and some a combination of animal and human. I see a ladder, but instead of ascending into the heavens like in Jacob's vision, it is descending from this cavern into the heart of hell. Instead of angels, demonic beings move up and down it in organized rank. We need to get these rocks cleared away."

"Sounds like my old foreman," said Kyle as he climbed up into the cab of the Hades IV loader.

"Remember the prophet I was talking about?" Levi asked, smiling at Kyle. "That's him."

The loader attacked the pile of rocks like a battering ram. When the opening was wide enough to pass through, Tony signalled Kyle to cut the loader's engine.

Caught in the lights of the loader was a macabre sight. Levi shone a light into the chamber, exposing more of the skeletal remains. "God, your word says in Galatians 3:13 that Christ redeemed us from the curse of the law by becoming a curse for us. For it is written that cursed is everyone who is hung on a tree. We cut off and break the curse of death and destruction over Drummingsville and the Stillmore mine. We sever the word curse spoken by Chief Issack over Drummingsville, and we sever demonic power and the legal right of demons to continue to enter the bloodline of the citizens of Drummingsville, from ten generations back in the history of our community. We repent of the sins of our fore-fathers—of their greed, murder, and immorality. Forgive us for our rebellion against you, God. We ask for your mercy, Father. We plead the blood of Jesus now upon the Stillmore Mine and upon the citizens of Drummingsville. And we ask, Father, that you release the angels of the Lord to drive these demonic forces from our midst and back to the pit."

When Levi finished, Tony explained to the others what he saw in the spirit realm. "As you were praying, Levi, I saw the spider web falling from our community to the ground. I also saw the angel of the Lord here in the mine, in all his brilliance driving the shrieking and screaming demons back down the ladder. As you spoke of the blood of Jesus, I saw several other angels—one of them carried a single drop of the precious blood of the Lamb, without spot or defect. The angel applied it to the top of the ladder, creating an uncrossable barrier, driving away the demons pleading not to be sent back to the pit."

"Lord," Levi prayed again, feeling inspired, "release your angels to stand in this place!"

Tony's voice rose in pitch as he continued. "I see two angels with flaming swords standing on the side of the ladder, like the guardians of Eden, and as watchmen on the community of Drummingsville's walls."

"Thank you, Lord," Levi said.

A sudden gasp turned the group's bowed heads upward.

"I found something!" Kyle yelled from inside the cavern.

"Get a picture of whatever it is," Rena instructed Rolf as he quickly set up a few portable lights.

"It looks like a gold pocket watch," Kyle said, holding up the watch in the light and blowing the dust off. "It's banged up a bit, but there appears to be an inscription on the back."

The cavern was cloaked in silence as Kyle moved his flashlight to better view the inscription. After what seemed like an eternity to those waiting, he finally read it.

"It says, 'To my love, Benson Thomas, on the day of our elopement, June 17, 1812.'"

"I remember that name," a woman's voice called out, shattering the stillness. Everyone turned to Selena Mendez, recognizing her as the mayor's secretary. "Mayor Thomas brought a book into the office a few months back which traced his family tree. I believe this pocket watch belongs to one of the mayor's relatives."

After another period of sombre silence, the decision was made to return to the surface. The elevator door opened and everyone slowly and methodically filed in. At the surface the elevator doors opened, and the occupants silently drifted across the mine yard as if they had just attended a wake.

Tony found himself silently walking by Kyle who after a few moments of silence decided to risk conversation. "Poor Thomas," Kyle said.

"Yeah," responded Tony, "but just maybe his family's blood cried out to God against him like Abel's did to God against Cain."

Rolf loaded the camera equipment back into the K7 News van with little enthusiasm. He jumped into the driver's seat.

"Well, I suppose that's it then, eh?" Rolf said to his colleague.

"Not really a fairy-tale ending," Rena said as she checked her make-up in a small compact mirror. "It's more along the lines of a bad dream. I don't even want to think about how it's been for the townspeople."

It's taking more makeup these days to hide the wrinkles, Rena thought to herself. *And just look at your hair. You look like a porcupine gone punk. It's the cost, I suppose, of being on the road so much. At least this is the real you. No surprises.*

She giggled as she closed the mirror.

"What's up?" asked Rolf.

"I was just thinking about the way I look, my hair being such a mess and all. What a nightmare!"

"I wouldn't worry. You can still turn heads, and I say that with experience."

Rena turned a little red. "It's a sad state of affairs when a girl feels the need to fish for compliments."

"On the contrary." Rolf started the engine. "A rose never knows its own beauty."

"A rose? I think you mean dandelions!"

"What's all this talk about dandelions then?" Inquired Rolf.

"I remember as a girl my father pulling dandelions in the front yard with a barbaric looking contraption. I'd pick the ones that went to seed while my father lectured me on not blowing them into the neighbour's yard. He looked so frustrated when I would blow them away."

"Is that it, then?" Rolf said. "Is that what we witnessed here in Drummingsville, the pulling out of a few dandelions or the blowing away of their seed? If it is, which neighbour's yard will the dandelion seed land in? Isn't that the real question?"

"I'm not sure. I just know that when it comes to dandelions, the fight never ends. It takes everyone being committed to the same vision."

"All that's gone on in this town ought to keep our ratings up," Rolf said, pointing out the silver lining. He pulled the van through the guard-house on the edge of the mine's property. "Just think what our ratings would be if we could tap into Tony Epson's visions."

Rena laughed as the van headed down the highway. "But we would be disposable. The station wouldn't need us to chase down every hot news lead. They'd just ask Tony, and we would end up spending our retirement on a porch playing string games."

"How about a little music?" Rolf asked as he reached for the radio, sending the van swooning down the highway to the brassy tones of "What a Wonderful World." They left their sobering thoughts behind them as they travelled away from town, possibly for good.

⌒

Frank Lacomb jumped in his chair at the sudden knock at his front door. He set his Bible down on the end table and progressed to the foyer. He took a deep breath and determined to swallow his pride, a usually difficult thing to do. Tentatively, he reached for the doorknob and pulled the door open, only to succumb to silence as he stared at his visitor.

"Uh, are you okay, Frank?" asked Levi.

"Oh. Yeah, sorry about that." Frank tried to work the lump out of his throat. "I'm just realizing that forgiveness is a lot easier to do in my head than in person."

"I think I can understand that."

"Well, excuse my poor hospitality," Frank said. "Please, come on in."

Levi followed Frank into the living room and sat down.

"Would you like a soda?" asked Frank.

"Sounds fine to me," answered Levi as Frank headed off to the kitchen.

A family photograph resting on the end table caught Levi's eye as he looked around the living room. He couldn't help but pick it up to take a closer look.

"She was a great lady, my Katherine," Frank said as he walked back in, carrying two tall glasses. He set them down on the coffee table in front of the sofa.

Levi placed the photograph back in its rightful place. "I'm really sorry. I didn't mean to pry."

"No, no, don't be sorry. You couldn't have known." Frank returned to his seat and sat down. He paused for a moment to ponder his memories of his late wife. "I remember the night Katherine lost her battle with cancer. I was like a madman, running mindlessly through the house, and then I ran out onto the front porch and yelled at the sky."

Frank reached for one of the glasses on the coffee table, holding it with both hands as he leaned forward and stared at the floor.

"I shook my fist at God and begged to know, why? Didn't He know we had plans? We were about to retire. We were going to travel from town to town as missionaries on twin Harleys. That's when I saw it—the brightest shooting star I ever saw, though my eyes hadn't really been looking heavenward until that moment. I heard His voice speak into my ear: 'Frank, it's my turn now. I know she has given you great pleasure, but how long I have waited by the roadside for my daughter to come home. You of all people should understand this.' When the quiet whisper stopped, I just stood on the porch smiling, thanking God for His good gifts."

Frank wiped a tear from the corner of his eye and took a sip of root beer.

Levi sat back, listening as Frank went on. He knew it was the best thing he could do for his new friend, after all he'd gone through.

"Sorry," Frank said. "I was getting used to the idea of Katherine being gone, but when Randy went and got shot, it triggered the emotion all over again. To tell you the truth, I've been feeling pretty bad lately about some things I said to Randy that I never had time to make right."

Frank looked up and met Levi's gaze. "I shunned you as an apostle, Levi, just as I shunned Randy as a pastor. For that, I apologise. If Katherine were here, she would never have let me get away with it. She would have told me I was no better than a sinner if I couldn't love my brother. I know I deserve to be stoned by you, rightfully."

"Well, Frank, if God stoned every one of His children when they made a mistake or failed Him, His family would be greatly reduced today. In fact, I might not even be able to talk to you myself." Levi chuckled. "Aren't you glad for the precious blood of Jesus, and that our sinfulness was exchanged for His righteousness on the cross? We are new creations. Everything about you at this moment is new."

"I know that, in my head," replied Frank with misty eyes. "Even after so many years in the ministry, the Holy Spirit is just now peeling off the layers of my pride like an onion. I suppose it's mostly been my own doing, the fact that the truth takes so long to become a reality in my life. But I tell you, Levi, just talking to you today has caused me to feel more alive than I have in quite some time. I feel like I've been refreshed. I guess I had a lot to get off my chest.

"I have to admit, I was threatened—possibly jealous—of how God seemed to show things to you and Tony. Then the Lord reminded me of how Andrew was willing to go look for Peter. What Jesus spoke to Peter didn't cause Andrew to be envious. I've been thinking lately about the offices listed in Ephesians 4:11 and how they should operate the same way as Andrew and Peter.

"Listen, I know I'm talking your ear off, Levi, but things are beginning to seem so new to me. Remember the king in the Bible who gave a feast, but the people who were invited didn't show? The king sent his servants to the highways and byways to bring in people, because there was still room in the banquet hall. What I'm trying to say is that I can't fill my Father's banquet hall by myself. God has allowed circumstances to back me into a corner. Now I seem to be seeing *God's* plans are for building His Church, not my own."

"I think I understand, Frank," Levi offered supportively. "I think it's wonderful what God's doing in you."

"I may as well start now, by swallowing my pride and asking if you'd be a mentor to me, to speak fatherly counsel into my life and the flock God has entrusted me with."

Levi looked up. "It would be a privilege. I've also been thinking about looking in on Randy's flock. I'm sure they'd be greatly blessed, Frank, if you were able to share your skills and wisdom amongst them periodically. Who knows? Together we may have a better chance of seeing God's people reach maturity and fill the Father's banquet hall."

"Maybe so."

The two new friends stood and began walking back towards the door.

"It's been a hectic few weeks and I really need to catch up on some long overdue sleep," Levi said, holding out his hand. "Let me shake your hand, brother."

The friends shook hands and smiled at the thought of their future collaborations.

"It really is true that unless a grain of wheat first dies, there can be no life," Frank declared, with a look of astonishment etched upon his face, as he waved to Levi from his porch.

"It's good to finally be driving again," Tony said out his driver's side window from where he was parked in Max's driveway. Roxanne was leaning on his shoulder and Jordan sat belted in beside his mother, playing a new video game she had bought him to keep him occupied on the trip.

"You take care, dude," Max said. "I think you could use this vacation."

"I've heard that before," Tony retorted with a laugh. "We figure we'll head out to visit a certain apostle for a while. After that, maybe we'll find a warm, secluded island to kick back in the sand and relax."

"Sounds great! Barbara and I will keep you in our prayers. But there's one thing inquiring minds want to know before you go. When the centre of the bridge descended and you were being pinned by the robed dude, what caused him to tremble so much when you both came up from the pit? I mean, what happened down there?"

Tony nodded. "I've been meaning to explain that to you. I believe your intercession invoked the Lord to take up His sword against the enemy. The robed figure was shaking because, like Balaam's donkey, he saw the angel of the Lord about to strike. The dark prince who was with him was blown away by another angel who put a drop of the blood of Jesus upon him."

"Wow, you saw all of that? That's incredible. Good to know our prayers are so effective."

"Hey, can you do something for me when I'm away?" Tony asked. "Can you keep your eye on Flora for me?"

"Consider it done," Max said.

"Great! Thanks a lot. Well, I guess the time has come." Tony backed his vehicle out of the driveway slowly. Leaning on his horn a few times, he yelled out his window, "Take care, buddy!"

"How about coffee in a month, when you get back?" Max yelled. "You ought to have a whole new set of visions by then, hey Joseph?"

Tony waved to Max and happily drove off with his family.

⌒

The phone rang in Sheriff Ryder's office, and he swivelled around in his wooden office chair to answer it.

"Sheriff Ryder's office. What can I do for you?" A pause. "Grant Timmons, you say? Yes, Mayor Thomas is being held here." A pause. "Well, I suppose I could unlock the holding cell just a second."

The sheriff stood up and walked out of the office, headed towards the holding cells. He unlocked the mayor's cell, then led Thomas back to his office.

"You've got five minutes," Ryder said, "so make them count!"

Thomas picked up the phone to hear Grant's voice on the line.

"I trust your new accommodations are suitable to you, Mr. Mayor," Grant said sarcastically. "I just called to inform you that Belial Enterprises is no longer interested in Drummingsville, so our construction company is withdrawing all finances from the mall and the Stillmore Mine."

"Grant!" Thomas sputtered. "Can we discuss this? They'll be forced to close if you do this."

"I don't believe that will be your concern for much longer. However, so that it doesn't cause you to lose sleep, I suggest that the town reclaim some money by trying to sell them. Or you could pave over the sites for parking lots."

"You can't do this to us!" Thomas screamed into the phone. "We had a deal!"

"You didn't fulfill your part of the bargain," replied Grant callously. "Thus our agreement is rendered void."

"No, please, listen! You can't do this to me!"

Click. The line resumed the monotonous sound of the dial tone as Thomas dropped the phone angrily.

"Ah, they don't love you anymore," Sheriff Ryder taunted. "Well, maybe there's something in my desk to make you feel better."

Reaching into the drawer, the sheriff pulled out the gold pocket watch that had been unearthed in the mine.

"I believe this belonged to a relative of yours." He handed the watch over to the mayor. "Sure is ironic how you and that Dylan character tried so hard to seal off that cavern. Now both of you are going to be locked up in a cavern of your own, and you'll have a good long time to think about your relative, now that you have his watch."

The sheriff walked the defeated mayor back to his cell. Justice had been served, he felt. He was glad to know there was still some form of even-handedness in his hometown.

Even spiritual justice had been wrought. Unbeknownst to most, a major victory had been won in the heavens.

～

Writhing in agony over her defeat, the queen was overcome by fear as an ominous black cloud filled her throne room. The ruling spirits were suddenly tossed about like trees uprooted by a twister. Blackness spread through the mid-heavens.

Then, as if slapped across the face, the queen reeled backwards.

"You will not fail me again," boomed an evil voice out of the blackness. "So that you are more intent on victory, I will remove a little of my protective covering from the Creator's light."

The queen tried desperately to shield herself from the slivers of the Creator's light that now filtered through to her. Her shrieks set all the ruling spirits on high alert.

"I will have more souls in my house," said the evil voice as the black cloud receded from the queen's throne room.

~

Out in front of an oceanside bungalow, Tony lay beside Roxanne on their beach chairs. Jordan looked for shells in the sand along the shore.

"Well, I think I've had enough sun for the day," said Roxanne. "I'm going to take Jordan in and start getting him ready for bed."

She stood up and walked over towards their son. Stopping halfway, she turned towards Tony, seeing that his eyes were following her. She brushed aside a few errant curls.

"I'll be taking a shower," she said seductively. "Don't stay out here on the beach all night."

"I'll finish my drink and be along shortly." With a smile, Tony closed his eyes and entered a peaceful sleep.

~

Grenfel led Morgan along the streets of Dremcon, which were still coated in coagulated blood, observing in awe the many unique acts of freedom being enacted by the citizens of the city. A woman stood in the street with bloody fingers, crying and thanking the Ancient of Days for freeing her from keeping up with the demands of spinning her broken wheel.

"Dremcon!" Grenfel muttered. "A people once walking in darkness now walk in the light."

Several people who had being cutting each other with knives now stood battered and bruised, embracing each other in an eternal hug.

A woman with bloody garments stumbled through the streets towards Grenfel. She fell before him and reached out a hand. "I'm so sorry about your father," she sobbed. "Can you ever forgive me?"

For a minute, Grenfel stood motionless, not uttering a sound. As he thought of his father again, a tear trickled down his cheek and he swallowed hard. For some reason, this woman reminded him of all the undeserved mercy and love he had received from the Ancient of Days.

Without further hesitation, he knelt down and whispered in the woman's ear, "You are loved by the Ancient of Days, who this day offers you his forgiveness. As do I."

The woman broke into more sobbing and prayers of thanks to the Ancient of Days.

Grenful rose to his feet and took Morgan by the halter, continuing on. Children who had been begging for food now danced and sang in the streets, proclaiming the Ancient of Days' promise that the righteous shall not beg for bread.

His mind drifted at the sound of the children's song, which reminded him of his mother's high, melodic cries. He envisioned himself and Morgan standing outside a huge walled city, its thick walls and gates made of iron and brass. He heard a voice like the Ancient of Days saying, "This is Meldrock's heart, his fortress Draiden! It must be overcome for Ascar to truly be free, once and for all."

His mother's melodic song continued, emphatically heralding, "This is a song of summoning. Behold, look!"

Grenfel saw talons glistening and heard the sound like the beating of many wings. Before him, an army rose up, responding to the song like life breathed into dry bones. The army carried no weapons, but they had brightly coloured banners bearing images of hawks. The voice of the army was as one and it seemed to join the queen's song.

The faces of some in this army were the same as those he saw on the street of Dremcon, while others came from Kutek's people. All were marching on the heart of Meldrock, the great walled city called Draiden. As the army moved throughout Ascar, people cried out, not from the grip of pain but from finally being released from it. The dead were raised, captives were set free, and nature itself was at the beck and call of this ever-growing army which worked powerful signs and wonders on behalf of the Ancient of Days.

"The thorned gem has fallen," the Ancient of Days said. "Meldrock's heart is under siege. My kingdom is returning to Ascar. Rejoice, you its people, and worship! Receive hope!"

As this vision faded, Grenfel heard the same voice whisper, "After Draiden falls, go to Tarmaze, for it is time for the flight of the hawk."

Abruptly, Tony's dream ended. Cold liquid spilled on his chest, forcing him to wake. He sat up with eyes wide open, clutching his spilled drink.

"A dream," he muttered as he breathed in the cool night air and folded up his beach chair.

He walked back up to the bungalow, rehearsing how he would make amends with Roxanne. But one thought threatened to push Roxanne right out of his mind as it repeatedly crashed against his mind like the surf: *It is time for the flight of the hawk.*